“Do you think it’s sabot

“Someone sabotaged the line?”

Garvey shook his head. “No. The trolley car coasted in like it does every day, right on time. Just odd that its passengers all happened to be dead. How it got in with a dead conductor is beyond me. Scared the hell out of the people on the platform. And besides, look at them, and the trolley. It didn’t crash. No sign of sabotage. But their wounds, it’s like they’ve been…”

“Stabbed,” finished Collins. “Like someone hopped on board and then ran through, stabbing them all. Stabbed all to hell.”

Hayes turned one over with his foot. They all had the exact same wound, a thin puncture mark about an inch long. “Maybe someone stopped the car and did just that.”

“I told you,” said Garvey. “Trolley was on time, almost exactly.”

“So?”

“Well, according to the stops from the platform before, the window for the murders is about, oh, a little less than four minutes.”

Hayes stared at him. “That’s not possible.”

“Yeah. That’s the crux, ain’t it?”

“Someone stabbed all these people to death in *four minutes*?”

“Or something did.”

“And none of them resisted,” said Collins, stooping. “Look at their hands. No scratches. No cuts. No bruises.”

Hayes frowned, doing the same. “And no witnesses.”

“None,” said Garvey.

Praise for
Mr. Shivers

“Compelling and truly horrifying, this debut novel is highly recommended for all fiction and horror collections.”

—*Library Journal* (Starred Review)

By Robert Jackson Bennett

Mr. Shivers

The Company Man

THE COMPANY MAN

ROBERT JACKSON BENNETT

www.orbitbooks.net

Orbit
Hachette Book Group
237 Park Avenue, New York, NY 10017
www.HachetteBookGroup.com

First Edition: April 2011

Orbit is an imprint of Hachette Book Group, Inc. The Orbit name and logo are trademarks of Little, Brown Book Group Limited.

Library of Congress Cataloging-in-Publication Data
Bennett, Robert Jackson.
The company man / Robert Jackson Bennett.—1st ed.
p. cm.
ISBN 978-0-316-05470-6
1. Labor union members—Crimes against—Fiction. 2. Murder—Fiction. 3. Corporations—Corrupt practices—Fiction. 4. Company towns—Fiction. 5. Corporate power—Fiction. 6. Technological innovations—Fiction. I. Title.
PS3602.E66455C66 2010
813'.6—dc22
2010011247

10 9 8 7 6 5 4 3 2 1

Printed in the United States of America

This book is for Ashlee,
who gave me a home.

THE COMPANY MAN

CHAPTER ONE

The canal was a gray, rotting thing, so polluted and turgid that what it contained could hardly be called water at all. It wound below the stone arches and the spiderweb trusses of its many bridges, and at each bend it gained yet more refuse. At one turning enough sediment and muck had happened to gather and dry to become something like soil. There small, mousy reeds grew and clutched at the passing garbage, forming a staggered little delta that curved out across the canal.

Hayes looked at the little nest and saw something shining on the edge. He examined the sludge around the channel and frowned at his shoes, then sighed and found the best purchase and leaned forward. He scooped up the prize and took out his handkerchief and cleaned off the mud. It was a coin, underneath it all. A politician's stern face glared back, on the other side a state bird or some creed. He smiled and laughed and held it up to the sky, trying to find a rare stream of sunlight falling through the towering buildings of the surrounding neighborhood. Finding none, he gave up.

"Hey!" called a voice.

He turned and saw Garvey looking down at him from the top of the hill.

"Yes?" said Hayes.

"We hooked him," Garvey said.

"Good for you," said Hayes.

"Come on over."

"Why?"

"Come on over," said Garvey again.

"I don't particularly want to. I'm enjoying myself here," Hayes said, gesturing to the river. "Look, I found a quarter."

"You don't want to see him?" Garvey asked.

"I don't need to see him. You're not going to file it just by seeing him."

"That's not the point. Come on, get over here."

Hayes walked to Garvey at the top of the hill, Garvey glaring at him all the while, and then they both descended into the other side of the canal. It was an immense construction, a blank gray canyon with shanties and tumbling lean-tos grouped down closer to the water. All of them had been abandoned as the police first invaded. Garvey and Hayes picked their way down around soiled vagrant beddings and miles of graffiti. On one spot there were the faded bones of a hopscotch game. Hayes tried to imagine children playing next to this reeking Styx and abandoned it.

The morning mist was lifting and Hayes could just make out the other officers milling away down on the bank. Something white and smooth floated out on the waters ahead. The air was so cold and wet it stung and Hayes pulled his scarf tight. On cold mornings like this he ached for the sour honey warmth of bourbon in his belly, but he steeled himself and tried to push those thoughts from his mind.

"Say, who is this on this quarter?" he said. He held it out. "I can never keep track of your politicians."

"He was spotted a ways down the canal," said Garvey, ignoring him. "Head down, drifting our way. Looks like someone sent him on a swim."

"Doesn't seem to be a very good swimmer," said Hayes.

"No. No, he doesn't."

They both approached the bank slowly. Garvey moved with the practiced plod of a harassed policeman, already resigned to face the terrible day. A uniform scurried up to match his pace and Garvey nodded absently as he rattled off a few facts and details about the sight ahead, none of which amounted to anything. The uniform waited expectantly, hoping for some commendation or at least acknowledgment from the big detective, but Garvey's face betrayed nothing. He just sniffed and put his hands in his pockets as though enjoying any pleasant stroll. Crestfallen, the uniform departed, and Hayes resumed his place at Garvey's side. The other officers watched him curiously. He was short and wispy and overdressed, and seemed queerly aristocratic with his long blond hair and expensive coat, which was several sizes too large for him. And whereas Garvey made a straight, slow trudge to the river, Hayes wound and wove aimlessly, distracted by odd things found on the ground, or perhaps lost in his own thoughts. To anyone's eyes the two of them seemed no more right for each other than they were for the neighborhood, yet when Hayes asked for a cigarette Garvey fished a tin from his pocket with his thick boxer's hands and lifted one out without a word. Hayes took it, murmuring a thanks through a small smile, and then passed his free hand over the cigarette in a quick flourish. It vanished, his fingers left holding nothing at all. With another flourish it had returned again, and Hayes planted it in his mouth, smiling cleverly. Garvey barely seemed to notice. His eyes stayed fixed on the river in the mist. Hayes sighed and stuffed himself farther into his coat and continued on.

Finally they came to the water's edge and looked. Had it not been for the hands you could never have told what it was. Facedown in the water it looked like some floating pile of rags, wet white towels twisted up and drifting alone. But the hands were visible down in the waters below, ghostly white and perfect, gesturing this way and that as they were buffeted by the currents. It looked like he was conducting some underwater orchestra, a soiled water nymph toiling through the runoff.

Hayes watched the officers struggle with the thing in the water, tugging it ever closer. "And he's a company man, I assume," he said.

"Don't know," said Garvey.

"What? You don't?"

"No. That's why I called you."

"You called me down here at seven in the morning on a body that might not even be one of mine?" said Hayes. "Good God, Garvey. I won't forgive you for that. I won't. I simply can't."

One of the uniforms reached out with a hooked cane and caught him on his side and pulled him close. They gathered around the bank with sticks and nets and Garvey helped them ease the dripping wreck ashore.

Hayes watched as they hauled him out and half-sang to himself, "Here comes another stray from my accursed flock, perhaps. My wandering lambs, my lost little babes. Where did you run to, little lamb? What trouble did you get yourself mixed up in? And to where can I lead you next?"

"Jesus Christ," said Garvey. He shook his head at Hayes, disgusted.

Once they had the body steady they laid him out on the ground. His face was waterlogged and almost formless, his eyes little swollen slits and his lips dumbly twisted. A ragged gash ran zigzag from one corner of his jaw to the top of the opposite collarbone. The injury was colorless, the flesh like custard or curd. No fish had been at him for no fish would live in the Construct canals.

"One of yours?" asked Garvey.

Hayes peered at him. "I can't say."

Garvey sighed and leaned on one of the nets. "Not familiar? Nothing?"

"No, I'm afraid not, Garv. McNaughton pays me for a great deal of things, but they don't pay me to keep a mental registry of every factory groundling they have." He coughed. "Anything in his pockets?"

Garvey reached in, fumbled around, then pulled his hands out and dried them off. "No."

"So just a man in his skivvies and an undershirt working part time as a buoy."

"Seems like it."

"Well. That's all I know, too."

They stood up and looked at the dead man. Thunderclouds of bruises lined his ribs and legs. The other officers clambered ashore and the gray river water from their waders left strata of silt across the dead man's heels.

"Four hundred and eighty-six," said Hayes.

"What?" said Garvey.

"This is Mr. Four Hundred and Eighty-six. Murder of this year."

"Oh. That's right, I guess. How'd you know that?"

"A rumor," said Hayes.

"That the only good rumor you know about this?"

"Oh, perhaps, Garv. Perhaps." He knelt and looked at the dead man's fingers. They were yellowed with nicotine and the nails were ragged. Several small pink cuts dotted the webbing of his hands and orange calluses floated in his palms below each finger. Hayes touched them, felt their firmness. Factory worker. Maybe a loader of some kind. Or perhaps he had been, once.

"I think he's one of mine, yes," said Hayes softly.

"Is he a unioner?" Garvey asked.

"Oh, I've no idea there." He gently placed the hand back on the cement and patted its back, as though reassuring the dead man everything would be all right. Several of the uniforms pulled faces as they watched the gesture, but Hayes was so used to the presence of the dead that he barely gave it thought. "But I'd certainly guess so."

"Are we good to take this, Detective?" asked one of the uniforms.

"Yeah," Garvey said, and sighed again. "Yeah, go ahead and pack him up."

They watched as the uniforms unloaded the corpse slickerbag and tucked him in and tied it up. Then they placed him on a canvas stretcher and began carrying him up the hill as a thin rain started. Garvey and Hayes followed.

"What I would give," said Garvey, "for something simple. A wife that shot a husband in front of the butcher. Two thugs getting into a tussle at a bar and one getting three inches of knife for his passion. Something nice, you know?"

"That's a rather morbid thought. But then, you have made a rather morbid career choice, Garv."

They began to crest the canal, the tops of distant buildings just peeking over the edge. "We're going to pass five hundred this year," said Garvey.

"Yes," said Hayes.

"Easily."

"Yes."

They left the canal and came back up to civilization, to the winding cement streets and electric lamps and the distant putter of cars. The scent of burning coal laced the morning wind and cries and shouts echoed from the tenements. Rag-wrapped beggars lay in doorways like sodden mummies, by all appearances dead except for the breath pluming from their hoods. And far beyond the rambling skyline the downtown towers of Evesden overtook the horizon, their windows and lights shining bright, jealously guarding their modernity. Every once in a while a spotlight stabbed up, calling out to some airship hidden in the clouds. The future was only a mile or two away but would come no closer to places such as these.

"You should have looked at him," said Garvey as they entered the warren of tiny lanes.

"I did look at him," Hayes said.

"Yeah. But you didn't want to."

"It's not part of my job. Or yours."

"Doesn't matter."

"You get too wrapped up in these things. It'll ruin your morning."

"He's a victim. A real victim, I think. I've got a feeling about him. Someone has to look, for things like that."

"Maybe. Do you think it'll file?"

"I think it might."

"Oh," said Hayes. He thought for a moment and said, "I don't."

"Hm. No," agreed Garvey after a while. "No, it probably won't." He sighed. "I hate Novembers. At least in December you know it's fucking done, or near enough."

As they left the canal behind, the neighborhood grew cleaner and the streets grew wider. Even though the dawn was lost behind the overcast the city was coming to life. Halfway up the side of a tenement a fat woman warbled something in Italian and draped patched sheets along a clothesline, her enormous white breasts almost spilling out of her nightshirt as she moved. A slaughterhouse ice cart rattled around to the back of a butcher's, and though its back was stained rose-pink from old blood there was no threat of any viscera spilling, not on a frosty day such as this. At Milligan's the barkeep opened the door and began kicking at three souses who'd slept hunched and penitent on the sidewalk, and the men moaned and scrambled away, cursing. Down at the corner four Chinamen sat on a wooden cage of geese, stoic and regal in their robes and caps as though they were foreign emissaries, and they watched Garvey as he walked by, sensing police. Garvey studiously ignored them, but Hayes gave them a sharp salute, and one of them favored him with a raised eyebrow. Across the street what had to be the world's oldest newsie peeled back his ancient lips to reveal a toothless mouth and bawled out the latest trumped-up outrage, something about how President Ballinger was once again sending the nation to hell in a handbasket. Three old men strode over, puffing in indignation, and paid for three papers and read them and shook their heads.

All in all, it was a morning like any other. It was hard to believe that somewhere in all this were rivers where the dead dreamily swam through the waters, or slept under upraised houses, or perhaps waited for the morning in an alley next to the previous day's trash. And yet Hayes knew it happened with regularity. They were simply another kind of citizen in these neighborhoods, a kind that waited to be dealt with by whoever had the time.

They found Garvey's car, a spindly affair that looked as if it should fall apart after four miles, and they both grunted as they climbed in. Garvey primed the car's cradle and listened to it whine as it fed into the engine. Then he eased up on the drive handle. The engine buzzed and sang its clockwork song, and he released the brake and they started off, down through the wandering alleys and out onto the trolley path and into the auto lane. Hayes leaned his head against the glass and massaged his temples and pinched his nose. He moaned a little as a trolley roared past and sank down into the underground. Then he took out a pair of spectacles with blue-tinted lenses, which he delicately referred to as his "morning glasses," and fixed them on his nose and stared out at the street.

"Late night?" asked Garvey.

"You know the answer to that," he said.

"Hah. Yeah. Why did you help today, anyways?"

"Pardon?"

"Why did you agree to come at all? If you'd been up so late, I mean."

Hayes didn't answer at first. They moved onto Michigan Avenue and started across town. The Nail rose in the distance, dwarfing the other buildings. It was at least twenty blocks north, but even from here every line of its architecture could be seen by the naked eye. Its ash-gray shaft stabbed into the sky, windows lining its castellations. At the top its jade steeple glittered with promise. They called it the Nail because to many it looked like one, with a fat head and a long sharp tooth, waiting to be hammered into something. Hayes had always disagreed. To him it looked like a finger, gray and thick, and at the top was its green fingernail, scratching at the sky. It was still a nail, but to him it was alive. Maybe growing.

Unlike many, Hayes was familiar with the inner workings of the building. He usually went there at least ten times a month. At its top silver letters spelled out the word MCNAUGHTON. His eyes traced over the letters and he sourly reflected that the same people who owned that marvelous piece of architecture also owned him, in a way.

"Well?" said Garvey.

"Mmm? What?" asked Hayes.

"Why'd you help?"

"Oh. I suppose just to have something to do," he said, and rolled to his side and tried to sleep.

CHAPTER TWO

Garvey wheeled the car toward the Brennan Bridge as the wind shook the last drops of rain from its back. They descended into the commercial streets and the sky was blotted out by a jungle of signs and advertisements dangling off the building faces, dripping gray water and runny ink. They parked underneath the shadow of the signs and walked down to a small corner diner, a dingy little eatery whose heat and noise spilled out onto the sidewalk. It was an early-morning place, filled with dockmen and construction workers and other tradesmen who awoke before the sun, a place where one could go and grudgingly wait the coming day. It was also a common stop for police, particularly ones who kept the most abnormal hours.

They had to fight their way through to a booth. Hayes thrust himself far into the corner and pulled his coat up so it made piles about his shoulders. He leaned his head against the window and stared out at the street, blinking languidly.

Garvey looked him over, frowning. "You look terrible."

"Well," Hayes said airily, "I rather feel terrible. But then, we just fished a corpse out of a river. How should I feel?"

"No, I mean you really look sick. Can I get you something?"

"Just water. Water will do me fine."

"Water? Your usual breakfast menu includes a beer or two, if I recall."

"No," said Hayes, and closed his eyes.

"No?"

"No, Garv. I won't have a beer. I won't be having a beer for some time, I should say." He tilted his head away from the window and smiled wanly at Garvey. "I'm giving it another go, you see, Garv. Trying to dry out once more."

Garvey raised his eyebrows. "Again?"

"Yes. Again."

"That makes this, what? Attempt number five?"

"Something like that," said Hayes. He sank lower in his seat.

"What's the occasion? Have another binge you regret? I can't imagine it'd be worse than the time you fell off the trolley."

"I suppose it's something of a special occasion," said Hayes. "But this is more professionally motivated."

Garvey looked surprised. "Really? The company's leaning on you to quit?"

"It's all very unspoken. Everything's done in subtleties. Courting a church girl is easier, I swear. Or at least I'd imagine it'd be, having never personally tried."

"How's it going?"

"How do you think?" Hayes snapped. "It's fucking awful. It feels like there's an army of nails trying to dig their way out of my head. How about you get me that water before I die right here in this booth, eh? Then you'll have another fucking body to deal with."

Garvey allowed himself a small smile, then nodded and left.

Hayes turned back to the window. Outside a chilly cement world tumbled by, filled with columns of steam and window-lined canyons and the colorless faces of crowds. He watched as people threaded through the alleys and the lanes to the waterfront streets. The Arch Street airship cradle was just a block or two down, its spire covered in glittering cables and panels, all tilting and shifting to correspond with incoming airships. Below that he saw the immense dark curve of the Brennan Bridge, the inner recesses of its arch lost to shadow. At the top two men sat dangling their feet through the railing and sharing some small meal. Their bodies steamed slightly in the morning air as though burning.

Garvey returned with a glistening plate of eggs and sausage and rolls. He put down a mug of water and pushed it over to Hayes, who lifted it up and maneuvered it through the lapels of his coat to his mouth. He sipped it once, then sipped again, deeper. "Ah," he said. "That's better. That's just what I needed."

Garvey carefully watched as Hayes placed the mug of water back on the tabletop.

"What?" said Hayes.

"So," said Garvey. "You've quit drinking but you're still hitting up the tearooms."

"Well. Yes," said Hayes, nettled. "I can't give up everything at once. I need a few vices. Just to function. Just to keep my head on."

"How long have you been dry?"

"Centuries, it feels like," he moaned. "Ages. Ages and ages and ages. Civilizations have risen and fallen in the time I've been dry. But I would guess a month, really. Two, at most."

"That's pretty good, for you."

"Mornings are the hardest. Mornings like this, especially. I need a little fire in my belly to stay on my feet."

"What'd you think of it, anyways? This morning?"

"I don't know," Hayes said, turning back to the window. "Do you want me to be honest, Garv?"

"Sure."

"I won't tell you anything you don't already know."

Garvey nodded, sawing through a sausage with slow, silent care. Grease poured from its mealy cross-section to pool around the eggs.

Hayes waited a moment. Then he said, "If you want me to be

completely frank, Garvey, I think you're fucked. Very fucked. I don't have any tricks to play here."

Garvey stopped sawing. "You can't at least check and see if he's one of yours?"

"If you can get a name, sure. I can check him against the factory rolls. But that's if you get a name, which I've got to think is pretty unlikely. Even though he wasn't dressed, he didn't exactly seem like a socialite. Not a well-known out-and-about-town sort. And even if you do get a name, there's been a lot of flux among the loaders and workers since the whole union business started. It's less organized than ever. It'd be . . . Well. It'd be impossible to nail it down."

Garvey's grimace subtly hardened. His limited range of facial expressions bordered on an inside joke among his fellow detectives in the Evesden Police Department. To the unobservant his face would seem to never move at all, his words just barely escaping his slight frown, yet to those who knew him the slightest twitch of his broad, craggy forehead spoke volumes. Garvey could tell you if he thought a body would file just by slowly lifting an eyebrow or pursing his lips. But his eyes never moved, permanently buried in the shadow of his brow. They were eyes that plainly said they had seen it all, or at least enough of it to feel they didn't really need to see the rest.

"Yeah," he said, and nodded. "Yeah."

"Like I said, it's nothing you don't already know," Hayes said. "I'm sorry you caught it."

"You said that already."

"I'm still sorry."

"You sure he's union, though?" Garvey asked, half-hopeful.

"Probably. You do, too, you just don't want to admit it. I mean, come on, Garv, you can't tell me you just fished a man who looks like a worker out of a Construct canal and haven't thought it has something to do with the lefties rattling around."

"No. Goddamn, I wish it didn't, though."

"So. How many does that make?" Hayes said.

"Make?"

"Yes. Union deaths in all. I'd expect you're all keeping tally marks over the morgue doors by now."

"Hm. Four," said Garvey reluctantly. "Four in the past five months. And that's not counting the beatings and other pointless violence that's been going on. I don't know how many we've had due to that."

"But four murders? Four genuine union murders?"

"Yeah."

"Hm," Hayes said. "Things are heating up."

"No doubt," said Garvey. He began speaking in the toneless cadence of work-speech: "All four were found very, very murdered, all in different but discreet areas of the city. Docks. Vagrants' cemetery, found one out there, pretty vicious. Most recent one was a union buster. He was found in a canal, like today. No one's getting anywhere with any of them. Now Collins has us all taking anything that even smells like union and making it high concern. 'Prioritization,' they're calling it. We're probably going to junk those four, though. I don't think there's any headway to make with them. Not with fresh ones coming in today, like this one."

"Goodness," said Hayes. "Your statistics must be terrible."

"Yeah. Four hundred and eighty-six. Jesus." Garvey shook his head. "Last month marked the highest yearly total of the century. The papers were all over it. The mayor's office is having daily panic attacks."

"Well. Nineteen-twenty can't come soon enough, I'd say. Happy new year, Garv."

Garvey muttered his agreement and turned back to his plate, sometimes shooting Hayes sullen looks as though he had personally engineered the foul morning, or possibly the bad year. Hayes ignored him, content to make his water vanish in little swallows.

Hayes was not, despite the beliefs of several scene-side cops and minor criminals, a policeman. He was often seen with the police or the district attorney's office and other civil servants, and a lot of the time he acted like a cop, with his constant questions and presumptuous manner, though he did seem to grin more than most. The one thing that really marked him as different was his English accent. But he had no badge, no gun, no pension, and no allegiance to the city or any jurisdiction. Those rare few who concluded that he wasn't police often wondered why he was tolerated among them, or why he wanted to be there at all.

Figuring out exactly who Hayes worked for would have been difficult for anyone. At the moment his paycheck came from a minor canning factory on the wharf-front, partially managed by a San Francisco shipping firm, which was owned by a prominent Chicago real estate corporation, which was in turn owned by a high-powered merchant bank overseas whose primary stockholder was, at the end, the famous McNaughton Corporation, linchpin of the city of Evesden and, according to some, the world. Hayes made sure to route how McNaughton paid him every once in a while, just to check. If he had done his work right, they changed its path once every six months.

Precisely what Hayes did for McNaughton was a mystery to most everyone. His chief overseer was James Evans, deputy director of securities at McNaughton, who often said Hayes's job was to be "a backroom boy, someone to make sure everyone follows procedure and that sensitive matters do not become unfavorable for the company's interests." Brightly, who was above even Evans as chief director of securities, chose to say that Hayes was "a fixer" or "our man in the field, but here at home." That was if he said anything at all, which he usually didn't.

Hayes thought of his job in very simple terms: it was his job to find out the things no one wanted him to find out and know the things no one else knew, all in the name of McNaughton Western Foundry Corporation. It often put him in many interesting situations. For example, this was not the first time he had been involved in a murder investigation, and while this one in particular didn't promise much interest for McNaughton as a whole, Hayes was always willing to help Garvey whenever he could. Garvey's high position in the Department and similar line of work made him an invaluable resource for Hayes, and after their working together for so long he'd also become the closest thing to a friend Hayes had.

"So I'm fucked," said Garvey to his near-empty plate.

"Maybe not," Hayes said cheerfully. "You could turn something up. You often do."

"Maybe. You say maybe. Maybe isn't probably."

"No. But if you keep at it long enough, it'll drop."

"Hm. Well. Give me a second while I pay," said Garvey, standing up.

"I'll be outside," said Hayes, and he gathered his coat about him and worked back through the throng.

It seemed to be even colder now that Hayes had felt a second of warmth. He huddled by Garvey's car, breathing deep and trying to stuff his hands ever farther into his pockets. There was a sour film on the back of his throat. His thoughts returned to the soft, white face rising up out of the river. Something mutinous began happening down in his belly, some minor organ pitching and yawing with a foul tide. He resisted it at first. Then began swallowing. A rumbling belch came up, followed by something that should have stayed down, and he instinctively flipped his hair and scarf out of his face before falling to his knees and retching. The hot clear fluids sent up thick clouds of steam as they spattered onto the icy stone. For the next few minutes he was wracked with the dry heaves, rattling burps that bubbled up from his deep inner recesses to come burbling out with festoons of spit and mucus.

Garvey emerged from the diner and stopped short at the sight. "Jesus Christ. I thought you said you'd quit drinking."

"I did quit drinking," Hayes said, wheezing and hiccupping.

"That's the classic drunkard's morning pose to me. Careful not to get any on the car."

"I *did* quit drinking," Hayes insisted.

Garvey took in Hayes's pale skin and the small puddle of thin, clear vomit. Then he sighed and scratched his head and said, "God. I know what this is. You gave up drink so you've been hitting the pipe double time. Is that it?"

"Fuck you," Hayes said, gasping for breath.

"The shakes in your hands agree with me."

"It's cold out."

"But not that cold." Garvey took out a handkerchief and handed it to him. "Here. Clean yourself up."

Once Hayes had wiped his mouth Garvey helped him to his feet and leaned him up against the car hood. They watched as a horse-drawn cabbie clopped around the corner, its lantern shuddering on its rooftop. A dark shadow passed over it, draping the cart in darkness, and Hayes and Garvey craned their heads up to see an airship crossing the clouds and blocking a rare shred of sunlight. It must have been very far up, Hayes thought, as he could not hear or feel the engines. That or he had become accustomed to the low buzzing in the ears and teeth you felt whenever a ship came near.

"How often do you do it?" asked Garvey quietly.

"Do what?" said Hayes. He wiped tears from his eyes.

"Go to the tearoom."

"Oh. I don't know. Every once in a while, I suppose."

"Why? Is it the voices?"

"I don't hear voices. And no. It's not. I suppose it's just something to do."

"Something to do," echoed Garvey.

"Yes."

Garvey had come to get him at four in the morning that day. Hayes hadn't been in his apartment, not the crummy little corner of the warehouse allotted to him by the good Mr. Brightly. But Garvey had known where Hayes would be. Tucked into a booth at the Eastern Evening Tearoom, far in the gloomy back passage lit only by blood-red Oriental lamps and the candles carried by the sickly girls in robes from table to table. But it wasn't tea they brought to their customers. Herbal maybe, but not tea.

The place was well known to the police. They'd tried to shut it down ten years ago, before Evesden had lost interest in a war on the opium trade. By the time Garvey had found him that morning Hayes had just been coming back from his little inner jaunt, his mind swimming with the peaty smoke of the tar, faintly cognizant there was a world going on around him.

Garvey said, "You know, rumor has it this prioritization stuff, that was an order. From Brightly to the commissioner."

"Brightly?" said Hayes. "My Brightly?"

"Yeah. And to the deputy commissioner and God knows who else. Said to junk whatever else we were working at and take any union murders we get and run with them. Sort of brazen, guy from the board of directors of your company telling the Department what to do. I was surprised when I heard. I thought you'd let me know it was coming."

"I didn't know myself," said Hayes. "They haven't contacted me in some time, actually."

"Really? Why?"

"Oh, I fouled something up. I think the gods are still mad at me. I'm on the shelf, I suppose."

"What'd you do?"

Hayes pulled a face. "It was an error of judgment."

"What the hell does that mean?"

"Well," said Hayes tentatively, "they told me to look into this one trader, a Mr. Ferguson, to see if he was doing anything shady. And their fears were well-founded. Let's just say he was dealing from the bottom of the deck. So I decided to... to put the screws to him and ask him about it, and, well, when I did he behaved somewhat erratically."

"What's somewhat erratically?"

Hayes sighed. "It means he panicked. Thought it was the scaffold for him, or prison, or something idiotic. And he weighed his chances and he . . . well, he leaped out the closest window when I had my back turned."

Garvey stared at him. He opened his mouth to say something but stopped as he did some quick math. "Wait, Ferguson? As in *James* Ferguson?"

"That would be the one."

"Jesus, you were involved in that? I read about that in the papers."

"Yes," said Hayes softly. "I'd expect you would have. They told me to go careful. I understand he was much esteemed. But I suppose I forgot."

"Would this have something to do with why you're drying out?"

Hayes smiled weakly at him.

"So you're on the outs," said Garvey. "Just when I need it least."

"I'm not on the outs," he said. He fumbled in his coat and produced a small slip of paper. "They sent me this the other day. Said to come in and speak to Evans. Later this morning, as a matter of fact."

"They sent you a telegram? Rather than talk to you?"

"Yes. I'm poison right now, I guess. Trying to keep me at a distance. Mind giving me a lift?"

Garvey glared at him. "I guess I can. I need you more than ever these days. I hope they're not just bringing you in to fire you for good, though."

"I hope so, too," Hayes said mildly, and climbed into the car. Garvey started it up again and wheeled it east, back across the city to the green-topped tower that seemed to dominate the horizon, no matter where you stood.

CHAPTER THREE

Each day in Evesden it was estimated that somewhere between two and three thousand people migrated to the city, more than anywhere else in America and possibly the world. This statistic was, of course, just short of a wild guess, since a fair majority of new immigrants came by illegal means, trafficked in from the Pacific in the bellies of immense iron ships, and so went uncounted. The workmen from the plains and the mountains to the east found more reputable passage, coming by train or by car or bus, and only the wealthiest and most privileged traveler came by air, drifting in on one of the many airship channels running that day. Much like the present population of Evesden, they were a motley band of people, coming from many states and countries and for many reasons, but it was always easy to tell new Evesdeners by the way they stared around themselves and the one question they would all eventually ask:

"How?" they would say, their eyes often resting on the enormous jade tower standing on the western skyline. How had they done it? How had McNaughton made the city and remade the world itself, and in only a handful of years? How had this tiny corner of the Western shore become the center of the globe overnight?

It was a perplexing question in the rest of the world, but in Evesden itself it was considered silly and naive, a badge of ignorance that marked the rubes. Answering it was thought great sport for most of Evesden's veteran population, forgetting that they had almost all been new arrivals once. They often answered with lies, or folktales, or silly superstitions, or they claimed some secret knowledge the rest of the city was not yet privy to. The seamstresses in the Lynn workhouses would often say that the Nail had always been there, that when the sea receded from the land it was revealed to be standing up like a huge spike, with all of McNaughton's astounding inventions already piled up within it. The trolley workers wryly told the new boys that the company brain trust had found hidden messages in the Bible. Why, they decoded passages of the Old Testament according to some codex, of course, and found the designs for their creations within the first pages of the Good Book itself. And still more whispered that the McNaughton Corporation had been kidnapping brilliant minds from abroad from the beginning, and forcing them to come up with ingenious new innovations. They could not possibly churn out wonders with such speed, they said, unless it was forced.

But for once, the truth was possibly almost as interesting as the myths. Historians and businessmen who were well versed in the actual story agreed that the origins of the McNaughton Corporation were practically predestined. Fated even. Its birth was so perfectly coincidental it had to be the hand of God himself, working just off the cold waters of Puget Sound.

It had inauspiciously begun in the summer of 1872 when lumber entrepreneur William McNaughton started scouting the fledgling port cities around the Sound, seeking a way to establish trade to San Francisco to the south. Yet before he could begin, his party soon came under storm and was forced to seek shelter in the house of a nearby fisherman, just outside what was then the tiny fishing hamlet of Evesden, a bit south of Discovery Bay. The old man who lived there was accommodating enough, allowing them to bed down and sharing what little food he had, and he introduced himself as Mr. Lawrence Kulahee.

Of the many essays that would come to be written about Mr. Kulahee, most of them would focus on his unspectacular appearance and lifestyle. To the average eye he must have seemed to be no more than a common fisherman, and the few photos taken of him showed a squat, dour-looking man with a head not unlike a potato and eyes both suspicious and shallow. The photos certainly didn't suggest their subject to be anything close to "the Leonardo da Vinci of the nineteenth century," as he would eventually be called. Later generations of phrenologists, denied the right to study Kulahee's remains, eyeballed the photos and proclaimed his skull structure synonymous with brilliance, but most scholars admitted they saw nothing in those little brown eyes. No spark of genius, no glimmer of intellect. It just goes to show, they all agreed, how appearances can be wildly deceiving.

After the storm ended William McNaughton found the road ahead was washed out, and while his companions chose to travel back he decided to remain with Kulahee and wait for the way ahead to become safer. Kulahee said it didn't matter much to him, so long as McNaughton was willing to help him out with a few of his daily chores. At first McNaughton dreaded the idea of being dragged around by the little old man all day, but his curiosity grew when they went around back to draw water and stopped at a curious little device mounted in the ground.

The machine immediately caught the eye. It was no more than two or three feet high, a strange creation of gears and pulleys set in a long, tight frame with a wide flat hat that kept the rain from entering its inner workings. On one end there was a crank with a small metal switch, and on the other was a short, slanted snout. Kulahee put the bucket before the snout, then began gently cranking the device, the little gears snapping and clacking like hail. McNaughton watched, curious, and then felt a slight vibration below his feet. Something shuddered and squalled and moaned down in the earth, just a few yards below the grass, and he stepped back, certain something would pierce the sodden ground and rise up. Kulahee paid no mind, still cranking away. The noises died to a low thrum and a small rope of steam grew from somewhere among the gears of the machine. It quivered slightly, as though in anticipation, and then it almost seemed to sigh as it produced the goal of all its exertion.

A thin stream of water began to trickle from the snout and down into the bucket. Kulahee stopped cranking and then pressed the switch on the side of the device. The trickle grew to a steady flow, filling up the bucket in moments. Then he hit the switch again, let the flow of water die off, and picked the bucket up and began walking away.

McNaughton stood and watched him leave, stunned. Then he struggled to catch up, asking, "What was that?"

"What was what?" asked Kulahee.

"That thing you used. What was that?"

"Oh," he said. "It's just a pump I made. A little hand pump."

"I've never seen a pump like that," McNaughton said.

Kulahee nodded, not paying attention.

"You say you made it?" McNaughton asked.

"Yeah," he said. "It takes the creek water. Not from the creek. But below it. Took me a bit to figure out how. But I did it. I make a lot of things," he added.

"A lot of things?"

"Yeah."

"What sort of things?" asked McNaughton.

"I don't know. Things that do different things."

"Like what, though?"

Kulahee turned and looked at him. Then he said, "All sorts of things. You... you want to see them?"

"Yes," said McNaughton. "Yes, I really would."

Once the day's work was done Kulahee led McNaughton to his

shed. There he showed him about a half-dozen other inventions of his, each staggeringly complex. There was one device that used a series of old lenses and mirrors to take the light from a candle and magnify it to illuminate an entire room with a clean, strong radiance. Another purified water, using a series of tiny rotating screens to filter out all manner of silts and then channel them into little concentric piles. And there was another that was just a fat, black egg, set in a glass dome with three small pipes running from its base.

"What does that do?" asked McNaughton.

"Gets hot," said Kulahee.

"Hot?"

"Yeah. Gets hot whenever there's a thunderstorm in, oh, say, three miles of here. Gets burning hot." He scratched his nose and said, "I use it to boil water. Make coffee."

McNaughton stared at it, then reached out to feel its radiance.

The future was born not in Paris or New York or Rome. It was born in a shed at five o'clock in the evening with two muddy men and a handful of mice as its only witnesses. Within a month McNaughton was sharing ten patent rights with Mr. Kulahee, who likely had no idea what he was signing away, and the McNaughton Western Foundry Corporation was scratched out on paper before Christmas.

McNaughton's venture began to pick up immediately, its first product being a streamlined version of Kulahee's hand pump. It was lighter, able to pull water from the worst wells, and through Kulahee's strange mechanical genius it did it all with a minimum of effort, amplifying force many times over. It seemed to pluck water from the very air, one journalist said. It was an enormous success, and the McNaughton Corporation skyrocketed. The company followed it up with a type of steam engine McNaughton himself suggested, taking Kulahee's understanding of mechanics from the pump and applying it to locomotion. This new model took much more refining, as Kulahee had never planned for his designs to be implemented on such a large scale, but at the end of their work they produced an adapted, faster form of locomotive that needed a quarter of the coal to run. By the time they introduced the conduits, those strange steam generators that ran purely off the discharge from nearby electrical storms, McNaughton was one of the foremost industrial barons in the world.

One thing struck McNaughton's investors as strange, however: upon forming the company, McNaughton refused to move the base of business away from the small fishing settlement where Kulahee had built his home. It would have been an easy thing to take the creations and Mr. Kulahee's valued mind back to San Francisco, where he could import resources, or even east to Seattle, which was a burgeoning city at the time, but McNaughton insisted that business come to him. Exactly why became a much-argued point. Some said Kulahee refused to move, forcing McNaughton to cater to the eccentric genius's rudimentary needs. Others said McNaughton wanted to become a strong voice in forming Washington's nascent statehood when it came to commerce, which he did. And still more claimed that Mr. Kulahee insisted he could do his work only when he was in a little cave far down in the valley, a place where he could go and meditate and allow himself to think. Perhaps it was there that Kulahee first dreamed up his famous airships, which would open up the skies to humanity at the turn of the century.

But no one could verify this. Both Kulahee and his designs quickly became almost fanatically protected company secrets. As patents became established the workings of any McNaughton product would naturally become known, but as for where the ideas came from and the research methods and principles that Kulahee had almost absent-mindedly developed, those became mysteries from the McNaughton Corporation's inception. Many took issue with it, but McNaughton was well protected. Not only did it often buy out its most vocal critics, but Washington state laws defended the company on every side, and as the corporation grew to become the powerhouse of the American economy it became protected on the national level as well. Generous military grants helped secure friends in all branches of government, and later it was generally agreed that if America had not threatened to become involved in Europe with McNaughton weapons at the vanguard then the entire German Crisis might have never been averted.

Evesden soon became an industrial city on a level never before witnessed. It sprawled out almost exponentially, with new neighborhoods and housing developments appearing overnight. Its growth was unaccountably messy, as blocks and streets and tangles of alleys were sporadically flung down and paved over. In some of the newer sections a rare street grid was enforced almost as an afterthought, but beyond a few blocks it always devolved into the usual snarl of pathways, splitting and curling away like bursting fireworks. The city lacked a genuine downtown section as well, choosing instead to absorb nearby townships and integrate them into its sprawl, and so Newton and Westbank and Lynn and Infield became neighborhoods trapped in the depths of the city, each with its own identity and customs.

But while the city planning left much to be desired, the city itself became a wonder of the world. Evesden was a place where the amazing became mundane, it was said. There towering cradles stood watch over the skyline, each a delicate, spider-spun array of cables and struts that embraced the shining gold airships that would come drifting down from the sky as though in a dream. Throughout the city, electric lamps bathed the streets in a soft white glow. Automobiles, a rarity in the rest of the world, choked the roads in places. On cold days the moisture from the shore would mix with the fumes from the plants, layering the thin, winding streets in a thick fog, and as you walked along one lane you would sometimes see a factory emerging from the curl of the clouds ahead, bejeweled with harsh blue lamps and covered in countless spires, like the deck of a ghost ship drifting mere yards away. And down below the city the underground trolley tunnels shuttled passengers from one end of Evesden to the other in minutes, sometimes even passing under the ocean itself.

But it was said that the trolleys were just the beginning, and that like icebergs only the tip of Evesden could be seen and the rest was far below, somewhere deep in the earth, even below the trolley lines. While it was true that McNaughton facilities were mostly underground, some said there were passages and chambers far below that the public never knew of, places where enormous machines did strange things for secret purposes, working day and night. Many Evesdeners testified that in certain places in the city you could hear a slow, soft pounding echoing up storm drains and sewers like some distant heart. Some even claimed there were words in it, a low voice speaking in the darkness in an unknown tongue, and indeed some clans of the homeless would perch around the deep vents and try to interpret its sounds, though this was universally regarded as madness.

Exactly when the city became the center of the New World was hard to say, but many agreed that the 1893 World's Fair was when it undeniably marked its place in the future. The choice of Evesden as the site outraged the rest of the nation: New York could not believe this frontier dock city had outbid it, and Chicago, hungry after years of denial and condescension, hardly took it any better. And after the Paris World's Fair and the Eiffel Tower, no one of sound mind could believe this ugly, improvised, industrial city could do anything half so graceful. Surely it would embarrass the country. But when the opening day came and journalists and sightseers gathered before the immense steel gates made just for the occasion, and then passed through and saw the Shifting Sky City and the Crystal Fountain and the Atrium of Arcs, the dissenters fell quiet. Many were moved to tears by the strange marvels silently displayed before them. "I just can't believe men made such things," one onlooker was famously quoted as saying, shaking his head. "I just can't. I never seen such before."

Evesden defied words, the journalists said. It was beyond description. Many simply called it unworldly. An alien city somehow wedged up on the coastline, something so foreign the mind could barely grasp it.

But the city had its problems as well. More and more laborers flocked to Evesden, hungry to work on the lines, and the city quickly found it could not keep pace. In 1884 it had a population just under nine hundred thousand, yet by 1900 it had six million. Smokestacks soon stretched down the coastline, McNaughton machines making yet more McNaughton products. Slums grew around the factories, disorganized and shabby, flung up in a matter of weeks. Shantytowns were built in the canals and on the pipelines and under bridges, swarming the docks and the train yards. City planners threw up squalid tenements, and after the shanty-dwellers stripped them of glass and plumbing they quickly grew overcrowded by the burgeoning populace, desperate for any place to stay. Corruption followed, feeding off the hunger. A miniature Chinatown sprang up by the piers that came to be known as Dockland, a place with its own laws and its own rules. And as McNaughton expanded, so did the crime rate, reaching first fifty murders a year, then a hundred and fifty, then three hundred, until finally at least four dozen people dropped a month.

Yet even as the city grappled to control itself, McNaughton kept nudging it forward, ever expanding. Products needed to be perfected, redesigned, and put to market. McNaughton Electric and Transportation Division quickly became the forerunner of the corporation, developing several projects a year, from construction equipment to telecommunications to the automobile and the airship. And with each release, thinkers and rivals all over the world wondered about the little old fisherman whose ideas had birthed a company, then a city, and then a world. How machines of such fantastic beauty and awe-inspiring possibility came from such a primitive character became one of the great questions the public was fond of toying with. Kulahee died in 1904, still in the same bed he had always slept in, though with a few more creature comforts that his respectable allowance enabled him to purchase. He took whatever secrets he still had with him. McNaughton himself died in 1912 and left no hint either.

Few gave it thought. The board of directors assumed control after they were both in the ground, nineteen shrewd men who were already worried about McNaughton's future in the world. As America assumed its place in the twentieth century, it was McNaughton that carried the standard, yet with each passing year its designs became ever more sought after. Word came of foreign companies and even countries that were disassembling McNaughton products and attempting to bribe high-level employees. Designs were abandoned and lost after bitter disputes. Internal movements developed, pressuring the top to spill. When designs for a different make of rifle barrel were leaked in a station in Italy, the board decided enough was enough. How can an empire bring wealth to the world, the company's leaders asked, if the world will not allow the empire to grow? They chose to answer the question themselves. McNaughton Western Foundry Corporation would arrange security to shepherd its strange little flock, and fight to keep its endless secrets at home and abroad.

CHAPTER FOUR

By the time Hayes got to the lobby of the McNaughton Tower his stomach was still rumbling but his mind was something close to steady. He swallowed, smoothed down his hair, and pushed open the doors and walked in.

The silence of the place was crushing. The lobby of the Nail never felt as much like a business place as it did a tomb. Gray-black pillars marched away from the front doors, all of them smooth and shining in the ghostly light of the lamps, which hung from the columns' sides like unearthly fruit. Suited figures paced in between the pillars, darting among the shadows to disappear down hidden halls. And high in the center of the lobby was the chandelier, a massive affair of dripping crystal and cruel, cold silver. It shone with a light so harsh and clean it was almost like starlight.

Hayes crossed the forest of pillars to the elevators on the far side and waited before the small bronzed doors. When they slid open the old black elevator man inside favored him with a wary eye and wordlessly motioned him in. Inside it was a tiny, shining coffin with buttons forming a wall of faintly glowing numerals. The old man mashed the one for the forty-seventh floor and they slowly began to rise, gathering speed as they slid through some unknown vein in the building's skeleton. When they arrived the doors slid open and Hayes stepped out into a small, high marble room, about the size of a very large closet. An orbed lamp hung several feet up, suspended in the shadows of the ceiling. On the far side was a tall metal door with a thick lock set in the frame, and a tin sign at the top of the door read, DENIED. PLEASE PRESENT YOUR KEY.

Hayes turned around and said, "Goodbye."

The word seemed to die as soon as he said it. The little old man just nodded. Then the elevator doors slid back together and he was gone.

Hayes sighed and walked to the closed door, then reached into his pocket and took out his key. It was not like many other keys: this one was about five inches long and had only one long tooth running along one side. On its surface were about two dozen minuscule dots arranged in a staggeringly complex pattern. A closer look would reveal that they were actually tiny lenses, each no bigger than a grain of sand, and that the end of the key was filled with a thick, clear glass. Hayes had never really been sure how the keys worked. Something about light having to shine through the end and then out through the tiny lenses in exactly the right way. Someone had probably explained it to him once or twice, but it was all math and gearhead talk and he usually tuned out pretty quick.

He walked up to the terminal and put the long key in the lock, fitting the single tooth into the provided slot. There was a whir from behind it and the door unlocked. The sign above flipped over to read, ACCEPTED!—47TH FLOOR and he pushed open the doors to reveal a much larger and grander hall, this one far more Old World than the lobby below, all floral carpeting and smooth dark wood. More suited emissaries paced from one office to another, slick and spotless, men of the moment. Hayes shambled out among them and some stared at him, curious as to why this shabby little man was here, but most of them looked away and went about their business.

It was the quiet that got to him, really. It was like being in church.

The Nail was almost a temple, a cathedral dedicated to the sole task of amassing wealth and power. Men passed one another like wandering ghosts, bearing their burdens of paper and numbers, moving from little room to little room and redirecting the fortunes of the greater world outside. And among them stalked Hayes, their keeper and reaper, protector and predator. He was not one of them, he knew that. He was an Ishmael atop Olympus, his hand against every man and every man's hand against him.

He walked to Evans's office and opened the door and entered. The ancient secretary looked up and peered at him and said, "You."

"Yes," said Hayes as he walked over to her.

"You're early. For once."

"Well, yes. Broken clock, twice a day and all."

"Hm," she said, rechecking the book. "Well. Go sit down. Along the wall. As usual."

"As usual," Hayes echoed, and took a seat. After a while he leaned back. His eyelids became leaden and his head grew warm and stuffy. He shut his eyes and sleep took him, warm and comforting. Old dreams swam up in his mind: dark stone passageways and doors and ceilings made of bars, and a haggard voice in the darkness begging for a cigarette or a drink of water, whichever one they might have, just please, give it to me, please...

He awoke to the sound of someone coughing politely. He opened his eyes and returned to the waiting room, yet he saw that now there was a girl sitting in one of the chairs along the wall with him, young but not too young, thin and tall with brown-red hair. She was dressed severely, almost in a nun's habit, and she was watching him curiously.

"Oh, I'm sorry," he said. "Was I snoring?"

"Muttering, actually," she said.

"I'm sorry, again. Doubt if many people sleep in waiting rooms."

"Not many, I should think," she said. She frowned at him. "Are you all right? You look very off-color. And you were sweating in your sleep."

"Really?" Hayes said. He examined his hands.

"Also, you have something on your knee."

Hayes pulled the leg of his trousers up and saw a chalky white residue on one of the knees. He guessed it was probably pigeon shit, no doubt collected when he had knelt in the middle of the street to retch up. He frowned and licked a finger and began to rub it off.

"Here," said the girl, taking a handkerchief from her purse. "Use this."

"That's really not necessary, thanks."

"No, take it. They gave me far too many when I first signed on."

Hayes took the cloth and saw the company insignia in the corner, an imperial M. "Very nice," he said. "I didn't get any handkerchiefs when I joined on."

"Oh," she said. She thought and then reached for her purse. "Would you like some, then? As I said, I have enough."

"No," said Hayes. "I think I'm fine with just one." He tried to gouge out what was left of the pigeon shit. Then he shook out the handkerchief and folded it and stuffed it into his front breast pocket. "Thank you," he said again.

"No, it's nothing," she said. Then she smiled politely and turned away. Hayes noticed she had an English accent, not unlike his, and what little of her skin he could see was burned smoothly brown. A sculpted drape of brown-red ringlets flowed down from the brim of her hat and across her brow before marshalling itself into a stern bun in the back. She held herself alertly, head fixed in the direction of Evans's door and the secretary beyond as though she was waiting for the next command, matronly and militant all at once. The pose was painfully overeager on a girl as young as she was.

"Did you just get in this week?" Hayes asked.

She turned to him, surprised. "Well, yes, actually. How did you know?"

"Just a hunch. That and Jim in there often interviews brand-new assistants for Security positions." He began rolling a cigarette. "Would that be right?"

She crossed her legs and respectfully looked away. "I'm sorry, I don't believe I'm at liberty to discuss that."

Hayes smirked. "I see. Well, you've got our stock response down. You'll be a natural at conversation, won't you?"

"Perhaps. That would bring this one to a rather abrupt end, wouldn't it?"

Hayes's smirk grew to a grin. "You know, you sound like me," he said, undeterred. "Like another wayward child of Her Majesty's kingdom. Where are you from?"

She looked at him, sizing him up and considering all the little wrinkles and stains that decorated his shirt. She eventually sighed a little and said, "Devonshire. Originally. But all over, really."

"Where would all over be, if you don't mind my asking?"

"Cairo, to be specific."

"Really? I've been there once or twice, believe it or not."

"Oh, really?" she asked, half-interested. "When?"

"Long ago. Long, long ago, when you were a mere babe, I'm sure. What's the change like, coming from there to here? I can't imagine the shock."

"It's quite something," she said glibly.

"Quite something? Ah, *there* it is," he said, smiling wider. "There's that magnificent English talent for understatement. It's been a while since I've heard it." He began to laugh, but the first few chuckles were cut short as something caught in his lungs. He snapped forward, hacking and choking and trying to ride out the deep, rattling coughs that started in the roots of his lungs and then ran up through the whole of his body. For a moment he thought he might vomit again, but then to his surprise the young girl stood up, sat down beside him, and then grabbed the back of his collar and pulled him upright. Before he could slide out of his chair she steadied the small of his back with her other hand, holding him still until air finally found its way into his chest again. He turned to look at her, wheezing.

"Air wants to go up and out," she said. "That is, if you don't want to choke yourself. You're a smoker, aren't you? I'd know that cough anywhere."

He nodded but could not speak, as he was still short of breath. She let go of him, then stood and smoothed down her skirt. "Well, it's a dirty habit. I know no one else thinks so, but it is." She gave him an appraising look. "You need to start taking better care of yourself."

"I take damn fine care of myself," he said. He readjusted his collar.

"Maybe so," she said. "But the bags under your eyes and the tremor in your hands say otherwise."

"What are you, a doctor?"

"Oh, no," she said, retaking her seat. "Just an assistant. But remember, sir, for the future: up, and out."

They both looked up as the doors opened and Evans came out of his office. He wandered over to the secretary to share a quiet word. As he turned he spotted Hayes and stopped where he was. Then he forced a smile onto his face and said, "Cyril. My boy, good to see you. So good to see you. Why don't you go in and have a seat? I'll be in shortly."

"Fine," said Hayes, and got up. As he left he glanced over his shoulder at the young girl. She was watching him, half-bemused, half-pitying. Then Evans closed the door behind him and he was alone.

Evans's office was far too large for one man. He often joked he had purchased his desk just to fill up space. Indeed, the desk was by far the largest object in the room, a massive medieval thing with all sorts of stern engravings crawling along its corners. A bookcase faced it on either end, both pitifully small, with four small paintings desperately trying to fill the rest of the wall space of the office. A tiny potted plant drooped in the corner, perhaps sent there as punishment. Through the windows at the far end one could see the rooftops of Evesden fall away like ugly dominoes.

Hayes sat down in one of the chairs before Evans's desk. The room was silent except for the click of the clock on the wall. The quiet seemed to stretch on forever.

He rolled and lit another cigarette to pass the time. The match trembled in his hands, its flame dancing around the end of the cigarette. He took a frantic drag and shook the match out and tried to calm his fingers. They would not obey, so he stuffed his hands under his legs and waited for the warmth to soak into them.

Hayes knew Garvey and that awful girl out front had been only partially right: the opium and exhaustion were definitely contributors to his shakes, but they weren't the main cause. No, the strange quakes in his hands had started the moment he'd read the telegram early that morning and realized Evans might be calling him in to fire him for good.

He drooped in his chair as he thought about it, chest still crackling with breath. He had never exactly loved his job, but he had little else. He could not imagine what he would do, what could be done, if he had no work to fill his days.

The doors snapped open. Evans walked in, turned and carefully shut them, and then walked to his desk, never glancing at Hayes as he went. He was a plump little man, only slightly taller than Hayes, with wire-framed glasses and a graying mustache and a glaringly bald head. People often thought of him as an elderly uncle, forever confused by how this strange new world worked. Hayes was more fond of him than he'd ever admit, but he knew this wasn't far off the mark. Evans had never really been cut out for this kind of work. He detested any hint of conflict, and often relegated any unpleasant duties to his small army of secretaries, whom he looked upon as his daughters regardless of their age. He was usually content to wander the upper floors, distributing duties with a vague, satisfied smile on his face before returning to the shelter of his enormous desk and evading meetings.

"You're early," said Evans as he sat.

Hayes nodded.

"That's unusual," said Evans.

"Well. Had to get up early."

"Oh? Why was that, I wonder?"

"There was a body, actually," said Hayes. "One of Garvey's."

"Why did he need you for that?" Evans asked.

"He thought it was one of ours."

"And was it?"

Hayes shrugged.

"Hm," said Evans, then cocked his head and thought.

"I've dried out," Hayes said eagerly. "Haven't had a drop. Not in a month or two."

Evans raised his eyebrows. "A month? Really?"

"Thereabout, yeah."

Evans studied Hayes's face and clothes and watched him rock back and forth in his chair like a toy. "You don't look well, though," he said, concerned.

"I keep hearing that. It's just the cold and the damp. It's murdering me."

"You aren't sick from... from not drinking?"

"That couldn't last. Not for a month. See?"

Evans sighed. "I suppose. I have been worried about you, Cyril. I admit it was a pretty curt way to end the affair."

"Curt?" said Hayes. He laughed harshly. "I remember the telegram very clearly. 'Abandon, stop. Return to your place of residence, stop. Await further orders, stop. Do not attempt contact, stop.' Wasn't quite poetry."

"No," Evans said. "But you had made a mess of it. A very big mess indeed."

Hayes lowered his head a little. "I... I know."

"Do you? The man's suing us, you know. For his injuries."

"Even though they were... self-inflicted?"

"Yes. Since now he knows how desperately we'd like to keep his dirty little trading a secret. That was the problem, you know. How public it was. We told you to look into him quietly."

"Yes."

"Very quietly," he said sternly. "You're supposed to be a scalpel, not a shotgun."

"But we never know what they'll do," Hayes said. "When you lay out all their wrongs in front of them, you never know which way they'll jump. I certainly didn't think he'd...that he'd jump out a fucking window."

"But we have you exactly because you're *supposed* to know things like that," said Evans, showing a rare flash of anger. "And we stressed beforehand, very clearly, use your kid gloves. This one is a public man, we said. He's got family. He's connected. Make sure this is all discreet. But you weren't. You, drunk as a lord, grilled him like he was a war criminal. And he fell to pieces. And now you've cost us money and reputation. That was only the most recent in a string of sloppy jobs. So you understand that we'd be perfectly justified in dropping you. Correct?"

Hayes screwed up his mouth and kept his eyes fixed on the carpet at his feet. Then he nodded.

"Good," said Evans. "But you're not fired. I want you to know that."

"I'm not?"

"No. You're not. Not yet, at least. We're keeping you, Hayes. We need you. Now, especially. We called you in to let you know there's a way back. Back into the fold." Evans pulled his coat off the back of his chair and settled it about his shoulders. He might have been the one person who detested the cold climate even more than Hayes. Then he pulled out a small pipe and suckled at it thoughtfully before saying, "Today, with Garvey. What did you talk about?"

"The murder he caught, mostly."

"Besides that."

"Well, the unions, of course. The Department's been told to prioritize. He said he heard it was Brightly who gave the order. Any truth to that?"

Evans smiled wryly. "I'm sure you know I can't say."

"Can't saying is often a yes."

"Forget that. What did he have to say about the unions? Besides prioritizing?"

"Well. He mentioned a few cases. Three of them."

"What sort of cases?" Evans asked quickly.

"Murder cases. Would that be it?"

"Yes. Yes, it's about those. What did he say about them?"

"They were murders, like I said. Union murders. Two lefties and a buster. One at the docks. Another at the vagrants' cemetery. He was junking them. Didn't want them. They'd make the Department look bad, I'm sure."

"And why was that?"

"Because there was no filing them. Solving them, I mean," he added, seeing Evans's confusion. "He was tossing them out."

Evans let out a breath. "Good."

"Good?"

"Yes, good."

"And why's that?"

Evans shifted awkwardly in his chair. "It would be best if the police left that particular matter alone."

"Why? What's going on with them? Why don't you care?"

"Oh, quite the opposite. We care. We care a great deal. You see, Cyril, we're all very worried about this... this union business."

"Oh, are you," said Hayes dryly.

"Yes. You may have heard that it's going to be violent. Well, that's wrong. It already is. We just wanted to be well informed. About the violence, at least."

Hayes suddenly looked at Evans, studying his face. The old man took off his glasses and looked away, disturbed by the scrutiny. Then Hayes's eyes lit up as if he'd been teasing at some hanging thread in his mind until the knot finally unraveled. "Which one was ours?" asked Hayes softly.

"I'm sorry?"

"Which one? Which of the union men was ours? The one at the docks or the one at Potter's Field?"

Evans shuddered and kept his eyes averted from Hayes. He sucked on his lip for a moment and said, "The docks."

"Right," said Hayes, voice still soft. "Right."

"Lord, I hate it when you do that."

"This is pretty cloak-and-dagger stuff, Jim. Running turncoats? How bad is the union situation getting?"

"Very bad. At first it was just a rumor. Something minor we needed to weed out. Now it's become... Well. It's become something akin to war. One of our most important and productive factories is just south of here. It manufactures some of the most delicate parts necessary for creating the frame for the engines of our airships. Recently there was an altercation."

"An altercation?"

"Yes. Specifically, someone tried to blow up one section of the manufacturing lines."

Hayes whistled lowly.

"Yes," said Evans. "Without that particular segment of manufacturing the entire factory would have been crippled. Do you know how much revenue that factory outputs a day?"

"I don't know. Some absurd number."

"Three million dollars."

"All right."

"It didn't work, naturally. If it had, well, word would have gotten out. No, the saboteurs mishandled the dynamite and it wound up going off in one of the entryways. We think he tripped and fell and blew himself up, honestly."

Hayes grinned. "How come this wasn't in the papers?"

"Because we didn't want it to be," said Evans simply.

"So that's when you decided to send some feelers into the union men."

"Brightly did, yes. And it didn't work well at all. I don't know how they found our man out but, well. You get the idea."

"And now you want me to work the unions for you."

"Yes. Yes. They've wormed their way in, God knows how deep. I need you, Cyril," he said. "Brightly needs you. We need your magic."

Hayes looked at him darkly. "It's not magic."

"It is to me," said Evans. "This is your way back, Cyril. All sins forgiven, after this. Everything forgotten. Are you willing?"

"You know I am, Jim."

"You're sure?"

Hayes nodded, eyes half-shut.

"Good." Evans shuffled the papers around on his desk more. They never seemed to go anywhere specific. "We do think the heart of the movement is here. Here, in the city, probably to the south, where most of our local plants are. Do you know how many major facilities there are in this region?"

"Eleven, if memory serves," said Hayes.

"Yes, that's right. More than any other city or state or even country in the world, and we do our most delicate work here. So this is where we need to be protected. But again, this is all relatively new to us. You can spearhead this for us, Cyril. Find something to work with and we'll put everything we've got behind you. And that's a lot. We're invested in you now."

"I feel tremendously valuable, yes," said Hayes. He stood and examined the bookcases. "All right. I'll run the usual rounds throughout this week. See what I can dig up, see where we want me to head. Probably can find some bar or name or something. Poor, hungry boys banding together, it sounds like gangs or clans or such. They probably have a name they like to trumpet. It shouldn't be hard."

"Right, but, Cyril…we're keeping you closer than that," said Evans slowly.

Hayes turned around. "Closer?"

"Yes."

"What's closer? How close?"

"In-house," said Evans. "You're being restricted to interviews in-house."

Hayes's mouth dropped open. "What?"

"Yes."

"You're joking."

"No. Interviews of lower-level men in the company."

"Lower-level?" said Hayes, outraged.

"Yes. Foremen, managers, team leads. Working-class leaders. Suspicious subjects. We have a list of names here, scheduled interviews, and you're going to interview them."

Hayes came back over and sat. "That's not...That won't..."

"Listen, Cyril, you're lucky they kept you on. They just want to start you out small and controlled. Build you up."

"Build me up."

"Yes. And we'll need to keep you stabilized, too."

"What's stabilized? What does that mean?"

Evans nervously scratched the back of his neck. "It means supervision."

Hayes's face went dead. All the thought in his wide blue eyes faded until they could have been painted on.

"Nothing in the way of an obstruction," said Evans hastily. "No interference. Merely someone to take note of your duties, schedule meetings and appointments, and report to me."

"A secretary," said Hayes.

"An assistant. An organizer."

"A spy. You're spying on the spy, is that it?"

"My God, Cyril, don't be dramatic."

"This is going to hamstring me. It's going to fucking hamstring me until I can barely move. You know that."

Evans sat forward. His voice dropped until it was dangerously soft. "I know this makes you mad," he said. "I know it does. You've been out on your own for so long, running your game. You did good for a while. But you've forgotten that there's a company behind you. That there's money riding on everything you do. You've forgotten that. But we haven't. So we need to watch you, and remind you when it's needed. You can see why giving you an assistant is both reasonable and necessary."

"I don't need one," Hayes said fiercely. "This meeting, almost being tossed out... That's enough. I've learned my lesson. I'll be a good boy. All right?"

"No. No, Cyril, it's not enough. We want someone on the ground with you. Matching you step by step. You've always been difficult to handle. We're just trying to curb you a bit."

"Curb me. Like a naughty dog."

"Cyril, you need this," Evans said. "You need someone to keep an eye on you."

"I have Garvey."

"You and Garvey are addicts. Dependents. Every month you run yourselves ragged over something, egging each other along."

Hayes pulled at his hair, bunching up the blond-white fronds and then teasing them out again. "What if I don't want to come back?" he asked quietly.

"What?" said Evans.

"What if I don't want to come back? What if I say no thanks, Jim, I prefer it the old way or no way at all? What about that?"

"Well. Then you don't come back. Then we go our separate ways. And that's the end of it. But there's no choice in this. You either take her or you're out."

Hayes's brow crinkled. "Her?"

"Yes, her," said Evans. "I think you'll quite like her. She's top-rate, a former army nurse. And she's well traveled, like you. Spent a lot of time looking after wounded British soldiers in Egypt before we scooped her up and brought her into the company."

Hayes kept frowning for a moment longer. Then epiphany flooded his face and he put his chin in one hand. "Really," he sighed.

"Yes, really."

"Was she last working in Cairo?" he asked, defeated.

Evans blinked. "Yes. She was. That was fast of you."

"That wasn't exactly intuition." He shook his head. "Well. Go on. Bring her in."

"Why?"

"Why not? We might as well get it over with."

Evans frowned, then stood and walked to the door. He opened it and stuck his head out and murmured something and then opened it fully. When the girl walked in Hayes was twisted around awkwardly in his chair, watching her through the fingers of one hand, his expression resigned and half-amused. She looked at him cautiously, as if she had just stumbled across a wounded dog and was not sure if it would bite.

"Cyril, this is Miss Samantha Fairbanks," said Evans. "Miss Fairbanks, this is Mr. Hayes."

She looked him up and down again. "Mr. Hayes?"

"Yes," said Evans. He put his hands behind his back and bounced forward on the balls of his feet like he had just presented a marvelous surprise.

Hayes shut his eyes and stuck one hand out in the air. The girl looked at it for a moment before stepping forward and shaking it.

"Well. We've gotten off on the wrong foot, Mr. Hayes," she said.

"Yes," he said. "Would you like your handkerchief back now?"

"No. Feel free to keep it for as long as you'd like. As I told you, they gave me more than enough."

"Handkerchief?" said Evans. "You've met?"

"In the waiting room," said Hayes. He opened his eyes and peered at her. "So. You're going to assist me. With all my inquiries and interviews and daily rounds. Is that it?"

"Yes," she said. "That's a simple way of putting it, but yes, it is."

"Sounds like it should be fun. Should be a grand old time. So when does this start?" he asked Evans. "And exactly what the hell are we doing, anyway, if you all are calling all the shots?"

Evans cleared his throat. "Well, the first interview is the day after tomorrow at nine at Southern Regional, but I thought it would be best if we showed Miss Fairbanks your station and you two could get somewhat—"

"No," said Hayes sharply. "No, it's best to hit the ground running. Get along better with plenty of work going on. Don't you agree, Miss Fairbanks?"

She surveyed him briefly, taking in his bone-white hands and haggard eyes. "I suppose I could, Mr. Hayes," she said. "If you think you're better in working circumstances then that's certainly where I'd prefer us to be."

"Fine," said Hayes. "Beautiful. I'm sure things will go swimmingly. You've done interrogations before?"

"Interviews," interjected Evans. "They're interviews."

"I've been present during them before," she said. "But never done one, no. I've been in plenty of stressful situations, regardless."

Hayes looked at her closely, leaning forward. She shifted slightly from one foot to the other, uneasy.

"Yes," said Hayes quietly. "You know, I almost believe you have."

"Excellent," said Evans. "Splendid. I'm sure you'll get along well."

Hayes fought to his feet. He pitched forward slightly and grappled with the chair back for support. Then he swallowed and said, "Yes. We will. The day after tomorrow. But until then, I'm off. Not...Not feeling well, you see."

"Off?" asked Evans. "Off to where? Will you be at your apartments?"

"No," said Hayes, heading toward the door. "No, Mr. Evans, I will not be at my apartments."

"So how will we reach you?"

"You won't," said Hayes. He opened the door. "Lovely meeting you, Miss Fairbanks."

"And you, Mr. Hayes," she said.

Then he shut the door and it clicked behind him.

CHAPTER FIVE

Garvey pulled a particularly thick file from the stack on his desk and flipped through it. After scanning a few pages he identified the case as an ancient one, not even his, an heirloom from a previous detective. He set it to the side, knowing that it had to die eventually, and then he pushed deeper into the stack of remaining papers.

Garvey was never entirely sure how much work he had left at any given moment. He'd often meant to arrange his paperwork according to some structure, but before he could begin he needed to clear out what was still left to do. After several months of delays he now saw little chance of that. Usually his desk resembled a battlefield, or even an architectural miracle; stacks of files slouched up against one another, propped up by cups or boxes or envelopes or even silverware, with corners or edges bent up to form little flags or markers whose meanings he soon forgot. Sometimes he thought his desk was sentient, lurking in the back of the Homicide office and soaking up the perfume of burned coffee and stale cigarette smoke that pervaded the upper floors of the Department. Every other day he'd prune it back, removing one of the more outrageous towers of paper and shuffling it off to elsewhere, but then the next day the growth of papers would have almost magically regenerated until it threatened to spill over the edges.

The mess of paperwork had only one consistent feature: a photograph that always peeked over a stack of old reports in the corner. The visible part of the photograph showed two little girls, each somberly staring at him over the reports as though hiding. Somewhere in the bottom of the photograph, concealed by the paperwork, was Garvey's ex-wife, seated before the girls and smiling. Some days Garvey felt the urge to lift the paperwork away and to show her as well. On others he felt like piling more on and covering up the photograph entirely so they could not see what he had to deal with each day. But mostly he did nothing, and so his two little girls remained there, yellowing and watchful, and somehow reproachful as he did his day's work.

That day had dragged on after the morning at the canal, a slow slog of repetitious conversations with starved men and women with sunken eyes. Now at the end he documented it all, scrawling down the essentials, ensuring that they became an immortal part of the Evesden Police Department's filing system.

He took out a small pad and read what he had written there to remind himself. Then he looked up and scanned the wealth of misery at his fingertips and selected the appropriate report and opened it.

This one a trembling mother who had stabbed her daughter's lover. The boy had clutched a balcony railing, a pair of knitting shears buried at the base of his neck. Mouth gaping like a fish, blood raining down on the street. Dozens of witnesses had seen her standing at the balcony door, howling obscenities at this terrified, dying thing, but few had stayed, and those who had did not wish to testify. Instead Garvey had spoken to her after. She had listened to him as he told her he understood perfectly, son of a bitch had it coming, why, I got two little girls of my own and if I'd been in your shoes...

At the end of the day she had been led to her cell, confident in his sympathy, assured that the world would turn out all right. He filled out her paperwork and set her judgment in motion. Fed her into the waiting doom that he created.

Garvey wrote it all down. All down.

His hand passed over another report. He remembered it from last May. A woman trampled in a stable, having been led there by a paranoid lover. The man had frightened the horses and then locked the door and leaned against it, trapping her inside. Garvey remembered the musty stink of manure and the scent of animal anxiety that had still sung in the air. He remembered her ribs broken and leaking, viscera pooling from her neck and hip. A jawbone so bloodless it was like old wood. Her killer had been found sobbing in an alley not more than a block away, urine snailing down both trouser legs. When Garvey had gotten ahold of him the trembling man could do no more than mewl "yes" or "no," but it was all Garvey needed, or at least all that was required by the city of Evesden.

That had been an easy one. Fallen and filed in minutes, hours. Garvey wrote it down, wrote it all down, and as he added on to the report he went over the names in his head. The bronzed list on the Pit wall. Names of the dead, hanging tags and labels for things long since departed. It seemed there were so many these days.

He pulled open a drawer, fingers dancing along the edges of the tomes. He dug up an old report for a fellow detective. He had found a man with the corpse of a little girl in his arms, rocking gently back and forth in the blackened corner of a burned-down building, murmuring, "I just wanted something beautiful. I just wanted something beautiful."

Garvey remembered it. He had been there. The girl's dusty skin had been the color of ripe melon, and both their cheeks stained with ashes, like survivors of an immolated world. They could not determine how she had died, since the fracture in her skull could have been accidental. There had been no witnesses, and the man had seemed mad since, so they could not say what had happened, not with certainty. Perhaps he was simply a crazed vagrant who'd stumbled across her where she lay. But a day ago Garvey had tracked down a street vendor who'd heard that the suspect had been awful riled up for young pussy, yessir. Awful riled up, but when wasn't he? And could you blame him? Could you, really?

Write it down, write it all down, he said to himself. If you don't write it and file it, then it didn't happen. Write and keep writing.

Another handful of pages, another memory. He remembered a little black newsie no older than sixteen, shot four times next to a newspaper stand. Keeled over with one hand clutched around the leg of the stand as if trying to anchor himself to life. He had held a sheet of newspaper over his face, trying to prevent passersby from witnessing his death. Some curbside Julius Caesar who considered his fellow man too common to see his passing.

They had not found his killer. It went unfiled. Still he wrote.

Then when Garvey was done he sat looking at this new report. John Doe, found floating in a man-made river, washed away like the other refuse of this city. There were only three pages of it so far. Almost nothing.

He wondered how Hayes would look at it. He probably wouldn't even bother. That was what made him good, plus the mad gift that ate his brain alive, thought Garvey. But it also made him weak. He would look for the flash and the glitter, things that intrigued and teased him. But without it there was no point to the chase. No fun.

This was not fun. Nor was it meant to be.

"Garvey?" said a voice.

He looked up and saw Collins sidling over, his hangdog face somehow even deeper and sadder in the light of the table lamps. "What are you doing here?" he said. "This isn't your shift."

"No, Lieutenant," said Garvey. "I'm just waiting. I've got a body downstairs. Gibson's going to start in on it in a second."

Collins shook his head and leaned over Garvey's shoulder to read his paperwork. His lieutenant was a big man, broad in the shoulders with a walrus mustache, but his droopy, pessimistic demeanor often made people forget his size. On the rare moments when he showed his anger he suddenly seemed to swell up and tower over people. Whether they were errant detectives or babbling suspects, it often had dramatic effects.

"Always gets to me," he said. "How you look. Most cops, they'd do anything to get away."

"I know," said Garvey.

"You think this one's got any promise?"

Garvey helplessly lifted his hands and dropped them. "It's a piece of shit."

"Hm. No one likes a floater, that's for sure. What about your spook? The blondie, did you bring him in?"

"Yeah. He didn't have anything. Makes sense. If our boy was McNaughton he was definitely lower-level. Insignificant, I suppose."

"I hate that little shit. I don't see why you run around with him."

"He gets bodies filed."

"I still don't like him," said Collins. "He stinks of that goddamn company he works for."

Garvey hesitated, tongue between his lips. "Lieutenant?"

"Yeah?"

"Mind if I ask you something?"

"Shoot."

"This prioritization thing. I heard that came in from Brightly. You know, over at—"

"I know who he is," said Collins sharply.

"Well. Is it true, sir?"

Collins eyed him sourly, hunching up his shoulders until the muscles bunched around his neck. His gin-blossom cheeks deepened in tint until they were nearly purple. "You know what, I'm going to suggest you put your attention elsewhere," he said. He reached out and touched the files on his desk with one thick finger. "Maybe on this, eh? Does that sound agreeable to you?"

Garvey nodded and stared into his desk. "Right," he said. He glanced sideways and sighed as he watched Collins hulk back into his office.

"Detective?" said a voice.

He looked up. A scrawny boy in a white smock stood peeking into the Homicide office. "Yeah?" Garvey said.

"We're about to begin," said the boy.

"All right."

Garvey stood and followed the boy across the rotunda and down the steps, then across the lower levels to the bleached tile stairs that wound down to where the dead slept and doctors did their best to make them speak.

The air grew cool down in the basement. The light was so lifeless here it was almost a different type of dark. Dusky jars of pink fluid lurked on shelves and blades winked from nearby rolling tables. The nauseating fragrance of formaldehyde and God knew what else floated in the room like a fog. And somewhere among it all was Gibson, overweight and darkly humorous, a cigarette dangling from his thick lips. No one had asked why he came seeking this job. It was the type of question you didn't ask because you might get an answer.

"Heyo, Garv," said Gibson. "Long time no see."

"Not long enough."

"You wound me, Garv," he said. "You wound me. Who's our lucky boy tonight?"

"No idea. That's the problem."

"I know. I was just making conversation." He led Garvey to the little cabinets that hid the dead. Their shoes were loud on the tile floor, painfully so. The morgue was usually silent except for the hiss and chuckle of the pneumatic tubes in the walls as messages and packages shot in from somewhere out in the city. Other hospitals and labs, perhaps. Garvey had heard the contents were often gruesome. There was a story of a jar of fingers that had been misdirected up to Vice with the day's mail, and Garvey wasn't sure whether to believe it.

Gibson came to one cabinet door and offered Garvey a small jar of perfumed salve. "Here you go," he said.

"I don't need it."

He chuckled. "You will."

Garvey looked at it, then at the wall of small metal doors. "You got a ripe one?"

"Riper than a homegrown tomato," Gibson said cheerfully.

"Then yeah. Yeah, I do."

He laughed again and tossed it to him. "Smart boy."

Garvey opened it and smeared a thumbful of the salve across his upper lip. Then he took a chair, put it next to the table, opened up the report, and began to write. Gibson and his attendant glanced at each other and Gibson smirked and shook his head. Then they opened the door, reached in, and pulled out the tray carrying the morning's load.

His color and thickness had changed slightly, but that was all. His face had drained off some water and perhaps he had lost more of what little blood he had left. But overall it was the same. Garvey looked at his thin, intelligent face, his retreating hairline. Strong, worn hands, scarred lower arms. Genitals shrunken against the inside of his thigh. A man like any other, washed up on cement shores.

"Well," Garvey said. "At least we know he wasn't killed by denners."

"What makes you say that?" asked Gibson.

"He's still got a face, doesn't he?"

Gibson chuckled and then began his inspection, chanting his litany of facts as he went along. Cause of death, estimation of age, summary description of wounds. The Latin terms for each body part formed some strange incantation in Garvey's head. He and Gibson's attendant wrote as fast as they could.

Garvey did this with nearly every homicide he caught. No other detective did, choosing instead to rely upon Gibson's reports. Gibson was a fine doctor and did his job well, and Gibson knew that it wasn't a sign of Garvey's doubt that he was down here whenever he could be, watching their grim procedure. He knew it was something else.

Garvey did not know the word "vigil," but he didn't need to. This was a ritual for him, even though it had no name. It was a process of documentation, of marking the passage of the dead and the beginning of Garvey's attempt to exact some sort of justice. And that was what their job was, at heart. They were men who noted deaths and attempted to change the world because of them. To put their killers to justice, perhaps, but what was that beyond a way of saying that this man mattered, that his life was important, and so his death should affect his killer's life in turn?

And so he listened. And wrote.

He was considering the official phrasing of one of his sentences when he heard Gibson say, "Did you hear that, Detective?"

"Hear what?"

"Tattoo. On the inside of his bicep. It's real faded. Hidden close to the armpit, probably so that you couldn't see it."

"What's it of?" he asked, and stood.

"Looks like a bell and a hammer."

"You mind?" Garvey asked, reaching for the corpse.

"I'm not married to him. Go on ahead."

Garvey took the flesh of the man's arm with his thumb and pushed it up. On the inside was a small black bell with a white hammer inside, acting as the clapper. It looked medieval. Some badge of brotherhood, almost.

"Ever seen it before?" asked Garvey.

"No," said Gibson, frowning. "Well, I'm not sure. Maybe."

"I haven't. You?" Garvey asked the attendant.

The boy shook his head.

"Hm," said Garvey. He looked at it a while, then picked up his file and sketched out the tattoo.

"Amateur stuff," said Gibson. He flicked the dead man's arm, the flesh as solid as rubber. “He didn’t know what he was doing at all. Probably just got some ink and a pin, maybe a razor, and went to it.”

“It’s the only identifying mark we have, though, right?”

“That’s true.”

Garvey sat back down, made sure to carefully notate the details of the tattoo, and then said, “Okay. Let’s continue on, then.”

CHAPTER SIX

Nights in Evesden were unlike nights anywhere else. As soon as the blue drained out of the sky all the cradle spotlights would come on at once across the city, shafts of hazy, dreamlike light stabbing up into the darkening atmosphere. They grew in clusters, positioned around each district's cradle. If the angle was right one could look up and see a forest of soft white trunks swaying back and forth, moving so slowly and with borders so faint it was hard to tell if they were moving at all, unless they happened to fall across an airship, in which case a bright, burnished gold star would suddenly light up above. Newcomers found it hard to sleep in the more exposed neighborhoods, as they were unused to the tides of porcelain light that came washing across their walls or ceilings, but veteran Evesdeners hardly paid attention. They scarcely noticed the strange waltzes that moved back and forth across the city as overnight traffic poured in from the skies.

It was generally acknowledged that the farther you were from them the more spectacular the view was, and in that case Dockland, which would not tolerate a cradle or indeed any real sign of modern civilization, offered one of the best vistas possible, although probably one of the most dangerous ones as well. The entire neighborhood was almost a sea of gloom buried among mountains of sparkling light.

Deep in the twisting bowels of Dockland the city did not sleep. As the distant spotlights flickered on the markets stirred and came to life, gathering in dimly lit rooms and doorways and alley entrances. Smoke tumbled across the tent covers and turned the voices of the barkers and the tradesmen into coarse growls, barely human over the din and clatter of trade. Whores grouped in well-lit spots and flashed mangled grins at passersby. In other places men positioned themselves around the entryways of inconspicuous shops, signaling to one another and screening visitors for whatever business happened within.

Hayes moved among them all like a ghost, weaving through the weak points of the crowds. He was riding a mean drunk and he had forgotten his coat somewhere and his scarf was stuffed down the front of his shirt, which was only half-buttoned. He tried to keep his senses about him. Dockland was probably the most treacherous part of Evesden except for some sections of Construct, where hobos and vagrants had holed up in the half-finished sites and lived in medieval savagery. He was familiar with Dockland, though, and its denizens were familiar with him.

Magic, he thought to himself as he walked. They need the old magic back in action, wheeling and dealing. Like always.

He knew he shouldn't feel angry at Evans. He wasn't the one who'd given the order to cut him off. The board, yes. Brightly, yes. But still, they had no issue dumping him off at the drop of a hat, and no issue calling him back just the same.

He shouldn't have come back. He should have just cut tether and run. He'd done it before. He'd done it overseas, in worse conditions than this. He was a consummate survivor. He could wander anywhere and find a future, should he want to.

Hayes scratched at his arm and realized he was shivering again. His nerves jangled with the needling tension that always took him at this hour. Cho Lun's Carpentry was only a block away but here in this loud, chattering chaos it seemed miles. He picked up his pace and skipped through a gap in the groups of people. As he did someone shouted, "Princeling! Hey, Princeling! Princeling's here!" but he did not respond.

He reached into his pocket to touch his savings. It was more of a wad of small bills, kept together by his sweat. He wondered how much time that would buy him. An hour. Maybe less. When he had first started coming to the dens he had bought out booths for the entire night, sprawled out on the cushions and teasing the girls for favors. Now it was utilitarian. Medicinal. He came to get his regular dose, and then he could make it through the next day.

He counted his cash again. It wasn't enough. Not for what he needed.

Hayes scanned the crowd and wandered for a bit before he found what he was looking for. In front of a closed warehouse a group of youths had set up a table game, the usual find-the-jack switch. They weren't working in shifts, which was lucky. Just one frontman and the rest of the gang organizing. It would be far easier to get a bead on things that way.

Hayes took up a station just down the alley from them and leaned up against the brick wall and waited. He listened to the leader's chatter, to his cajoling and wheedling. Watched the movements of his hands and the blur of the cards.

Then he took a breath, let it out, and tried to pay attention.

It took about an hour for Hayes to start getting it. It helped that all the boys were watching the game at once. Soon the sensations started leaking in, the joy of the con and the careful attention of the bait and hook. Let them win a little, let them lose more. The greed burned inside Hayes and he began to hold the pattern in his mind, the way one thought and feeling segued into another, the way the night was supposed to work for these young men. It was faint and not much to work with, but Hayes didn't have much time.

He stepped out from the shadows of the alley and got in line for the game. When he stepped up the young man grinned and said, "Up to try your luck, try and get the jack to bleed green?"

"I am indeed," Hayes said.

"All right then, sir, let's see the wager you're willing to put on his crown. Hopefully your bundle'll stay put and not topple, eh?"

"Hopefully," he said, and put down his money.

The young man looked at it. "That's an awful lot."

"I'm awful lucky."

The boy frowned, judging him. He nodded. "Fair enough."

Hayes felt the pattern change in the boy. Change tempo and direction, almost. Hayes struggled to keep his attention and watched the cards. Lose once, win twice, and walk, he said to himself.

The boy turned the cards up, showing him the jack. Hayes barely looked. Then the boy flipped them over and began smoothly swerving them in and out, chanting quietly as they moved. Hayes anticipated the turn and felt the boys burn white-hot with anxiety. When the cards stopped moving Hayes pointed to the wrong card and the lead boy smiled and flipped it over.

The boy grinned. Already he had the gray teeth of an old man. "Sorry, sir. You're not lucky today, it seems."

"Imagine that," said Hayes. "Try again?"

The boy began laying cards down again. But Hayes knew the game now. On the second try he won his money back handily. On the third he placed his money down and made a triple bet and watched the jack spin by, the boy desperately maneuvering it through the other cards. Hayes almost missed it. When they came to a stop he took out a finger, waved it along the line of cards, listening carefully. The boys watched and as his finger passed by the third card he felt a whine of fear ring out in all of them like a chorus.

Hayes tapped the card. "That one."

The boy stared at him, then flipped it over. The jack looked up at them both. The boy leaned close and said, "What the fuck you doing here?"

"Taking my winnings."

"What'd you do? What'd you do to the game?"

"Nothing," said Hayes. "I just won it."

Spectators around them started to applaud. The boy looked up and suddenly remembered himself.

"Here," he said. "Here. Take your goddamn money and go."

Hayes counted it carefully, then tipped an imaginary hat and walked away, the crowd still applauding. As he turned the corner a faint headache started to pound. He silently cursed himself. There had been too many people there and he had stayed far too long.

No, this was not magic, he thought to himself as he walked. He didn't know what it was. It was just his. Brightly called it his "talent" or his "knack." Evans preferred not to speak about it at all. And Hayes needed no word for it. It was just something that happened.

Sometimes when the wind was right and everything was still, Hayes could feel ripples running through him. Echoes from the minds of those around him. Most of the time they were deathly faint, but they were there. And sometimes he could learn things from them, or even mimic them.

It had taken him a long while to realize he could do it at all. To him it felt natural, like breathing. Like seeing patterns in mathematics and solving them, or sitting down with a pencil and knowing how to sketch a tree. It was just something his mind did without asking.

The boys at McNaughton had quizzed him about it at great length when Brightly had first hauled him in. Physicists and biologists and psychologists. Only a few, as Brightly wanted to keep any information about Hayes as restricted as possible. Hayes always told them it was like listening to music you had never heard before being played over and over again in the next room: you could hear something in the background but you weren't really sure what it was, but if you stayed there long enough eventually you could pick out the trumpets and the bass line, and if you stayed even longer you'd be able to complete the melody in your head without trying. Pretty soon you'd be humming along.

Much of it seemed to be based on time and proximity. After five minutes Hayes could sense when people were around him, within ten or twenty feet or so. After eight he would have a pretty good idea of where they were in relation to him. After thirty minutes he would get "the pangs," occasional flashes of how they were feeling, but unless they were having extreme emotions those were always difficult to determine. After two hours he would have a reasonably decent idea of their level of anxiety, depression, stress, or whatever else. After four he would begin to form a concept of how they felt about various things, some of them minutiae, others possibly important. And then, after spending six hours of close contact with a person with no other individuals around to interfere, Hayes could have a good sense of personality and some strong ideas about the problems that loomed particularly large in their mind, along with some habits unique to that person alone.

Yet even then, after slogging it out with that person for a quarter of a day in a tiny room, he still might not come up with anything too helpful. Just a handful of useless moments, skating across the edges of his thoughts.

It also meant he couldn't be in a crowd for more than an hour, as the noise would be unbearable. How it worked was a mystery to him and everyone else. It was just there. Always muttering and eating into him and burning him up. Drink or the pipe were the only things that killed it. Those, and work. The thrill of hunting through the city helped him forget it, or perhaps it drowned out whatever part of his mind could listen. But he'd take whatever was available. Whether it was a drug or a chase, he needed to keep a little flame burning in his head to beat back the murmurings that always followed him.

Cho Lun's was just ahead. Hayes spotted the three lookouts casually dawdling down the street by the door. He walked up and entered, the darkness and the aroma of the den closing in on him like a curtain. Half-finished legs of stools and chairs made a tangled forest around him in the dark, and a single candle burned on the front desk. Above it Hayes could make out the eyes of Chinese Charlie watching him calmly. Two other men moved somewhere in the room to stand somewhere behind Hayes, but it was Charlie who ran the place. Hayes could only assume his name was meant to be humorous, as Charlie was well over six and a half feet tall and about as red-haired and blue-eyed as they came.

"Hello, Princeling," said Charlie quietly. He threaded his fingers together on the table.

"Evening, Charles. How are you today?"

"The Princeling's back quite early today, isn't he," said Charlie. "Usually the Princeling doesn't show his face until midnight. It's only ten. Isn't it?"

"It is. I missed the ambience. Didn't realize we needed a reservation."

"We don't. Not usually. It's just that when little Princelings start coming back more and more their money starts getting smaller and smaller. Ain't that right?"

Hayes reached into his pocket and took out his winnings. He held them out and one of Charlie's boys snatched the money away and showed it to Charlie, who looked without touching. He nodded.

"All right, then," said Charlie, and he stood and crooked a finger and led Hayes to the back, candlestick in hand.

They went down a small wooden hallway. The ceiling got low and the air grew humid and smoky. There was laughter somewhere and moaning and someone kicked at a wall and wept. They emerged into a low, thin room with curtains and veils hanging from every corner, some silk, some no more than rags. Small girls in robes wove and dodged through the silken jungle, trays in their hands and long, curving pipes resting on their shoulders. They walked to nearby booths and swiveled the pipes around like brightly-colored insects maneuvering their antennae, sensing profit.

Charlie called to one in Mandarin, belittling and cursing her. She scurried over and he continued his tirade as she set up Hayes's booth.

Hayes could catch only a few words of it. Chastising her for her laziness. Reprimanding her for her impish whorishness. Not this time, he told her. Not with this one.

Hayes lay down in the booth and the girl set up the pipe. Charlie stood over him, frowning grimly with his arms crossed.

"You don't like me much, do you, Charlie?" asked Hayes.

"I like your money just fine," said Charlie.

"Then you must like me very much, as I bring so much here."

"I like you just as much as you can afford."

The little girl held his pipe still and Hayes suckled at it as she held the flame to its end. He drew in once, twice, fumes enveloping his head, then filling his lungs. It was just a taste, but its soft, stinging breeze was already wiping the day away. He leaned back, smiling.

"Tell me, Charlie," he said softly.

"Tell you what, Princeling?"

"What do you know about unions?"

"Unions?" Charlie's brow wrinkled. His sweat shone and in the dim light he looked like a man made of fatty wax.

"Yes."

"Which unions?"

"Any unions. Trade unions. The ones they're trying to make at McNaughton, for instance."

"I'm no working man, Princeling."

"You work very hard, Charlie. You're always here."

"I don't think they're going to make a guild of denners, then. Why you want to know about unions, Princeling? What patch of ground you got your ear to?"

"All of them. I'm just interested. Just curious."

Charlie cocked an eyebrow. "You sniffing for Mickey Tazz?"

"What?"

"Mickey Tazz. He's the union man out of the Shanties, or at least that's the rumor. He's the man with the shit-stirring stick."

"No. No, I never heard of Mickey Tazz," said Hayes. The pipegirl gently took his head and maneuvered it, her little fingers like ice. She brought the pipe up and Hayes sucked at it again. Numbing tendrils worked their way into his chest and then deep into his spine and up into the base of his brain. The light shuddered and yellowed like the soles of a man's feet and the girl's eyes were swallowed by inky blackness, some beautiful nocturnal creature with moth eyes and a pouting mouth waiting on his every word.

"I wouldn't go sniffing for Tazz, Princeling," said Charlie's voice from far away. "Tazz is a hard boy. He'll fuck you up good and proper. Maybe even more than you fuck yourself up, see?"

Someone began laughing, dry, smoky chuckles that rattled deep down in their chest. It took Hayes a moment to realize it was him.

"I see," he said. "I see."

CHAPTER SEVEN

Samantha awoke especially early to take the trolley from Newton down to McNaughton Southern Regional Office in Infield. She had read all she could about the trolley system, not willing to step on until she absolutely trusted it. After she woke she reviewed the stops and the timing, committed the schedule to memory, and then walked down to the station and reluctantly consented to be a passenger. Her planning quickly disintegrated as the malformed lump of machinery trundled up to the platform and released a rush of people that nearly bowled her over. The trolley did not look like a vehicle for transportation as much as it did a decrepit dance hall organ, covered in peeling gilding and bronze pipes. She clapped her hat to her head and squinted through the sea of bobbing heads to see the line number, and dashed aboard at the last moment. Once inside she shrank up against the wall as the vessel shuddered and lurched forward.

She watched as the dark stone walls began to fly by. It was like they were speeding over black waters. The other passengers took this with no reaction, coughing or fingering newspapers in the low light. From time to time a conductor shambled through the aisle, looking scruffily regal in his porter's uniform, his epaulettes askew and one brass button missing. A dogend was stuck behind his left ear and he groused and hassled passengers for tickets. When he demanded Samantha's he studied it and then returned it as though it had personally insulted him.

She came to Infield at eight minutes past six, fairly late by the schedule she had made for herself, and then headed off toward Southern Office, keeping to the route she had picked out the night before. She had taken the map with her, but the streets resembled the map in name only. What were straight lines on paper were meandering, dilapidated paths in real life. Shop fronts and home expansions tumbled off the sidewalk to squeeze roads into spaces just a few feet wide. In some places the streets ended entirely, without warning or explanation. And as she walked she began to realize there was something else wrong with the streets of Evesden, something more fundamental. After a while she realized it: there were no paving stones or cobblestones here. No seams, no cracks, no worn-down edges. The streets of Evesden were all smooth cement, almost like they were one huge piece, and the curbs were all sharp-cornered, having never seen the years of traffic common to other cities. She wondered what sort of machine could make a whole city block in one piece, especially when they were as tangled as this, and soon gave up, feeling somehow she had to be wrong.

By the time she arrived at Southern Office she was disoriented and somewhat sweaty, but still forty minutes early for her meeting. She stopped in a small café to collect herself, ordered a small cup of coffee that was too hot to sip, and then began to carefully make the proper corrections to her map. She was not sure if it was at all possible to make an accurate map of Evesden, as all those available seemed misinformed to at least some degree, but she was willing to try anyway.

It had been a strange trip here to Infield, but the journey to Evesden had been even stranger and longer. Samantha had never expected to be here, even under these circumstances. When she had been a child following her father from military base to military base in the East she'd heard of this wondrous city out on the edge of the ocean, but it'd never actually been real to her, at least no more real than Heaven or Fairyland. Then when she'd begun serving in the hospitals it had slowly become more present. Officers and engineers she had met in the service began getting bought out by the famous McNaughton Corporation, forever extending its grasp. "Turning company," they'd called it, and it was always "the company," never just "McNaughton." There simply wasn't another kind. And then when one once-corporal had mentioned in friendly conversation that she seemed to have a solid head on her shoulders and they could use her sort in the company, she'd found herself agreeing to a position and suddenly she was receiving communications from this mysterious jewel on the other side of the world.

When she'd been given her new assignment and transferred to Evesden she hadn't been sure what to expect. To Samantha, McNaughton was synonymous with order and institution. She'd found her true calling in the arms of the company, trawling through their labyrinthine files and setting their information to rights, and they'd greatly appreciated her work. So she had expected the home city to be something new, a place ruled with intelligence, perception, and efficiency, a paragon of the ideals McNaughton valued and rewarded. Yet she'd found something very different. Evesden was the most confusing city she'd seen yet. You couldn't walk a block and stay on the same street. Not even the maps made any sense. And how disappointed she'd been to find McNaughton treated rude, shabby little men as if they were the most important employees in the world, for no reason she could see.

Samantha sketched out her latest route but stopped as she questioned one adjustment. Then as she glanced around the café she noticed a blond, rumpled figure slouching in a booth by the windows. It was Hayes himself, a mountain of cigarette butts in the ashtray before him and an entire pot of coffee cooling beside it. He wore a curious pair of small blue spectacles that he kept pushing farther and farther up his nose. Stacks of files sat in a heap on the table and in the booth, one open in his lap. She recognized them as the ones she had prepared the day before for their first set of interview subjects.

Sighing inwardly, she stood and walked over to him and said, "Good morning, Mr. Hayes."

He nodded slowly without taking his eyes off the file. He did not seem at all surprised to see her.

"How are you doing?" she asked.

Still he did nothing. One of his eyebrows may have twitched a bit, she wasn't sure. Then he reached forward and salvaged one cigarette from the graveyard on the table and took a smoldering drag. He vanished behind a cloud of foul smoke. Samantha turned her head away as it drifted toward her.

He said, "These are very good."

"Pardon?" she said.

"These are very good. These files."

"Thank you."

"Very thorough. They'll make my job a lot easier."

"I'm surprised you got them so quickly," she said. "I sent them late last night."

"Mm."

"You must have gotten up early to get them."

"I never went to bed," he said.

"Oh," she said, startled.

"Your coffee's getting cold."

"I'm sorry?"

He nodded at the other side of the café. "Your coffee. At that table over there."

"Oh, yes. May I sit with you?"

"If you can find space."

She went and got her cup and made a small clearing across from him and sat.

"How'd you get these so quick?" he asked. "I mean, I learned who we're supposed to be interviewing just today."

"They gave me a day's head start," she said.

"And you managed to pull... what was that, doctors' records in a day?"

"Yes. They should be valuable, too."

"Doctors' records? In what way?"

"In many ways, if you're, well. Creative."

Hayes smirked. "I'll try my best. But let's hedge our bets. Please enlighten me."

"Well, for example, Mr. McClintock is an alcohol addict."

"So? Are we going to tempt him with gin?"

"Nothing so grotesque," she said, sliding out the relevant file and flipping it open. "I have him scheduled to be redirected here as soon as he gets in to work, which I think should be about nine, if his time cards are anything to go by."

"So he'll be too exhausted and half-drunk to be much of a liar," said Hayes. His smirk turned into a smile.

"That's the idea. And for tomorrow, Mr. Vanterwerp has significant digestive problems, so—"

"So I'm going to guess that you have him penciled in right after lunch."

"Yes."

"That's pretty dirty pool."

"It'll work."

"I have no doubt." He went back to the pile, shaking out one sheaf. Samantha frowned as several papers slid off the table into the opposite booth, but said nothing. Hayes read in silence. As he did she noticed he was wearing the same clothes from the last time she'd seen him. One cuff was trapped far up in his coat sleeve and his tie was barely hanging on. A serious stubble was collecting on the line of his jaw and clouds of black hovered below each red-rimmed eye.

"Who do you think is the most likely?" she asked.

"The most likely for what?" he said.

"To be working for the union. To be a saboteur."

He smirked. "None."

"What?"

"None of them are working for the union."

"How do you know?"

"Well, I don't, for sure. But I can say that these are foremen and overseers with rather high-paying jobs in comparison to others below them. They've been working for twenty years to get this sort of security. They don't want to lose it. Their men, on the other hand, have no security at all," said Hayes, and flipped over a page. "They work relatively unskilled labor for shit wages, wages that have been undercut twice in the past three months. So it's their boys who are trouble, and the foremen, as men with much to lose, will probably give a few of them up. Even the alky. What's his name again?"

"McClintock."

"Right," he said. "Have some more coffee."

At seven they walked down to Southern Office with the mass of files stuffed under Hayes's arm. The building was very utilitarian, not half as lavish as the Nail. Its cement walls were hastily painted and naked bulbs flickered in the ceiling. Workmen, not clerks, sauntered through the halls, eyeing them suspiciously. Hayes spoke to the front receptionist, a greasy little man named Neal who had half his shirt unbuttoned. Hayes passed the reins over to Samantha, who began scheduling all the interviews at an hour apiece.

"No," said Hayes. "Three hours."

"Three hours? You're sure this will take three hours?" she asked.

"Yes. Three. Apiece."

She frowned but then rescheduled them with Neal, who was none too pleased to take orders from a fancy downtown woman, but did it anyway.

Hayes made only one other request apart from the time. He asked that Neal reserve two rooms for the interviews, small ones isolated from the rest of the building, but next to one another.

"Put our interview subjects in one room, and I'll prepare in the other," he said.

"You need two rooms?" Neal asked flatly.

"Yes."

"What if we don't have two rooms?"

"Then we'll wait. And when the Nail asks where we are and what the holdup is, you can tell them."

"Fine, fine... What's all this about, anyways?"

"Promotions," said Hayes simply. "There are some spots to fill and we're screening our prospects."

They set up in a tiny corner of the building on the third floor, one room a small meeting room and the other practically a broom closet. Hayes dragged a chair into the closet and set the files on the floor.

"All right. I'll stay in here and get ready," he said.

"You want to stay here?" Samantha asked.

"Certainly. You sit in the meeting room and wait for Mr. McClintock. When he comes, tell him he's to be interviewed by, oh"—he thought for a bit—"Mr. Staunton, and then come and tell me he's here. Then go back in and tell him I'll be in in a bit."

"But why?"

"I want to make him wait."

She went back to the meeting room and sat at the table, confused, but said nothing. At eight forty-five McClintock stumbled in, a short, squat man with a bloodred face and fat butcher's hands. He looked extremely wary. Samantha wondered if he had ever been in the Southern Office before.

"Please take a seat," she said, and gestured to a chair at the little table.

"Okay," said McClintock, and sat.

"I'll go and tell Mr. Staunton you're here."

"All right."

She walked out, shut the door, then walked two feet over and opened the door of the broom closet. Hayes was seated in a chair and was leaning its back up against the wall, hands behind his head, eyes somewhat closed like he was dozing.

"He's here," she said softly.

"Mmm-hmm." He did not open his eyes.

"When will you be in?"

He shrugged, then waved dismissively.

Samantha returned to the meeting room. "He's somewhat delayed," she told Mr. McClintock. "Please make yourself at home."

McClintock blinked his red eyes and settled down in his chair further. His head drooped forward inch by inch and within a few minutes he was asleep. Samantha watched as his shoulders rose and fell, then sighed and checked her watch. After a half-hour she got up and walked back to the broom closet. Hayes was still in the exact same position, gently rocking back and forth on two legs of the chair.

"Well?" she said.

"Well what?" he said quietly.

"He's asleep. If you're trying to rattle him he certainly doesn't know it."

"I'm not trying to rattle him."

"Then what are you trying to do?"

"Please go back in and do whatever it is you were doing. Note-taking, or whatever. It's very important." He waved her away again.

More time passed. Samantha slumped in her chair, taking notes every five minutes, mostly out of spite. Twenty minutes later the door burst open, causing her to jump and Mr. McClintock to snort and sit up. Hayes swept in and slammed McClintock's file down on the table before him, saying, "Sorry I'm late, this place is incredibly confusing. Now give me a minute, if you please, because I'm not entirely sure why I'm here." He dumped himself in the chair before McClintock and put his feet up on the table with a groan. "You don't mind, do you?" he asked.

"No," said McClintock, bewildered.

"Great. Grand," he said, and began studying a report that, if Samantha was right, he had read twice already.

After several more minutes McClintock asked, "Why am I here, exactly?"

"Promotion, this says," Hayes said. He slapped the paper. "You're up for one, it seems. I'm to screen you."

"To what?"

"To screen you. I'm Staunton, Andrew Staunton, Personnel." He stuck out his hand. "Nice to meet you."

"Nice to meet you," said McClintock, shaking.

"Great," said Hayes. Samantha noticed he no longer spoke with an English accent. This was harder, American, inner-city.

"Did you say I'm up for a promotion?" McClintock asked.

"Seems that way," said Hayes.

"To overseer?"

"That would be the one, it says," said Hayes. "But there's just a few general questions we need to ask first. You know, a procedure they send me around to have everyone go through. It's nothing, just hoops everyone has to jump through. I've got a bunch more scheduled for today, very basic stuff. All right?"

"Sure," said McClintock, still rubbing sleep from his eyes.

They did start out basic. They went over his job title, amount of time worked at McNaughton, marriage status, children, current wages, expected wages. Health, date of birth. Output. But eventually they shifted slightly, just slightly. Any issues on the line, Hayes asked. Problems with workers? Accidents, even? When? How long ago? Specific reasons for each? Were you present for these occurrences? McClintock became noticeably perturbed by these questions. He sat up straight in his chair and blinked as he tried to focus on Hayes and insisted that he ran a clean ship, you know, and he wasn't sure what all these questions were about but he didn't like them one bit. He'd been working diligently for more than thirty years and he didn't like having such accusations tossed in his face at the crack of dawn. Hayes immediately understood. Course not, course you don't, you wouldn't be here if you didn't run a clean ship, but no career goes by without a blotch or two. "It's just for the records," Hayes explained. "Just for records. I hate record-taking as much as you do." Then Hayes took a deep, exhausted breath, glanced surreptitiously at Samantha, and leaned forward to softly ask McClintock something. Samantha could not hear what he'd said, but McClintock looked astonished. Then he half-smiled in disbelief and nodded. Hayes produced a small porcelain thermos from his coat and took a sip and passed it to McClintock, who drank deeply. Samantha opened her mouth and wondered if she should say something. Hayes did not look at her to communicate any message and so she chose to stay quiet.

From then on the two men were like brothers. They sat the same way in their chairs, the familiar bar slouch with their elbows on the table and their chests propped up against the edge. They talked the same and they laughed the same and they took the same dismissive attitude to Hayes's questions. It stopped being an interview and started becoming a conversation. Hayes didn't seem interested in the man's accidents but in his war stories.

Then Hayes asked, "This one incident, about four months ago. Fella who got burned by the conduit. Remember that?"

"God, who wouldn't," said McClintock. "I remember. I never heard so much screaming. Everyone was shook up for weeks."

"What the hell was that about? How does something like that happen?"

"Tricky job. They just happen. It's part of it."

"So there's no specific reason?"

"People get tired. They go out one night, can't sleep, come in, and don't know what they're doing. And they pay for it."

"That's how they all are?" asked Hayes. "Just honest mistakes?"

"Pretty much."

Hayes watched him closely. His eyes took on a dreamy look, filmed over and sightless as if seeing someone else entirely. "What about that one with the hands?"

McClintock looked at him uneasily. "How'd you know about that?"

"Rumor mill," said Hayes. "Something that vicious, well, you hear about it."

"He got them caught in the cincher. It happens."

"I can see one hand getting caught. But both? That's a little odd."

"It was odd. It was horrible, too."

"Did you see it?"

"No. No, I didn't see the accident. I saw them wheeling Tommy away, though. Belts around his wrists and cloth all over them. He'd passed out."

"Who did see it?"

McClintock thought for a moment then and shook his head. "It's the strangest thing."

"What is?"

"I don't know who saw."

"You don't?"

"No. Sometimes..." He tried to think again, but the words would not stop coming now. "Sometimes I can't trust the boys who are down there. You know? They said it was an accident. I wasn't there, I didn't see. They said it was. But I couldn't be sure. Tommy never said who did it. He died not long after. Infection. But he was scared when he was alive. And Tommy was never..."

"Never what?"

"Never liked so much."

"Why not?"

"Some damn thing," said McClintock. "I don't know. Something about wages. They don't talk to me about those things, you know? I'm their boss, not their friend."

"I know. You're right. But they should still trust you that much."

"They should. They absolutely should. I've never done them wrong before. Not ever. I've fought for them time and time again, I've fought to keep jobs and shifts and wages. Things keep getting scarcer down there, moving labor around. But you look at them and they're all looking right back at you and you can see it. Right there. They don't trust you. They don't trust anyone who's not with them. Who's not suffering same as them. But I was on the line way back and I suffered plenty. I just survived long enough to get up to where I am. You know?"

Hayes watched him silently, eyes still unfocused. Then he said, "They were for Mickey, and Tommy wasn't."

McClintock nodded. "They were. Tommy didn't want to truck with it. Didn't care for it."

"Who were the ones involved?"

"I don't know."

"But who would be likely?"

"Naylor and Walton, I'm almost sure. Those bastards. The fucking bastards. And Evie's always palling with them, too. The past few months I got no idea what's going on with those boys."

Hayes nodded. "I see," he said. "All right."

He asked more questions. Asked about the social life of McClintock's team, about where they went to drink. Not professional stuff, just two boozers chatting and loafing. Sure, said McClintock, they hang at the Third Ring Pub, down where Southern meets the Shanties. Hayes asked about girls and McClintock said sure, they have a few, what working man doesn't? Rumor had it John Evie had a few boys, but he couldn't say for certain. Peggy had been Naylor's girl, maybe still was, off and on. Little redheaded thing, he said, he'd seen her with him more than a few times. Got to be a good fuck, but any fuck's a good fuck if you've been as dry as he had, and he prodded Hayes with an elbow and the two of them laughed. More names breezed by, just idle gossip being passed along. And in the corner of the room Samantha wrote them all down, every single one.

At the end of the three hours Hayes and McClintock both wobbled to their feet and helped one another to the door, laughing and stumbling. They went to the hallway to chat and left Samantha to finish up her notes. When she was done Hayes returned, sober and distracted again, hardly drunk at all.

"Who's Mickey?" she asked. "I don't have any record of a Mickey in here."

"Mickey Tazz is the union man," said Hayes as he sat. "He's the boy Evans painted the target on, whether he knows it or not."

"How'd you know that?"

"Rumor mill."

"Would that be the same place you heard about the hands?"

"Sort of. We have ten minutes 'til our next interview, right?"

"We do."

"Right," he said, and put his feet up and fell genuinely asleep this time.

There were three others that day: Mueller, Ferdig, and Andersson. Each time Hayes waited in the broom closet next door, and each time when he emerged he began an interviewer and ended a friend. Always there with a sympathetic ear, always smiling sadly or nodding in concern. For Mueller, who oversaw the booking office in the detailing facility, he was stiff and cordial, the consummate bureaucrat, asking detailed questions and receiving detailed answers. Lovers of due process, the both of them. For Andersson, who was so big and dour and blond, Hayes was a comrade, a fellow soldier, another hard worker who was paid for his efforts with more problems, more bullshit, more lazy coworkers. The more advanced the world gets the less everyone gives a shit, they both agreed. And for Ferdig he was a coconspirator, the two men finding some neighborhood link in their histories, some district or corner they both used to frequent, and they traded rumors and cigarettes like old thieves.

Each one had names. None quite so many as McClintock, but names nonetheless. And each had heard of Mickey Tazz, the shining hope of the Shanties. A clean, smart man supported by a nasty crowd, there was no doubt. He was riding the lightning, wasn't he? Some days he seemed like Christ himself.

Andersson seemed to almost support the man. "He is not a criminal," he told Hayes. "He is not dangerous. These are just dangerous times. He is just voice. Speaking of unhappiness, yes?" Hayes nodded, understanding. He worked his way close to the melancholy Swede, the two of them frowning and sharing small scraps of their days, Hayes as a simple paper-pusher, Andersson as a spot-welder for the Tramlines. Hayes professed some admiration for Andersson's admittedly dangerous job, and the man took pride in that. When he left Hayes walked him all the way out of the building, sharing oaths and gloomy head-shakes along the way, and Hayes returned with a small bevy of information about the union leader.

Mickey Tazz, born Michael Tazarian, half-Irish, half-Czech. Came from the Shanties, worked on the dock and rose up to foreman damn quick. When the Chinese and the blacks started eating up wages he tried to fence them out and put a freeze on the wage levels. Started his own little band of stevedores, they say, but wasn't a thug about it. He was a political animal, right from the start. Wanted to talk to the big boys. Full of high ideas about the rights of man. Naturally, things got ugly and a bunch of them got arrested, including Tazz. He wound up spending a nickel spot in Savron Hill, but on getting out he started to organize, looking to band everyone together under one big banner. If Evesden was the city of the future, then Mickey Tazz was the man who would make it a future where everyone lived in peace. Tomorrow is coming, he told everyone. We just have to make it the tomorrow we want.

"That's a charming little picture," said Samantha at the end.

"Yes," said Hayes. "It is." And he sat down and waited for the end of the long day.

CHAPTER EIGHT

The next three weeks passed in nearly the same way. Each day a new list of names. Each morning a new set of blank little rooms with blank men. And at the end of each day they had a new list of their own to deliver to Evans, who would then presumably deliver it to Brightly, or at least someone higher up on the Security chain.

However, what happened after that was never made known to them. Hayes was not sure if there were arrests made, or inquiries, or if other investigators were following up on the allegations brought to light by their interviews. Samantha once asked him about it, wondering if this was procedure, but Hayes could do no more than shrug. This union angle was completely new to him, he admitted. He'd no idea what the procedure was, or even if there was any.

Then one day on one of their rare free mornings Hayes swung down to Payroll and checked on a few suspicions he'd been nursing. He frowned when he heard the answers to his queries, and then took the elevator up to the Communications Office for Securities and sent off a telegram directly to Brightly, asking to meet. Then he sat in the waiting room of the office and watched the gray clouds drifting by outside.

It was extraordinarily difficult to get a meeting with Brightly. The man moved constantly. As far as Hayes was aware he didn't even have an office. There was a rumor that the short, red airship that they saw hovering near the McNaughton cradle so often was his own personal vessel, ready to swoop him up and drop him down wherever and whenever he needed it. Hayes felt sure this was a lie. Brightly wasn't one for flash and style. Whatever he was, he was far from Father Christmas.

Suddenly the telegraph came to life, rattling and clacking, and the clerk ripped the reply message from the machine's teeth:

> CURRENTLY IN ENG SUMMIT STOP COME TC OFF 1100 HRS STOP USE BCK ENTR STOP
>
> —B

Hayes was surprised. He'd hardly expected a response, let alone one so quick. He thanked the clerk and then headed out to the street to catch a cab over to the Telecommunications Office.

He arrived early and waited across the street from the dull gray building. It had none of the flair of any of the other McNaughton structures, but then like most McNaughton buildings much of the work was done in the spacious basements and offices underground. At ten-thirty a crowd of men in cheap suits and shirtsleeves threaded out, talking and babbling to each other. Engineers, he guessed, from whatever meeting they were holding. No doubt Brightly had wanted Hayes to steer well clear of them.

Finally at eleven Hayes sauntered around to the alley behind the office and found the back door. Although it was made of wood and iron a light key slot was set into the side. Hayes took out his own light key and slid it in. There was the familiar whir and clunk and he pulled the door open. He hadn't been positive it'd work; his light key was accepted by most McNaughton doors, but some areas, like the Records floor and some labs and engineering bays, were specifically off-limits to him.

He entered a long, empty corridor. The lights were mostly off, and as he walked in he felt wary for some reason. Then as he passed two swinging doors he looked through their windows to see Brightly lounging at the front of what looked like a large teaching auditorium. Arced desks descended down to the front stage in concentric circles, and most of the lights were off. The desktops were covered in papers and pencils and all sorts of clerical rubbish. At the front of the room was a large blackboard and many graphs and charts, and before them sat what looked like a large iron lamp on a pedestal.

Hayes pushed open the door. Brightly looked back, surprised, and then stood. An easy smile played across his face, but his right hand quickly reached into his pocket to pull out his pocket watch. He glanced at it, then called up, "Good morning, Hayes. You're early. Or, actually, on time."

Hayes grimly reminded himself that Brightly wasn't checking his watch to see if he was early. "Yes," he said, walking down. "Had some minutes to spare. Thought I'd skip over early. Who were those boys leaving just now? Pale, unwashed-looking chaps. I guessed they were your scientists. That so?"

"Yes."

"I suppose you had me come in after so I didn't hear what they were saying?"

"I didn't want any interruptions," said Brightly, his voice fruity and jovial as though they were discussing news at the club.

"Or perhaps so I wouldn't hear what they were thinking?" asked Hayes.

Brightly's easy smile didn't twitch a bit. But then, however much Hayes needled, it almost never did. Brightly was an impenetrable wall of a man, physically and spiritually. He was six feet tall with bulky shoulders and the build of a powerful man happily gone to seed. He was somewhere in his early fifties, but his head was crowned with leonine, prematurely white hair. He always had the smile of a boy just leaving grade school, wickedly delighted at the way the world was perpetually coming to his favor, which perhaps for Brightly it was.

Hayes knew very little about him, but he'd heard he'd cut his teeth in Africa during the Boer Wars, when his salesmanship to the Boer Republics had pushed the war in their favor. At least until Britain put up a better bid, and it all went to pieces for them. It was supposedly after Britain annexed the Republics that Brightly orchestrated McNaughton's unspoken alliance with the British Empire. After all, it was said, since McNaughton was clearly going to be the dominant empire of the coming years, they might as well learn a few tricks from an old hand. Some even said Brightly had sold arms to the Boers just to get Her Majesty's attention and attract a bid.

"Nonsense," said Brightly. "Our secrets are, naturally, your secrets. You're company, after all. So what can I do for you?" As Hayes came before him, Brightly checked his watch once more.

"I want to know what we're doing with the unions," said Hayes.

"With the unions?" said Brightly, faintly confused. "That's obvious. We're investigating sabotage and propaganda."

"Yes, yes," said Hayes. "But we're not *arresting* any of them. I went to Payroll today. All of the men we identified as saboteurs are still working. Still coming in for their shifts. We're still *paying* them, for God's sake. Doesn't seem to add up."

"That assumes we're doing simple addition," said Brightly. "You're thinking too small."

"Am I? Then please, broaden my mind."

"Hm. How far would you say the union infiltration goes, Hayes?" asked Brightly cheerily. "How far do you know, for sure?"

Hayes shrugged.

"Exactly," said Brightly. "We don't know. Or at least we don't know much. You just have a few thugs."

"A few killers."

"Killers, yes, but thugs all the same. They're superficial, low-level. So why flush them out so early, when we know so little, and our product so far is so meager? Why startle them by arresting just a few violent brutes, when we'd much rather have bigger fish on the line?"

Hayes thinned his eyes. "You're talking about Tazz."

"Time!" called Brightly, still smiling. Then he abruptly turned and walked away from Hayes to the far corner of the room without saying another word. He stood there with his back to him, silently looking at his watch in the palm of one hand.

Hayes did not follow. Instead he grimaced, and then silently counted off a full minute while Brightly did the same. Once it was done Hayes followed him to the corner of the room.

"So we're not making any arrests until we've got Mickey Tazz, is that it?" he asked.

"Tazz, or whoever," said Brightly. He checked his watch again. "We just don't know. And until we know, we won't make arrests, now will we?"

"It's still not safe," said Hayes. "Leaving saboteurs working at your plants. They've killed, you know."

"I'm aware," said Brightly mildly.

"They may kill again."

"Precautions have been taken," said Brightly. "We're keeping our eyes on them. They won't be doing any more damage."

"You're keeping your eyes on them, but not too close because you don't want them spooked?" said Hayes. "Christ. You know that'll never work."

Brightly smiled placidly. "I think I'll judge what works and what doesn't. We need to know everything we can. There may be other groups of them, committing crimes we can't see. Hidden pockets in other plants. If we eliminate one, we leave others still functioning. Or maybe doing worse damage, since they'd know we're onto them."

"If you want me to find out if there are any others, let me grill the ones we've identified. I can work them over and find out everything they know. You haven't even let us bring in Naylor or anyone else connected."

"That's assuming they know anything," said Brightly sternly. "And you know we're not going to let you do that. Not after Ferguson." He sighed a little as though disappointed. "You know, this is not normal procedure. You honestly shouldn't be going above Evans's head on this."

"Evans doesn't know what you're doing either," said Hayes. "And Evans can't give me what I want."

"And what's that?"

"To go after Tazz directly, on my own," said Hayes.

"Time!" said Brightly, snapping his watch shut. Then he lumbered away back down to the front of the room.

Hayes opened his mouth to say something, but refrained. He stared at the ground at his feet as Brightly took the steps up to stand on the edge of the stage, humming to himself with his back to Hayes. Hayes counted off another sixty seconds, then crossed the auditorium and followed him up the steps.

Brightly turned to face him as he approached. "Now, Hayes, you know we can't let you do that."

"Why not? It's Tazz you're after, that's obvious enough."

"Is it?" said Brightly. "Are you sure it's Tazz we're after? Tazz seems a politician to me. A rabble-rouser, albeit a secretive one. There may be other, nastier men who do his ugly thinking for him. Tazz, after all, probably has to stay clean."

"I can ferret them out, regardless of who they are," said Hayes. "I just need..."

"Need what?"

"Need more rope," said Hayes. "And I need to be on my own."

"On your own?" said Brightly merrily. "You mean without Miss Fairbanks?"

"Yes. She's not bad, but she's... She's slowing me down."

"Is she? From my perspective you're doing better than you've ever done before. Rather than your usual erratic bursts of product, Hayes, you're delivering small payloads of gold every day. Do you know that? Have you even been paying attention to what's going on?"

"Yes, I have. We've turned Securities into a sausage factory. We're too timid."

"You mistake sloppiness for action," said Brightly. "Miss Fairbanks, while lacking your formidable talents, is an invaluable compass for your investigation. And the little woman's no fool herself, you know that. Do you know we've been allowing her to select your interview subjects for you for the past week? And you've been bringing home kills, each time. You've seen that, haven't you?"

"I haven't," said Hayes stubbornly. "I don't know what happens when I report something. No one tells me anything anymore. And no one tells her, either. No one even told her what I could do."

"Time," said Brightly, looking at his watch. He did another about-face and walked down the steps and up to the edge of the auditorium. Hayes watched him go, frowning, and began counting seconds for the third time.

Whenever he spoke to Brightly, which was very rarely, the conversation was always conducted this way. That, or it was extremely short. Brightly was well aware of the limits of Hayes's abilities, and he'd always been very careful to prevent Hayes from overhearing anything he shouldn't. So every four minutes Brightly would interrupt their discussions to move outside Hayes's vaguely defined range, and then wait a full minute to continue the conversation again. Yet for some reason Brightly never felt comfortable shouting across a large room. He felt it was improper, and refused to consider it. And so rather than their continuing the conversation as they marched across the large auditorium, Brightly would turn his back and pretend Hayes wasn't there at all, and they'd both stand in silence while Hayes's slippery grasp on his errant thoughts faded.

Hayes didn't like it, but he'd grown used to it. At least Brightly was kind enough to move himself, rather than making Hayes walk away. But still each time he met with Brightly he felt powerfully small, as though he were no more than a supplicating little creature forever trapped in Brightly's shadow, and scrambling to keep up with the man's heels as he steadily moved away.

As Hayes counted he looked to his right at the large iron lamp on the pedestal. It must have been the subject of whatever summit Brightly had held there. Unlike that of other lamps, its glass chimney was extremely small, no more than three inches tall, and it was nestled within columns of complicated-looking wires and plumbing. Strangely enough, the little chimney seemed to be holding some sort of clear fluid.

Hayes turned away from it as the minute ran out. He walked up to Brightly and saw that at the back of the auditorium where he stood there was another lantern on a pedestal, only this lantern was much smaller.

Hayes ignored it. "So what am I supposed to do?" he asked.

"Keep on doing what you're doing," said Brightly. "We'll have everything planned out for you."

"And Sam?"

"She'll do what we plan for her as well. I don't understand why there's friction between you two, I understand she's a lovely girl."

Hayes paused. "She doesn't know about me. And no one plans to tell her."

Brightly shook his head. "She doesn't need to know. It'd only trouble her. And besides, you've already turned her inside out, haven't you? Read all the words written on the inside of her skull? What more could there be to protect?"

Hayes did not answer. Brightly turned to look at the little iron lamp on the pedestal and cocked an eyebrow, thinking. "Here," he said. "Here, Hayes. Do you want to know why we're having you do this? Why we're stressing security as much as we are, and making you do all these tasks?"

"Because they're sabotaging our factories, of course."

"Yes, yes, but there's more than that."

Hayes just shrugged. "I just assumed it was for profit."

"Well, yes," said Brightly, eyes glittering. "I'd be a liar if I said it wasn't. But there's more. Much more. Here. I'll show you." He leaned over and hit a switch on the smaller lamp. It began humming very,

very softly, a low hum that seemed to build but never grew truly loud. Once it was on he walked down to the stage, leaving Hayes behind once more.

"Is this part of your minutes of silence?" Hayes called to him, but Brightly did not answer. Instead he switched on the larger lamp and stood back.

"This may take a bit to warm up," he called up from the stage. "They need time to recognize one another."

"Who?" said Hayes, but again Brightly said nothing.

Eventually the lamp on the stage seemed to hit some threshold. Brightly smiled, walked to it, and called, "All right, now—watch."

"I'm watching," said Hayes.

"Are you watching closely, though?"

"Damn it, yes."

Brightly adjusted some dials on its side. Then, glancing up at Hayes, he held one hand over the top of the lantern and pushed a button. Immediately the little glass chimney lit up, glowing with a soft blue light. At first Hayes was unimpressed, and he opened his mouth for a smart remark, but then he noticed the chimney in the lamp beside him had lit up as well. Brightly released whatever button he'd tapped, and the lights went out in both. Then he tapped it twice more. Both lamps flashed blue simultaneously. Then he began tapping out a little rhythm, each lamp flashing with the long and the short beats exactly.

"What are they?" said Hayes.

"They're our newest prototype," said Brightly. "And they're going to revolutionize everything. And I do mean *everything*, Hayes."

"Just these . . . these lamps that light up?"

"Not just light up. They light up *instantaneously*."

Hayes stared at him blankly. "So?"

Brightly frowned and released the button. The lamps went dark. "They're called the Siblings, or at least that's what we're calling them for now," he began. "I rather like the name. Gives it a fraternal feel, like a family. Something the average man can appreciate. They're crystals, Hayes, crystals that are paired together. Very, very small ones, just the size of molecules. But they're remarkable, because if you split them up and put a minute charge through one of the crystals—just a very, very small one—then the other crystal immediately experiences symptoms of that same charge. Even if it's not physically touching, which you can see as there's one half floating in each lamp here. And they do it *instantaneously*. There's no delay at all."

Hayes looked at the lamp beside him. "None?"

"No," said Brightly. He tapped out another rhythm on the lamp, and the other one flashed with it. "And usually everything has a delay. Radio waves. Electrical impulses. By God, even light has one," he said, laughing. "But, as far as we can tell, these crystals don't have any. They conduct the same tiny charge, no matter how far apart... to an extent."

"An extent?"

"Yes," said Brightly. "It's mostly limited by proximity and duration. Depending on the machine that powers them, they can instantaneously conduct charges within a certain radius. With these it's, say, half a mile. And, as you saw, it takes several seconds for them to recognize each other. They can only do it in pairs for now... But can you see what use this would have, Hayes?"

Hayes stared at the little lamp, thinking. "Communication," he said.

Brightly beamed. "Exactly. If you make chains of them, paired across the world, you can conduct messages with almost no delay at all. But even better, if we can get them powered so they broadcast far enough, we won't even need chains—you'd be able to communicate with the other side of the globe, immediately. People could pick up the phone and call France if they'd like and hear a voice right away."

"And generals could communicate the movements of the enemy to their separated troops," said Hayes.

Brightly's smile thinned. "What a nasty idea."

"Yet a lucrative one, isn't it?"

"Possibly," said Brightly. "The military possibilities of the Siblings have not gone unacknowledged. But we can't decide what people do with the things we make, can we? Is that burden for us to bear?" Somehow his smile became even more placid.

"How many does the government have now?" asked Hayes flatly.

"Oh, none. These are prototypes, and crude ones at that. We're experiencing some mathematical problems. Theoretically, they shouldn't be limited at all, by either time or duration, and we still haven't increased the range as much as we'd like... but we're still figuring it out. We won't be ready to go into production for a year, at least."

"And what does that take?" asked Hayes.

"Well, that's a bit more complicated," said Brightly, turning off his lamp. "Apparently it involves some very hot temperatures, some high-speed collisions of some very small things, and some very tricky math. Of a sort."

"Of a sort?"

"Yes. You see, they had to make up a new kind."

"A new kind of what?"

"Of math," said Brightly simply.

"Of *math*?"

"Oh, yes."

"How did they do *that*?"

"Come now, Hayes," said Brightly. "Surely you can't have forgotten our patron saint?"

Hayes thought, then rolled his eyes. "Kulahee, again."

"Yes. The man spent hours and hours toying with equations. Making numbers do things they'd never done before. It's taken years to decode some of his scribbling, but we did it. And now we can stand on the shoulders of his giant figure, and move the very stars."

"Very nice, Brightly," said Hayes. "You ought to write that down."

Brightly glowered at him. He marched up the stairs and said, "Turn off that one and come with me."

"Right, right," said Hayes as he left. He turned to the little lamp and examined it. It had several knobs and buttons and switches on it, all of them pretty incomprehensible to him. He stuck his tongue in the corner of his mouth and leaned in, peering through the panels.

...messenger...

Hayes snapped back and stood up. He looked around, but found the room was empty.

"Hello?" he said. But, of course, there was no one there.

He blinked. He knew that sensation. It was the feeling he got when someone came close and a lone thought slipped from their mind to his. That one had just been one word, just "messenger." Yet there seemed to be no one near.

He looked around again, curious. Then, shrugging, he turned the Sibling off and followed the path Brightly had taken. Hayes found him in a large side room off the corridor, this one much more industrial. As usual, the second he walked through the door Brightly checked his watch and marked the time.

But Hayes barely noticed. There in the center of the room was a Sibling, like the ones he'd just seen, but it was enormous, the size of a cathedral bell. Cables the size of his arm coiled through the many columns, and there nestled in the center was the same little glass chimney, no larger than the ones from the previous lamps. Hayes whistled as he looked the device over.

"Yes," said Brightly. "This was for an experiment. We loaded this one's paired Sibling onto a tanker ship, timed a team of watches down to the nanosecond, and floated it out into the middle of the Pacific. Then, at the exact agreed-upon moment, they recorded themselves tapping out a signal on it, and we recorded the reception on our end. When they returned to shore, we compared the two recordings. They were exact. The only delay involved was basic human reaction time. Even though there were countless storms in the way.

"When we first made the airships we thought oceans and seas didn't matter. We could cross them without thought. But that was just a passing fancy. Now we know better. Now those great distances are truly immaterial. We're going to make a new age, Hayes. In the next few years, the world will get smaller and smaller. Do you see?"

"I see," said Hayes.

"Now do you understand why your task is so important?"

"Just for the Siblings?"

"Not just for them. This is but an example. One that may truly revolutionize the world."

Hayes thought, then shrugged. "I still don't see why I can't go after Tazz."

Brightly's smile shivered a bit. He stiffly shook his head. "By God, sometimes you are the most useless fool I've ever met," he said through his grin. Then he pushed open the doors and walked out.

Hayes smiled after him. He'd never gotten him to do that before. He turned to look at the massive Sibling and scratched his nose. He saluted it, though he didn't know why, and then walked toward the door.

...messenger...from afar...

He stopped short and whirled around. "Hello?" he called out. "Who's there?"

There was no answer. Only the low thrum of the Sibling. He checked behind it but could find no one hiding there. Then he stared at the device and moved closer, holding his hands out as though trying to feel any effects.

Had the Sibling spoken to him? Was it even possible for him to overhear a machine? He'd certainly never experienced anything like it before. Perhaps it was a transmission he'd overheard, somehow... But wasn't this one a prototype, built only to see how far they could transmit? Or could someone else have somehow been sending messages through it?

He shook himself. It was a silly idea. It was much more likely there was someone on the floor above or below and Hayes had just happened to get close to them.

Hayes left and caught up to Brightly, who was standing with his hands behind his back at the end of the hall. He was wearing his traveling coat and his hat now, and he'd shed the smile for a dour glare. Yet no matter how angry he was, the second Hayes came near he checked his pocket watch and marked the time. Hayes would forever be a tool to Brightly, he knew, one that came with liabilities that required careful use. Every second Brightly allowed was one with a purpose, however hidden.

"I hope this has not been a waste of my very valuable time," he said. "Has it, Hayes? Please tell me you've learned something useful?"

Hayes was silent. He gave Brightly a piercing look, then nodded slightly.

"I hope so," said Brightly. "I honestly do. Some days I'm not sure why I've kept you on. We ask for you to do one thing, one little task, and we set the bar so low for you, and still somehow you find the need to buck us. But pay attention, now, because I'm going to keep this simple—if you *don't* do these little, tiny, easy tasks we've set for you, you'll be out. Out right away. No exceptions."

"I just want to do my job. To get after Tazz."

"No, Mr. Hayes," said Brightly. "You are a man of addictions. And some of your addictions go far beyond any chemical or bottle. You want to chase Tazz the same way a drunkard needs his tankard. It's simply another exciting little diversion for you, isn't it?"

When Hayes did not answer, Brightly nodded. "Then it's as I thought. Let's hope this is one compulsion you can overcome, for your sake. Good day," he said, and pushed through the doors and walked out to the street.

CHAPTER NINE

On her fifth week on the job, Samantha began to feel disappointment creeping in on her. She still organized rigorously and kept both herself and Hayes to the plans laid out for them, but the days went by more slowly. Looking back on the past weeks, it was difficult to say what they had accomplished. Her work had become condensed to mere paperwork and research, just facts and figures to feed Hayes before each interview. Conversations about violence and horrible suspicions drifted by, and she wrote them down without any expectation of redress. It became difficult to remember that often there were fortunes at stake when the day seemed to repeat itself again and again, with no hint of progress gained.

Hayes seemed to feel similarly. Each day he swept into the room, his eyes alight with a mad, dancing spark as he did his little performance, and then when he was done he shambled out, little and tired again. They did not speak much beyond work. They nodded hello and went about their business and then parted. Each time she reflected that she really knew very little about the man she was paid to assist.

So it came as a surprise one day when, as they packed up and prepared to leave, Hayes turned to her and said, "Well, Sam, I believe that went rather well, didn't it?"

"I would say so, yes," she said.

"Care for some dinner?"

She thought about it, wondering if it was some ploy. "If you're sure."

"Of course I'm sure," he said. "Bit of food would do us both good."

They ate boiled beef and cabbage at a bar across the street, a dim and murky place built of weeping wood. They sat at a scarred table in the corner, and she had a glass of stale tea and he a porter, telling her offhandedly that she was not to tell anyone about that as he was supposed to be bone-dry, you know, but every once in a while a man has to put a toe out of line. They exchanged curt comments about the food or about work, and Hayes drank beer until his lips were a thin black-brown and his cheeks gained color. Eventually he asked her where she was staying, and when she said Newton he cried, "My God. You're practically living among royalty. How did you land that?"

"Mr. Evans arranged it for me, actually. It is quite nice," she said haltingly.

"A bit too nice?"

"Maybe a little. I'm not really used to such treatment."

"Oh, it's nothing. Evans is just fond of young girls in the most boring way possible. Thinks they're his children. I'd ride it out, if I were you." Hayes sloshed down more beer and said, "Where did you live in Cairo, if you don't mind my asking?"

"In my father's house," she said.

"Do you miss it?"

"Yes. Yes. Very much."

His eyelids fluttered. "Would you tell me about it?"

"What? Why?"

"Because I'm curious, I suppose. I have you watching over my shoulder all day. I thought I might learn a bit about you. Can't I order you to tell me, or something?"

"You are not my direct superior," she said.

"Well. You're my assistant. Just assist me with it, then."

She sighed. She looked at Hayes and saw that familiar light in his eyes she'd seen in their interviews, that hunger to take a person apart and learn their story, like studying and dating a fossil found deep in the earth.

"My house?"

"Yes."

"It was small," she said. "Very small. We lived on the second story. I did, I mean. Below us was a large family. Their father was a tradesman. He dealt in spice, and downstairs it always smelled strange. Strange but beautiful. People sang in the mornings and throughout the day, calling people to prayer. I never prayed with them, it wouldn't have been appropriate. But I often wish I had. I don't know why."

Hayes shut his eyes. He took a deep breath as though he could catch that same exotic fragrance. "It sounds very nice," he said.

"It was. Very nice."

"What did your father think of your transition to here?"

"My father has been dead for ten years."

"Oh. I'm sorry to hear that."

"It's all right. It was ten years, after all."

"If it was all so nice, why did you accept this position?" he asked.

She put her spoon down as she considered the question. "Well. It would have been impossible to say no."

"Why?"

"Because... because this is *Evesden*. This is the most famous city in the world. I mean, I've worked for McNaughton for a few years, but never here, never at the main office. At the *Nail*. I had been looking for a chance to go further, and when this came along I couldn't refuse."

"Yes. I suppose I forget how this city seems to the outside," he said. "Do you regret it? Taking the position, I mean?"

"No. Should I?"

"Well, you seem like a capable, career-minded young woman. It's lucky you're working for one of the more liberal places around, but you could really get a leg up if you did something else here."

"This is a leg up," she said.

Hayes lit a cigarette and spat smoke out the side of his mouth. "No it isn't."

"This is a position of extreme importance, operating for some of the most powerful people in the country. Of course this is significant."

"Oh, all right, but beyond that? Beyond wanting a pat on the head from the fogies upstairs?"

Samantha glared at him. "I don't want a pat on the—"

"I apologize," he said, immediately and insincerely. "Very sorry. Totally out of line. But honestly. What do you want, beyond the prestige?"

"It's also putting things to right," she said, trying to believe it. "Keeping things safe. Protecting people. Prosecuting the murders in the lower ranks."

Hayes was quiet. He swilled his beer around at the bottom of his glass, watching the slick muddy tide wash up and down the sides. "There was a man once," he said. "A man named Teddy. Teddy Montrose. This was a few years ago, mind. Engineer. Worked in Telecommunications, Teddy did. Teddy handled a lot of high-security designs. Oversaw a lot of important information being passed back and forth. Then one day Brightly calls me up and says, Hayes, my boy, we think there's something amiss with our dear friend Teddy. In fact, we think he's running something on the side. There's a lot of Russian traffic up north along the coast, and there's talk that someone in Telecommunications is going to pass some information about trade agreements on to them. Teddy's our weak link, my boy, the chink in our armor. The likely spot, yes? So why don't you look into

Teddy and make sure everything's tip-top. And of course I say sure, Larry. Sure thing."

Hayes sat up and hunched over his glass, blond head crooked on his shoulders. "So I did. I did look into Teddy. I followed him for about a month. Spent a lot of time in empty rooms, staring out the window. Spent hours watching his family. He was a nice fellow, Teddy. Two kids, Honoria and Jessica. They liked the river market, I remember that. Nice wife. Sort of dull, though. Elizabeth, I think her name was. Liked horses. I told Evans that, said he'd get along with her. Jim's a horseman, you see. And I keep following him and following him, and I keep telling Brightly that there's nothing here. This man's straight as an arrow. Pure as the driven snow. Waste of time. But he just tells me to keep sitting on him. So I do.

"Eventually it breaks. Teddy told friends and family he was going on some business trip overnight, but I had no record of it. Instead he went east. East to Dockland, suitcase in his hand. To a little building. Next to where the painted women walk, the daughters of joy. But there were no women in that place. I checked, you see, went inside once he had done his bit and left. No. No, they just had a line of little boys. About seven years old, I'd say. All lined up on the wall in nice clean smocks. Bare legs, hands clasped before them. Heads bowed like they were waiting for teacher. The man in the front told me I could take my pick.

"I left. Thought about it for a while. And told Brightly."

He licked his lips. "Brightly seemed satisfied by this. Very satisfied. Said I did a good job, and thank you for your discretion. But I found out later that there was no Russian connection. No leak on Teddy's part at all. I asked Brightly about it. He got all shirty with me. Said that didn't matter. When or if the time came that Montrose's devotion wavered, he said, well, they had the stuff to get him in line, and now fuck off and forget about it. So that was that. And I never heard more about it.

"We still have Teddy working for us. I don't think he knows we know. And it's not my job to care, I guess. After all, this is what we do for a living, you and I. It's a dirty game, but it's the winning game."

Then Hayes looked at her, eyes thin. "But we have our own game, too. Some of the things we've dug up in the interviews are very valuable. There are things I need to keep to myself, or give to my contact in the police."

"The police?"

"Yes. Favors are pretty important in my business. Your business, now. Are you all right with that?"

"What would you give them?"

"Those boys McClintock talked about. I have someone who'd like to know about them. A detective. And we're not taking any action on them, so someone might as well give it a go. So is that all right, Sam?"

She thought about it. She didn't feel it was appropriate to contact the police, but then it didn't seem like their investigation had done much at all so far, nor was it going to. It had been a sad thing to record horrible crimes but never act on them, and she was secretly desperate for it to end. And after hearing what Hayes had said about the nature of their position, she wasn't sure if their investigation had much to do with justice in any way.

She nodded.

"All right," he said. Then they stood and walked out to the street. It was raining again, a cold, soft sting that tickled the neck.

"I was wrong about you," he said. "I thought you wouldn't last, at first. But you might."

"What makes you say that?" she asked.

"Because you're not stupid. Not by a long shot. But this isn't a desk job anymore, Miss Fairbanks. This isn't an ordered world of archives and hierarchies, no matter what you'd like. We don't live for the approval of our betters, no matter how happy it may make us feel. And the truth here is soft and runny. I know you'd like to stay in the back room, reading and writing and hunched over a desk, but that's not the way now. See?"

"I see." Then a thought came to her and her skin went cold. She peered at him and said, "Mr. Hayes, are you trying to turn me?"

"What? Turn you?"

"Yes. Like you do everyone else I've seen you speak to. Make them your friends, even though they hardly know you. Tell them whatever lies they need to hear. Is that what you've just tried to do, to me?"

He stared at her, and somehow he seemed to grow even smaller and older in his coat. "No, Sam," he said softly. "No, I haven't tried to do that with you. You'd know, wouldn't you. Since you've seen me do it so often."

She still watched him suspiciously. "Was anything you told me the truth?"

"Yes," said Hayes. "It all was, actually."

"Even Teddy Montrose?"

Hayes nodded.

"And he's... he's still working for us?"

"He's climbed a few ladder rungs at Telecommunications now. Gone up a pay grade or two. But yes."

She thought about that. "Why are you telling me this?" she asked.

He shrugged hopelessly. "Because they're keeping things from us. From me, and from you. And because I don't want Naylor and his boys to go unpunished or to do anything more, and I don't think the unions will be spooked by the police nabbing a few thugs. I've seen organizations like theirs before, they're too disparate. Their reactions are too slow."

"Is that all?"

He stared at her for a moment longer. With his wet hair and soaking coat, he suddenly seemed like a lost child. "And because I want you to trust me, I suppose."

"What? Why?"

"I don't know. I suppose I just know you now, Sam." Then he bid her good day, turned, and disappeared into the crowd.

CHAPTER TEN

Garvey paced up and down the canal bank, clambering over hills of soft wet loam and crumbling cement. He had been roving up and down the canal for four hours, scanning the water and the sludge. There were disturbances, plenty of them. Footprints and cigarette butts and strange scores in the mud. None of them were very distinctive and none of them told him anything. It had been too long.

Garvey eyed the half-finished structures of Construct in the distance, the skeletal tenements and cement pillars standing up like monstrous fenceposts. A many-segmented crane sat hunched in their center, a hibernating predator in a distant, alien land. Garvey knew that somewhere on the northern side of Construct were the foundations of the Lady of Industry, Evesden's once-intended answer to the Statue of Liberty. She'd been meant to stand along the shore, holding up a great gear that would glow a soft pink at night, the luminescence visible for miles down the Strait. It'd generally been felt that the placement couldn't have been better, since Construct was right next to the Kulahee Bridge, which reached all the way across to Victoria, so northern visitors to Evesden would have seen the rosy gear slowly cresting the horizon as they approached. But the planners had gotten only so far as casting her feet and putting up her supports when the troubles with Construct began, and they'd been forced to abandon her along with the rest of the project. Now two enormous gray feet sat out by the waters, the waves just licking the toes, as though some giant had gone diving into the sea and left its curiously anatomical slippers behind. Garvey had seen the pictures. They'd run in all the papers when Construct had first started sinking.

Garvey shook himself and returned to the work at hand. If they'd had a body in tow they would have gone through Construct, he decided. Almost certainly. Much of it was abandoned now, and there would be a thousand places for a quiet murder in Construct. Excavated basements and foundations, collapsing canals and office sheds. But they wouldn't have lived there. They would have gone over the Royce Bridge, or somewhere nearby. It was the only dependable route.

Garvey climbed back into his car and drove to Royce Street and surveyed the shopkeepers and homes. He took out a small photo of the dead man and began approaching the cabbies and the newspaper stands, the late-night cafés and the morning bakeries. None recognized him. But then, they said, it was tough to remember. Most nights seemed the same as any other. Garvey wrote down what they could tell him. Then he showed them a sketch of the tattoo on the man but none of them recognized that either.

"What you looking for?" asked one man at a newspaper stand. "Somebody dead?"

"Somebody's always dead," said Garvey.

"Yeah, yeah. But who is it this time?"

Garvey walked away and did not answer.

He moved outward in a spiral, hitting the row homes and the slums, flashing his badge and the picture and asking if there had been any disturbances or sightings of the man. The people came to the door with their eyes meek and watchful, like rabbits approaching a wolf at the entrance of their den. In many homes the reek of shit and urine and rotting wood hung in the air. Sometimes a child cried from somewhere in the depths of the house without ceasing. They knew nothing.

At one home a dog was chained up in the alley beside, panting as though delighted with the day. Garvey knocked on the door and an elderly woman with cataracts the color of oyster shells answered. When he asked her about the picture she had to pull it close and peer at it with one eye as though she were looking at it through a microscope. Then she said, "Oh, yes! I've seen him."

"When?" asked Garvey eagerly. "About three, four weeks ago?"

"Oh, no. Long before that, I think. Last summer. He had a little boy with him. Little boy, used to play with my dog while I watched. The man asked if it was all right and I said certainly it was."

"He had a little boy?" said Garvey, mentally groaning.

"Yes. He gave Arthur the high point of his day."

"Arthur?"

"My puppy. Arthur's his name." She smiled blindly in the general direction of the little dog, who almost seemed to smile back.

"What was he doing out here? The man, I mean."

"I'm not sure. He used to come out here on walks with his boy, I think. There's a playground nearby. Then they used to go over and look across the waterway at Construct. He said he told his little boy giants played there."

"Did you get the man's name?"

"No. It was months ago and he only came a handful of times. More than half a year ago. I probably wouldn't remember if it hadn't been for Arthur. And it was before my eyes went, you see."

"Sure, sure. Any idea where he lived?"

"Oh, somewhere around here, I assume. I'm not sure where. He always came from up the road," she said, and pointed.

"From the Shanties?" said Garvey.

"The what?"

"The Shanties. The Porter neighborhoods."

"I suppose so, yes."

"What did the little boy look like?" he asked.

"Like a normal boy. About ten. Underfed a little. He was about so high and he had brown hair and brown eyes," she said, sticking a quivering hand out breast-high. "That's about all I remember. I think the boy's name was Jack, but I can't be sure."

"Jack?"

"Something like that."

"All right," said Garvey. Then he bade her good day and went back to his car and sat, thinking. He looked at the photo of the dead man, then shook his head and said, "Christ. A kid," and sighed.

Being a policeman of any type in Evesden meant you saw a lot of things, many strange, some funny, and plenty terrible. You armed yourself with a strong dose of black humor and used it to belittle the sights you saw, to make the tragedies and stupidities trivial and easy to handle. A friendly, joking discussion between average police, or possibly the medical personnel they worked with, would probably shock or outrage any outsider who hadn't yet had a taste. One popular joke was to discuss victims as if they were plumbing, noting leaks and broken U-bends and pointing out the areas that needed soldering. Usually the victim wound up being a toilet in these bizarre, comedic metaphors.

But no matter what anyone had seen, no matter how many bodies they'd filed or marked off, the mere presence of a child changed things. Delivering news to families, and especially about children, aged a man in ways unseen by the naked eye. And cracking the plumbing routine about a dropped child was unthinkable. Any police who dared bandy a joke of any kind about in such a situation would probably wind up with a whaling. A murdered-child case was a curse, the worst possible event, changing the demeanor and very workings of the Department for weeks. The fraternal greetings gave way to furtive nods, and the detective stuck with it was practically considered the victim of a terminal illness. Conversations died when he came near, and he'd find himself receiving earnest condolences and whispers of good luck. One detective, Wolcott, had received a child case as his very first on the job. It had never gotten filed, and Wolcott had been removed from the Department after he was found weeping at his desk a year in, the child's name still on the bronzed list on the wall. Garvey heard he was working a beat now, dropped back to being a regular uniform. So it went with such poisonous tragedies.

While Garvey couldn't say if the boy, Jack, was in any danger or involved in any way, it still left a bad taste in his mouth. The man had been poor, Garvey could tell that just from looking at him, and if the old lady was right he'd made his home in the Shanties, a rough neighborhood if ever there was one. God only knew what would happen if the boy went looking for him when he didn't come home. Abandonment was common in the Shanties, but that didn't make it any less brutal. Garvey hoped the boy had a mother out there, and that the John Doe's murder had nothing to do with his family.

He rubbed at his eyes and leaned his head back and sighed. After a while he slept.

He awoke with a start, sitting up at a harsh tapping noise. He peered out the window to see a patrolman standing there, half-stooped and waiting.

"Fuck's sake," said Garvey. "Leave me alone."

The patrolman kept tapping. Garvey swore and pulled out his badge and slapped it up against the glass. The patrolman shrugged and Garvey rolled down the window.

"What? What the hell do you want?" he said.

"Detective Garvey?" asked the patrolman.

"Yeah?"

"My name's Clemmons. You're needed, right away."

"By who?"

"Lieutenant Collins. He needs you in the Shanties. Something's happened."

"Collins?" said Garvey. "Why does he need me?"

"He just said to find anyone. Anyone."

Garvey blinked the sleep away and squinted at the patrolman. He couldn't have been older than twenty-two. He was pale and clammy and Garvey noticed his lips and fingers were trembling. He smelled faintly of vomit.

"What happened?" asked Garvey.

"I can't say, sir. You'd have to see it for yourself."

"Something bad?"

"You'd... you'd have to see it for yourself," he said again.

"How'd you know I'd be here?"

"I didn't. I've been driving around for an hour in this neighborhood. I just happened to find you. You want to follow me?"

"Where to?"

"On Bridgedale. It's the trolley station, sir."

"All right."

The patrolman started walking back toward his little car. Garvey stuck his head out the window. "Can't you at least give me a hint?" he called. "Something? Anything?"

The patrolman did not seem to hear him. He climbed into his car and it shook as it started and Garvey followed it down toward Bridgedale.

Three blocks in they came upon the crowd. Throngs of people stood in the street, gawking down toward the corner at the trolley station. Garvey and the patrolman tried to nose their cars through but gave up and got out to push through on foot. Eventually they came to a fence of patrolmen with batons and truncheons, nervously handling their weapons and calling to get back. Garvey pushed past them to where the trolley station steps yawned open. Down on the station floor a half-dozen uniforms and detectives were pacing back and forth, looking off at something Garvey could not see.

As he went down the stairs the stench of the trolley tunnels embraced him, a scent of sewage and coal-tinged smoke. The strange, dry breezes that always surged through the lines played with his hat and tie, prodding them this way and that. He clapped his hat on his head and spotted Collins standing under one of the stark white station lamps, nodding as a patrol sergeant gave him a bad rundown. Garvey had always hated the trolley station lights, specifically how they looked just like street lamps but somehow misplaced here, far under the earth. It was as though the designer had tried to make this strange underground normal and in doing so had made it even stranger. An average street scene, but trapped in eternal night.

When Collins saw him he said, "Oh, thank Christ."

Garvey approached, worried. His lieutenant rarely expressed gratitude or fondness for any of his detectives. "You called for me, sir?"

Collins waved away the sergeant. "I called for anyone. But it's a damn good thing they found you. I could use someone decent around here."

"Why? What's happening?"

Collins considered it. There was a queer look on his face. It took Garvey a moment to realize he was terrified. "Well," he said. "I suppose you'd better come and see for yourself."

Collins led him left, down through the empty station and past the deserted ticket booths and newspaper stands. It was like some subterranean ghost town, yet there at the far end was a ring of officers standing clear of something dark and still at the end of the platform. After a while Garvey realized it was a trolley. He had never seen one without its lights on.

All of the other officers were watching it silently. They kept their electric torches off as though the thing were asleep and they feared its waking. A low rumble filled the tunnel end, the faraway passing of other trolleys and trains. Garvey felt blood pumping in his ears as they walked toward it. He could see shapes and forms slumped up against the glass of the trolley, but he could not make them out. As he neared he smelled an electric copper scent that stuck to the back of his throat like a film. Blood, he figured, very fresh.

One of the uniforms shook his head as Garvey and Collins walked by. "Just came out of nowhere," he said. "Sailing out of the dark, like a ghost ship."

"What is it?" said Garvey. "Who's on it?"

"No one," said Collins. "Or at least, no one anymore." Collins flicked on his torch and kept the beam on the dusty platform floor as he braced himself. Then he lifted it and let it glance over the trolley door. It did not show everything, but it showed enough. Garvey saw human forms slouched on the seats, red tongues sprouting from their backs or heads and running down in tendrils to spread across the seats or floor, other corpses curled around the trolley bars. Some were slumped against the glass, their skin as pale as sea foam. His eyes traced over where the crimson and rust-colored pools melted with the shadows, where the fingers and arms became motley tangles. It felt impossible to tell them apart, to distinguish where one ended and the others began. Trapped in that little trolley car, their ruined faces and figures seemed to blend into one another until they were one red-and-white mass laid out on the creaking seats. Then Collins switched the light out and they were shrouded once more.

Garvey could not imagine their numbers. To his eye they had seemed limitless. Still no one spoke. Then Garvey turned around and walked over to a bench and sat.

When the message came to Samantha and Hayes they were on their last interview of the day, awaiting a McCarthy, Franklin. The man from the front desk walked in and handed a telegram to Samantha, who read it and handed it off to Hayes and began quickly putting on her coat.

"Where are we going?" he asked.

"Bridgedale, apparently," she said.

"Oh? Why?"

"To meet a Mr. Shroff. Any idea who that is?"

"One of Brightly's men. Newspaperman, usually tips us off about things going on in the city." He scooped his scarf off the floor and added, "Which probably doesn't bode well at all."

They hurried out to the street, where Hayes tried to pay a cabbie an enormous amount of money to take them across town. With some persuasion Samantha managed to convince him to try a trolley for a fifth of the cost, yet when they began to enter the trolley lines the ticket vendors and conductors turned them away.

"No rides today," one said. "No trolley today."

"Why on Earth not?" said Samantha.

"All lines are down. No platforms taking any passengers."

"Yes, but why?"

He shrugged. "Can't say. Official broadcast came through about an hour or so ago. We're all shut down. You'll have to take a motor-cab, or walk if you can."

"This is the first time in my memory, short as it is, that the trolleys have been wholly shut down," said Samantha as they walked back to the street. "What could have happened?"

Hayes simply shrugged, irritated to have been made to walk so far.

They took a cab to Bridgedale and the address specified in the message, yet they found it surrounded by a thick, babbling crowd that shielded everything from view. The police had made a large clearing at the front, cutting off the street at either end and shutting down one intersection. Horses and purring cars bucked back and forth as they tried to negotiate their way out, swears and shouts ringing over the buzz of the crowd. People huddled close to one another in the chilly air, bobbing where they stood to glimpse through brief cracks in the groups in front of them. Steaming breath unscrolled up from the crowd in a hundred places, giving it the strange impression of a ticker tape parade.

"What in hell is this nonsense?" said Hayes as they climbed out.

Bystanders couldn't tell him, shrugging and shaking their heads. Soon he was flagged down by Shroff, who was so short he had to jump to make his hand seen over the crowd. Hayes worked over and pulled him close and said, "What the hell is going on?"

"Trouble," Shroff said. "Big trouble, down in the underground. Someone's dead."

"Dead? Who's dead?"

"Don't know, really. Cops have the entire area cordoned. They beat the hell out of one ass who tried to push through. Pardon my language, ma'am," he said to Samantha, and tipped his hat. "I bet there's a lot of them, though."

"A lot of who?" asked Hayes as he slipped through the crowd. Shroff and Samantha struggled to keep up.

"The dead," said Shroff. "But no one knows how many or who."

When they finally got through they found they faced the trolley station entrance, the big rusty tin T hanging over the steps. They could see nothing down below except for the faint lights of the station.

"Looky there," said Shroff, and pointed. "There's your detective friend, eh?"

Garvey was standing at the top of the steps, speaking to another officer who was leaning against the railings. He looked paler and grimmer than usual. He kept his face at a sharp angle to the underground station, like he did not want to look inside or perhaps smell its curious breeze.

"Yeah," Hayes said. "There he is." Then he tugged off a glove, stuck his fingers in his mouth, and whistled piercingly.

The police and some of the crowd looked up. Garvey blinked and did the same and saw Hayes standing in the front. His grimace deepened and he strode over and said, "What are you doing here?"

"Same as you, I think," said Hayes. "Only there's truncheons in the way." By now he was flush and grinning with excitement.

Garvey thought for a moment, then said, "I guess it'd be worth you seeing." He nodded to the patrolman, who let Hayes pass but kept Samantha behind.

"Who's that?" asked Garvey, gesturing to her.

"My assistant," said Hayes.

"Your assistant? You have an assistant?"

"Sure. She's new. Secretarial duties and such."

"God. I got to pity you, lady. Come on then," he said, and helped her through.

"Thank you," she said to him. She stood up and readjusted her hat and blouse.

"Don't mention it," he said. He stopped halfway down a step and turned to extend a hand. "Don Garvey."

Samantha awkwardly shook and introduced herself breathlessly, still fighting past the dour stares of the patrolmen.

"So what's going on, Garv?" asked Hayes.

Garvey began to lead them down the steps of the station. "I don't know," he said. "I really don't."

"Rumor has it people are dead."

"Rumor has it right."

"Was it an accident?" asked Samantha.

Garvey stopped and looked at her. "A what?"

She faltered under his sharp eye, then rallied. "An accident. A trolley accident. Like a derailing."

"Oh," he said. "No. Not an accident. That'd be the reasonable conclusion, wouldn't it? But no."

"Then what?" said Hayes.

Garvey said nothing. He just motioned them farther down into the tunnels. Hayes glanced to the side and saw bile and chunks of half-digested beef drying and curling on the station floor.

"Bad one?" he asked.

Garvey said, "The worst I've seen."

They walked down the platform, ignoring the curious glances of the other officers. Then a shout rang out: "No. Not him. No."

They turned. Collins was striding toward them, a half-dozen officers in tow like furious ducklings. Collins pointed at Hayes and said, "Will someone please explain to me what in God's name this little shit is doing back here? It had better be plenty impressive, too. I mean it."

Garvey stepped forward into Collins's path. Even though Garvey was tall in his own right, Collins loomed over him like a storm cloud. He glared at Hayes over Garvey's shoulder, but Hayes dawdled on the platform and looked down the tunnel with a mildly interested eye. Samantha gripped her briefcase and looked to him for some excuse for their intrusion, but he was barely aware of Collins's furious outburst, let alone her frantic looks.

"I invited him here," said Garvey quickly. "I gave the order to let him through."

"I guessed that," Collins said. "What in hell did you think you were doing, bringing a mad thing like that into a scene like this?"

"I thought he could help."

"Help? Help with what?"

"Unions. He might know something. He almost always does."

Collins turned to Hayes. "And? Do you know anything?"

"I don't even know what the hell is going on yet," Hayes said. "Did you say this is union stuff, Garv?"

Collins gave Garvey a warning look. Garvey winced. "I think it is," he said slowly, reluctantly. "I think it's got to be."

"Don't go stirring up shit you can't shovel, Garvey," said Collins. "Don't go doing that now. Not at a time like this."

"Let's at least show them to him," Garvey said. "Just to see."

"See who?" asked Hayes.

"Our passengers," said Garvey. Then he grabbed Hayes by the arm and dragged him down the tunnel to where a darkened trolley car sat in the shadows. Behind them Collins shouted at Samantha and the other officers to stay back. Garvey hauled him through the broken bronze doors of the trolley, Hayes fumbling with the steps, and suddenly he was aware that there were people in the darkened trolley car with them, sitting silently in the seats or lying on the floor. The coppery taste of blood filled his nose and mouth and he suppressed a gag. Then Garvey flicked the light on and Hayes saw the trolley car fully.

As he tried to take in the room around him he felt as if he were in the belly of something alive and malignant and hungry, and there littered on the floor of this monstrous stomach were staring eyes and grasping hands and faces dull and blank and soulless. His eyes adjusted and he tried to count the figures in the dark. There were around a dozen of them, it seemed. More brutalized than in any murder Hayes had seen in years.

"Oh, my," said Hayes softly.

"Yeah," said Garvey. "Oh, my is right." He shook out a handkerchief and stuffed his nose and mouth into it. Hayes did not, for even though Garvey was murder police Hayes was far more used to the scent of blood and putrefaction.

Hayes swallowed and shook off the shock. Then morbid curiosity took him over, an old and not entirely welcome friend, and he began studying the bodies nearest to him. He found their poses were queerly passive, as though they had simply dropped, as if something had passed through the trolley car and pulled the life right out of them. And yet they were so ravaged. One man sat in his seat with his back and neck open in a dozen places, one hand still on his handhold. Behind him a woman sat on the floor, sunk to the ground with her knees and thighs below her, smooth white flesh spattered with arterial spray and her face calmly fixed as though contemplating a troubling question. At the end of the car the conductor lay facedown on his control board, still in his seat. Behind him a group of three men lay in a heap around one of the poles. Had it not been for the wounds dotting their chests and thighs you would have thought they had simply become tired and decided to lie down to sleep.

There were more. Many more. Propped up in the seats or prostrate on the floor. Each of them serenely drooping as if the little motor that made their hearts beat had simply stripped a few gears and given up. Behind them the windows were lined with hairline cracks, but there was no sign of impact in the car.

"Do you know anything about this?" said Collins behind him.

Hayes looked at them. Took in their shattered figures and glassy stares. Then he stooped and said, "Well."

"Well what?" said Garvey from behind a handkerchief.

Hayes looked into one's face. He put a finger on the man's white chin and moved his head up to look into his eyes. The skin sagged at the edges, like he was wearing a mask and his true face was hidden somewhere below the paling flesh. "I know this one," Hayes said softly.

"You do?" said Collins.

"Yes," said Hayes. "I do. Edward Walton. He works—worked—in the Southern District. Can't remember what he did. He worked under McClintock. Fellow I interviewed. That's how I know him. He's a unioner. Remember, Garv? I sent you some information on him. Just yesterday."

"I've been out of the office for the past two days," Garvey said.

"Damn," muttered Hayes. "Too late, I suppose." He stood and moved through the mass of corpses, carefully stepping among them with wobbly, balletic jumps. "There's Naylor," he said. "And Evie. And Eppleton. And Craft. They're dirty, all of them. Only a few are suspected murderers and saboteurs in my book. The others are just sympathizers. I don't know who the women are. That one's a whore and no mistake." Hayes took a seat between two corpses, surveying the mute crowd. "They're all mine, for the most part. Or were. All McNaughton boys, and all dirty."

Garvey and Collins stared around their feet. "Jesus Christ," said Collins. "Why didn't I hear about this?"

"Do you think it's sabotage?" asked Hayes. "Someone sabotaged the line?"

Garvey shook his head. "No. The trolley car coasted in like it does every day, right on time. Just odd that its passengers all happened to be dead. How it got in with a dead conductor is beyond me. Scared the hell out of the people on the platform. And besides, look at them, and the trolley. It didn't crash. No sign of sabotage. But their wounds, it's like they've been..."

"Stabbed," finished Collins. "Like someone hopped on board and then ran through, stabbing them all. Stabbed all to hell."

Hayes turned one over with his foot. They all had the exact same wound, a thin puncture mark about an inch long. "Maybe someone stopped the car and did just that."

"I told you," said Garvey. "Trolley was on time, almost exactly."

"So?"

"Well, according to the stops from the platform before, the window for the murders is about, oh, a little less than four minutes."

Hayes stared at him. "That's not possible."

"Yeah. That's the crux, ain't it?"

"Someone stabbed all these people to death in *four minutes*?"

"Or something did."

"And none of them resisted," said Collins, stooping. "Look at their hands. No scratches. No cuts. No bruises."

Hayes frowned, doing the same. "And no witnesses."

"None," said Garvey.

Hayes turned to look out the window down the tunnel. It was black as night behind the car. He wondered what was wandering in there, or what might be waiting down the rails. Then he lifted his hand and touched the cracks in the window before him. They ran throughout the other panes as well, all of them slightly broken but never wholly shattered. He looked up. The bulbs in the roof of the car had completely broken. Little half-moons of white glass stuck out of the sockets, the filaments of the bulbs completely exposed.

Then Hayes cocked his head suddenly, like he had heard something. He made a soft *hmph*, then turned to walk down to the conductor's chair.

"Where are you going?" said Garvey.

"There's something wrong down here," he said. He looked carefully from body to body.

"What do you mean? What's wrong?"

"I just...I think there's someone else," he said.

"Someone else? Someone else what?"

"Someone else in here with us."

Garvey gave Hayes a sharp look. "You sure about this?"

Hayes nodded absently as he looked through the trolley.

"Are you sure this little shit has all his dogs barking?" Collins asked.

"I'd let him work," said Garvey. He crossed his arms and fixed his eyes on the floor like he was pretending not to see anything.

"It's definitely over here," Hayes said. He looked down at the conductor. The man's cheeks and forehead were streaked with blood. He grimaced. "Maybe down below?" He stooped to look under the conductor's brass control panel. He grunted, then pushed on the conductor's leg to move it aside.

"Goddamn it, Don, don't let him move stuff around," said Collins.

"I'm not moving stuff around, I just...I swear, I heard something."

"Heard what?" Collins asked.

"Something," Hayes said irritably. "I just can't see." He shoved at the conductor again.

"Get out of there," said Collins. "I've got plenty of shit on my hands right now, I don't need you—"

But his words were cut off as the conductor jerked once, shuddered, and then lifted his head to stare into Hayes's face where he squatted beside him on the floor. They gaped at one another for a moment, and then both of them cried out and leaped backward, but the space was so small and cramped that they both crashed into the wall, Hayes cracking his head as he did so.

"Holy God, he's alive!" Garvey shouted.

To everyone's disbelief the conductor swiveled his head to look around him, face terrified, and stared at the bodies beyond. His eyes rolled madly, and he thrust himself up against the windows as though he was trying to force an escape. A strangled noise started from somewhere within the man and grew into a flat-out scream. He lifted his hands to his face and began clawing at his cheeks, howling wildly until his cries formed words: "No! No, no, let me go! Don't hurt me, let me go!"

"Goddamn it, get ahold of him!" shouted Collins, but it was too late. The conductor shook his head and barged through the trolley car and out the broken doors. He leaped down onto the trolley platform and then wheeled around when he was met by an enclosing ring of officers. A few of them brandished revolvers, uncertain where to point them.

"Don't shoot!" Garvey yelled. "Don't shoot him, damn it!"

The officers shouted for him to get down, down on the ground, but the man would not listen. He reeled back and forth, eyes still wide and mad, raising his arms and shouting for them not to hurt him. Finally one of the larger detectives tackled him and wrapped around his legs, bringing him to the ground. The conductor wept and struggled with him and clawed at the floor. Several patrolmen ran to him, and one took out his truncheon and raised it high.

"Stop!" shouted a voice.

The officers looked over their shoulders to see Samantha furiously striding toward them. They paused, unused to dealing with well-dressed women, particularly ones who were shouting at them.

"Stop?" said the policeman with the truncheon.

"Yes, stop!"

"Why? We fucking said to get down and he didn't!"

"That's because he's deaf, you damn fool, can't you see?" she said angrily. She pushed through them to kneel beside the conductor's head. He stared at her, still crazed and babbling, but she gently took his head and held it still. She touched his ears. There was a small flow of blood running from within them and down his cheeks. "The man can't hear a word you're saying. Can you?" she asked the conductor kindly.

"Don't hurt me," he whimpered. "Please, don't hurt me."

"We won't," she said. She shook her head widely so he could see, then fixed her face with the most comforting and gentle expression she could. "We won't hurt you."

Collins, Garvey, and Hayes climbed down out of the trolley car to join them. "He's deaf?" said Collins.

"Yes," she said. "His eardrums have burst. He just hasn't realized it yet, I think." She began making strange gestures before the conductor's face, looping and knotting her fingers and sometimes tapping them together. The conductor stared at her in confusion.

"What's that you're doing?" Garvey asked.

"Sign language," said Samantha. "What little I know of it." She sighed and dropped her hands. "But he doesn't appear to know any at all."

"He doesn't?"

"No."

Hayes looked at the man a moment longer, then stared back down the tunnel. "So he's been recently deafened," he said. "Probably by whatever happened to the trolley car. Wouldn't you say?"

Samantha did not say anything to that. The conductor had begun weeping, and she took out a handkerchief to dry his tears.

Collins and the other detectives took the conductor and sat him before a small blackboard, where they scribbled out questions. It took some time to convince the man he was deaf, and when they finally succeeded he broke down again and wept for some time. Finally he came around to read their questions and loudly answer them, often rambling on incoherently, ignorant that the officers were signaling for him to slow down. Samantha and Hayes sat in the dark on a station bench a ways away, watching.

"Fuck me," said Hayes. "I hope none of the others spring to life. I nearly shat myself." He turned to look at her. "Where'd you learn sign language?"

"When I was a nurse. There'd be young men who'd been shelled and were deafened. I didn't learn much, just enough to ask questions."

"Well, you're full of surprises, aren't you."

"That man needs medical attention," she said. "He's in pain."

"They don't want the crowd to see him yet. They'll want to keep this controlled for as long as possible and get all the answers they can."

"But he's in *pain*, Mr. Hayes."

"If they didn't, they'd have a riot, and we'd have a lot more pain."

Samantha sighed and stared at the trolley car beyond. "What happened here, Mr. Hayes?"

"I don't know," he said. "Did you see?"

"See?"

"See them. The bodies."

"From a ways away. When Mr. Garvey had the light on. Or Detective, I should say." She swallowed. "I wasn't sure what I saw."

Hayes nodded. "I'd be fucking glad of that."

They both shivered. It was cold down in the trolley lines, close to the ocean and far away from the warmth of the city, and with the station so empty it was a gray and eerie place. The officers became dark figures passing back and forth in the spectral light of the station lamps. After some time with the conductor Garvey walked over to them, reviewing his notes.

"Well?" asked Hayes.

"His name is Gilbert Lambeth," he said. "Been a conductor for the Evesden Lines for nearly five years. Knows his trade, talks in a lot of engineering gobbledygook."

"Did he say anything useful, though?"

"I wish. He says he was making the stops, as usual. Turns out it's mostly automated. He hadn't made any adjustment to the trolley's schedule, not a second. He left the last platform, the Stirsdale platform, at the right time and was just going through the tunnel as normal when he heard a..." Garvey flipped through his little notebook. "A loud noise. A high-pitched squeal, he says."

"A *squeal*?" said Hayes.

"Like metal on metal. Then there was a pop like a bomb went off, and the lights went out, and he passed out. The trolley car coasted in automatically, but Gilbert wasn't awake to tell it to continue. Then he just sat there until you woke his poor ass up. And that's it. That's all he's given us."

Hayes thinned his eyes. "That almost sounds like a planned attack."

"Yeah. It does."

"Why would anyone want to do that?"

Garvey sighed. "I have a few ideas. I found something interesting." He took out a sketch of a little symbol of a hammer inside a bell. "See this?"

"Yes?" said Hayes.

"This was tattooed on my John Doe. In the canal."

"Who?"

"The guy. The guy you helped me fish out of the damn canal? Six weeks ago or so? Mr. Four Hundred and Eighty-six?"

"Oh. Oh, right. Wait, so that sign was tattooed on him?"

"Yeah. It was on his arm. And there's eleven dead passengers in there, and nine of them have the same tattoo. All in the same place." He tapped his arm. "Right there."

"*How* many dead?" said Samantha softly.

"Eleven."

"Good... good Lord."

"Yeah. This is the worst yet. The worst by far." He paused. "Someone is killing unioners. And anyone they're close to."

There was a pause as Hayes and Samantha considered that.

"Have you seen many unioners with that tattoo?" asked Hayes.

"Well. No. Just the recent dead ones."

"But even so, who would want them dead?" Hayes said, standing up. He walked to the edge of the platform and looked down at the sooty rails and the blackened stone floor. "I mean, who'd even be able to do something like this? Slaughter everyone on a trolley without even slowing it down?"

"You sure those names are all you can give us?" said a voice.

Hayes turned to see Collins standing not far off, watching him with harsh eyes. "What?" he said.

"You sure there's nothing else you know? At all?" asked Collins.

Hayes shook his head. "Nothing."

Collins looked at him for a long time. Eyes uncertain. Hands at his hips, uncomfortably close to his gun.

"What?" asked Hayes.

"There's nothing you're hiding from us?" Collins asked, this time quieter.

"Hiding? No. Why are you asking?"

But Collins just shook his head and walked back to the other officers.

"What the hell? What was that about?" asked Hayes.

"He's just worried," said Garvey.

"Well, I can see that."

"No, he's worried about you. And McNaughton."

"Why?"

"Oh, come on, Hayes," said Garvey, exasperated. "You come in here telling us that about half these men are responsible for murders in your company, and then all of them suddenly drop dead? Not to mention that it was on the day after you sent me their files. That's sort of odd, isn't it?"

"You think McNaughton could have done this?"

"I don't know. Do you?"

Hayes stared into the tracks at his feet. "No," he said. "They don't have the guts. Besides, those files I sent you were nothing. Just enough to give you a lead."

"You sure?" Garvey said.

"I doubt if McNaughton is capable of murder, either," said Samantha. "Particularly *mass* murder. But before we're asked to start incriminating ourselves, are we involved with an official police investigation, Detective Garvey?"

"Well. Not official, no," said Garvey.

"So on what grounds are we here?"

"You were just asked. By me. And Collins. And Brightly, probably. Consulted, maybe. Your company pulls a lot of water around here. People are usually pretty happy to just do whatever the hell they say. But I have a hunch that's going to change soon."

They turned to look at the conductor, who was shouting about something once more. The policemen around him frantically tried to flag him down.

"And all he knows is he heard a loud noise," said Hayes quietly.

"Yeah," said Garvey.

"And then all those people were dead."

"Yes. And only he survived, out of all of them," said Garvey. Then, quieter, "Want to sit with him for a while? See if he's telling the truth?"

Hayes shook his head. "Not in a crowd. Later, maybe. I'm already getting a headache. And you think your John Doe may have something to do with it?"

"Maybe. I'd talk about it but I don't know when I'm getting out of here. It'll be hours for sure."

"How many other detectives are on this?"

"Right now we're all just running around, bugshit crazy. I'm guessing it'll come down to two murder police and then a shitload of High Crimes. I'll be on it, maybe. Labor detail and all. Probably Morris, too."

"Shit," said Hayes. "Morris is worthless."

"Yeah. Goddamn. Usually I love a murder in the Shanties. All these little tennie weasels do is talk. Cooped up in these goddamn tenements, what else are they going to do but talk about who killed who, and why? But this is going to be the pits." He moved to spit, then glanced sideways at Samantha and stopped. He coughed and said, "Want me to swing by and kick you out of bed later?"

"That'll work," said Hayes.

"I need to get back. It was, ah, nice meeting you, Miss Fairbanks," he said, and tipped his hat. The he walked back to the distant, dark figures grouped around the trolley.

"John Doe?" asked Samantha as they walked back up through the streets.

"Unnamed murder," Hayes said. "Garvey caught one a couple of weeks ago. Man found floating in a Construct canal, throat cut. Dragged him out right before I met you, in fact."

"Oh. And, excuse me, but what exactly is Construct?"

Hayes stopped and looked at her cockeyed.

"I mean, I've heard everyone talk about it," she said. "I've just never seen the name on any of the districts and boroughs or anything."

"That's because it's not a real name. That's odd. You're usually pretty on the ball, Sam," he said. "Construct is the great stillbirth of Evesden. Here, you can see it from nearby."

He led her out to the edge of a bridge and pointed at the northwestern horizon. There beside the massive form of the Kulahee Bridge two dozen tall cement pillars stood like ancient monoliths, bare and gray and silent, each bigger than most buildings. Around their bases were skeletons of scaffolding and iron framework and silent construction equipment. They seemed like the ruins of a primitive temple, as though some savage fragment of history had somehow found itself wedged against the shore.

Samantha frowned. "So it's just…"

"You probably know it as the Isle Projects," said Hayes.

"Oh. Yes."

"No one calls it that here, though. It was going to be a section of city-funded, McNaughton-approved, and McNaughton-built tenements. Domiciles. Towers of apartments. Whatever the hell. Some were going to be bigger than the Nail, they said."

"And what happened?"

"Well, for one thing, most of the land around the city was already used up. So some engineering prodigy decided they'd make their own."

"Their own *land*?"

"Yes. After all, it had worked for the Kulahee Bridge. See, that area designated for Construct wasn't good for foundation, not at all. Part of an ocean runlet, or something. But they gave it a good try and laid down cement and steel and redirected the streams and gave half the damn shore a complete overhaul. Reclamation, they called it. Brought in some Dutchman to do it, apparently they're naturals. Eventually they had just miles and miles and miles of buildable foundation, some of it right out in the ocean. Or so they thought. North section started experiencing real trouble with the dredging and it put the rest of the plan on a tilt. They said you could put a marble on one end of Construct and it'd travel four miles before going into the water, on a dry day at low tide, that is. Then the contractors and the real estate folks started crying foul and there were problems with backers or whatever, and everything devolved into some sort of huge litigious feud. It's been in limbo in court for years. There's a lot of money to be made there, you know. It's Evesden's great humanitarian effort.

It was going to turn it from a valuable hole to the shining city on the hill."

"How do you mean?"

"Hum," said Hayes, thinking. One hand roved through his coat for a match. Finding one, he lit it and puffed at his cigarette distractedly. "That's a bit more complicated."

"Please try, if you would."

"Well, see, if you go from one end of this city to the other you'll find a dozen towns in between. All with different names, all with different people. This city exploded and people grouped together and lived where they wanted before the government could say anything about it. But the poor got the short end of the stick. They..."

He stopped and looked at her. Her pad was out and she was scribbling away.

"Are you writing this down?" he asked.

"Yes," she said.

"Why?"

"Because I want to know this. Go on."

"Well. Suit yourself. Anyways, the poor got the short end of the stick. They got the in-between places. They got Dockland. They got the Shanties. They got Lynn. We're in the nice part of the Shanties now, almost none of it is this presentable. Construct was going to be new living. The rich extending a hand to the poor. Instead they made the world's biggest graveyard. So the poor stay where they are, stuck in their little neighborhoods, and everyone tries to forget about it." He sneaked a glance at her. "Newton is far and away the most advanced section of town. It has the elevated train and it has the conduits. You're living in the twentieth century we were all promised, while the rest of the city's still fucking medieval. Hope you like it." He stamped out his cigarette. "Come on. Let's go see Evans and find out what the word is."

CHAPTER ELEVEN

After they cleared the bodies Collins mustered up a group of men, armed them with rifles, and had them sweep the trolley tunnel, torches wheeling through the dark as they ran. Though the lights faded their shouts somehow remained, echoing through the many atria of the tunnels. Garvey sat on the station bench once they were gone, waiting. Sometimes he got up to examine the trolley car again, especially the door. He touched where it had crumpled in and traced his fingers over the strange cracks in the glass. Each time he would sit back down, chin in his hand.

A half-hour later a patrolman came down from the street and reported a call from Collins saying they had found no suspects, no assailants, no nothing, and to continue his investigation, this time down into the tunnel. Garvey nodded as he heard the order. It was not unexpected, but that didn't mean it was welcome.

They paired him with a trolley maintenance overseer by the name of Nippen, a short, thick man in blackened overalls who seemed entirely too cheerful for such dark work. He ferociously shook Garvey's hand, ignorant of the grease stains he was leaving on the big detective's palm, and then gave him a tin hat and hopped down onto the rails. "Come on down, Detective," he said. "Let's wander a bit."

Garvey, not liking at all the way he said "wander," put on the hat, lowered himself down onto the rails, and followed him into the dark.

"They stopped the trolleys, right?" said Garvey as they entered the tunnel. He flicked on his torch and the rails before him lit up like dusky ribbons. "I'd hate if they followed up something like this by crushing my ass."

Nippen laughed. "They stopped everything. Our whole system is fucked for a day, for a whole day. No money today, not for anyone." He laughed again, as if the thought cheered him.

"Any idea what we should be looking for?" Garvey asked.

"Not a one," said Nippen. "You get all kinds of odd stuff down here."

"Really? I thought they kept the trolley lines clear."

"Oh, no," said Nippen. "Well, we *try*. We *try* to keep the tunnels clear. But shit obeys gravity, and all things eventually want to go down. People. Animals. Garbage. But if anything keeps the tunnels clear, it's the trolleys themselves. It's hard to argue with a few tons of iron and steel. They just push it all out, see?"

"You get people down here?" said Garvey.

"Oh, sure. The bums love it down here. It's warm in places. The crazies all seem to come down here, eventually."

As they passed under one juncture a deep moaning and squalling filled the tunnels around them. Garvey ducked down and sent his torch beam dancing about. "What the hell is that?" he said.

Nippen stared up at the tunnel roof, smiling. "I don't know," he said thoughtfully.

"You don't?"

"No. You hear a lot of things in the tunnels. There's a lot of machinery below the city you forget about." He listened as the squalling tapered off. "That? Oh, I'd say that was probably a pneumatic messenger tube shooting across town. Probably trying to force through a thick spot of mail. Maybe."

"It sounded awful big."

"It may have been," Nippen said. "I hear McNaughton has pneumatic tubes the size of people. That they shoot people back and forth through the tubes. That true?"

"I doubt it," said Garvey.

"I thought so," said Nippen, and laughed. "I thought that story couldn't be true."

"You sure there's no one down here with us?"

"Yep. Your lieutenant ran through here just a while ago, guns drawn. He'd have shot anyone, no matter what they were doing. I hear they blew up a rat. Scared one of the cops and then just *pow*, rat was all over the place. That true?"

Garvey reluctantly admitted that that rumor, at least, was probably truer than he'd like, and Nippen laughed.

They continued on. The underground tunnels were a strange, alien place to Garvey. Ribbed metal shafts curved around him like immense tidal waves, sometimes giving way to old, scarred brick crisscrossing over the roof. Passageways of old stone slowly turned into tunnels of shining, alloyed brass. Pipes and tubing would surface along the wall and run for several yards before submerging below the stone. The walls themselves gurgled and chirped and squeaked as unseen things worked for the city above. And all of it stayed down here in the dark, buried here to be forgotten save for those few stragglers like Nippen, or the vagrants who wandered these midnight paths.

As they walked Nippen showed him the maintenance tunnels and the air shafts and the sewage pipes. They were all means of connecting with the surface, one way or another, though all of these were locked tight. Beside each one was a little tube with an earpiece, which Nippen told Garvey connected them to the maintenance man on duty, whoever that was. "It's usually no one, unless there's a scheduled check," said Nippen.

"And there's one on duty today?"

"Oh, yeah. Everyone's on duty today. If there's anyone running around in the tunnels right now, we'll know."

But there was no sign anyone had been in the tunnels at all. The rails were clean, or clean enough, with no signs of disturbance. After nearly thirty minutes of fruitless searching they came to an intersection where another tunnel branched off and sloped up into darkness.

"Which way?" said Garvey.

"Let's see, that trolley that got hijacked, was it the ten thirty-five?"

"Yeah. And no one ever said it was hijacked."

Nippen laughed and ignored him. "If it's the ten thirty-five, it came through this way," he said. He flashed his beam on the tunnel to the right.

"You sure?"

"Oh, sure enough," he said gladly.

"What happens if you're wrong?"

"Then we'll come to some other platform and come out. Most of the time."

"Most of the time?"

"Well, yeah. Some of these older tunnels don't lead to the trolleys."

"They don't?" asked Garvey.

"No."

"Then where do they go?"

Nippen shrugged. "Who knows? Listen, this city was built long before we installed the trolley lines. And a city is a big thing, people forget that. There're opposing forces at work here."

"There are what?"

"Opposing forces. Everything's got to balance out. You build big buildings and fill them up with people, all piled up on the rock, so to balance that out you have to make a big underground, pushing back, anchoring it. It's all floating on the surface."

"Is it?" said Garvey, giving him a dubious glance.

"Yeah," he said. "When McNaughton and Kulahee first made the city, they made it deep. The trolley just fills up the empty spaces, really. The spaces they spared for us. You can tell which ones are the old tunnels, they used red brick when they first made them. You see patches of it here and there. I don't go in the McNaughton tunnels."

"You don't?"

"No."

"Why?"

"I don't want to know what's down there," he said simply.

Garvey stopped. Something white and crumpled was lying beside the rails. He flashed it with his torch, then walked over to it.

"What's that?" asked Nippen.

"A trash can," said Garvey, picking it up.

"A trash can?"

"Yeah. And it's been beat to hell. Is it normal to find a trash can here?"

"On the rails, no. Maybe in the maintenance tunnels or one of the shafts. But not on the rails." Nippen scratched his chin, leaving a twist of grease below his lip like a goatee. "Not unless someone threw it out the window or something."

"Hm," said Garvey. He tucked it under his arm and continued walking up the rails.

"That evidence?" said Nippen.

"Maybe," said Garvey. "What's the strangest thing that's happened in the tunnels?"

"Oh, hell, I don't know," he said. "There's plenty of stuff me and my colleagues have done that was strange enough." He laughed hoarsely. "But I hear stories. Real stories. About things Kulahee made and they just stuffed down here, stuff they didn't want to use or think about." He stopped smiling. "Once I heard there was a maintenance crew sweeping through here and they heard someone. Someone coming out of the McNaughton tunnels. And they followed the sound, listening to the footsteps. And then they saw him. It was a man, but all white."

"White?"

"Yeah. Like you or me, but totally drained of color. Like it had just been sucked out of him. Even his clothes were white. He turned around and looked at them, his eyes pink as a grapefruit. He'd been picking up cans that had settled in the tunnels. He just looked at them for a while, then he turned around and wandered on, deeper in. They didn't follow. I wouldn't have either."

He and Garvey walked on for a stretch longer, not speaking. "Still," said Nippen, "they're just stories."

They kept moving, Garvey examining every maintenance hatch or sewage pipe. They still had not seen a sign of the platform yet. Garvey was surprised. The trolley had taken only four minutes to go from one to the other. It must have been moving at a tremendous speed.

Suddenly he stopped by one maintenance tunnel, then tilted his head, listening.

"What?" said Nippen, but Garvey held up a hand to shush him. Garvey unlocked the hatch, then drew his gun. He nodded at Nippen to step back, then flung the hatch open. The maintenance tunnel was low and poorly lit, but they could still catch a flurry of movement as someone scrambled down another passageway. "Stop!" Garvey shouted, and bolted after them with his gun drawn and the trash can still under his arm.

He swung around the corner, finger not on the trigger but ready to get there, and stopped. A ragged man was sitting on the floor of a small closet before him, trying to pile scraps of paper and refuse over him in an attempt to hide. His face was covered in sores and his hands were no more than bandage-wrapped claws. He kept his face averted and would not look at Garvey.

Garvey lowered his gun. "Shit," he said. "Who are you? What are you doing here?"

The man shook his head.

"I said, what are you doing here?"

"Ain't nothing doing," mumbled the man. "Ain't nothing worth doing."

"Oh, Christ," sighed Garvey, and reholstered his gun. "Nippen!"

Nippen came running up the passageway, breathing heavily. When he swung around and saw the vagrant, he said, "Oh, no. Morty! Morty, guy, you're not supposed to be here!"

"Morty?" said Garvey.

"Yeah, he's a regular down here. He sneaks down into the maintenance tunnels all the time. We keep telling him to stay out, but he always manages to get in somehow. Morty, come on." He squatted before the vagrant. "You know you can't be here."

"Ain't nothing worth doing," said Morty again. "Ain't nothing worth doing in the whole wide world." He kept uselessly shuffling through the papers with his bandaged hands.

"Here," said Nippen, taking his arm. "Come on, Morty, get up."

"Hold on," said Garvey. He took out his notebook. "You've been in the tunnels? Have you been in here all day?"

Morty would not answer, still looking away.

"Were you, Morty?" asked Nippen.

Morty nodded reluctantly.

"Did you see anything?" Garvey asked. "Hear anything?"

"Hear all kinds of things," said Morty.

"Like what?"

"Like trains. And pipes. And machines in the walls. Machines that speak to each other with light. Winking at each other. Blinking songs to one another. And crying. Always crying."

"Crying?"

"Yuh," said Morty, nodding. "Everything real unhappy down here. Crying."

"All right," said Garvey slowly, waiting.

"And everything sand," added Morty.

"What?"

"Everything sand. Minutes. Seconds. Tears. Yesterday."

"Everything's sand?"

He nodded. "We come in. Stumble about. Holding bit of sand to our chest," he said. One bandage-wrapped hand formed a cup against his breast. "Fall through our fingers all the time, all the time. We don't even know. We don't even know. We all dying and we don't even know. But ain't nothing last. Ain't nothing last forever." Then he peered up into Garvey's face and said, "Watchman. The watchman way down low, down below the city, he coming. He got his hand clutched on things, too. Not sand. Seeds." He leaned forward. "You know what they are?"

"No."

"They're tomorrow. More seconds. More futures. He giving them to us. He coming for us. He tries to tell us but we don't listen. We can't."

"So you didn't see anything?" said Garvey. He flipped his notebook shut.

Morty began rocking back and forth, shaking his head.

"Nothing at all?"

Morty stopped rocking and stared at him. "There are islands down here."

"Islands?"

"Yeah. I've seen them. Islands, lost in the dark. Islands and buildings made of metal, floating around. All abandoned, lost in the dark in between the walls. They speak to each other. Speak to each other as they float. Flick lights on at each other. I hear it, the lights in my head. But sometimes the watchman makes them say other things."

"Does he?"

"Yeah."

"What does he make them say?"

Morty shook his head. He clasped his knees together and began rocking back and forth again.

"What does he say, Morty?" asked Nippen.

Morty said, "I am a messenger, sent from afar. You must listen to me. You must listen."

"I'm listening."

"I am a messenger, sent from afar. You must listen to me. You must listen."

"Jesus," said Garvey. He turned around and began to walk away.

"Sorry," said Nippen after him. "He gets like this."

"I am a messenger, sent from afar. You must listen to me. I am a messenger. I am a messenger. I am..."

Garvey hopped back into the trolley tunnel and smoked a cigarette as he waited. Another guttering moan rolled through the tunnels, tapering off into the sound of distant thudding, which soon faded. He wondered what it was. Perhaps the whole city had shifted above, one block moving centimeters over, almost tectonically. He found it hard to believe he could climb a nearby rung and find the normal world still there. The city and this winding, nocturnal labyrinth could not possibly exist together, separated only by a few feet of stone.

Nippen eventually climbed out, then picked up the earpiece set in the wall and bellowed into the tube, "Hey, Charlie? Charlie? It's Jeff here. Listen, Morty's in maintenance tunnel"—he stopped to check—"AC-1983 again. Yeah, yeah, I know. He almost got shot by a detective just now. No, you don't, there be a lot of paperwork if we had to get rid of a goddamn body. Yeah. Yeah. Have a good one." He hung up and returned to Garvey. "Sorry, again," he said. "Morty's like that. He comes down here to listen to all the noises. He thinks he hears voices in them."

"Really," said Garvey.

"Yeah. But he's harmless. Just your average street crazy."

They began walking down the trolley tunnel again, still waving the torches over the walls and the rails. Soon they saw a string of small, pearly lights far down along the tunnel wall, unmoving. It was disturbing, like seeing only one star in a black night sky.

"That's the last platform," said Nippen. "You can just barely see the lamps. It's farther away than you think. Some people walk for hours, thinking a platform's just ahead. It's like that."

With a sinking heart Garvey continued toward the lights. He'd spent nearly two hours in the dusty tunnels and found no more than a trash can and a homeless man, neither of which seemed to carry much importance for his case. It felt like it was his job to catch the murders that couldn't possibly file.

"Sometimes I think Morty might not be wrong," said Nippen at his side.

"About what?"

"About the voices. The voices in the tunnels. I mean, sure, it's just sounds and all, but if you spend enough time down here it does sound like they're saying something. What, I don't know. Maybe I've just been down here too long," he said as Garvey climbed up to the platform. He looked off into the tunnels, thinking, then smiled up at Garvey. "Maybe if you spend every day in the tunnels you imagine things."

"Maybe," said Garvey.

"Is that it for you? You done here?"

"I sure hope so." Garvey took off his tin hat and handed it to Nippen. "Thanks," he said. Then he walked away, smoothing his hair down as he did so, and left the little man leaning up against the platform.

"You have a good afternoon, Detective," said Nippen. His voice echoed throughout the empty station.

"Goodbye, Mr. Nippen," said Garvey.

"And good luck with your case!" he called, and laughed.

It was not until much later in the day that any of Garvey's efforts were rewarded. He sent the trash can uptown to the Department, vaguely mentioning it might be evidence, and then began walking the blocks near all the previous stations the trolley had stopped at. It was dreary work, and he was not entirely sure what he was looking for. Just seeing if there was something nearby that those people on the trolley had been doing, some indication of who they were and why they'd been there.

He was deep in the Shanties in one of the poorest sections of town when he saw it. A sign hanging on the front of a bar, made of old, weathered wood; yet painted on the sign itself was a white hammer set on a black bell, and below that were words telling passersby it was the Third Ring Pub.

Garvey took out his sketch of his John Doe's tattoo and held it up. It matched perfectly.

It was about as far from an upscale place as he could imagine. It stank of old beer even from the street and the door had been broken in numerous times, the innards of its heavy lock exposed in the shattered wood. Garvey braced himself, then pushed the door open and walked in.

The ceiling was low and the splintered wooden floor was covered in sawdust. Garvey began to take measure of his surroundings, but before he could he realized the quiet susurrus of bar talk had died the moment he walked in. He looked around. The corners were packed with men in overalls and threadbare canvas pants, all of them standing up to look at him. Their forearms thick and scarred and their faces bright red with drink and years of work. They stared at him, hardly holding back their contempt, and Garvey became intensely aware that this was a union bar through and through, and he was wearing a suit and a demeanor that screamed police as loud as it could.

Garvey smiled, tipped his hat, and quickly walked out.

CHAPTER TWELVE

Hayes and Samantha rode up the elevator to find the forty-seventh floor of the Nail had erupted. Runners bolted back and forth from office to office carrying messages. Every other room was filled with shouting. Evans had been called away to an emergency meeting, and Hayes and Samantha waited before his office for three hours. Hayes slept and snored and would not quiet no matter how many times Samantha woke him. After the fourth time she gave up and sat as far away from him as she could.

When Evans tottered in he looked decades older than when they'd last seen him. He looked at them bleary-eyed and said, "I see you got my message."

"No," said Samantha. "I don't think we did."

"Oh. Then you just predicted it. Come in. Some people very much want to talk to you about this."

She began following and on the way in kicked Hayes, who awoke with a snort. They both sat down before him, Hayes still yawning. Evans was silent for a very long time before saying, "You know what this is about."

"Yes," said Hayes. "The Bridgedale Station."

"Yes. It's very bad for everyone."

"McNaughton's not connected, though," Samantha said. "Not really. Right, sir?"

"No. Only vaguely associated. But the public wants to see it. After all, we helped engineer the trolley lines, and it's already rumored that the passengers were union members. They want to see us exploiting the workers and sending them to slaughter. You know how it is. Have you talked to anyone?"

"Talked?" said Hayes. "Besides Garvey? No."

Evans looked at Samantha. "You?"

"I don't know anyone to talk to," she said.

"Hm. That's good."

"Anything else?" asked Hayes.

Evans checked his watch. "Give me two minutes."

"Why?"

"Because Brightly's on his way here now."

"Oh, goodness," said Hayes drily. "He'll be in a right state, won't he."

Evans nodded. Then they all sat in silence, thinking.

The doors opened and Brightly himself rushed in, moving at top speed. Samantha was surprised to find he was a giant of a man, sporting a strained smile. The smile vanished as Evans stood up. Brightly said, "Oh, no no. No, that's fine. Sit right there, Jim. I'm fine. Hayes," he said, nodding to him. "And you must be Miss Fairbanks, how nice to finally meet you. Jim here has nothing but good things to say about you."

"Why, thank you. It's nice to meet you, too."

"Yes, yes. Pity we have to meet under such circumstances. The work you're doing is fantastic, simply fantastic. You're invaluable, my girl." He came and delicately sat on the edge of Evans's desk, close to her, casual but domineering. He reached into his pocket, pulled out his watch, and checked it before replacing it. Then he put his hands in his lap, bowed his head as though in prayer, and said, "Well. We all know why I'm here. You were at the scene today, correct?"

"Right," said Hayes.

"How was it? In there, in the tunnels?"

Hayes thought for a while. Then he said, "Do you remember that October at the vulcanization plant?"

Brightly looked surprised. "What? Yes, of course I do. How could I forget?"

"It was worse than that. Far worse."

His eyes grew wide. "Dear God... Worse than that, even?"

"Yes. We're lucky the police sent everyone packing," Hayes said. "I was in that damn trolley car. If the press had gotten a snap of it we'd have panic in the streets, I'm sure of it."

"Christ almighty," said Brightly. He exhaled hugely, then gathered himself. "All right. And people saw you there?"

"Well. Yes."

"Good. All right. Now, your previous investigation was highly classified, which is good. But Shroff, well, Shroff got word that you identified all the bodies at the scene. Is that correct?"

"Somewhat. I only identified a few."

"Hm. And they were all from your recent investigation?"

"Pretty much."

"I want names," said Brightly. "All of them. And what you've got about them. Every little thing."

Hayes gestured to Samantha. She said, "I'll have them to you by the end of the day, sir."

"Yes. Good. Give them to Evans here. Yes?"

"Certainly," said Evans.

"All right," said Brightly. He took another deep breath. "Now. As your inquiry was so classified, Hayes, I don't think too many people know that, well, we had a list of all the people who died, not to mention good and *documented* reason to dislike them. So thankfully that pretty concrete association is still not public. But listen: to counteract the bad press, we're going to have to do something. I'm launching a full public inquiry into anything we might have on what happened in that trolley. Anything that McNaughton might have had to do with it. Extremists, malcontents, anyone with any connection. I'm going to announce it later today with the board. Make sure it gets into the right papers. We hope to have something solid for them by Christmas. And, naturally, you'll spearhead, Hayes."

"And the union investigation?" asked Hayes. "What about that? Are we still worried they'll throw off your... production time on your big projects?"

"Forget the other nonsense," Brightly snapped. "Forget rooting out unioners. People are starting to think we've killed a dozen people, and they *will* think it by the time word gets out. Most of the city still doesn't know. We need to act fast."

"Right. And this time if we do find something, we'll do something about it, right? Or will we wait to see if we can find out more?"

Brightly eyed him coldly. "That was a strategic tactic. You know that."

"Yes. Very strategic and very effective. If we'd done otherwise, why, all those boys would be safely locked away in cells, and we'd still be in the clear. Thank goodness we didn't."

"If you think I don't regret that decision, you're wrong," said Brightly. "Dead wrong. It's for that very reason we need to be even more vigilant in this new investigation."

"Please, Cyril, just keep doing what we tell you to," Evans said. "Especially now, in this emergency."

"Oh, I will. I will," Hayes said. He took out a cigarette and began walking it along his knuckles, the cigarette disappearing below his pinky at the end and reappearing on his thumb to start again.

Brightly got off his perch and squatted before Hayes. He was still taller than Hayes by an inch. Brightly reached forward and plucked the cigarette from his hands and crushed it into dust. Hayes watched the tobacco rain onto the carpet around his feet.

"Look at me, Cyril," Brightly said softly. "Listen to me, please. I know I made mistakes. I admit that. But we need you to be on your best behavior now. We need you to do everything you can. Everything else, everything else that's happened before, that's in the past. We need your help. Will you give it to us?"

Hayes frowned. "All right. I'll do what I can."

Brightly nodded and stood up and took a breath. "Good," he said. "Good then." Then he reached into his pocket again, checked his watch, and walked to the far corner of the room, where he looked out the window with his hands behind his back.

Evans jumped in, taking up some unseen cue. "A list of tasks is being compiled at the moment. You'll get them in the morning. You'll follow them up and report to me. Based on this information another set of tasks will be compiled. And so on, until we're satisfied. We'll relate your findings to our Public Affairs Division and, in due time, release them to the public. This is all happening independent of the police, mind."

"Independent?" said Hayes.

"Oh, yes," said Brightly calmly, returning. "People already suspect we're somehow puppeteering the Department around. Like anyone could gain control of something so corrupt and disorganized. But this is all going to be about appearances. I don't want to see anyone with a badge coming near us for a while."

"That means Garvey, Hayes," said Evans.

"I know what it means," he said.

"Naturally, neither of you will be named," continued Brightly. "The information will be credited to a variety of sources. But your efforts will be greatly appreciated, and you'll be compensated in your own way. Clear?"

Hayes nodded wearily. "Clear."

"And you, Miss Fairbanks?"

"I understand," she said.

"Good. Now, girls and boys, I'm afraid I'll have to ask you all to leave. Evans and I have more appointments today. Many, many more." Then Brightly went and looked out the far window again, hands behind his back and face carefully kept clear of them both, and did not look at them again until they left.

"God, who could envy us now?" said Hayes as they rode down the elevator together. "If you thought our old work was dull as dirt, this one's going to be worse."

"I didn't think it was *too* dull," said Samantha. "It was mostly records work, which I did all the time before. It's not that bad."

Hayes studied her with a disbelieving eye, as if she were a strange breed of creature he'd never seen before. "Every once in a while I think you're pretty smart," he said, "but then you go and say something like that."

She rolled her eyes. "Exactly what do you think is going to make this new work so terrible, Mr. Hayes? Everyone on the board will be paying attention to us. This is our chance to prove ourselves."

"But we won't actually be *proving* anything," said Hayes as the doors opened. "Sure, we're supposed to be looking for any connection, but what would happen if we actually *found* something that implicates the company in what happened on that trolley? It's the last thing they want."

"So what do you think we'll be doing?" Samantha asked. They crossed the lobby to exit through a side entrance.

"Putting on a show," Hayes said. "A real song-and-dance routine where we talk and talk and report all day, and find nothing. Just something to make the newspapers feel safe. But it won't work. They'll panic anyway. Personally, I'm looking forward to hearing what Tazz has to say about this."

"Tazz? Why?"

"Because a lot of his problems just got solved, I should think. Several violent undesirables acting in his name just got eliminated, and now they look like martyrs for his union. With blood on McNaughton's hands and everything. His reaction will be very telling, I'd say."

Samantha considered this. "Well, for whatever it's worth, I very much doubt if the company could have ever been involved in something like this."

"Your loyalty is almost charming," said Hayes. "But for once I agree with you."

"You do?"

"Oh, yes. McNaughton's powerful enough that they don't need to kill anybody. And Brightly was afraid back there. Terrified. Him and Evans. Neither of them has any idea what's going on. They're innocent. Or ignorant, at least."

As they walked through the hallway they were forced to the side by a crew of men maneuvering an enormous painting up onto the wall. Several of the workers climbed up and stood on ladders to help guide the painting onto the hooks in the wall. Samantha and Hayes stopped to watch, caught up in the stress of the moment.

The picture was a strange one. It showed two men standing in a cave, one off to the side with his arms crossed and his face serenely satisfied. He was short and dumpy, dressed in furs and shabby clothes. Samantha got the impression that the painter had been directly told to make him "rustic." The other man, who was the primary subject of the painting, was much more civilized, wearing a gentleman's idea of outdoor clothing and sporting a patrician mustache and sideburns. She immediately recognized him as William McNaughton. He was cradling something in his hands, a delicate device made of frail, silver gears. It seemed to be giving off a faint sheen of light, like it was a holy relic.

"That's McNaughton," said Samantha. "And that's Kulahee there? On the side?"

"It would be, yes," said Hayes. "They took this one out for touchups the other day. Looks like they're done."

"What's that in his hands?"

"Oh, some machine," sighed Hayes. "I suppose they told the painter just to paint 'an invention' and he did the best he could. Or maybe it's symbolic. McNaughton offering Kulahee's creation to the world."

"Why are they in a cave?"

"Kulahee spent a lot of time in the caves around his home," said Hayes. He grunted, then squeezed his eyes shut and pinched his nose. "He...he kept some things down in there. Spent a lot of time digging around in them. Famous local myth, the caves of Kulahee."

"Are you all right, Mr. Hayes?"

"Yes. I'm fine," said Hayes. "Just...had a headache since we went down into the tunnels." They began walking down the hallway to the doors. Hayes kept one hand pressed to his temple. "The air down there really got to me."

"Are you sure you're well?" asked Samantha.

"Yes."

"You're shaking."

"No," he said. "No, I'm...I'm..."

He coughed and pitched forward. One knee buckled and he fought to stay upright, but then it failed again and he crumpled to the floor, the other leg askew behind him. Spasms wracked his body and his skin turned the color of bleached bone and something red-black ran from his nose. Samantha ran to him, shouting out his name. She grasped the sides of his head and pulled his mouth open to show his tongue thrashing about in his mouth. Then his eyes rolled up into his head and he went still.

CHAPTER THIRTEEN

Samantha stood over Hayes, not sure what to do. She looked up and down the hallway but saw no one. She wondered if she should call for help. Then a tremor shook through Hayes's body and he surged gasping back to consciousness. He grabbed her arm and panted, "Get me out of here."

"What? Why?"

"They…can't see me like this. They can't." He struggled to say more, but then his eyes watered and he shook his head.

Samantha pulled him to his feet and hefted one of his arms around her neck and began to hobble out of the Nail. She worried that the people outside would stop them and demand to know what they were doing, but no one did. They hardly looked at them at all.

"Where am I going, Mr. Hayes?" she asked him.

"Home," he whispered. He barely seemed awake.

"Home? Yours?"

He nodded and his head lolled back. He raised one trembling finger and pointed down a back alley. "Through there," he whispered.

She grunted as she maneuvered him into a better position, then began limping down the alley with him. He was extraordinarily light for a man. Underneath his enormous coat and all those clothes he must have been a pigeon-boned thing with hardly a scrap of fat on him. He muttered deliriously as they walked, singing little songs to himself and speaking to invisible people. Many times it seemed to be in a foreign language. Samantha did her best to ignore it, but as she readjusted her grip on him his head fell forward and she happened to catch a few rhymes of one of his little songs.

Her eyes shot wide and she dropped him. He fell in a heap in the alley, yet kept muttering. She stood over him, breathing hard. Then she stooped to listen again. She swallowed, terrified, and then shook her head. "No," she whispered. "No, I don't believe it."

"What?" said Hayes. He blinked and licked his lips. "Where are we? Are we nearly there?"

Samantha's mouth compressed until it was a bloodless line. She swallowed again and said, "Yes. Nearly."

She picked him back up and continued through the maze of back alleys, following his semi-lucid directions. Finally a set of warehouses loomed before them and Hayes gestured at the cracks between them and murmured, "There."

They emerged onto a small abandoned cobblestone lane. "Now where?" she asked.

He pointed at one of the largest warehouses.

"You live *there*?" she asked.

"Yes."

"Mr. Hayes, is this a joke?"

"No."

She dragged him to the big wooden doors and Hayes slumped against them and fumbled through his pockets. Litter and empty cigarette tins rained onto the ground, small bits of loot stolen at impulse, pens and paperweights and cheap jewelry. Finally he rummaged up a massive iron key. He worked it into the lock and turned it and something clicked and clanked loudly inside the door. Then it swung open and they stumbled in.

Samantha's mouth opened in shock as Hayes led her inside. The warehouse was enormous, nearly fifty feet high. Small rows of windows filled the upper portion of the room with the gray light of afternoon. Hundreds of stacks of books sat on the bare cement floor before them, anywhere from three to five feet tall, with oil lamps standing between them here and there. Chairs and beds and cabinets and tables were scattered throughout, most of them dusty from lack of use. At the far back was what had once been the manager's office, although it seemed to have been renovated as a small home of some kind. Two mealy-looking ferns sat before the front door.

"What is this place?" asked Samantha.

Hayes walked forward and began staggering through the stacks, grabbing cabinets and ripping them open and digging through them. Finally he found a small green bottle, and he sat on the floor and opened it and drank. He sighed deeply and leaned back against the cabinet and shut his eyes.

Samantha walked forward and looked at the bottle. "Laudanum," she read.

"My medicine," he said.

"For what?"

"Attacks."

"What kind of attacks?"

Hayes did not answer. He got to his feet and walked toward the office in the back. He dragged a small iron brazier out of the piles of junk and filled it with coal and stuffed paper in the cracks and lit it. Then he sat before the small fire, huddled in his coat and rubbing his hands.

Samantha found a chair and brought it up to sit beside him. "You live here?" she asked.

"Yes."

"Why?"

"For the quiet. Lots of room, lots of peace and quiet. I asked Brightly and Brightly delivered." He stoked the coals with what looked like a conductor's baton.

Samantha watched him for a long time, her face oddly frozen. "How do you know what you know about people, Mr. Hayes?" she eventually asked.

"What?"

"I'm curious. How do you know the things no one else knows?"

"I don't *know,*" he said. "It's just guesswork. That and I have my sources."

"Are you lying to me, Mr. Hayes?"

"What? No."

She looked closer at him. "Are you sure?"

"Why?"

"Do you... do you not remember what you said?"

"Said? When?"

"Just now, as we left the Nail. Do you remember what you started saying on the street?"

"I think I gave you directions," he said slowly.

"Before that."

"No. No, I don't. Probably just crazed muttering."

"It wasn't."

"Then what was it?"

She was silent for a good while. Then she said, "It was a good-night rhyme my father used to sing to me when I was little. Then you started quoting Twain. My favorite Twain story. From *Roughing It.*"

Hayes stoked the fire again and did not look at her.

Samantha was breathing hard now. "Can you... can you read... minds, Mr. Hayes?" she asked softly.

"No," he said. Then, "Yes. Sometimes."

"What do you mean?"

"It's hard to explain."

"Please try."

Hayes took a deep breath and shook his head. "They just... Well. They leak in."

"What do?"

"Thoughts. Things."

"What do you mean?"

He screwed up his mouth. "Sometimes... sometimes if I am alone with a person for a very long time I can begin to act like them. And talk like them. And then eventually I know small things about them. Little things. Opinions. Feelings. Worries. They seem to come from nowhere." He blinked and scratched his face, streaking it with soot. "That's all."

Samantha looked away. The silence marched on.

"Don't be afraid," said Hayes.

"I'm not afraid," she said. Her voice quivered. "I'm angry."

"What?"

"I'm angry you had... that you subjected me to... You *know things*!" she shouted, and she stood, fists shaking at her sides. "You know things about me and I don't know how you know them and I don't want you to know them!"

He nodded. "Yeah. Yes. You're mad."

"Of course I'm mad! I've never felt so violated in my life!"

"I don't know any big things about you! Nothing private. It's just a taste, a smell. A feeling. Like... like smelling something you haven't smelled in a long time and remembering things and all the things associated with it."

"Like spice from downstairs," Samantha said.

Hayes did not meet her eyes. He played with the little baton in his hands. She walked away through the stacks of books and found another chair and sat in it, hidden from his view. "Damn you," she whispered. "What are you?"

She heard him stoking the fire once more, maneuvering the brazier about. Then she heard him coughing. She leaned around to look and saw he had a hand placed at the side of his head again and he was bent over, knees touching his chest.

"Are you all right?" she asked.

Hayes took another sip of laudanum. He shook himself and said, "I'll be fine."

"An attack?"

He didn't answer.

"What are those attacks? Is it part of your—"

"I don't know," he said.

"What do they do?"

"They hurt."

She stood up and walked back to the chair beside him. Neither one looked at the other.

"Who else knows?" she asked.

"Brightly," he said. "And Evans. And Garvey."

"Garvey?"

"Yes," he said.

"That's why Brightly rushed us in and out so fast, isn't it? He doesn't want to be around you. Doesn't want anything to . . . to leak in."

"Yes."

"And that's why you live alone like this."

He nodded. "It's quiet here."

"Is . . . is this what you meant when you said they were keeping things from us? From me?"

He nodded again.

"Why didn't you tell me?"

He laughed miserably. "How could I? Listen, Sam, I've been on this earth for forty-something years and I've not yet found one good way to tell someone what I am that wouldn't end up with them screaming their heads off or me knifed for my trouble. How would you have told someone, Sam? Tell them your head fills up with the garbage their minds leave in their wake?"

Samantha sighed and shook her head. "You still should have told me."

"But I couldn't. How could anyone? I'd much rather just . . . let it lie."

There was a knock at the door, the sound shooting up into the rafters and then drifting gently down. The door opened and Garvey stepped in. He looked at the two of them and called, "Am I interrupting something?"

Hayes and Samantha shared a look. Then Samantha sighed and turned away and sat down far from Hayes.

"No," said Hayes. "Come on in, Garv."

"So what's the news?" Garvey asked as he strode forward, weaving among the stacks. It took him a good twenty seconds to walk over to them. He found a chair and sat beside Samantha.

"McNaughton's panicked over the bad press," said Hayes. "Guess who's got the job of finding out if there's any connections."

"Ouch."

"Yes. It's going to be especially hard because I think they want us to find nothing at all."

"Do they know you sent me those files yesterday?" asked Garvey.

Hayes thought about it. Then shook his head.

"You sure?"

"I'm pretty sure. They have a hard time keeping track of the things I make disappear. So I don't think it's connected. Anything on your end?"

"I have a few things, sure," he said, easing back into his chair. "Gibson came and gathered them up. Shuffled the deck, you could say. I canvassed the area but no one saw anything. Spooky place, down there. We're putting something in the paper about it, asking people to please let us know if they hear anything. I don't expect much more than bullshit." He glanced at Samantha. "Apologies."

"For what?" asked Samantha absently.

"For swearing. Sorry. Don't deal with ladies too often, these days."

"Oh," she said, and nodded.

Garvey looked at both of them queerly and said, "What's with you two? Did I just walk into something?"

Hayes turned to glance at Samantha, sighed, and said, "Sam's just figured out where I get my little hunches from."

Garvey's eyebrows rose. He uncrossed his legs. "Oh," he said. "Huh. Is that so?"

She nodded.

"That's... Well. That's pretty fast."

"What?" said Hayes.

"I said it was fast." He grinned crookedly at her. "It took me a few months for him to tell me how he did it, and only then because he was slobbering drunk. You're pretty quick, Miss Fairbanks."

She stared at Garvey. "That's what you have to say? That I'm pretty *fast*?"

"Well, yeah."

"Aren't you horrified? Aren't you offended?"

"No. Don't have much to be offended over."

"But he can just... he can just listen!" she hissed in a stage-whisper as though Hayes were far away. "Like he's got his ear to the walls of your mind, listening to everything you say to yourself!"

Garvey shrugged. "I guess. But it's not like he can stop it."

"He can't?" she asked, looking at Hayes. "Is that true?"

Hayes looked up at her from the folds of his coat. He searched her face for a moment as though he had forgotten what they were talking about or maybe just who she was. Perhaps it was the dimness of the warehouse or the light from the small fire before him, but suddenly he looked older than any other person Samantha had ever met before. She had seen such things only once before in her life, when she had been an army nurse and had treated wounded men returning from battle. They had been boys, always boys, no more than twenty, and when they'd walked back through the carnage and the savagery and sat waiting to be treated anyone could look at them and see that they were creatures interrupted. Boys who would never become men now, never become people. They were something wounded and crippled. Something broken that could not be fixed.

"No," he said. "I can't."

"Oh. You... you really can't stop it?"

He shook his head.

She sighed. "I see. I think I see, at least."

"Are you all right?" he asked. "All right with this? And with me?"

"I don't know. I suppose I could be."

"That's good enough," he said. "Good enough for me."

They discussed the usual. How it worked. When he had figured out he could do it. His boundaries, both physical and moral. Samantha found herself both relieved and frustrated to find out how limited it really was. She asked about Evans, and Brightly, and especially the board, whom Hayes said he had been practically forbidden to ever come close to. She asked about the worst people he had ever read, whom he could barely recall, and the best, whom he recalled even less.

Garvey told her of the first time he had met Hayes, stinking drunk and sleeping off a two-day bender in the tank. They had come to haul someone out of lockup and as they dragged him through Hayes had reached through the bars and grabbed Garvey's arm and slurred, "That right there is a guilty bastard if I ever saw one. Ask him about the tack hammer and he'll weep like no tomorrow." And he had been right. The suspect's next-door neighbor had murdered his dog with a tack hammer, and the suspect had done only what he thought was right in return. Hayes claimed he had no memory of this event, and had been extraordinarily confused when a Detective Garvey came calling the next day.

"Anyways, what the hell was that you had?" Garvey asked. "A fainting spell?"

"An attack," Hayes said.

"What do you mean?"

"I don't know. Sometimes I'm out walking and it's like a thunderbolt hits me. Like someone just opens up my head and pours things inside. Never good things."

"Is that all?"

"There's a few things I do after. Vomit. Cough. But yes. That's all."

"Christ," said Garvey. "How long has it been going on for?"

"About half a year."

"Are you sure you're all right?"

"Yes," said Hayes irritably. "I'm fine. Let's talk about something important, eh? Like the bodies we saw today?"

Garvey reluctantly consented, starting with the Third Ring Pub. "They didn't want me there, hoo boy," he said, scratching his head. "I've had murderous looks before, but never so many at once. So I called for support and got a half-dozen patrolmen to accompany me in to speak civilly with the owner and the patrons. They didn't want to talk at all, but they gave us something. Turns out Naylor and the rest of them were regular patrons there. They were there nearly every day, and they were there that morning before the Bridgedale trolley mishap. If 'mishap' is the right word. They left all together, probably heading to work or maybe to one of their homes, which explains why they were all on that trolley at once."

But as to who could have done something about it or why, neither Garvey nor Hayes could possibly guess. With no witnesses and no leads and the primary suspect being an entire company that, according to Hayes, seemed to know barely more than the police, they all figured it was going to be an ugly mess indeed.

"Something else odd," Garvey said. "You know the door? The trolley door?"

"I suppose," said Hayes.

"It was broken in. There were marks on the front. Impact marks. From what, we're not sure. Looks like a battering ram, maybe."

"Someone hung on the side of a moving trolley and rammed the door in?"

"Maybe." He sighed. "You know what, we could send shit back and forth on this for hours." He slapped his notebook shut. "You just can't think about this normally. You just can't."

"You think this might be related to the man in the canal?" asked Hayes.

Garvey turned the question over in his head, handling how it fit. "I don't want to say anything too fast," he said. "But I'm tempted to."

"Is the union situation really this bad?" asked Samantha. "For something like this to happen?"

Hayes shrugged. "That's the big question, isn't it? To be honest, I can't say. I rarely deal with the working-class levels of Evesden. You want to answer?" he said to Garvey.

"There's not enough work," said Garvey. "And what work there is isn't paying enough. Not by a mile. But that's the way it is. The dockworkers want one pay, the smelters and foundry workers want another, the airship assembly teams want highest of all. Everyone says they want a little more, just enough to survive, they say, but they don't. Not really. They just want. I know them all, I've listened to them all, I've hauled in people from each of their damn clans. And who's going to tell McNaughton how to run their company? And how will they set their standards? One pay for all workers or certain levels only for a few? And how will they figure that out? I don't know. I can't think of a solution. I just clean up."

"So what's going on?" she asked. "Out there."

"Out there? They're starving. As is expected, I guess. Things got too big. There's too many of us," he said, and lit a cigarette. The bright orange flare seemed strange in that colorless place. "You can say all you want about greed and evils and economics, but that's what it comes down to. They all came here looking for work and a lot of the trades they came here with got put out of business, and now there's too many people. So they'll turn to vice and violence and make a living as best they can. I guess you can't blame them. But I have to. It's what they pay me for."

* * *

Hayes dozed off as night came on, the bottle of laudanum half-empty between his feet. Garvey and Samantha rose and left him there among his books and his dusty chairs with the coal fire smoldering before him.

"He'll kill himself drinking that poison," said Samantha.

"Maybe," said Garvey.

"No. It's really poison. It's opium."

"I know. He does, too. It's been, well... manageable for a while now. Here, let me take you home."

He led her to his car and they climbed in. He hit the lights and asked her where she lived. When she told him he whistled. "Newton is pretty fancy," he said.

"It does all right," she said, smiling.

After a while of riding they turned down Grange Avenue and the lights and white stone buildings of Newton swam into view. The thin, smooth tunnel of the train ran between the building tops like calligraphy, and here and there it dipped to the platforms, its car windows strobing in its descent. Up above the streets an arched glass walkway stretched from one building to another, and though it was empty the starlight refracted through it to make a ghostly prism suspended in the sky. Down on the corner a theater let out its patrons, all of them standing in the flickering lights of the marquee bulbs, arranging their coats and discussing the show. Cabs descended on them in a flurry, sensing the hefty fares of drunk rich folk who'd forgotten precisely how far they'd come. On nearby restaurant rooftops men and women in furs laughed and their merriness rebounded off the walls to rain upon the street. Champagne laughs, lily-petal laughs, pretty and sweet and perfect.

Samantha remembered what Hayes had said about the twentieth century and remembered the fairy world she lived in compared to the rest of the city. A tiny bubble of promise that would come true for only a select few.

Beside her Garvey explained that Newton was like a birthday cake, with many layers, all interconnected. Even below the street, where an entire marketplace filled the corners and cracks of the trolley tunnels and you could eat exotic food from all over the world, provided you didn't mind a roof made of piping. And down there more mechanisms and devices kept the city running, more than you could ever imagine. Though, considering what had happened today, who would want to imagine it?

"There's no going back, is there?" Samantha asked suddenly.

"Huh?" said Garvey.

"Oh. I'm sorry. It's just... something I thought of."

"What is it?" he asked.

"There's no going back. It's what I said. What I said when I first came here, on the airship. I'd never ridden one before. And as I got off another one came into the cradle. It was like seeing the sky open up. It shone like a shield with a little glass button on its belly, only the button was full of people. Then its engines turned all around and it lowered itself into the trusses. Workers came forward and looped the lines around its nose. And it floated in. Lowered itself down between the buildings. Like a tiger in the jungle."

"I've seen it," Garvey said. "Never been on one. But I've seen them dock in."

"There's no going back, I said. The world changed right underneath my feet. And I almost didn't notice it happening. But now there's no going back."

"No," said Garvey. "There isn't."

"And to think all this came from a fisherman," Samantha said. "Thought up decades ago."

"Kulahee? Yeah. He's worshipped like a god in some places around here. People have spent lives trying to figure out how he did what he did. But whatever the secret is, McNaughton isn't telling."

Samantha watched as they passed by a pneumatic mail post, its dark glass chutes sprouting up from the cement. The brasswork around its nozzles was done in intricate leaves and vines, and each nozzle was unlocked and open, ready to devour whatever canister the next citizen was willing to feed it. "It's almost like men could never make these things at all," she said as it disappeared behind them.

"Yeah," said Garvey. "Sometimes I feel that way, too."

He dropped her off at her apartment. She stood below the awning and turned to look at him. "Thank you for the ride," she said.

"Not a problem. Sometimes I need an excuse to see the nice parts of town, you know?"

Samantha laughed. "I suppose."

"Sleep well," he said.

"I will."

He drove away. She stood and watched as the headlights faded and disappeared into the night.

CHAPTER FOURTEEN

The story of the murders spread quickly. The southeastern areas shouted it first and then it leaked to the outer districts. It was a steady build, like a storm piling clouds up on the mountains. When it had finally gathered enough momentum the rumble became a scream and the city filled up with wild questions.

The mystery and vagueness of the murders brought the police into question immediately. Either they were fools for not knowing enough or crooked for keeping information repressed. Badges were bought with money, everyone knew, and it didn't matter where. Down in the Docks where brothels and dens paid to keep the patrols strolling, or up in Newton and Westbank where the police kept only the laws the locals approved of. And McNaughton men were gods to the police, that everyone agreed. The very name became an even dirtier word in Dockland and the Shanties in the wake of the Bridgedale trolley. The overseers at McNaughton were untried war criminals in a city where the war had not yet begun. Surely they had somehow engineered this, everyone said. After all, hadn't they been the architects of the trolley lines? Could any trolley line be trusted, now that they could be turned into slaughterhouses the second anyone entered them?

McNaughton's Bridgedale Inquiry seemed to die at birth. Several times a day Samantha was handed a list of names, locations, and dates, and sometimes she accompanied Hayes to the interviews and sometimes he went alone. On the days when she went with him each hour was a chain of enormous blank facilities honeycombed with tiny rooms, filled with silent, sullen people who answered questions with questions. The company had gone frigid and suspicious in the aftermath. Most of the time Samantha stayed either on her feet, running between Hayes and Brightly or Hayes and Evans, or buried up to her neck in research. She logged hours in the company's Records floor, a dark, labyrinthine cross-section of the Nail that seemed to be mostly locks and doors. Samantha was granted one of the highest-clearance light keys for this work, and she soon learned that Brightly and Evans were logging its use, matching the daily tally with the number of records she pulled. It was unnerving and exhausting work for her, especially under such scrutiny. She prepared the most bare-bones accounts for each of Hayes's interview subjects, just enough for him to be ready. He sat with most of them for hours and caught no whiff of deceit. Only terror and anxiety. To try and prepare more would have been a waste of time, he said.

Garvey did not fare much better. As he had suspected, he and Morris were appointed to the detail, with Morris working as the primary detective. Morris was a relic, a supporter of the fine old days when effective police work usually meant beating confessions out of whoever seemed most suspicious. They were usually foreign or black. He was a towering man with a puffy, Welsh face and beady, furious eyes. Ironically enough, he was also a devout Christian who refused to tolerate any foul language, which turned any conversation with Garvey into short, clipped sentences that barely made sense.

Morris's approach to the murders was similar to McNaughton's: they looked for extremists, both religious and philosophical, a term Morris and Lieutenant Collins interpreted as referring to all socialists and unioners. But if Hayes met a brick wall it was nothing like what Morris met. Whole neighborhoods of people stayed dead silent on the subject of unions, and especially Mickey Tazz.

Mickey Tazz, the people murmured to each other. Tazz will set us right. Tazz will set everything right. The working-class messiah, suited up in overalls and brogans. Out there in the slums somewhere, and strangely silent.

Garvey had better luck with one of Walton's ex-girlfriends. When she came in to view the body he sat with her in the Central's lobby, passing her cigarettes and sandwiches. Eventually he asked her about the tattoo.

"Why?" she asked.

"Just idle curiosity. They all had them."

"Yeah. Mikey and Frank and them all got them." She shook her head. "Idiots. All the guys at the Third Ring. It was like they were part of a gang. Said McNaughton could never flush them out."

"Flush them out?"

"From the lines. Pay kept dropping and they kept firing people, but Frank and them had been working there for years and said they'd be the fly in the ointment. The sand caught in the gears. Said they'd never leave. It was a guy thing. A stupid thing."

Then he showed her the picture of his canal John Doe. She did not know him. Another unknown body, falling through the cracks.

Garvey then compiled a list of things he'd found in the trolley and began trying to account for each of them. Most of them seemed random. A set of keys. A ball of yarn. A medallion. A pair of scissor handles and a book collection, lost by God knows who. Giving up, he returned to the one thing he'd found during his trawl through the tunnels: the little white garbage can. He sat it on his desk and stared at it, chin in hand, as if they were opponents in a chess game. He turned it around in his hands, feeling its battered indentations. Then he realized something.

He returned to the Third Ring Pub, but this time did not enter. Instead he took the garbage can and matched it to the ones found outside the diner across the street. When he asked the diner's employees about it they identified it as the one that usually stood outside the front door but had gone missing, though they were unsure when. Garvey went and stood at the front door of the diner, looked back at the pub, and smoked and thought. Then he drove to where the trolley was being held in a police impound lot, looked at the broken door of the trolley, and held the garbage can up to its crumpled front. The two fit.

"So what the hell does that tell us?" asked Collins when Garvey told him and Morris.

"It shows us that, whoever it was, they busted into the trolley with a garbage can, of all things," Garvey said. "One taken from right across the street from the bar the unioners had left. Which means that the assailant had been watching them just minutes before the murders. Which suggests that this all was . . . well, improvised, at least as far as I can tell."

"How does that match with the deafness and the four minutes and all?" asked Morris.

"It doesn't. Not yet. I'm explaining what I can and taking the stuff I don't know and leaving it hanging. For now."

"Great," said Morris. "Just beautiful."

"It's all I have," said Garvey. He shook his head. "All I could find."

Collins nodded, chewing his pipe to the point of dissolution. "What do we have on the street level?"

"Not much," said Morris. "No one likes to talk about unions. Especially to a cop. There's a few boys I know who are reliable snitches but they don't know anything. But we're working it. Slowly and surely, we're working it."

Afterward Garvey went down to the morgue, which had become chaotic in the wake of the murders. Gibson and his attendants were working triple shifts to handle the incoming family of the Bridgedale. When Garvey arrived he found three corpses laid out on the floor rather than in the cabinets. He gave Gibson a disapproving look.

"What?" Gibson said.

"That's not very respectful," Garvey said.

"It would be even more disrespectful to not examine them. Are we not here to investigate, Detective? We need more workers. More room. An actual doctor's surgery. But we make do with what we can. Right?"

Garvey sighed and looked at the shrunken, gaunt remains of the prostitute, flecks of makeup still clinging to her drying face. "Right."

"I don't see why I even look," Gibson said, shaking his head. "It's the same damn thing."

"Which is?"

"Stabbings. Stabbed all to shit. But from the look of it, it was all done with the same weapons. These ones, in fact." Gibson picked up a small cloth sack and dumped it out on the table. Inside were two blades with no handles, each about four inches long. One side of each was dull and the other sharp. The sharp sides had several small pieces missing and the tip of one was gone.

"Found these in Mrs. Sanna," Gibson told him. "Occupation barmaid, it seems. I suppose whoever killed all these folks got to her last. Must have snapped off in her. They were way the hell up in her back. The tip of that little bit was in Mr. Evie. In his neck."

Garvey picked the pieces up, handled them. Then he placed them back on the table and picked up his report and flipped through it.

"What?" said Gibson.

"There was a pair of scissor handles in the trolley," said Garvey.

"Oh. Jesus Christ."

"Yeah. I'm guessing they were there for...Hell. Who knows. I think I saw a ball of yarn in there, maybe someone was knitting on the train. I don't think the scissors were brought there by the murderer, though."

Gibson took what was left of Mrs. Sanna and wheeled her back into her dark little cupboard. "Scissors are usually not the weapon of choice for the prepared assassin, no."

"Ignoring all the things I can't explain, this feels like a crime of passion," said Garvey thoughtfully. "Whoever went in there was irrational as hell. Just grabbing things and going nuts. Busted in with a garbage can and started killing people with a weapon found on the scene."

"But how could they have done that on a moving trolley?" said Gibson.

Garvey turned the blades over on his palms. He felt the notches in them and wondered whose bones the splinters had found a home in. He thought about who had held them before and what they had done and tried not to imagine the possibility that someone had assaulted and murdered an entire carful of people single-handedly, and in only a handful of minutes to boot.

"I don't know," said Garvey. He put the scissors down. Then he wiped his hands and thanked Gibson and left.

Christmas in Evesden came and went, though it was more somber than ever before. The Christmas Eve Parade was paltry in comparison to the previous ones, and only a handful of people turned out to watch it trundle along Michigan Avenue. The St. Nick they'd hired to ride the sleigh waved halfheartedly at the few children present, who were skinny things with sunken eyes. They solemnly watched him go by and did not wave back. When the parade finally came to a halt at St. Michael's it was said St. Nick climbed down from his ride, drank deeply from a bottle he'd hidden in his red coat, cursed the parade and everyone in it, and stormed off.

Neither Samantha nor Garvey celebrated in any significant way. Samantha tried to attend Midnight Mass at the church down her street, which she felt slightly guilty about since she was in no way Catholic, but it turned into a moot point when she spent too much time at the office on Christmas eve and couldn't bear to enter the church late. Garvey made one of his rare jaunts to see his family out in the country, and he spent his brief holiday awkwardly dancing around his ex-wife, who made it clear that his presence wasn't necessary, and his two young girls, both of whom he barely saw these days. He felt very much like an intruder in their home, as he had in the waning days of his marriage when his work had begun eating up every hour; their holiday was their own, separate from him, and he was only an observer. On Christmas day he sat on his ex-wife's porch and watched the sun set on the chilly countryside, and he thought about the bodies waiting for him back in the city, and what would happen to his career if they went unfiled, and also, very briefly, about the pretty girl Hayes had brought to the trolley station.

Hayes did not realize it was Christmas until after the day had passed, though he did vaguely wonder what all the candles were about.

Then just before New Year's McNaughton and Evesden received yet another blow, just when they needed it least. It did not fall in the city, however, but far up the coastline, just off the shores of the Alaskan town of Ketchikan. It came on a dark but clear night, with the stars very visible early on in the evening, but soon a few residents of the town noticed something different about one of them.

One of the stars was red, it seemed. And it also seemed to be growing.

As word spread, people were drawn out of their homes to gather and watch as the red star grew until it flared bright and arced across the night sky, never losing its deep red hue. It sailed down to the sea, and though some *ooh*ed and *aah*ed, many were disturbed by its sanguine color. It seemed a baleful sight to them, but they could not say why. One local, a photography enthusiast, managed to capture a magnificent shot of the star's descent, and when the photo was developed it seemed to show that the star was splitting the sky in half.

Some reckoned that the falling star had landed not far off the coast, and a handful of fishermen decided to take their boats to investigate. It was not hard to find the place that it'd hit, as a thick column of steam was still rising less than a half-hour afterward, but to their surprise the fishermen found that the star had not sunk, as had been expected, but was floating. It was obviously still incredibly hot, as water boiled and steamed around it, and they had to wait some time before they could approach it.

When they did it soon became apparent that it was not a star at all, but some sort of vessel. It resembled a fat, silver-white tack, and though it had melted in several places they could still see where three engines were attached to its back. It also seemed somewhat incomplete, as though it had disassembled itself as it fell. As the fishermen marveled at this strange thing floating in the waves, another ship began to approach on the horizon, this one no fishing craft but a much larger cruiser of some sort. It began signaling to them to leave the site and return home, but before they paid any attention to it the thing in the water turned over to reveal an insignia on the side—a thick, imperial M.

By the time the cruiser had pulled up to confiscate the device, several fishermen had already returned to the city to report what they'd seen.

When the photograph hit the papers and word got out that this craft was man-made, and somehow made by McNaughton, the country was swept up in surprise and outrage. What was it, they demanded. Where had it come from, and why had it fallen? Was it an accident? Was there someone in it? And why had the government not been notified? McNaughton's delay in addressing the press cost it dearly, and when it finally did answer it did not satisfy much. It was, the company said, a new airship of a sort, but this one was meant to sail higher than any other, and then boost itself up and pierce the outer limits of the atmosphere. McNaughton had launched the unmanned prototype from a station in the north of Alaska, and had not intended for it to fall so far south, or indeed to fall at all. According to their research, said the engineers, sounding more nervous with every minute, if it went high enough then it would simply float, and never come back down. Obviously, they had miscalculated somewhere.

The public was shocked, and the governments of both America and Canada were furious. How could they risk dropping airships onto civilians' heads? And for what, simply to see if it was possible to send an airship as high as it could go? The Canadian government was especially angry, saying that the United States had best learn to curb its alpha pup, and most of America agreed. It was a preposterous idea in the first place. How could McNaughton ever have thought it could work?

This time the McNaughton response was immediate. They *knew* it could work, the company said coldly. It was just a matter of adjustment. When the authorities asked for some evidence to support this, the McNaughton spokesmen recited the usual litany of private entrepreneurial rights protecting the company's research, and everyone threw up their hands in frustration. Indictments were drawn up, yet few expected them to get anywhere soon.

In Evesden the news was received with deep dismay. In the wake of the murders the city could hardly bear the disapproval resulting from the Red Star Scandal, as the press—somewhat enthusiastically—had labeled it. Everyone was overtaken with superstitious dread, interpreting the falling star as somehow connected with the eclipse that had happened earlier in the year, and it was said that this did not augur well for the city at all. Soon an almost medieval gloom spread throughout the streets, and each day people shook their heads as though surprised that the sun had chosen to rise at all.

Hayes, who had been dimly aware of the experiment (and the stress between the many internal factions both for and against it), was perhaps one of the few people in McNaughton who understood how this would seem in the wake of the murders. He sensed immediately that the city would feel that the sky was falling; that McNaughton had somehow pushed the limits, and the world would soon cave in; that the technological foundation upon which it had built the city was unsteady, and would soon crumble; and that the Age of Wonders that the company had ushered in across the globe was failing, and perhaps the threat of war that had come not so long ago had never really left. Maybe this, the city would say, was the end. After the union murders, it could only be more fuel on the fire.

But Hayes did not mention any of this to Brightly before he and a few other Security chiefs went north to assist. He simply sat and smoked and watched the northern skyline for a few minutes on New Year's eve, the sun slowly disappearing behind the Kulahee Bridge and the staggered columns of Construct, and then, alone, returned to work.

And in the morning when the sun dawned 1920 dawned with it, an inauspicious birth for a dreaded year.

CHAPTER FIFTEEN

"Let's do something in the Southern District today," Hayes said one morning as he sat in Samantha's office, draped across one of her chairs.

"What?" she said.

"Southern District. Let's do something there. Some interview."

"We have our interviews laid out for us," she said. "Preplanned."

"Oh, I know. But let's find some excuse to go out there and babble. I'm sure there's got to be one."

"Why?"

Hayes did not answer. His face was hidden below the lapel of his coat and he might have been sleeping again.

They went to the Southern on the tenuous lead that one interview subject, Ramirez, who had been out previously due to the recent death of his father, was now available. But Ramirez knew nothing and was confused as to why they had even chosen to speak with him. His father had died before the trolley murders and he had been away in California for the funeral when they took place. Hayes nodded and agreed and after two hours of it they went to lunch. An hour later Samantha and Ramirez returned to continue their discussion, but Hayes instead chose to walk the three blocks down and across to the Tramline production facility.

Who am I today, he wondered to himself as he crossed the railroad lots and the small service roads. He reached into his pocket and took out six identification cards, each with different names, different titles, different access codes for whatever machine. He found the one for Andrew Staunton and tucked it into his front vest pocket and walked up to the loading dock. Men in greasy jumpers were milling about, backing up trucks and shifting cargo. They looked up and frowned at this little suit who was walking toward them with some official-looking papers in hand. They called to the foreman and he tore his eyes away from his clipboard and advanced on Hayes. Hayes held up his identification like a shield and shouted, "Staunton, Personnel section. Here to see Mr. Martin Andersson."

"Andersson?" repeated the foreman, straining to make his voice heard over the clatter. "No Andersson on the dock."

"Believe Mr. Andersson works on the spot line."

"Spot line? Oh, all right then. You're nowhere close." He peered closer at Mr. Staunton's identification and came away impressed. "That's way inside and down. Mess up your clothes, you know."

"That's fine."

"I'll try and grab Collier, that's the lower deck foreman. He'll be able to get Andersson. Come on." He walked over to the cement wall and slapped a button. A horn sounded somewhere and the iron mouth of the loading dock began to draw back. The facility, like all McNaughton sites, was shaped like a bunker. At the ground level it was a huge cement loading dock, with an enormous upper warehouse facility and manufacturing decks below and foundry lines sunk down in the far back. Hayes rarely visited the factories, but he'd handled plans and schematics plenty of times. He'd bought a few of them off the odd cunning bastard and sold others with significant structural integrity problems designed in. But he never remembered the size and scale and scope of the things.

Inside it was a vast cavern with a roof and walls so far back light could not touch them. Strings of chains and hooks looped down over tracks that wound off through the stations, each one designated by a different-colored light standing on poles at the intersections. Piping sprouted from the cement floor to meet above the loads and trusses, and some dripped scalding water and others dripped a substance that resembled water but was freezing and smoky. Hayes could just see the foundry's crucible in the far back, enormous and round, the molten metal within its black lip glowing a gleeful unnatural orange that turned the workers at its base into wicked, fiery sprites with black glass eyes.

The dock foreman found the lower deck foreman, presumably Mr. Collier. Mr. Collier listened to the dock foreman's shouts and grimaced in dismay and waved Hayes's identification forward. Hayes handed it up again and it was scrutinized once more and Collier was impressed like the others.

"Oh, all right," he said. "This way. You know, this guy meant it when he said you really shouldn't have dressed so well."

"I don't mind a spot of grease."

The foreman laughed and walked to a set of lockers set up against a scuffed cement wall. He reached in and pulled out a mottled brown jumper streaked with ash and reeking of sulfur and tossed it to Hayes. "Not grease," he said. "I just don't want to see your clothes catch fire on you."

Hayes awkwardly suited up and they both put on immense black goggles, and then they went to one grated stairway and began the descent into the bowels of the factory. Soon orange light filled the charred walls from some unseen source below. The passageway grew immensely hot and moist. Every pipe and hose and rivet glistened. Hayes felt as if they were not in some creation of men but instead in some living machine, wandering its fevered breast as it struggled to push air and metal through its passageways. As they descended a dozen workers staggered up the steps, their faces sooty and their heads half-hidden by the liquid-black lenses of the smelter's goggles. They watched Hayes and the foreman walk by with blank faces but Hayes was not sure they could make another kind.

They walked until they came to the elevator and then climbed aboard and went two flights down until they hit a rotunda. Immense gears squalled and churned around them and the entire rotunda swiveled until they were in a different sector of the facility entirely. They walked on.

Hayes watched as the machinery moved above them, shining with grease and screaming with fatigue in places. How many men had died to make this place, he wondered. This temple of industry, this hidden hall of production. When ancient peoples had knelt before the carven faces of their gods and imagined fabled crypts and castles their thoughts could not have touched what men had made here, hacked into the bones of the earth itself. Hayes watched as one Tramline carriage rolled past on a beltway, its structure fine and smooth like a dragonfly's skeleton, its half-built engine as delicate as the smallest clock. A goggled worker trundled along, the glassware receptors for the radios packed into a straw crate on his wagon, spindled glass like fine ice. He passed by them as though none of this mattered. Not Hayes or the foremen or the fragile wonders in his care.

They walked to the spot-welding line and Hayes could tell Andersson by his height. He held a long, sparkling welder in one hand, a sputtering magic wand. He knelt and set his solvent with the mindfulness of a man playing the cello, carefully placing his long, delicate instrument along the strings of the Tramline carriage, then drawing back slowly. The foreman waited until he was done and then waved down Andersson and his team. Andersson stood and frowned at the foreman until his eyes fell upon the little blond-haired, fair-skinned man who was clearly wearing goggles for the first time in his life. Then he laughed and opened his arms and cried, "Mr. Staunton! What are you doing here! What are you doing in such dangerous place as this!"

Hayes grinned and said something in Swedish. He wasn't sure where he had picked it up or what it meant but it made Andersson laugh all the harder.

They retired to a sailor's bar, full of tattooed men with thick black coats and raw faces. Andersson and Hayes spoke quietly over fish soup and black ale, and Andersson listened as Hayes gave him the news, describing how the very top was now paranoid of how they appeared to be murdering their own workers.

"Appeared," growled Andersson. "Appeared. Idiocy. Nonsense. They did not appear. They did. It was them. They killed those men. How, I do not know, but it was them."

"Why would they kill their own people?"

"Please, Andrew. Do not be telling me that you are such an idiot. I know you. You are a very clever man. You know that those men, the dead, they were the more violent sort. The more passionate sort."

"Sort of what? Of union man?"

"Of Tazzer. Yes. The accidents, yes?"

"Ah, yes," said Hayes, suddenly appearing to recall. "The accidents."

"Yes. Some say this is the right thing to do. To fight. To kill, if necessary. I do not know. Killing is always bad. It will only lead to trouble. But some say this is what we need to do. To send message," Andersson confided softly. "To bring attention."

"Some say this will rally the lower classes. That the deaths of their own will unite them."

"Who says this?"

"People. As they always do. Some say Tazz did it himself," Hayes said slyly. "Or a Tazz supporter."

"No!" Andersson said, shocked. "That is nonsense!"

Hayes shrugged. "You just have to pay attention to who's going to gain the most from this. It seems those men were causing trouble for

Tazz. Doing bad things in his name. This way he gets two things, he gets some bad business out of his way and he gets something to rally everyone around. And no one would ever suspect him. Has Tazz denied it?"

"Yes," said Andersson angrily.

"You saw him? Saw him deny it?"

"Well. No."

"You didn't see him?"

Andersson frowned into his beer mug. "Tazz has said nothing about the trolley murders."

"Really? Nothing?"

"Nothing," said Andersson.

"Not even anything about the Red Star?"

"He is not coming out anymore."

"What? Coming out of where?"

"Union men died, Andrew," Andersson said softly. "A lot of union men. There is danger, they say. He is in hiding."

"Hiding?"

"Yes. In some place. Safe place. Place where no one knows where he is except only a few. Only his most trusted men. And no one knows who they are. This has become a deadly secret game, Andrew," said Andersson, shaking his head. "Trust no one. That is the way it now goes for us down here, in the Southern."

"That's how it always goes, I think. Now, tell me, Martin," said Hayes, "where did he spend his time in the clink?"

"Clink?" said Andersson, confused.

"In jail. Tazz was in jail, correct?"

"Yes. After the docks protest."

"Where was that? Savron Hill?"

"I think so. Why?"

"Curiosity. That's all. Just curiosity."

"I see." Andersson looked away, then asked bashfully, "Andrew, would you mind if I ask you a question?"

"No."

"Even if it is a very silly question?"

"No. I don't mind at all."

"All right." He frowned as he considered his words and said, "Andrew, you are not a little man. Well, in some ways, yes, but in business ways, no. In the city, no, in the company, no. And all I hear is of McNaughton's magic. With its genius-men who think these things up. And I just wonder, eh—"

"Where McNaughton's secrets come from? Or what the big secret is?"

"Yes. Yes, that is what I am wondering."

Hayes smiled. He considered telling one of his more fun lies about secret scientists smuggled in from abroad. But he had developed a soft spot for the big man and decided to tell him the simple and boring truth, as far as he had it figured out, which he thought was pretty far.

"Well, internally they say it's marketing," said Hayes.

Andersson frowned. "Marketing?"

"Yes. Marketing. Like, the way you pitch something. The way you lie to someone else in the marketplace about what you're selling. They say it's not designs, not mechanics, no. The real secret to everything is the McNaughton approach to sales."

"It is this? Just a thing of sales? You believe that?"

"Well, they do," Hayes said with a smile. "You know what I believe?"

"You do not believe it's marketing?"

"No. I believe it's all a load of shit."

"Shit? What is shit?"

"Everything. The very idea of it. Horseshit. Poppycock. Tripe. I do think there were, oh, a half-dozen neat things Kulahee came up with long ago. And that was a good start for the business. And then McNaughton just said there were a hundred more things, but they were all secret, and you could buy them but never know where they came from. So, naturally, everyone wants to buy and invest in these wonders. But it's nothing special. It's just normal things developed by some well-paid men. That's what I think."

Andersson thought that over, frowning, and settled back in his chair, fingers twined together and resting on his belly.

"Why do you ask?" said Hayes.

"Oh, it is just something I have seen over the years," said Andersson. "Some of the more advanced devices... Some of them seem to have not been made for people at all."

"What? Then who? Elves? Imps? Bloody fairies?"

Andersson stared at him as his internal translator tried to make sense of that. "Oh, no," he said after a while. "Not like that. It is just that over the years, I have been promoted a few times, assigned manufacturing of some of the more specialized items. And many of those... Well, it seems like the designers spent a lot of time trying to figure out how to make them used for people. Like they just had to put in levers or consoles or, say, on the airships, walkways and cockpits and passenger cells and such. Like when they were first designed, they did not have people in mind at all. Maybe it is the way Kulahee first thought of them. But why would he design a thing that way? And if you are right, and it is not Kulahee at all but our own people, why are *they* doing it that way?"

Hayes was quiet as he considered this. "Then who were they made for, originally?" he asked.

Andersson just shrugged. The two men drank their black ale in silence for a bit. Then Andersson sat forward, leaning over the table. "Some of the men in Telecommunications," he said softly, "they say that some of the things they build, they talk to them."

"What?" said Hayes. "What talks? The machines?"

Andersson nodded dourly. "Yes. Talks to them." He tapped his temple. "In their heads. Whispers to them."

"Well... What are they saying?"

"They cannot tell. They only get the feeling that they are talking. The machines want something from them, they guess. But maybe they are crazy. Who can say?"

Hayes thought quickly. "These machines... Do they have little crystals? Are they like lamps, that light up blue? Some big, some little?"

"Lamps?" said Andersson, confused. "No, they did not say they were lamps."

"Are you sure? No little lights, nothing like that at all?"

"No, I've never heard of that. They just said the machines whisper to them, if they spend enough time around them." He drained off the last of his beer. "Perhaps you are right, though," he said. "Perhaps it is just marketing."

"Maybe so," said Hayes, disturbed, and then he thanked the big Swede for his insight and paid and left.

When he returned to the Southern Office the interview room was empty except for a single note on the table that said, YOU COULD HAVE TOLD ME. Hayes smiled and put it in his pocket and found a semi-decent restaurant with a phone station. He put a call through to Garvey and left a message with the number for the station. Then he ordered a drink and downed it and wadded up his coat and used it as a pillow and slept in the booth. A waiter came and asked him to kindly clear the hell out and Hayes shoved a ten-dollar bill into his hand and told him to bring him a sandwich and another drink. As he ate the phone rang and Garvey answered, his voice faint and exhausted.

"Listen, I have a favor to ask you," Hayes said.

"Oh, boy."

"Mickey Tazz has gone underground."

"What?"

"Tazz has gone underground. After the murders."

There was a pause. "How'd you find that out?"

"I know a few people."

"Huh. Where'd he run to?"

"No idea. Sort of the point, really. I don't like it, though. This would be a rallying point, wouldn't you say? Everyone else is seeing McNaughton's hand in it, why isn't Tazz crying it in the streets?"

"For God's sake, Hayes, I don't know anything about this Tazz guy," said Garvey.

"I know. But I do, a little. And I'd like to know more. You still have that friend up in Savron?"

"You mean the guard? Weigel?"

"Yeah. Yes, I mean Weigel. He still there?"

"I think so."

"Check out Tazz's record there for me. I understand that was where he was penned up. Did you know that?"

"No. No, I didn't. You got that from the guys you interviewed?"

"That's the rumor," said Hayes. He grinned in the booth and tossed his sandwich away. "Garv, my boy, I'm going to give you a positive payload. I'm going to give you the gold. I'll give you everything I have on Tazz, and then I'm going to go down and identify your canal John Doe for you."

"What?" said Garvey. Hayes could hear him sitting up on the other end. "What the hell are you talking about?"

"I don't have anything certain. Not right now. I just know some people who may recognize his face, I think. I'll talk to Samantha tomorrow and have her package up what I have on Tazz and ship it to you. Then we'll go and see what we can find about your tattooed John Doe."

There was a pause. "Does Samantha know she's doing this?"

"Not yet."

"Does Evans or Brightly?"

"No. I don't plan for them to, either. Ever since the Red Star the oversight for our investigation's been slackening, so I don't think it'll be noticed."

"Jesus. Why the hell are you doing this, then?" said Garvey.

Hayes thought for a moment, then said, "Don't know. Talk to you later, Garv," and he hung up.

CHAPTER SIXTEEN

When Samantha returned home that night she was surprised to find Garvey leaning up against the wall outside her apartment building, reading the paper. When she approached he looked up, smiled, and said, "I'm glad you're here. They tend to hustle a guy along if he's wearing a suit this cheap in this neighborhood."

"Even if he's a policeman?" she asked.

"Especially if he's a policeman."

"What would a policeman be doing out here, anyway?"

"This particular policeman just wanted to check in on you. See what's up."

"With Mr. Hayes? Well. Mr. Hayes was surprisingly difficult today."

"Yeah," said Garvey slowly. He pushed his hat back and scratched his head. "That was mainly what I wanted to talk to you about, Miss Fairbanks. He's probably going to make tomorrow difficult for you, too."

"What makes you say that?"

Garvey summarized what Hayes had told him on the phone, trying to fill in for the leaps of logic Hayes tended to make. Samantha was silent for a good while as they stood outside her building.

"Oh, yes. The McClintock interview," she said softly.

"What?"

"Mr. McClintock was the first man we interviewed about the sabotage cases. He was the one who listed most of the men in the Bridgedale trolley. Hayes chummed up with him and they talked about women and friends and family. He gave us a dozen names, at least. Friends, family. All of them the men who've been murdered. They all seemed to run in the same circles. If the man in the canal is connected with the Bridgedale murders, I suppose it's likely one of the people McClintock listed knows him. Well. Knew him. We might even have his name already, we just don't know it's him."

"And I was never sent any of that? Any of that information?"

"I believe Mr. Hayes originally sent you a few files..."

Garvey shrugged. "It wasn't much. Just enough to start a case. To let me know something was going on."

"Yes. We've been told to keep our distance from the police. There's too much implication there, they say, though they've hardly been paying any attention since what happened in Alaska. Besides, I think it may have just slipped our minds in the recent chaos."

"Beautiful," said Garvey.

"Is it that important? One murder in the wake of so many?"

Garvey was silent for a while. Then he said, "Yes. The man in the canal, I think he's a real victim. I smelled it on him when I first saw him."

"A real victim? How do you mean?"

"A lot of the bodies we pick up didn't die innocent. They died doing something they shouldn't have. Robbing a store, or making tar shipments. But others die minding their own business. For no damn reason at all. Those are the real victims."

"I see," said Samantha quietly.

"Yeah. And he had a kid."

"Did he?"

"Yes. I'd like to find out what happened to him. What he did when his dad didn't come home one day."

"Oh," she said, and thought. "Well... If you can get me a sketch or a picture of the man you found in the canal, I'll try and see if I can help Hayes in whatever silliness he's going to try."

"I'll make sure to get you that," said Garvey. He pinched the bridge of his nose and shook his head. Then he took a deep breath. "You know what, I don't even want to talk about the case anymore. Nothing about the union, nothing about Hayes."

"What do you want to talk about, then?"

"I don't know. You hungry, Miss Fairbanks? Want to grab something to eat around here?"

"Like what?"

"Anything. I never eat around here. I'm willing to go anywhere about now." He smiled lopsidedly at her. It was like a crack in his face, breaking through all the fatigue and the frustration to the rangy, wiseacre boy hiding behind. Samantha found herself smiling along with him in spite of herself.

"All right," she said.

He took her to the northern end of Newton, where the apartment buildings dwindled and the clubs and band halls began to sprawl across the shore. She had passed through that part of her neighborhood before and heard the bands playing from somewhere nearby, but she had never tried to attend any of the shows. The customers and crowds of Newton had seemed forbidding and impenetrable then, the women all glamorous and preening, the men regal in their top hats and tails. Yet now they all parted before Garvey, who plodded through their ranks without a care in the world, amiably discussing weather or baseball or the offenses of his coworkers as Samantha struggled to keep by his side. He walked as though they were alone on the street. Samantha felt a thrill of guilty pleasure each time they broke through a line for a show and attracted countless foul looks.

At one corner Garvey glanced at her with a crafty look in his eyes, and mentioned that he knew a place nearby. He then led her to a club called Mirabelle's, a thoroughly modern affair with alabaster pillars and needle-thin spotlights that flashed up through the evening air. It sported the longest line of any club Samantha had yet seen, but Garvey passed them by and casually walked up to the maître d', who first gave them a sour glance but then blinked in surprise as he looked again. As Garvey strode forward the maître d' smiled in recognition and reached out to shake his hand, and he greeted them both as old friends, enthusiastically asking how Detective Garvey was these days, and where he'd found this beautiful girl to grace them all with her presence. Samantha blushed hugely at that. The maître d' hustled them inside and the other patrons waiting in line shouted their objections, but he and Garvey seemed totally unaware of it.

Samantha almost gasped as they were led in. The interior of the club was almost entirely done in white—white marble floors and walls, white pillars, and a wooden center stage painted a gleaming white. It seemed wintry and fragile and impossibly beautiful, as though the arches and pillars might melt at any moment and it would all collapse. Tables were crowded around the center stage, and waiters in white dress coats threaded through the narrow lanes, delivering plates and drinks with demure smiles as though they were used to treating customers far more reputable than these, but were kind enough to bear the ignominy without mention. Behind the corner of the stage a full brass band played an unobtrusive jazz number while a sharp man in a three-piece suit stood beside them, sucking on a cigar and watching the crowds. When Garvey walked in a light went on in the man's eyes, and he smiled slightly and pointed at Garvey and then to one of the choice corner tables, where they were immediately ushered to sit.

"*This* is a place you know?" asked Samantha in awe once they were seated.

"Sure," said Garvey. "They know me here."

"I can see that. How on Earth did you ever manage this?"

He shrugged and smiled mysteriously. "I did a favor once or twice."

"A favor?"

"Yeah. The owner's daughter was in trouble once. Nothing serious, but it could've been. I kept it quiet and sorted it out." He nodded at the man with the cigar, who just barely nodded back. "They've been kind to me ever since. I come here every couple of months or so. What do you think?"

"I must admit, I'm shocked by it. For a moment I thought you were going to threaten them with your gun to get us in."

He smiled. "No. I don't have it on me, anyway."

"You don't? Why not?"

"I forgot it," he said. "It happens all the time, actually. Today was one of those times."

"I thought all policemen carried their trusty revolvers with them."

"Not murder police. We don't do the shooting. We just clean it up. The gun has nothing to do with the job."

They ordered martinis and calamari, and laughed and spoke quietly as the band played. Samantha was astonished to learn that Garvey's previous job had been as a librarian, but the more he talked about police work the more that seemed perfectly apt, as it seemed to be nothing but filing and papers. She soon noticed he had a curious way of conversation, however—where before he'd seemed a very quiet man, now he was so enthusiastically candid about his life that Samantha couldn't help but volunteer some of her own history, telling him things she'd almost never tell any other acquaintance. It was an almost invasive sort of sympathy, this big, lanky boy of a man bounding forward to make himself utterly vulnerable at your feet. You soon found you were giving yourself up to him, telling him everything you ever thought he'd want to hear, just to match how exposed he'd made himself. She wondered if it was a tactic and if he handled his suspects the same way, or if it was just his nature. She figured it probably was a bit of both, and then she couldn't help but compare him to Hayes, who was so evasive, forever changing names and accents and stories until you didn't know what was sitting on the other side of the table from you.

At ten o'clock the club host announced that the show would soon be starting, and Garvey excused himself and slipped off to the restroom. Samantha drank the rest of her martini, and soon the lighting in the club changed, the tables growing dimmer while the spots on the stage grew bright. As the patrons began standing Samantha followed suit, and found herself with one of the best views. The band started playing, picking up a soft, waltzy tune, and then there was a whir overhead. She looked up and then laughed in surprise as the ceiling above the stage seemed to be snowing, the flakes drifting down from some machinery hidden above. She caught a few and found they were real ice that melted on her fingertips. Soon the stage was almost hidden by a veil of soft white snow, yet through some cunning nature of the machinery it snowed in bursts that lined up with the beat of the song. Then two dancers came swooping out from the side of the stage, and the crowd gasped in surprise. One was a man in a black-and-white tuxedo with tails, the other was a long, slender-limbed woman in a glittering white dress that seemed to be made of snow as well. Once they came to the center of the stage, they began to dance and sing together.

Later Samantha never could recall what the song was about. It felt as if it was partially in French, with only snatches of meaning scattered throughout the words. But the words were a mere excuse for the performance. The dancers' clothing was adapted so that at times it blended in with the flakes of ice, and as they swung one another in and out of the light they would flash bright and then seem to vanish, flitting across the stage in each other's arms. It was powerfully mesmerizing, these faint white-and-black figures slipping among the bursts of the falling snow. She had never seen anything like it. She doubted if it could have been done anywhere else in the world.

It was never clear when the dance was done. Between the lighting and the camouflaged outfits, it was difficult to tell if the dancers were really there or not. But then the song came to an end, and everyone suddenly remembered themselves and started clapping furiously.

"It's a seasonal thing," said Garvey's voice over her shoulder.

She turned and saw him standing beside her, watching the snow end. "Pardon?" she said.

"It's a seasonal thing. They have different shows for winter, summer, spring. The fall one's my favorite, they do some interesting stuff with leaves. But we missed that."

"Unless we stick around for a while," she said.

"Well, there's that."

She looked back at him again, and noticed there was something different about him now. He carried the faint smell of violets and lavender about him, and it looked like his hair had been carefully combed. Although she could have been mistaken, she felt sure he'd paid the bathroom attendants to tidy him up as best they could. She was suddenly reminded of a boy headed off to church, frantically trying to arrange himself. She smiled at him and laughed, then clapped one hand over her mouth to stifle it.

"What?" he said, and nervously stroked one side of his hair.

"Nothing," she said, still fighting a smile. "I simply enjoyed the show, that's all." She looked back up at the machinery hidden in the ceiling. "How did they produce the snow?"

"You tell me," said Garvey. "You work for the people who made it."

"Ah," she said. "Aren't we popular."

"Something like that," he said. "Say, you still hungry?"

"Why? Do you know another place?"

He smiled that wide grin of his again. "I know a lot of places."

This time they went down, descending through a trolley tunnel outside and then taking a hard right away from the lines, toward the middle of Newton. The tunnels themselves seemed almost deserted, as almost all had been since the murders.

"Is this safe?" she asked, but Garvey only shrugged.

As they walked through the tunnels she heard the sound of music and gabbling, and then they emerged into what looked like the heart of an Oriental market of some kind. Little wooden booths and tables were set up against the walls, and paper lanterns hung from the piping overhead. There was hardly any room to move, and considering that the market had to be emptier than usual, like most of the underground, she could hardly imagine it during peak hours.

Since there were so few visitors the vendors and the shopkeepers descended upon them immediately and began hounding them for their custom. She saw that though most booths had an Eastern look about them, more than a few of the vendors were as white as she. Garvey took out his wallet to pay, fumbling with his badge as he did so, and as soon as the light found the glint of his shield the vendors all calmed somewhat, and some disappeared entirely. He sneaked Samantha a sly grin, and then purchased some sweet, crackly honey cakes and strange, spiced meats on wooden skewers, and paper cups of soup with vegetables and fruits of many colors. They drank spiced wine as they walked through the subterranean marketplace, Garvey ducking through the lanterns as they moved, and he showed her many strange goods and services that could only be found here, or possibly at the shore, he said.

She nodded, believing him entirely. She felt suddenly that Garvey knew the city better than any other living soul, and though to her it offered only lonely, scarred alleyways and skies of gray smoke, for Garvey it behaved differently. He could sweep aside all the loneliness and the struggle and find gems and wonders hidden among its many crooks and niches. He knew its subtle joys and eccentricities as one would know an old, wayward friend. And as he showed her each oddity, rich or poor, tasteful or gaudy, she saw in his eyes that he truly loved this place, this anomalous city on the edge of the world, a hodgepodge of towns and technologies and peoples that should not ever be.

They ascended to find the streets had emptied of cars and a light rain was falling. One by one the street lamps flickered on with an angelic hum, filling the streets with pearly light.

"Sometimes I think this city has a voice," said Garvey as they walked.

"What does it say?" she asked.

Garvey thought for a long while as they walked back to her apartment. He finally said, "That it's dying."

"Dying?"

He nodded.

Samantha thought about this. It seemed an impossible notion after he'd shown her so many colorful veins in the city, still alive and thriving. "Dying of what?" she asked.

"Of itself. Under its own weight. And when it's done, more than Evesden will hurt."

"How do you mean?"

He kicked at a pebble in the gutter. "You remember what almost happened in Europe?"

"Yes, of course."

"Yeah. All those bastards out there are just waiting to get at each other's throats. The only thing that keeps them from doing it is McNaughton, because the second a shot gets fired, they turn off the tap. No more airships, no more telephones. It'd be bad for commerce. I don't like your company, Miss Fairbanks, but they've made a peace, of a very tense and bastardly sort."

"You can call me Samantha. And I'm aware of the agreement that was laid down after the Crisis."

"Yeah. I should have figured that. I'm just venting. Samantha," he added.

"I know. What do you think we can do?" she asked.

He sniffed, thinking. "We just hope we catch this goddamn killer and end this union nonsense in the cleanest way possible, I guess. It wouldn't be a victory. And I don't know if it'd be easy to live with.

McNaughton would just keep doing what they're doing. But it'd keep the blood to a minimum. I hope."

They came to her apartment and the porter tipped his hat to her. She waved back.

"What time is it?" asked Garvey, searching for his watch.

"It's half past eight."

"Hum. Well. Thanks for the dinner."

"But you paid," she said.

"I can still thank you, can't I?"

"I suppose. For going to a Newton restaurant?"

"For having an excuse. Yeah."

She nodded. "Have you ever seen a Newton apartment?"

Garvey stared at her, dumbstruck. Then he quickly recovered and said, "No. Never have."

"Would you like to?"

He stepped back and looked up the face of the apartment building. "It's awful tall."

"It's a long way up. But it goes by fast."

They took the elevator up and she led him to her apartment. It did not yet feel like home to her, but it was a warm, dark place, with honey walls and a carpet a deep shade of red. Yet everything was covered in papers, every surface stacked with khaki reports and files, reams of parchment and miles of writing. She felt she should have cared about this, and wanted to clean up, but that urge was strangely absent.

"You take your work home, huh?" Garvey asked.

"I do."

She walked over to a cupboard, where she pulled out a bottle of port and poured two glasses without asking. He walked to the balcony and looked out at the buildings across, their faces spectral and luminescent in the night.

"You know, some people would have a thing or two to say about a divorced man being unaccompanied in a woman's apartment," he said.

"You're divorced?" she asked.

"Oh," he said, sheepish. "Yeah. Yeah, I am."

"I didn't know that."

He nodded.

"People would probably have a lot more to say about you being divorced," she said, bringing him a glass.

"Yeah. They probably would."

"But this is the twentieth century, and this is the city of the future, isn't it?" She sat beside where he stood and crossed her legs. As she did her dress rode up, revealing most of her calf, and the tips of her toes brushed the back of Garvey's knees.

"I guess." Suddenly he seemed to falter, and he looked at the glass in his hands, then up at her. "Think this is a good idea?"

"What is?" she asked.

He didn't say anything. Just stood there handling the little glass of wine.

"Oh," she said. She blinked and sat up. "I...I suppose I didn't really think about it."

"This could fuck a whole lot of stuff up."

She sighed and put down her glass. "It could, couldn't it."

"Yeah."

They were quiet for a long while, their drinks untouched. Then Garvey said, "It's snowing."

They rose and went to the balcony. Small white flakes were spinning down through the air to the street. It looked nothing like the show at the club. Currents formed between the buildings and they could see where the air turned into waves and horns and spheres and slants. As if the atmosphere itself were made of clockwork, telling time or some glyphic truth to only those who would look up and watch. Or perhaps the message was meant for something else. To something external. Invisible and waiting.

"Look," said Samantha, and pointed up to the tops of the buildings. They could just make out the conduits sitting on the edge of the building crowns, fat and black and round, like strange rooftop fruit. Steam poured out of the cracks in their housing in thin strings that whipped wildly in the flurries.

"They say they glow blue when a storm comes near," said Samantha.

"I've heard that. It's not true."

"No?"

"No. But if it's a really bad storm they will dance and wriggle. And get fucking hot."

They watched as a small airship trundled down out of the sky and made a slow pass of the rooftops. A spotlight stabbed down and illuminated the conduits for a moment before blinking out. The little ship had to fight the wind and they watched as it nosed along the rooftops, furiously trying to make its way, like a beetle caught in the ocean tide.

"Checking the conduits," he said. "This must be the first part of a pretty bad one, then."

"It must be."

"I suppose I should go."

"I suppose so."

He moved away and said, "I had fun tonight."

"I did, too."

"Can I see you again?"

She looked at him. "I thought it wasn't smart."

He shrugged. His face was painfully motionless.

"I suppose it couldn't hurt, could it," she said.

"No," he said. They went to the front door and she let him out and he bade her goodbye and went back down to his car. She watched from the balcony as he crossed the street. He stopped before the car door, as though struck by a thought, and she wished he would look up at her. But he did not, and climbed into his car, and drove away.

CHAPTER SEVENTEEN

The small storm lessened as the dawn came, and with the last few flakes Hayes rode the elevator up to Samantha's office. He had expected some smart remark or a chilly silence when he arrived, but instead he found her patiently waiting for him with a sketch of the dead man and, more impressively, the last known address of Peggy Kennedy, the girlfriend of Naylor that McClintock had rhapsodized over.

"She's the most likely connection to the man in the canal, if there is one," she explained. "She was romantically involved with Frank Naylor, who seemed to be the de facto leader of their little group, and she was practically one of the boys. She saw everyone and spoke to everyone. In a social setting, of course. I doubt if she was involved in anything more unsavory than grousing about the company from time to time. And she's apparently a very pretty girl," Samantha said. She sniffed. "She was very... popular."

"Very good. But how are you ahead of me?" he asked as she stood.

"Never mind that," she said irritably. "Do you want to go or don't you?"

"Well. Sure?"

They took a trolley down to the edge of the Shanties and then caught a cab the rest of the way in to Peggy's apartment. The people there told them Peggy had moved out weeks ago and was now staying with a Turkish jewelry salesman, rumored to be a ferocious loan shark. They found the man's shop not far away. It was run-down and full of cheap baubles and the stench of soggy tobacco. Peggy was tending the counter, and Hayes sent Samantha out while he pretended to browse.

He found Peggy was indeed a very pretty thing, and she knew it, flashing her eyes at him as she tried to pitch him some cheap paste jewelry. She was far less willing to help with the missing man, so Hayes presented himself as an affiliate of a well-known religious charity, the Saint Catherine's Foundation for Deprived Children. Concerned about the man's child, he told her smoothly. The boy had been by their establishments several nights in a row and had left a fake name, Hayes said. For some reason the boy had listed Mr. Naylor as a contact, but he was not to be found and they were redirected to her. They had managed to get a rough sketch of the father, and presumably the boy would be with him.

Peggy looked at the sketch of the dead man sadly. "What was he deprived of?"

"Sorry?" said Hayes.

"You're the... the Foundation for Deprived Children?"

"Oh. Oh, yes. Deprived of social and maternal figures. That's why most of them come. For the community. For the friends."

"I see."

"Did you or Mr. Naylor know the boy or his father?"

"Frank's dead," she told him.

"I'm sorry?" said Hayes.

"Frank's dead," she said again, then realized his confusion. "Oh, no. No, no, no, not the boy or the father. Frank. Frank Naylor. You know the papers? That thing in the paper?"

"Yes?" He affected surprise. "Oh, my goodness, you mean..."

She nodded but did not say anything or take her eyes off the sketch. "The father's name was John. John Skiller. The boy's name is Jack. I remember that."

He asked her if she knew the boy's address. She told him that once when Frank was roaring drunk they had swung by a tenement where Skiller lived. Skiller had been livid to see Frank so wild and coming into his home in the middle of the night with his boy there. Tossed them out cold. The place wasn't much to speak of anyways, she said, and certainly didn't warrant such pride. She gave him the directions and he thanked her and left.

Samantha was down the street having a cup of thin coffee. He grinned at her and said, "We have a name. A name and an address. Garvey will be delighted, don't you think?"

"Yes," she said simply, and stood up and made to go.

"You all right?" he asked.

"Yes."

"You sure?"

She nodded but said no more. They went back out on the street and headed off to the address.

Skiller. Mr. John Skiller, thought Hayes as they walked. Strangely dead long before his friends. His death was no less grisly than theirs, but perhaps the same man or woman who had killed him had also killed everyone in the Bridgedale trolley. But how or why was beyond him.

Garvey had once said that most crimes were never solved by the why. Ask a cop why someone killed another person and he'll probably tell you that he doesn't give a damn, and he'll mean it. And he'll be right. You don't find them by the why, because anyone can kill any person for any reason. One of the defects of the species. But another defect of the species is good old-fashioned stupidity, and that means you can almost always catch them by the how. How they went in, what they used to kill with, how they got it and where it went, and who they talked to and what they did afterward. You can almost always catch them by that. This is a finite world of a limited amount of matter, Garvey would always say, and on their way to and from a murder they probably fucked up plenty of shit.

Hayes tended to agree. But he found it to be a very boring way of looking at the world. Garvey was forever inspecting every little item and every line of dialogue, trying to arrange the murder in his mind. Hayes found people more interesting, and especially getting them to tell him what he wanted to know. Investigation was as much a con game as it was a science. You lied and wheedled and smiled until finally people found themselves giving you the truth bit by bit, against every ounce of their better judgment.

"Is that it up ahead?" asked Samantha.

Hayes peered up the street. He saw a soaking wreck of a building, four stories tall with broken windows dotting every floor and uneven streams of smoke pouring out of the roof. Men in stained shirtsleeves loitered on the front walk and they eyeballed Hayes and Samantha as they approached.

"Hey, Princeling!" called someone across the street. "Hey! Hey, it's Princeling!" They laughed.

"Who's Princeling?" said Samantha.

"I have no idea," Hayes said calmly.

They came to the front door of the tenements. Inside children cried and moaned by the dozens. The wallpaper drooped down around them like petals of a dying flower, its folds stained coffee-brown by the leaky ceiling. Hayes and Samantha stepped around the dripping spots and walked up the stairs to the second floor. Some doors to the rooms were open, others were missing entirely. One couple argued in the hall in some garbled patois, throwing their hands up in the air and sometimes making to strike one another, but never doing so. Hayes smelled shit somewhere, not the scent of rot or stagnation but genuine human shit.

They walked to the next flight of stairs. As they passed by the rooms the people within took no notice. Inside one room a man lay asleep on a pile of newspapers and dishrags, cigarette butts trailing across his chest like droppings. In another a dog watched them from the shadows of a broken kitchen cabinet and whined piteously but did not emerge. And in another room five children lived in unadultered squalor, none of them older than six, their mouths toothless and their eyes bright and their clothes stained with shit and sick. In the corner were three wooden buckets full of excrement, and above them a forest of flies twitched and shuddered. One child pounded on a back door, calling for someone. Her head was covered in flies, blue-black backsides crawling around her ears. She brushed them away absentmindedly as though they were barely there.

"My God," whispered Samantha. "My God, Hayes, they're just children."

"Come on," he said gently. "Come on. Up the stairs we go."

"No, we... we can't leave them here. There's got to be something we can do. Someone we can call. An orphanage. Something."

"Yes."

Samantha shook her head. "We have to call them, Mr. Hayes. Have them come and take care of this."

"Yes," he said, his voice still gentle and soothing. "Yes, we will. Of course we will. Now come." Then he padded up the stairs. He waited at the top and watched as Samantha stared into the room. He needed no special talent to understand she was trying to reconcile her life in Newton with a place such as this. How could people live this way with machines performing marvels only miles away? But as he watched a queer sense of unease grew in him. It had been a long time since he'd ever looked at anything as sadly as Samantha did now. He could not remember the last time he'd matched her sorrow, or her horror. He often forgot how young she was. She had to be several years shy of thirty, he remembered, and as he did he felt terribly old. Eventually she turned and made her way up the stairs, shoving tears away from her eyes as she did.

"Are you ready?" he said. "It's possible it may get worse."

She shook her head, thought, then nodded.

"All right."

Near the top of the building cold drafts ran through the rooms in invisible rivulets and they clutched their coats about them. Hayes searched among the room numbers and found Skiller's at the end. He knocked, waited, knocked again, then tried the knob. It was unlocked and he pushed the door open a crack.

"What are you doing? You can't just walk in!" Samantha whispered to him.

"Keep a lookout," he said.

"What? I can't—"

"Keep a lookout. I don't think anyone will notice or care, but keep a lookout."

She stood down the hall from him, clutching her hands and fretting. He opened the door, motioned for her to stay there, and walked in.

The room was not like the rest of the tenement. Although shabby, it was well kept, with clean floors and scrubbed walls. A hole in the glass of the far window was carefully sealed with newspaper and chewing gum. There were two beds, one large, one small. Nightstand between them. An oil lamp with plenty of fuel. An opened envelope lay on the floor, its flap clumsily torn open. A wooden car sat next to it, paint completely peeled off.

Hayes returned to the door and gestured to Samantha to come in. She was speaking to an ancient old woman, her head bowed and her back stooped, muttering to Samantha through thin lips. Samantha nodded along and hastily bid her goodbye.

"Who was that?" asked Hayes.

"Some old woman," she said. "She's senile."

"What was she saying?"

"Something about how she was a messenger, and machines making lights in her head. Was there anyone in the room?"

Hayes shook his head and they entered together. "Check the closets and drawers," he said. "Check under the beds. Look everywhere."

"For what?"

"Anything."

There was not much in the drawers. Trinkets and small knickknacks. Several candle ends, the tallow soft and greasy. The cabinets contained moldering bread and rotting potatoes. More flies whined out of the shadows as Samantha opened them and interrupted their meal. Hanging on the wall cabinets was a calendar. The year was wrong. Above it was a yellowed picture of Christ riding a donkey, with faded, ragged peasants laying palms on the road before him.

Below the smaller bed Hayes found a tattered box full of newspapers, each of them covered in a child's drawings done in coal. Drawings of the moon and of the city and of mountains. Men with swords, faces bright and clean. And the sun. Nearly all pictures featured the sun. It was an enormous thing, floating above the small Earth the child had scrawled out, full of promise. Hayes leafed through them, his fingers tracing their folds. It seemed wrong to handle them, to take the dreams of the dead or missing and treat them like no more than articles in a case. When he was done he put them back in the box and replaced it under the bed.

"What was that?" asked Samantha.

"Nothing." He smoothed the bedsheet down. "Look for a letter."

"What?"

"A letter. Something. There's an envelope open, look for a letter."

"What if they took it with them?"

"Then they took it with them."

After searching for a bit they found it furiously crumpled and tossed into the corner, hidden behind a chair. Samantha opened it up and read it, then shut her eyes and turned away.

"What is it?" asked Hayes.

She didn't speak at first. "It's a goodbye," she said after a while. "A goodbye to his son. If he doesn't return. My Lord."

Hayes took it from her and sat down on the bed and began trying to work around the misspellings and the clumsy grammar.

"To my darling Jack," he began. "You are a good boy. A very good boy. I know that. I hope you know that. And I hope you know that there are things I must do so you can be a good boy. I love you. Very much. That is so. If you have this then I have not come back and that is okay. It is all right. Do not worry. You must go to Auntie Margaret's by the sweetshop with the big red sweets and stay there and you must wait for me. I hope I will see you. But I may not. That is okay. It is all right. Do not worry. I love you. You are a good boy. A very good boy. I love you. I love you. Daddy."

Then Hayes put the letter down and they both sat in the little empty room and did not speak.

"Where is the boy?" asked Samantha hoarsely.

Hayes shrugged and folded the letter up and put it in his pocket. Then he thought and took it out and held it out to Samantha. She withdrew from it as though it were poison.

"Take it," he said fiercely. "You're better at this sort of thing than me. Take care of it. File it away."

"I won't. I won't *file* it away. Damn it, Mr. Hayes, it's—"

"It's evidence. It's useful. File it away and keep it and remember it."

She took it and stuffed it into her small briefcase. Then Hayes stood and looked around. Looked at the empty remains of a humble life. He tried to envision the man and the boy sleeping in the beds and eating at the table and reading together and living together, but he could not. This was a dead place, a silent place. Full of nothing but small items, quietly falling into disrepair.

"Come on," he said.

Samantha stood and they walked out to the landing. The shouts and screams of the neighbors seemed muted and dull, reduced to incoherent babbling. Hayes heard himself telling her to tell Garvey, to give him the letter and tell him the address. Garvey would want to come and look. Garvey was better at those sorts of things. Better than most.

As they reached the bottom floor a filthy child peeked out at them from beneath the stairs and reached out to touch Hayes's trousers. Hayes stopped to see what it wanted but the child did no more than rub the fabric of his pants between its fingers, slowly and lovingly, as if it was savoring something. Its eyes opened wide and it cooed and Hayes realized it had never seen or felt fabric like that before. He turned away and passed on.

I am tired, he thought. I am so very tired.

They came to the front walk. All the men outside had left except for three of them. One looked up and watched them keenly, thin-eyed and soft-chinned. The others joined in and Hayes felt that animal sense ripple through him, cold like a night breeze, that feeling like somewhere in the whisper of trees they were being hunted. He was not surprised. After all, to most it would just seem like two dumb townies had wandered into the Shanties, ripe for the picking. It had been just a matter of time until someone tried something.

They walked down the steps. Samantha was not paying attention. Hayes took care to look not at the men but several feet before them. He reached inside his coat and gripped the little three-inch flick knife he kept there. He slipped it in his sleeve up against his wrist, then disguised the movement with a cough and started counting. They would make their move in twelve seconds, he gauged.

They sat up in eleven and began to move. He knew the positions immediately, saw the one on the right wander away to block the street east and the one on the left sauntering forward, pretending to walk into the building. The soft-chinned one waited, placing ten feet of space between himself and the one on the left. When the man on the left passed Hayes the soft-chinned one got up and followed, sandwiching them between him and his partner.

Hayes guessed it would happen in seven seconds. He wasn't sure how but he was already picking up their positions, unconsciously aware of their exact placement around him. It never happened so fast, usually it took minutes, even hours.

"Samantha?" he said softly.

"Yes?" she said.

"Listen."

"What?"

"Listen, you—" But the soft-chinned one was already pulling a strip of iron from his pants pocket. Hayes heard the man behind them spinning around and sprinting back at them, moving for the backstab.

Hayes shoved Samantha to the ground hard and the little knife popped out of his sleeve and into his palm. He stabbed it down and felt it sink into the thigh of the man behind him before he could make contact. The shock of the impact shook Hayes's wrist. Their attacker cried out and stumbled, and instead of tackling Hayes he crashed into him. The flick knife stayed deep, grinding through gristle and tendons, and as the man tumbled to the ground the blade was ripped from Hayes's hands. He collapsed beside the wounded man and saw the leader and the one on the right rushing forward.

Samantha reacted much faster than Hayes ever would have imagined. She got up and drew close to him, clutching her briefcase before her and backing away from them. Then she knelt and ripped the knife from the wounded man's leg. He screamed and a flash of blood marked her shoulder, and then she stood and held the knife out before her. She licked her lips and shouted to stay back, stay away. Hayes dimly felt like applauding her. The remaining attackers faltered, uncertain as to exactly how many knives their prey had hidden on them. Then without any warning the one on the right froze, looked across the intersection of the street, and gaped at something before screaming wildly and running away.

Hayes, Samantha, and the remaining two assailants all watched him go, each of them confused. Then they stupidly turned to look at what he had seen.

When Hayes saw it he was not sure what it was. At first it looked like no more than a blur, like some error of the light hovering on the sidewalk. But it was not, as the fluttering thing began to move toward them.

He realized it looked something like a person, pale and ghostly like a dying light. Hayes saw arms and fingers and legs and a mouth somewhere in the blur, just flashes of each as if they were there for a fragment of a second before dissolving into nothing. It staggered forward toward them, and then there was a sound like all the metal and steel in the world squalling and screeching under enormous stress, high-pitched and furious. Hayes and Samantha and their attackers all clutched their ears and cried out. They could barely hear themselves. Hayes's eyes watered and he struggled to look through the tears, but he swore he could see a face somewhere in the advancing blur, wild and crazed.

Then it hit him. Hit him like a meteor, like an artillery shell. A sense of such powerful grief and madness that it overwhelmed him. It boiled in his heart and ate his throat from the inside out and he suddenly saw the world as a cruel, vicious place where no act was just and all that lived in it deserved to die, and to die horribly, to die screaming.

He screamed with it. The noise was like a needle in his mind and he doubled up and the world faded around him.

CHAPTER EIGHTEEN

Hayes awoke to the sting of alcohol in his nostrils. Everything around him was a muted roar, throbbing and pulsing. There was a cold ache where his sinuses met his throat. Then he moaned and he heard his voice faintly as though it were coming from the next room and he opened his eyes.

He was lying on a bed, surrounded by white curtains. Clean white daylight fell in rays upon the bedsheets in his lap. Through the cracks in the curtains he could see people darting past, wearing white. He guessed he was in the Hamilton, the big, well-trafficked hospital on the edge of the Shanties. It was a hospital of fairly low repute, as it saw more than its fair share of questionable wounds and the staff could be paid to keep quiet about them. It was also rumored they ran a small drug trade, though Hayes had once been personally frustrated to learn those rumors were not true.

He held his hand up in front of his face and snapped his fingers. He could hear it, very faintly. Then he checked his joints, his hands, his elbows, his knees and ankles. They seemed to be working. He checked his face and couldn't feel any lacerations, but the linen bandages around his ears were troubling. Then he surreptitiously eased a hand down toward his crotch, found that everything familiar was still there, and lay back.

The curtain twitched. A nurse stuck her head through and said something to him but he couldn't catch much of it. Then she checked his bandages. She nodded and leaned close and said, "You probably can't hear well right now. One of your eardrums burst, you'll have diminished hearing for a while but it should come back eventually."

Hayes let loose a long string of swears. They must have been louder than he intended because the nurse recoiled slightly. Then she asked, "Is there anything you need?"

"A fucking cigarette," he told her. She made a soundless sigh and walked away.

He lay in bed for a few more minutes before the curtain opened again and Garvey sidled in. He looked at Hayes's head and grimaced.

"Your bedside manners are terrible," said Hayes.

"Not so loud," said Garvey. "Can you hear me?"

"Somewhat. Where am I? The Hamilton?"

"Yeah. You've been here nearly a day. You should get good treatment, they know me here. They'll be surprised I'm not here to see some weasel or a denner with five rounds in his legs."

"Cigarette?" asked Hayes hopefully.

Garvey reached in his pocket and took two out of his tin. First he lit Hayes's, then his own.

"What's going on?" Hayes asked, exhaling. "Where's Samantha? Is she all right?"

Garvey was silent a while, thinking. Then he said, "She's fine. That's what they told me, at least. I missed her. They let her out before you, about a day ago." He coughed. "You had some sort of... I don't know. It looked like you were in a coma. It wasn't the ear thing. You were attacked, you know, but Samantha didn't see you catch any blows to the head. Did you fall and hit it on something?"

"I fell. Didn't hit it on anything. I think..."

"Think what?"

That it was almost like an attack, thought Hayes, but he waved the question away. "Never mind. What was that thing? That thing we saw?"

Garvey pulled up a chair. He sat down beside Hayes and pulled his tie loose and took off his hat. "Why don't you tell me what happened."

Hayes described it, word for word. From Peggy in the jewelry shop to when they saw the twitching thing walking toward them in the street. He even described the attack he'd had, the sense of grief and sadness and fury that brought him to his knees. Garvey nodded along, his face growing wearier and wearier as he listened. At the end he said, "You shouldn't have gone there. Once you had the name and address you should have come straight to me."

"I should have," Hayes said. "Probably. Yes."

"You should have given me everything you had on Skiller the second you knew anything."

"I was trying to help."

"Damn it, Hayes," he said angrily. "We could have jumped on this. *I* could have jumped on this. Time matters in these things, damn you."

Hayes frowned as he looked Garvey over. The skin under his eyes was dark, like little smears of coal. His hair was oily and unbrushed and his collar was a faint yellow.

"What's going on?" Hayes asked. "What's wrong?"

Garvey sighed again and rubbed his face. Then he stood and took off his coat, moving slowly and unsteadily. He sat back down and stared into the linens on the bed and said, "It's surfaced."

"What has?"

"Our killer," he said. "There's been two more murders. In a jailhouse this time. Northeastern District Jailhouse."

"Oh, God," said Hayes, and lay back.

"Yeah. In Newton."

It had happened two nights ago, he said. The very night Hayes and Samantha had been attacked outside Skiller's tenement. He had gotten the call at three in the morning, just as the aching swirls of a hangover were beginning to settle in. He had woken and pulled on whichever clothes he could find, not knowing he'd be wearing them for the next forty hours, and dragged himself down to Newton, where a crowd was already forming.

Charles Denton and Michael Huffy. Two scummy little tennie weasels from deep in Dockland. Both had a long record of breaking and entering and one charge of assault. Put most of an ice pick in a cornerstore shopkeeper who had walked in on them filching cigarettes. Spent a few years in the Hill, got out for good behavior. That night they'd hopped a trolley down to Newton for the high and righteous purpose of throwing rocks and bottles at the cars and passersby, chivalrous gentlemen indeed. Then they were caught, roughed up a little after they stoutly resisted arrest, and tossed in the drunk tank at around midnight.

That was the last anyone ever saw of them. By two-thirty a.m. they were dead and no longer recognizable. Only way to tell it was them was from the front desk log books.

Garvey had walked into the jailhouse to find it was in a shape similar to that of the Bridgedale trolley. Two of the on-duty officers were completely deaf, a third partially. Garvey had followed the trail of destruction back to where the jail cell was blown in. This time a paperweight had been used to hammer off the lock. Inside had been the two winners of the evening, the lucky boys who had gone out looking to hassle some townies and instead had gotten a few worlds of hurt for their troubles.

A tin plate had been the weapon of choice for the occasion. Used the edge like an axe and bent the damn thing like it had been chewed up by a machine. Huffy and Denton didn't have much in the way of faces afterwards, just the backs and bases of their skulls and a bit of their ears, just a bit. Garvey probably would never forget the moment when he had been slowly walking up the hall to the jail cell, making a note of each of the items found disturbed along the way, and had spotted something twinkling and golden and squatted to look carefully at the object before realizing it was a golden tooth, still stuck in the remains of most of a man's jaw, a quarter-inch of lip smiling right below its shine.

Garvey had kept hope at first, which was dumb of him. Huffy and Denton both had unsavory records, but nothing in the way of legitimate employment. Just some idiots who had never developed brains past the delinquent days of seventeen or so. But then he had spoken to some known associates of the fellows and learned with a sinking heart that why yes, they had recently found steady work, and where else but at the McNaughton Vulcanization Plant as loaders? And most certainly, they had come into contact with the burgeoning union movement, and had become reformed, passionate men, suddenly reinvigorated and moralized upon realizing the strife of the lower classes.

"No tattoo, though," said Garvey to Hayes. "So that's something. Or maybe it's nothing, at this hour I don't know shit."

"So the policemen in the jail didn't see anything?"

"Same thing as the conductor. They heard a noise, blacked out. Woke up an indeterminate time later to find the place in ruins. Whatever it was, it tore the jailhouse up something fierce." He sniffed. "There was one more thing, though. There was blood on the outside of the cell door that was broken into."

"Not Huffy's or Denton's?"

"I don't think so. Wouldn't make sense, from that angle. I think he or she or whatever the fuck it is hurt themselves. I sent a few uniforms out to hospitals to see if there were any strange injuries. Something on the hand, probably. Nothing, of course. This bastard case won't go down that easy, it was dumb of me to think it would."

"How's the public handling it?"

"Bad. Bad as hell. We're under fire and no doubt about it. No one's paying attention to the deafened officers, no one cares if the two bodies once lived a lifetime of sheer fucking stupidity. No, they just see two union men, dead in Newton, slaughtered under police supervision. Jesus Christ, sometimes I wish America would just shit this city into the ocean and be done with it. Harry Mills over at *The Freedom* is screaming his head off about it."

"Oh, Lord."

"Yeah. Saying it's the beginnings of a blood feud, says that every man in a pair of brogans can barely expect to sleep well tonight. Someone found out that the two men were beaten before their incarceration. Well, of course they got beaten, Denton tried to bite off a patrolman's fingers. They were lucky they weren't here in the Hammy, with you. Not that they're lucky now or anything. But that doesn't matter. People are throwing rocks at officers out there. Shouting at us as we walk by. *The Freedom* isn't alone, Benby in *The Times* is starting to question us, and the goddamn mayor is starting to listen. Or starting to pretend he's listening, everyone fucking knows he's funded by, hell, I don't know, some suit at the Nail. They say McNaughton's figured out a way to murder people from miles away. Murder whoever they want." He looked sideways at Hayes. "They say McNaughton has a monster working for it."

"It's not a monster," said Hayes dismissively. "If it *is* the killer."

"Then what was it?"

"I don't know. Something. But not a monster. What did Samantha say?"

"She says pretty much the same thing as you. It was like a person, a person who couldn't stop moving. It was spotted again, you know. People said they saw a ghost, way out in Lynn. Shuddering under the moonlight and screaming, or something like screaming. From their testimonies that would have only been a few minutes before the murders."

"That can't be right," said Hayes.

"It's what they said. It crossed the city in a handful of minutes."

"They're wrong. It's bullshit. You've chased bullshit witnesses before, right?"

"Well, yeah."

"Of course. Things like that aren't real."

"You both saw it," Garvey insisted. "You both heard it and were nearly deafened. It's the same thing, whatever it is. We're still tracking down the other thugs that tried to beat your head in but if we find them, which I doubt we will, we'll probably hear the same thing."

"Are you seriously considering the scenario of a boogeyman running around murdering unioners?"

"No. No boogeyman. Just something. Someone, maybe. How, I don't know. What, I don't know."

"Oh, please, Garvey. Don't be stupid."

Garvey clenched a fist and bit the knuckle. Then he took a breath and said, "Listen, you bastard. Look around you for once. We live in a city powered by thunderstorms along with the usual coal and oil and what have you. The things your company makes here are things the entire world fucking wants. Things that can fly and never have to land. Cranes with arms and legs that can build a whole town in a week. And you. They have you, you crazy bastard. Whatever you are. I've lived here all my life and by now I'm willing to believe a lot."

Hayes shook his head. "That doesn't matter. It can still be explained. Somehow."

"Then explain it. Explain to me what's happening."

"Someone's mad. Maybe at the unions, maybe just at these men. I know you love the how and not being able to figure this one out is fucking you up but good, Garv—"

"Of course it is!" cried Garvey. "Eleven people, sorry, *thirteen* people drop dead within a *very* small space of time, no sign of resistance, no sign of alarm or of a struggle! How does that happen?"

"I don't know yet, some sort of bomb or gas!" said Hayes.

"That makes this sound planned, and this *wasn't* planned. All the evidence points to anger, to a stupid crime."

"Not all the evidence, just everything you want to look at."

Garvey fell silent at that. He sat down and buried his face in his hands and breathed deep.

"We have to find the link," said Hayes. "These people were murdered for a reason, and we need to find out why."

"The link is your company. That's what the link is."

"It isn't. Or it isn't just that."

"You want to talk about stunning bombs and gases, who do we know who makes that?"

"I'm telling you, Brightly has no idea what's happening. Evans, either. I'd know."

Garvey looked at him coldly. "Would you?"

Hayes sat up in his linens. He leaned forward and glared at him. "What?" he asked. "What's that?"

"Would you actually know?" Garvey said. "Are you still that under control, even?"

"Oh, here we are. Here, I know why I must have misheard you," Hayes said, and he ripped the bandages from his ear. "There, now." He cupped one hand to the bloodied side of his head and said, "All right, what was that, Donald? What was that you said to me? Because I know it wasn't what I *thought* you said, I know it had to be—"

"Be reasonable!" shouted Garvey suddenly. He got to his feet, fists at his side. "You're having fainting spells! Swilling opium at every chance you have! You forget to give me Skiller, you fucking *forget*, and now I'm stuck chasing more bodies and I missed something that may have helped keep my whole damn Department from looking like common thugs for your company! For your company, for your fucking company!"

"All right, you want something?" said Hayes, sitting further up in his bed. "You want to look at something? Look at Tazz! Look at the unions! If the papers are saying you're thugs, why isn't Tazz? Why hasn't the figurehead for this whole damn movement weighed in on what's happening? Or have I missed something? Has he piped up?"

A nurse rushed in, drawn by the commotion. She raised her hands and clasped the air as if she were trying to strangle out the noise itself. "Gentlemen, you have to—"

"Have I missed something in the past two days? Have I?" asked Hayes.

"—You really must—"

"Hayes..." said Garvey.

"Come on, Garv, tell me. Tell me that."

The nurse pressed on Hayes's chest, murmuring to sit back, to please sit back.

"Come on, Garv," Hayes kept on. "Go on, tell me I'm wrong."

Garvey shook his head. "All right. No. He hasn't. He hasn't said a damn word."

"Not a word!" shouted Hayes. "Not a fucking word! How'd I know? Huh? How did I know that one?"

"*Please* be quiet," pleaded the nurse. "You absolutely—"

"All right," said Hayes to her. He put his hands in the air, surrendering. "All right. We'll be quiet. We'll be good little boys. Now run along. Run along and go cut on someone for me, would you?"

The nurse glared at him, then turned around and stormed out. Garvey and Hayes sat back down and they both stared into their laps.

"What did you find on Tazz?" asked Hayes finally. "Tell me that. You went to Savron, didn't you? Went up to the Hill and tugged on your guard friend's coat, right?"

"Yeah. Yeah, I did."

"And what'd you find there? What'd you dig up?"

"Almost nothing," admitted Garvey. "Which wasn't what I wanted."

He had gone there the day Hayes and Samantha had seen Mr. Skiller's lodgings, he said, just before the new murders. He'd surprised Weigel, who said he never thought he'd see Garvey again. They'd once worked Robbery together, way back when Garvey was just cutting his teeth and they both thought being a cop would be grand fun.

But Weigel had found the realities and complexities of police work a little too daunting, and so had taken up a job as a guard for the state, as he found that work much more direct and satisfying. According to the records, Weigel had been stationed at Savron when Mickey Tazz first got thrown in.

Which is where the problem came in. Weigel had heard of Tazz, naturally. Everyone knew a little about him. But he'd been stunned to hear any news that Tazz had been at Savron at all, let alone when he was keeping watch. If anything, Weigel had said, Tazz was there before him, years before him, before anyone here, because that'd be something you'd hear about, wouldn't it?

Garvey had agreed and then produced a bottle of whiskey, and the two men sipped and bullshitted each other. Eventually he'd persuaded Weigel to check and they both walked down to the records in the basement. Weigel, slightly drunk and dubious of Garvey's suspicions, reluctantly began digging, and after a little less than twenty minutes they found what Garvey was looking for, to Weigel's amazement. Michael Tazarian, a happy denizen of Savron Hill from 1912 to 1917, South Sector C, Cell 145, under Corporal Dobbs. Who, of course, Weigel barely knew of. The man had retired two years ago, he said. He had no idea where he'd be, they weren't exactly buddies.

From there the file was nothing but framework. Nothing but scraps and locations. Behavior reports, none. A bare handful of appeal hearings and even those pretty skinny. Physical reports, nonexistent. Tazz's stay in the Hill had been a quiet one.

"No one's that clean," said Garvey. "No one passes through Savron and leaves that tiny of a paper trail."

"No," said Hayes, thinking. "No one ever does. Think there was anything missing?"

"I can't say. Had all the essentials. It was weird, though. Weigel asked the other guards if they remembered him. Some said they did, a little."

"But they weren't sure."

"Not sure, no."

"Hm. I'll want those records, if you can get them. Give them to Sam for me. We'll store them somewhere for further examination."

"Why?"

"Skeletons in the closet," said Hayes. "Everyone has a few misdeeds in their past. And if those records turn out to be lying, then Tazz's must be pretty sizable, wouldn't you say?"

"How are you going to come at it?"

"By asking him," Hayes said simply.

Garvey laughed. "He's in hiding. You said it yourself. No one knows where he is. How do you plan to crack that?"

"You leave that to me. What are you going to do?"

"Get what I can on Skiller from Samantha. She's going to be turning it in at Central later today. Then I'll work that and I'll keep working the trolley and the tennie murders. Just keep working it until I've worked it to death and then I'll take the corpse apart. And yeah, I'll catch other murders in the meantime. Pile them up if I have to. Can't work them, this is priority."

"What will your squad think of that?"

"What they usually think. That I'm fucking odd. For working alone and working with you, and working directly under Collins. And they won't like me for it, but what are you going to do."

"Hm," said Hayes contemplatively. "You know, I remember the first time I was quite impressed with you, Garv."

"Oh, yeah?"

"Yes. That rifle robbery down close to Blanton. Old man had been shot three times and someone spotted a boy running away with an ancient Winchester. Fucking cowboy gun. But you had no other witnesses and nothing to go by. So you trawled every gun shop in town, legal and otherwise. Took you a few weeks, and I don't know how you kept it as quiet as you did, but you did. So you got word of a Winchester belonging to some wharf rat down at the docks, something he had taken out to show off to the other firearm fans, and when you couldn't win a warrant you sat on the house in the freezing cold, day and night, for four days. And then the little bastard tried again. Caught kicking in the door of some old biddy's house, cowboy rifle in hand. He folded like a wet napkin once you sat him down in the cells. Then you caught a cold and were bedridden with a fever for a week after. I thought you wouldn't make it. Remember that?"

"Yeah."

"That was good. Good police work. Just working it to death, something always shakes loose, yes?"

"Sometimes. Other times not."

"Think something will shake loose here?"

"I don't know." He took his hat and ran a finger along the brim. Then he said, "Thanks, by the way."

"For what?"

"For identifying my John Doe. For finding him and his boy. I appreciate that."

"All part of the fun."

Garvey stood and made to leave, then he stopped and looked back at Hayes from the edge of the curtain, eyes hooded and wounded all at once.

"What?" said Hayes.

"You know, if you stopped chasing the dragon for a while you'd do a better job," he said.

"Fuck you," said Hayes. He turned his face away.

"You would, you know."

"If I didn't take my medicine I wouldn't be able to work. My head would burn up."

Garvey nodded, thinking. Then said, "No. It's not that."

"Fuck you. What do you know?"

"I know that you were going to the dens long before you ever had an attack," said Garvey. "So it must just mean you don't care about the work that much."

Then he walked away and left Hayes to sit in his bed. It may have been his ears but the sound seemed to die away until everything was silent.

CHAPTER NINETEEN

At the end of the afternoon Samantha finished compiling everything she had on Skiller, having turned the man's story into a hard, stable little pile of sanity in the center of her cluttered office. It had taken less time than she'd originally imagined, yet she'd been somewhat disappointed by how unremarkable his life was. After all this time of Garvey thinking of Skiller as his sad little Grail she had expected his story to be more dramatic, more meaningful. But she found he was just a man after all, his least important moments laid down in the McNaughton records like everyone else's.

John Neil Skiller, born 1882 in Lincoln, Nebraska. Hired by McNaughton in 1902, one of the very first members of the Air Vessel Foundry, back when the alloys were still experimental and no one was entirely sure how they'd behave when cooled. No supervisor complaints or acclamations for him, nothing more than "adequate." Sometimes if the supervisor was feeling particularly generous he was also "punctual." He seemed to be a quiet man, always in the background, yet never catching any attention. Rarely commended, never promoted. Just had his wages cut down year after year, dollars shaved off bit by bit. Suddenly she thought of Garvey, sitting beside him in the dark morgue of the Department, and she could think of no one better to shepherd the man's memory to justice.

She picked up the file and went down to the front to hail a cab. She was interrupted by one of the company limousine drivers, who waved her down and told her a gentleman was waiting for her. She approached the limousine cautiously. Then her heart sank when she saw Evans seated in the back of the limousine, knees together and hands quaintly in his lap. He smiled wide when he saw her and said, "Miss Fairbanks! Please, come closer and let me get a look at you."

"Good day, sir," she said. "Are you doing well?"

"Oh, well enough. It's very good to see you up and about. Are you hurt? Or ill?"

"No, Mr. Evans, I'm fine."

"That's good to hear. Excellent to hear, really, it is. Would you care to take a ride with me today?"

Samantha hesitated, then said, "Certainly, sir."

Evans leaned to the left to speak to the driver as she climbed in. "Cheery and Fifth, Willie?"

"Yes, sir," said the driver, and shut the partition. The car spun up and soon they eased off down the street.

"I was aghast to hear what happened to you, Miss Fairbanks," Evans told her once they began moving. "Just stunned. It's hard to believe such things happen in this city. It really is, isn't it?"

She nodded.

"That strange apparition. You saw it?" he asked.

"Yes. I suppose I did. Though I'm not sure what I saw."

"Certainly, certainly. Have you... adjusted, though?"

She attempted a smile. "I'm alive and working. It's easier not to think."

"I suppose I can understand that. And how is Mr. Hayes?"

"I'm not sure. When I left him in the hospital he was alive and well but still asleep. Have you seen him?"

Evans shook his head. "Mr. Hayes's health is being taken note of. Just not by me, personally. I was somewhat surprised, however, to find your investigation had taken you out into the city," he said. He frowned a little. "Especially so far as the Porter neighborhoods. Unless I'm mistaken, I believe at the time you were supposed to be speaking to Mr. Ryan? Of the Vulcanization Plant?"

"Yes... yes, well, Mr. Hayes had discovered that there was another link between McNaughton and the Bridgedale. A previous homicide being investigated by one of the detectives working the murders."

"Detective Garvey, I presume."

"Yes," she said, uneasy. "I know you said you wanted to keep this in-house, sir, and away from the police investigation, but—"

"That I did."

"Yes, but when something that concrete comes along you have to check it. Our orders were to check everything, if I recall. And Detective Garvey is an honorable officer."

Evans laughed. "My dear, I hadn't planned on going so far as to suggest Mr. Garvey was a danger to anything."

"Oh. You hadn't?"

"No. On the contrary, Mr. Garvey is one of the most trustworthy men I've ever met. No, no, what I'm worried about is you." He took off his glasses and began polishing them on his tie, watching her sadly.

"Me, sir?"

"Yes. Miss Fairbanks, you know we brought you here to, well, to stabilize Mr. Hayes's investigations. To bring them to heel. What you did the other day damaged your reputation with your superiors. With *my* superiors. Those above even Brightly. They no longer know if they can trust you, you see. And that worries me. You are a promising young lady. It would be terrible if your career were to become irreparably damaged after coming so far. And we need you."

He put his glasses back on and stared out the window as the building faces slipped by. "Our company has accomplished very great things in its time," he said. "Very great. But the greatest things are still to come. They are still being made. I can personally attest to that, and I know only of a handful of them. And all of them, *all* of them are being made right here, here in this city. And yet here is where we find the most opposition. In our home. Where we have brought wealth and industry. These are grave times for us, my dear. We are building the frame around which the future will be constructed, and yet here at the height of our powers everything threatens to collapse. But I still believe we can do good. I do. Do you believe this?"

Samantha hesitated.

"Go on, my dear," he said. "You can be frank. I may be a sentimentalist, but I'm no fanatic or idealist, or anything so distasteful."

"I don't know," she said finally. "I don't know anymore. When I first heard of where I was being sent I was overjoyed. But now that I'm here and I've seen these places…I don't know. It's not what I thought it would be."

He nodded, his face tired. "I know. I felt the same way."

"You did?"

"Why, yes. No reasonable person could feel different. But I find it difficult to think of another way this city could have been built, another way we could have made what we made. It's said by men far smarter than I that the most efficient way to organize progress is through business, to harness our own desires, and…and, well. I don't know what to say. There are casualties, I suppose. Effects. Like the slums. Like the unions. But tell me of a way that we could hire everyone we wanted and pay them all what they wanted and not handicap our own goals, our own dreams? I know that sounds clichéd, that those are arguments you're sure to have heard before. Patronizing ones as well, arguments anyone can poke holes in. I thought so, too. But after being here and seeing what we can make, they stopped being so clichéd to me. I spent all four of my years here trying to think of a way to reconcile them. I've given up."

"Four years?" Samantha asked, surprised.

"Yes," said Evans.

"You've only been here four years?"

He smiled. "How long did you think I've lived here?"

"I don't know, sir. Longer than that."

"I guess you think I've spent a lifetime here. I mean, I've been longer with the company, more than forty years. But no. I've only been at the heart of things for four."

He reached below his seat and pulled out a small silver tray and two small glasses with a little bottle of gin. He poured himself one and sipped a little, then drank the rest in one gulp. He offered her a glass, apologizing as he did as though he would never wish to watch a lady drink, then replaced the set when she refused.

"I believe that was one of Mr. Hayes's innovations," he admitted. "The traveling bar." He paused and considered something. "Do you know how I came to be here, Miss Fairbanks?"

She shook her head.

"I am here for the same reason you are here, really," he said. "My transfer took place a little over four years ago, as I said. Through Brightly, actually. I was in Pakistan. Far, far away. Working as McNaughton's chief negotiator for mining claims in the mountains. I was a civilized man in what I thought was an uncivilized land. I had gone there looking for adventure but found more bargaining and more talk and more money. Same as always. Business as always. Then one day I got a telegram. Emergency telegram, with the executive emergency access code at the end. Had to dig out the rule book to even figure out what that meant. It was from some man I'd never heard of, man by the name of Brightly. Said to get in the saddle and head due east, to Nalpur.

"So I did. I rode and I rode and I rode all day, to Nalpur, and there I was summoned to the town prison. Nasty place. Most of it was underground, the cells were pits with bars over them. It was like a crypt. And inside I found at least a dozen men in suits, like they had come right out of New York or Chicago or Evesden. McNaughton men, you see.

"I was directed to Brightly, in the back. I'd not heard of him before, but he was quite enthusiastic to see me. I asked him exactly what his position was and he smiled and told me he operated under a lot of different hats, but the hat of the day was Personnel and Acquisitions and he was here to get a man and he needed some executive backup. My backup, he said. Said I was the premier agent in the region and, somehow, I had negotiated for jurisdiction over our own employees in the country. Like we were our own nation. I didn't recall that but I went along with it and asked what sort of employee we were here to get. And he said, 'A man of talents and knowledge.' Just that, and he said I was to hire him. This seemed strange, he wasn't our boy yet so how could we have jurisdiction, but Brightly waved that aside and said all I needed to do was interview the fellow. I balked and he said, 'No, no. No, no. He's a harmless little thing, an Englishman, civilized and sophisticated like you or me.' And he showed him to me. Took me to one of the cells and had me look in.

"There was a table in the middle, and at the table was this little man. A towheaded little man with an immense beard and his hands and ankles all done up in chains. Slight as a blade of grass and still as a monk. And for some reason, I felt sad for the little prisoner. He seemed so alone. So alone in that awful place.

"So I said I would do it. Brightly congratulated me and gave me this enormous interview file. I said it would take hours to get through and he said that was fine, fine, just fine. And he smiled at me. I remember that.

"I went in there and I sat down with the little man and, well, I started talking. Hullo, I'm Jim, you seem to be in a difficult situation and I'm here to help, so on and so forth. Just like bargaining with any of the locals, you see. And for a long while the little man didn't speak. Just stared at me, dead-eyed. Eyes like glaciers. Only way I could get him to talk was by offering him a cigarette. He almost ate the thing, he was so happy to have it. And then we started our discussion.

"I asked him what he was here for. And he said, 'Robbery.' And

I said, 'Oh, and you're innocent, of course,' and he said, 'No.' And I looked at him. Let him think it over. I asked, 'You're guilty of robbery?' and he said, 'Yes.' I asked him who he had robbed and what he had stolen. He said he had stolen fifteen cases of pistol rounds from a McNaughton shipment. Us. He had robbed us. He had stolen our goods to sell to some warlord or another, and he didn't give a damn, it seemed. That was a bit of a nasty shock. I couldn't imagine why we would want such a man. But, well, I recovered and we went along.

"But as we spoke he seemed to change. It took place gradually, over a few hours, but I noticed after a while. His accent changed. Became American, Southwestern, like mine. He loosened up. And then we started talking. Not talking about work or prison or his past, but about me. About becoming Presbyterian. About Nap Lajoie and horses and Kipling. Things I loved. And we talked for hours. Hours and hours.

"And suddenly I had no idea why I had been so worried about this prisoner. He was a great fellow, smart and cheery. Like a kindred spirit. I told him so, told him I was astonished to find him here in prison. And that was when he cracked a little. Just a little. He looked at me, so sad, and asked if maybe he didn't belong there. Maybe prison was where he should be. I told him no, no, a man like you is made for great things. Prison is no place for a man with such potential. And he nodded like he was agreeing. But, you know, I don't think he ever really believed me. I think he would always believe that he belonged in that prison. That he deserved it, somehow.

"But I signed him. And when I came up I found Brightly and his men busy as bees, writing down this and talking about that. They had been watching, you see. I told them I had no idea why such a man was in prison, he seemed like a worthy man to me. Surely he must have had understandable reasons for his actions. And Brightly smiled at me and he said, 'Evans, did you even get that man's name?'

"Well, I was astounded. I'd forgotten, and I couldn't believe it. I started to tear open the briefcase to see what he'd signed on all the forms when Brightly told me not to bother. They knew who he was. He was a smuggler and raider out of India, ex–British colonial. Son of an ambassador, they figured, been living off our shipping lines for years. They'd tried to catch him but, well, he always seemed to know when we were coming. It was like trying to catch a ghost. When they caught him it wasn't out of any cleverness of their own, he was raving drunk in some bar and bragging. Then they tossed him in prison, and…and he survived. Which, really, was remarkable. Do you know, by any chance, how long a white man survives in a prison over there? Or any man? I can guarantee it's not long. But he survived. Like he just knew when trouble was heading his way.

"And then, Brightly said, there was what he'd done in the cell in there. Hadn't he changed? Hadn't he somehow turned into the man I wanted to meet, the man I'd most like to talk to? And made me a friend. Did it in less than four hours, too. Said he'd done it to three other inquisitors. Turned them around and made them his. And then Brightly explained." Evans frowned, thinking. "He said… Well. Child, you may think I'm mad for saying this, but—"

"I know what he can do," Samantha said quietly.

Evans looked at her, stunned. "You do?"

"Yes."

"How?"

"Just from watching him. And from things he said. Then I asked and he explained it to me himself. It doesn't seem like a gift too often. It seems more like a disease."

"Yes," said Evans, still shaken. "Yes, I rather expect it does. You're cleverer than me, my girl. Cleverer by far. Were you mad? Angry?"

"I was. At first." She paused. "I do wish you had told me," she said, stiffly.

He smiled feebly. "I wished I could have. Believe me, I know the anger you felt. I was furious at him. And at Brightly. I was furious he had exposed me to that man, but he said he had to see what would happen, just to see if what the prisoner had done to the other interrogators was coincidence. He'd been doing it all day, you see. And they needed a real signature on that paper, he said. A real executive. I didn't know that was a load of hooey at the time, of course Brightly outranked me, he always has. But I believed it, and Brightly told me how a man like that might be useful. Might be useful for the company in these dangerous times. 'Come on, man,' he said. 'Think of the company. Think of Willie, do it for Willie.' Willie being William McNaughton, you see. And I said, 'Do what, exactly?'

"And then he asked me if I was happy. Happy there in Pakistan. Using outhouses and riding horses everywhere and having to learn a new damn language every ten miles, he said. Asked me if I'd like to take up a job here, at Evesden Central Control. In the Nail itself.

"Well, I was stunned. I'd only been here once for a geology conference. Put on a presentation for a bunch of keen, clever young men who tore me apart. I asked him what I would do. And he said all I had to do was take care of their new man. The man downstairs. They didn't really even know his name or how old he was. Said I had to learn that and then it was up to me to control him. To be his better. To make him useful for Willie and the company.

"And so I went downstairs. And he introduced himself for the first time. And that's how I met Hayes. We talked some more and he signed on and laughed like it was all some grand joke. Maybe it was. I'm not sure."

Evans sat in silence for a great while. Then he sighed and adjusted his glasses. "I'm not stupid. I know Brightly handpicked me as a go-between. Between himself and Hayes. Brightly doesn't want anything in his head to get into Hayes's, that's for sure. Hayes was and is his star pupil, his big find. How he found him in Nalpur is beyond me, but he engineered it and he got us both from there to here, me dragging this mad dog by the leash. I suppose you're wondering why I'm telling you this silly story," he said, smiling weakly again.

"Well, I'm not sure, no."

"My point is, I was a tool to them. To the higher-ups. As Hayes is. As you are. And I knew it. I did, I knew it. When I bought in I knew what they wanted me to be, and I still know now. Now that I've paid. But, you see, I know that it's been worth something. In these past four years, well, we've made marvels. Things you wouldn't believe. Things that may..." He paused, smiled, and said, "Well, I shouldn't tell you this. We're working to make things that may one day leave here and land in Europe in only a few hours. And more. They say these same devices may one day touch the sun and the moon and maybe beyond. The very stars, Miss Fairbanks. We'd reach the stars themselves. It's very primitive right now, very primitive stages, as, well, I think we've made apparent through some recent mishaps, but it's growing. And there's more than that, child. I don't know all the mechanics, but there's one thing..." He trailed off, then shook his head as if he couldn't believe it himself. "You know the Earth turns, Miss Fairbanks?" he asked.

Samantha nodded.

"Turns like a top, in space?"

"Yes."

"What if you could somehow harness that power? Develop something that was sensitive to that turning... and began to turn the other way as a reaction? What sort of power would that generate?"

She thought about it. It seemed like a simple enough suggestion but then as she put more thought into it she realized the enormity of the idea.

Evans chuckled. "Yes," he said. "Everyone thinks of, oh, the trolleys and the phones and trains and airships. The conduits and the cranes. But there's more. The bigger things are still being developed. How they come up with them, I don't know. It's like they pull these ideas from another world entirely. But we're making a new age, Miss Fairbanks, right now. And we are but a part. Hayes is a part. I am a part. You. This city, even those in the slums and those in Newton and, yes, those in the Bridgedale neighborhood. We are all parts in a greater mechanism. Hayes alone has done more to protect the development of these ideas than he could ever know. The men he's turned and bought and sold... He didn't even care what he was doing it for. He just thought it was great sport. But he's changed this company. One man has changed this company. And we will change the world in turn, in ways it can't even expect."

The car came to a stop. She and Evans looked around, surprised. Samantha found they were in front of a large, unmarked warehouse.

"Oh, dear," said Evans. "We're here. I forgot to tell Wilford to drop you off. We'll have to cut our conversation short, I'm afraid."

"No, no," she said. "No, please. Go on, if you have a bit more time."

He considered it, then smiled. "Here. Come. Walk with me. You'll accompany me inside and then Wilford can drop you off."

"What meeting do you have to go to?"

"Oh, it's a demonstration," he said. He stepped out of the car and unfolded his umbrella. "This is one of our test facilities. It's a basic meeting, I have them once every few months. About what's next on the regional agenda."

He gave instructions to Wilford and offered Samantha his arm. They walked together, past the barbed wire fence and the guards out front, to whom Evans explained that Samantha was only there to help him in. The guards grudgingly let her pass and they crossed the lot together.

"Tell me," said Evans. "Why should I allow you and Mr. Hayes to continue on this tangent?"

"I'm sorry?" she asked.

"Why should I let you go on running amok in the Porter neighborhoods? Instead of chastising you, I mean. Humor me, please."

"We have a chance of finding out who's behind the Bridgedale trolley and the Newton murders," she said. "We can tell everyone the truth. That it's not our company. That it's someone else."

"Hm. Yes. That's a goal, yes. But why do you want to do it?"

"To do it?"

"Yes. You worked quite a bit when it was just you, preparing the day for Hayes. But now you work overnight, and never even mention overtime. It's not business, then. It seems personal now. Why is that?"

She thought as they walked to the front doors. More guards nodded and let them by, twirling their truncheons.

"There's a boy," she said quietly. "A little boy. Skiller was his father. He was the canal man they found with his throat cut."

Evans's walk slowed. He nodded. "I see," he said faintly.

"We don't know where he is. There was a letter his father wrote to him. A goodbye."

"Yes," said Evans.

"And there's more. There's more and, and...I don't know," she said. She found she was suddenly fighting back tears. "I don't know. I stood in that little boy's room and I looked through their things and they won't ever be the same again. Won't ever be touched. It won't ever be a home again. And there's Garvey. And Hayes. And this, this means something to them. I don't know what it is but it gives them something I haven't ever seen before. Something real. And I want it. I want it to do the same to me as it does to them."

"Here, here," Evans said softly. "Here. Calm down. Calm down. We can't go in with you upset."

"I'm sorry," she said. "I'm usually not like this. It's just, I saw their home and there was this little girl with flies all over her head and she was crying, she was crying and waiting for someone to come, and what Garvey and Hayes are doing...It's like they think if they fix this one thing it'll fix everything else. Even Hayes seems to think so, in some perverted way. And maybe it will. Maybe it will."

"Yes," Evans said. "Maybe it will." He sighed and wiped the rain off his glasses. "I just wanted to see if there would be a good reason for me to explain all this to Brightly," he said. "That's all. And there is. Now come," he said, offering her his arm again. "Come and see me in safely."

She sniffed and dried her eyes. Then she took up his arm again and they walked in the front door. Inside was a long, low cement hallway with closed metal doors at the end.

"Do you think Mr. Hayes is of sound mind, sir?" she asked quietly as they walked.

"Oh, I'd say Mr. Hayes is of exceptionally sound mind, considering the things he's seen," said Evans, and pushed open the other set of doors.

Samantha nearly gasped. Before them was the largest room she had ever seen, or maybe it seemed that way because it was completely empty. The walls were gray and blank and made of enormous cement slabs so well put together that the seams were mere hairlines. The opposite wall had no markings at all except for a small door, beside which was a guard posted in a chair, reading a book.

"This is where you're having your meeting?" asked Samantha, awed.

"Yes," said Evans delightedly. "I told you, we're *making* things here."

They crossed to the small doorway. It took nearly a minute. She was reminded of Hayes's warehouse, which was no more than a third of the size of this place. Then she realized it and this place and the common McNaughton facility schematics were similar. There was the warehouse portion, then something sunk down in the back, and then much, much more below…

The guard stood up and smiled at them. "How are you today, Mr. Evans?"

"Fine, thank you. How is *Little Women*?"

"Oh, it's excellent. Thank you for recommending it to me."

"Well, I want to make sure the time passes for you, Henry. Metal as usual?"

"Yes, sir," said the guard. "And, she, uh…"

"Oh, nonsense, Henry. Miss Fairbanks just wanted to make sure I made it in all right," said Evans. "She won't be going down to see." He winked at her, then took out his watch and his wallet and handed them over, and then removed his spectacles and put on a pair whose frames were made of wood. He removed his keys, the change he had, and then his belt. Henry took them all and stored them on a nearby table.

"Keep an eye on them, Henry," said Evans.

"Oh, I will, sir. Always do."

Samantha found herself staring at the wall. Then she looked down at her hands and her arms. She could not explain it, but she felt some strange prickliness standing here, like an electrical field, but somehow deeper. It was as though this section of the building was different from what she had passed through, and perhaps different from any other place she had ever been. She felt she was in some boundary or somehow *soft* place, a border beyond which things changed imperceptibly.

She looked up to find Evans smiling at her. "This is where we part," he said. "I had a lovely chat with you." He leaned close and whispered, "You feel it, don't you? Don't you?"

"Yes. What is it?"

He shrugged, then laughed. "I can't say. Company policy. Let me know how your inquiry goes, Miss Fairbanks! I'll watch it with interest." Then the little old man waved and walked off into the dark hallway. She watched as he vanished into the shadows and the sounds of his footsteps faded into nothing. Then she stood there, unmoving.

"Are you all right, miss?" asked Henry.

"What? Yes. Yes, I..." She trailed off, then took a step forward. Henry stood to block her way.

"No, no," she said. "I don't want to go in, I just wondered if you'd mind if I..." She gestured at the walls.

Henry looked at the wall and smiled. "Sure. I do it all the time."

Samantha nodded faintly and walked to the towering cement walls. She placed one hand on the stone and for a moment was disappointed. There was nothing. It was just cool cement, like the street outside. But then she felt it, very faintly...

Vibrations. So low and deep they could barely be felt at all. She paused, then put her ear to the wall. She heard a low, steady, measured pounding, like some enormous machinery operating somewhere nearby, behind the wall or below the floor, something moving to a tempo she could not identify but felt she had known her entire life.

Then she sensed it. The flow around her. Something moving. Changing. As if whatever operated below was bending and changing the very structure of the world as though it were no stronger than any other metal found in the hills.

She listened for some time. Maybe hours, maybe minutes. Then Henry coughed and she awoke from her trance. She walked away, head held high, and went and had a coffee before delivering her package to the Evesden Police Department and returning home. But for some reason she avoided sewer grates and street vents, and would not go near the trolley stations.

When she came home she found Garvey waiting in the mezzanine of her floor, seated in a chair and playing with his hat in his lap. He looked up and then stood when she came near, and ran a nervous hand through his hair. He looked pale and weary, as though he had been up for days.

"Oh," he said. "I wondered when you'd come home."

"How long have you been waiting here?" she asked. "I was just at the station to drop off what we had on Skiller."

"I haven't been here too long. Sorry to make you go all the way to the station when you could have just held on to it." He paused, then said, "Are you all right? Are you hurt? I missed you at the Hamilton. I wanted to check in on you."

"My ears keep ringing," she said, and she began to walk toward her apartment door. "And I may have sprained my wrist. But otherwise I'm fine. Much better than Mr. Hayes."

"That's good to hear," he said, following her.

"I'm sorry for delaying your case, which it seems is what I was doing. I should have made Mr. Hayes stop once we had Mr. Skiller's address and then given it to you, shouldn't I?"

"That's not what I'm here about," he said. "I just wanted to make sure that you were okay."

"Well, you can see that I'm fine," she said, trying to believe it. She opened her apartment door slowly. The memories of the previous days bloomed in her head, the filthy, abandoned children and Hayes reading the goodbye letter as he sat upon the empty bed, and she badly wanted to think of something else, anything else. She looked at Garvey and saw he felt the same, perhaps. Blood was pounding in her ears, and she was reminded of the warehouse Evans had showed her, and the echoes in the deeps.

She entered and turned to him. "Why don't you come in?" she asked. "You look like you've been awake for days."

"That's because I have," he admitted. "I don't even know what time it is."

"Then why don't you come in?"

Garvey hesitated. "I was just... seeing if you..."

He trailed off. She waited, but he did not say anything.

"Donald," she said slowly and gently, "why don't you come in?"

He looked at her, desperate and uncertain, and then nodded, still fumbling with his hat in his hands. He walked in and sat on her couch, and stared up at her earnestly. A cagey young thing, she thought, wearing years that lied about his true heart. Then, smiling slightly, she shut the door, and went to sit beside him.

CHAPTER TWENTY

Hayes lay in bed in the hospital, perfectly still. The nurses who looked in on him sometimes thought he was sleeping with his eyes open, but he was very much awake. He'd retreated deep inside himself and gone deaf to the outside world so that he could work in peace, slowly assembling his next move. He rifled his long and twisted memory for contacts and friends and reliable sources, for favors owed and debts unpaid and veins of information he could mine. Most of them were worthless, and these he laid aside. More troubling were the ones he started considering before remembering that they were not in Evesden at all, but belonged to some other city, to some sandy outpost or distant fringe country. He'd left them all behind long ago. And others that he'd summon up would turn out to be no longer in the world in any sense, having gone on dangerous voyages and never returned, or been laid low by a stray bullet, or met the noose and danced on the scaffold, or simply expired.

Most troubling of all were the people he remembered vividly, but could not recall meeting or having a conversation with. These, he figured, were not his memories at all, but were ones stolen over the years, mnemonic castoffs that'd somehow been caught within his mind. Sometimes he forgot he lived and worked mostly within a world of abstracts and dreams.

His work went slowly, and soon he realized he was distracted. What Garvey had said had nettled him, somehow. Garvey's disappointment stung deeper for him than others'. As he'd come to know Garvey over the years of bleary cases and casual atrocities, Hayes had begun to feel the same admiration for him that a young boy does for his older sibling, even though Hayes was several years older than him. The way Garvey saw the world felt at once true and impossible, full of a sort of wisdom that had always been beyond Hayes. It was as if Garvey's life was the way Hayes's should have been, yet he had failed utterly at it, and now could only watch.

Most of it was that Garvey knew what Hayes could do, knew that Hayes listened to his thoughts, and simply did not care. The idea that someone could live so unashamedly and without self-disgust baffled Hayes.

Samantha cared, that was for sure. Ever since she'd learned of his abilities her nerves had sung like razor wire, every minute. But it was not the loathing and paranoia he'd expected. Instead Samantha almost welcomed his examination, and both perversely hoped for and dreaded his judgment. He had never met someone so desperate to prove themselves to someone, to anyone.

He'd forgotten how young she was, he realized, or perhaps what it was like to be young at all. It pained him a little, like the ghostly ache of a lost limb, but Hayes could not recall when he had lost that part of himself.

He shook his head, disgusted at his own self-pity. For the rest of his stay he continued to work, and did not spare a thought for either of them.

When he got out of the hospital the nurses gave him a list of medicines to purchase at the drugstore. He crumpled it up as soon as he was out the door and tossed it away. Then he went to work.

He guessed that Dockland would be the place to start so he took a trolley east to the Conver Bridge and then walked to Dover and 177th. He stood and looked at the buildings and tried to refresh his memory, then headed north along the Conver Canal and counted the sluice gates set into the side. When he got to the sixth he sat on the edge of the wall, waited until the street was clear, and lifted himself up and over.

He slid down the cement to the edge of the sluice gate, took out a pocket knife and undid the grate. Then he crawled into the small tunnel, cold water running over his shoes and his ankles, and stopped when he came to a drainage pipe leading up to the street. He reached up into the pipe and felt around until his hand found the little shelf inside and the wax paper bundle waiting on it. He tugged the package out and carefully opened it. Inside were four hundred dollars in cash, three birth certificates and identification cards for various purposes, a handful of light keys, mostly fitting locks throughout the Nail, and a .22 pistol with twelve rounds, separately wrapped in more wax paper. He took the money out, counted off two hundred dollars, split the bills up into three parts, placed two of them in his pockets and the third in his sock, and put the rest of the money back in the pack. After that he picked up the pistol. He handled it, spinning the chamber and sighting it up along the drainage pipe, but shook his head and put it back. Then he rewrapped the bundle and replaced it in the drainage pipe.

He crawled out of the sluice gate, soaked up to mid-shin, and climbed back up the cement bank and crouched by the wall, waiting. When it was clear he vaulted back over and walked briskly into the heart of Dockland, shaking off the drops as he stepped.

He had seventeen such packages hidden throughout the city. Some were in hotel crawl spaces, others were in banks, others were under the floorboards of basements that were easily accessible from the street level. One was in the park, buried in the children's playground and guarded by a tin dragon boys and girls could ride. Each package held the same things in the same amounts, though the IDs and keys varied depending on where the drop was. It had taken him about a year to place them all. Until now he had not breached one.

Hayes checked his money again, then straightened his tie and tried to wipe off his shoes. Then he set off.

The Princeling came to The Grinning Evening in Dockland that night with money in his pocket and a spirit for party. He dropped bills left and right, bought cigars and drinks and romanced the ancient waitresses, to their delight. He got Stanley the bandmaster to play a drunken version of Mahler, the trombone sleazing its way along the symphony, and they all laughed and sang. He persuaded one man to down half a pint of vermouth and they all cackled as he sprinted to the sink, and the Princeling stood on his chair and started up the band to cover up the sound of the man's sick. Then he pulled a few members of the crowd to a dim corner and whispered into their ears that he was looking for company, company with the great Mr. Tazz, and no other would do. He tucked some green in their pockets and they listened and nodded and returned to the party, their smiles dampened by the call of business. And without a word of goodbye the Princeling was gone.

He made an appearance at Moira's Black Kettle, passing by the pimps and the johns outside to go straight to the back room. There he lounged with the girls, drunken beauties draped over the stained and ragged pillows, their breasts and thighs hanging loose and their eyes bored and distracted. Idly scratching the coarse down between their legs, so casually and carelessly exposed. The Princeling brought them cigarettes and held the girls close and murmured things into their ears that made grins bloom on all their faces, and then he spoke to Moira and danced with her and they sat on the pillows like old traders and spoke of business. Of pimps and joes, of girls cut and men cut in turn, of the lure of the pipe and how strong the calling beat in their veins on the hot afternoons of late summer. They spoke of tradecraft and drops and the wandering patrols of the bluecoats, so weak-boned here, not city police at all, not in Dockland. Different breed. And then he asked her if she had heard tell of a man named Tazz, and said that the Princeling wished to speak to him. He needed palaver with the union man, he told her, and quick. She listened and nodded and gave him her word. Then the Princeling left, his baser desires unfed, his billfold only slightly dented.

He went to the vagrant's hutch by the wharf and found Macklevie sitting among his ragged wares, sharpening a knife of bone. The Princeling laughed and danced down to the old beggar and tossed a bottle of Glenmorangie to him and Mackie crowed with delight. They both had a dose and then the Princeling perused the commodities, handling a knife for balance, weighing the heft of a pistol, biting the odd bullet. He sniffed Mac's secondhand tar and smiled indulgently as Mac gave his pitch, whispering that this was the stuff, this right here, this'd light your fancy and burn you deep. The Princeling bought a set of charms made from crow bones and silver, and the old beggar counted his take with glee. Then as the fog mingled with the wharf fumes they stood in the septic light and spoke of rumor and gossip and who had buried whom, and of the union man, the Dockland specter, Mr. Tazz himself. His boys and his aims and his dreams and wishes. Mackie had some pamphlets from back in Tazz's early days, *The Ladder Up*, sure to be a valuable commodity once this all turned doomsday, but the Princeling said he wanted not printed word from the man but verbal discourse, sir, and try and let it be known, if you would be so kind, try and let it be known.

Then the Princeling passed by Cho Lun's Carpentry, the sound of hammer and saw absent as always. The corner boys watched him go by but he did not enter. Just laughed and saluted and skipped on.

He strolled over to The Underground, the dance hall set up in the abandoned trolley tube, where girls and boys sweated in their suits and skirts as they whirled one another about. Stevie had a rouser going that night and no mistake. The orchestra was fired up and the dancers on the stage were succumbing to the madness. Sometimes the people on the floor took one another into the bathroom stalls, and there a passing visitor could spy the surge of flesh or hear a gasp of passion. But the Princeling passed through them without remark and came and crouched with the orchestra under the stage and spoke to Stevie, their bandleader. He asked if union boys had come Stevie's way, and had they danced to his tunes or maybe suckled at his tar, which he understood was sold in the backstage passageways, or maybe they got serviced in the rooms upstairs, if the rumors the Princeling had been hearing were true. Terrible rumors they were indeed, especially if Moira or any of the other neighborhood high muck-a-mucks heard about them. Stevie listened and grew white as the Princeling listed his misdeeds and whispered no, no, I haven't seen him, but if I ever hear one word I will let you know, sir, I certainly will. The Princeling nodded and told him that was good, and then he walked back through the stench of sweat and sex and out to the chilly city and the wind's embrace.

He stopped then briefly, mopped his brow, and steeled himself for his next stop. It had been the first name to come to his mind, but he'd known he'd want to be riding full and fast by the time he came to it. He licked his lips and turned down a side alley and wound his way through to a small string of little shops. At the end was a place called The Far Lightning, which to the casual eye was no more than your average gin joint. But still Hayes walked up and knocked at the door and was admitted by a huge man with stooped shoulders who glumly asked if he'd like a beverage.

"Oh yes, a Negroni, if you know how to make one," said Hayes.

The doorman nodded, motioned with one hand, and led him around the meager bar to a small door, which he opened and then stood beside, waiting obediently. Hayes entered and walked down the short staircase until he came to a low, wide room that was lit by oil lamps, and among the many shadows were tables of roulette, of craps, of poker and of blackjack. At each table men sat hunched and anxious, so lost in their games they did not even notice Hayes entering. All except one.

Hayes saw him at the back immediately. He barely had to look, for he knew his man would be in the same place as always. Seated beside his shabby little wooden table and his checkers game and his newspaper, dressed in his old jean overalls and a red striped shirt, one hand fixed on the ebony cane between his legs. Hayes watched as Sookie Jansen's eyes zeroed in on him immediately. The old man raised one twisted claw and waved him forward, and Hayes obeyed.

No, he thought as he walked. One didn't prostrate oneself before Sookie Jansen without a heart full of confidence and some secrets to share. Of all his contacts throughout Evesden, Sookie was the best and also the worst, because Sookie's company was like his many games: gaining something was possible, but losing something was certain, no matter what talents you had. Hayes considered him something between a friend and a rival, which was saying something, because Hayes felt he had few of either.

"Well, well," said Sookie. He leaned his head back and squinted at him. "Come here so I can take a look at you."

"Hello, Sooks," said Hayes. "How's business?"

Sookie did not answer. He just looked him up and down, and Hayes had the uncomfortable feeling of being x-rayed. Like Hayes, Sookie was from overseas, being the unwanted son of a supposedly chaste Catholic missionary in China. His upbringing had been brutal beyond words, and he'd soon shed the grasp of God for the more lucrative one of the streets, where he'd made a minor king of himself, Hayes had heard. He'd been one of the first immigrants to Evesden, as Sookie'd always had a nose for profit, and he'd served as a pillar of the underworld ever since. Not that anyone knew. Sookie was decidedly a businessman and never a gangster, and his reputation only existed where he felt it was necessary.

You'd never think it to look at him, though. He was a short old man so wrinkled and aged he was almost beyond race. His blue eyes were alien in his faintly Asiatic face, and a brambly scrap of hair was forever riding below his lip. He'd learned his English from some far-flung dockworkers, and so he spoke in a queer Southern patois. He wore the same overalls and the same shirt and the same porkpie hat every day, and he'd come down to his club at the start of every morning and load his lip up with tobacco and sit and watch and idly play checkers. Hayes had never once seen him spit. He felt sure the old man simply swallowed it.

"Well, now," said Sookie finally. "Something's got ahold of the Princeling. Something's got a burn on him. That's for sure." He turned to his opponent across the checkerboard. "Hecker, I hear there's a nice breeze coming in. May bring some clean air. How about you check that out for me?"

Hecker rose and left and Hayes took his seat. "You didn't answer my question," said Hayes.

"No," said Sookie pointedly. "I didn't. What the hell you doing here, Princeling? You're bad news. People paint their doors with lamb's blood to make you walk by."

"I'm here to trade," said Hayes. "To tug on your earlobe, dear Sooks."

Sookie grunted. "Heard you was at Moira's spinning a few wheels. That so?"

Hayes tilted his head but said nothing.

"Yeah. Yeah. So why didn't you come to see old Sooks first, Princeling? That's real rude, as far as I can see."

"I needed something to trade with, of course."

"Of course," said Sookie, and sighed. "This'd be about the unions, eh?"

"Yes, Sooks. It would."

"Hm. Unions, unions," he mused. "You know, you ain't the same anymore, Princeling."

"No?"

"No. You used to be dirty. Dirty all over. Dirty and mean. And dirty and mean is dependable, and Sookie likes dependable, see?" He poked Hayes in the arm. "What the hell happened to you?"

"Don't know what you're talking about, Sooks."

He grunted and peered at Hayes again. The he grinned. "Oh, no. No, no. Don't you go telling me old Hayes got bit by a *woman*? Is that the case? I think so." He cawed laughter. "You know, I heard a rumor about you running around with a girl, but I didn't believe it was true. Now, though, I got to say they was right. I can tell it just by looking at you."

Hayes smiled and shrugged. Sookie always toyed with you before giving anything of worth.

"It is," said Sookie. "You got that look about you. You got the shine. I guess what they say is so. Old Hayes nudged up against some pussy and it burned him but good."

"It's not like that."

"Oh, sure it ain't. I'd never think I'd see the day. Especially 'cause lately I hear you ain't exactly a fan of pussy. Is that so?"

Hayes grinned wider and shrugged again.

"Ain't nothing wrong with that," he said. "A man wants what a man wants." Sookie shook his head. "I can't believe it, though. You always seemed like a hard little thing. Like you'd cut through the world like a knife. And now you twisting in the wind for a woman."

"I'm not a romantic, Sooks. You know that."

"But there *is* a girl."

"A young thing with fresher eyes than mine, yes. But she has nothing to do with this."

Sookie flexed his lower lip and sucked on his wad of tobacco. "Mm. Maybe not. But something's different in you. I never seen you run out in the open like you are right now, especially not over something like the unions. Just unwise."

"Say what you like," said Hayes. "I'm going to do it anyway."

Sookie sucked on the chaw again. "Let me tell you a story, boy. I had this cousin, see? Call him Archibald. Archibald, he wasn't a smart man, not by a long shot, but he inherited this old 'lectric printing press. Only one in town. So he does a fair bit of trade, gets his dollar, follow?"

"I follow."

"So day after day he runs his little print. Don't need no repairs. Don't need nothing extra. Just runs that machine. And then one day he got the idea, hey, why not make the press faster? Stronger? Sort of beat-up thing, beat-up and old, why not spruce it up, make it better? So he think on it and think on it. Never realize he don't know shit about a printing press. And then one day he shuts it down, gets under there, start fooling about with its insides, and then, *snap*." Sookie held up one hand and drew a finger across the knuckles. "The damn thing cuts off all his fucking fingers. Like butter. Like they was butter. See?"

Hayes nodded.

"What I'm saying is... don't fuck with what works. Don't do nothing extra, nothing special. Don't try and fix shit. Even if it seems broke. Just do what you do. Just do what you do every day. And forget about everything else. Hear?"

"I do," said Hayes. "But I still want to hear about the unions."

Sookie shook his head. "There's no angle for the unions for you. Nothing to play."

"I'm not here to play. Come on now. What's the word you have on them and the Tazz-man, Sooks?"

Sookie frowned and sighed, as though ruing the foolishness of the young. He regarded Hayes for a moment longer, then said, "Rumor has it that Tazz went underground."

"I know that."

"No, when I say underground, I mean *really* underground," he said. He pointed down. "Down there. In the catacombs, or whatever the hell they are. You know they're there. I hear that's where he run."

Hayes sat up. "Why the hell would he go there? That's where the killer is."

"Can't say. But I hear he's looking for something. Trying to figure something out. What, again, can't say."

"But what have you heard, old Sooks?"

Sookie turned away and sat back. His chest and shoulders sank in and his belly rose up and suddenly he was just another old man, trying to think of what was upsetting him so. He pawed at his newspaper and said, "Hm. You hear this thing in the paper about fields?"

"What? Fields?"

"Yeah. These fields them scientists are discovering."

"No. No I have not," said Hayes, growing irritated.

"They say they're finding these fields, like magnetic fields, but different. They're holding everything together. All together, even at the smallest level," he said, and held up his thumb and forefinger to show how small. "They make everything whole. Ain't that something? And now they're saying they can break those fields. That they can break stuff up. And do a lot of crazy shit with what come out. Think that's true?"

"I don't know."

"I think it is. And you and I know that McNaughton ain't going to let no one talk about stuff unless they've already figured out how to do it. And done it themselves a couple times over." He set the paper down and gazed out over the crowd. "I think this city's like that."

"Oh?"

"Yeah. People come here, looking for something. Money. Future. Whatever. And instead it just breaks them up. Makes them forget what makes them them. I know. I've seen it rise and I'll probably be around to see it fall, if it ever does. They lose that little field inside of them. And they give up what they got to the city. To bad men like me." He grinned and sat up straight. Then he poked Hayes in the arm again. "You lost your field, little boy. You're falling apart. You're forgetting what makes you so mean and dirty, see?"

Hayes did not smile this time.

Sookie looked at him sidelong. "I've heard that McNaughton's got all kinds of machines down there, underground. In the catacombs. Maybe Tazz wants to see for himself. And maybe get one of his own. Think that's possible?"

Hayes sat back. "I think maybe," he said softly.

"Yeah," said Sookie. "If a man could learn how to control those things down there, whatever they are, maybe he'd be able to control the city. Maybe. Neat idea, eh?"

"Yes," said Hayes, troubled. "Very fascinating."

Sookie sniffed. "So. What you got for me, Princeling? What's there that you can trade?"

Hayes shook himself and returned to the game at hand. "Merton's buying up wharf property," he said smoothly. "Thinking about importing, maybe."

Sookie waved a hand. "Don't give me garbage. Give me something good. You know I want something good."

"John Flax died the other night," said Hayes. "In Savron. The guards were in on it and they buried him in the basement."

"Chicken feed. Complete chicken feed. If you want to show your face here again I suggest you pony up, son."

"All right," said Hayes. "You know that senator's kid? The illegitimate one?"

"Ronald, I think his name is," said Sookie. "Fathered on a Chinese whore not much older than a mayfly."

"Yeah, maybe. Well, rumor has it... rumor has it he's no longer... whole."

"Whole?"

"Yeah," said Hayes, and glanced down at his crotch and back up at Sookie. "Whole."

Sookie's eyebrows rose. "Oh, really?"

"Yes. Mishandled one of Moira's girls. Things got ugly. Leastways, that's the rumor."

"You get that from Moira?"

He shook his head. "She'd never tell."

"No. I guess she wouldn't." Sookie nodded. "Huh. I've been looking to get ahold of that senator for some time now."

"Well, there's your foot in. Hope it does you well, Sooks." Hayes stood to leave.

"That's all?" said Sookie, surprised. "You don't want me to tell someone about how you want to see Tazz?"

"Oh, no. I know Sookie's mouth isn't big enough to help," said Hayes.

Sookie smiled crookedly. "That's so."

Hayes turned to leave when the old man's hand shot out and grabbed his wrist. "You be careful, Princeling," he said. "You got a disease in you. A new one, for you. I seen it before in others. I see it in your face. You're pulling out all the stops because you don't plan on coming back from where you're going. If it's the girl that's doing this, then fuck her and forget her, I say."

"And if it's more than her?"

Sookie frowned. "Then you better be damn sure about where you're going. You hear?"

"I hear," said Hayes. Then he bade Sookie goodbye and walked through the tables to the stairs and the rest of his chores.

Six hours and 191 dollars later Hayes washed up on the sidewalk before a grimy little all-night diner in Lynn. He had crossed the city in one night, touching those in the know and giving them the message. He was exhausted and reeling from drink and drugs, but he felt he had accomplished something. He had at last made headway.

The smile faded from his face. He had torn free of the madness and the high now drained from his body. Loneliness welled up in him, diamond-sharp and silent. He felt lost among the small, winding night streets, populated only by strangers and stragglers who were dark and silent as they passed on the other side of the road.

Hayes staggered through the front doors of the diner and dragged himself up to the bar. The place was empty save for a few. A cop on his beat and a cabbie who was nursing a watery glass of orange juice. A thickset woman who sat in the corner before an empty plate and sometimes cried noiselessly to the notice of no one. A bent woman with dishwater-blond hair pushing a broom between the tables though there seemed to be no dust. Lonely survivors, left behind by the day before.

Hayes sat with his head in his hands and tried to ignore the voice in the back of his mind that wished he would die, this terrible thing, this wretched empty vessel that was unable to enjoy even the dalliance of sin. He felt ill. In that moment he did not really know what he had done that night or why he had done it. If his life followed any direction right now, he guessed, it was due to nothing more than sheer momentum.

The waitress came and took his order. Minutes passed and she came back with a plate of steak and eggs. To his weary mouth they tasted only of cigarettes and retch. The policeman left and a woman came in and sat next to Hayes and ordered eggs. She opened up a newspaper and read in silence. After a while Hayes dozed over his plate.

He dreamed of deserts and the lone moon seen through a roof made of iron bars, of the smell of horseflesh and the lightning flash of carbine fire on barren slopes. Then he dreamed of the city as seen from above, a handful of blinking lights grown along the edge of the Sound like cobwebs caught in a corner. He listened to the lights below and realized they had a voice, one voice speaking together. After listening for a while longer he realized the lights were weeping.

"Meal subpar this time?" said a voice.

He awoke. The woman with the newspaper was smiling at him over the top of a sheet.

"What?" he said.

"The meal," she said. "I noticed you haven't eaten much of it."

"So?"

"Well then, it can't be very good."

"Why?" he demanded.

She faltered, then said, "I've just seen you in here."

"Seen me? Where?"

"In here. You come here pretty often and eat the same thing, steak and eggs."

"Here? I come here?"

"Yes."

Hayes thought, then squinted at her and asked, "Why are you watching me eat?"

"I'm... I'm not."

"You know what I eat here."

"No, I just come in here sometimes and I... I see you, so I was just curious."

"Curious."

"Y-yes. I thought I'd make chat." She looked down, then said, "I'm sorry. I didn't mean anything by it." Then she stood and put down some money and walked away.

"No," said Hayes as she walked out. "No, I didn't mean to..."

She did not hear him. She went through the front doors and did not look back. Hayes hung his head. "Shit," he said softly to himself. "Goddamn it."

He cursed himself a while longer and then paid and hobbled out. He wasn't sure what he would say to her if he caught up to her or even why he cared. In the end it did not matter. By the time he reached the street she was gone.

He walked past the Nail to the web of side streets that made his neighborhood. He did not go to the warehouse but instead went to a small shop across from it with a FOR RENT sign hanging in the glass. He took out his keys and opened the door and went past the empty front room to the stairs in the back and then up to the second floor. It was unadorned except for a mattress in the middle of the bare floors, lying perfectly in line with the window, which looked down upon the front door of his warehouse and all the small alleys that went to the back. He had purchased the shop for that very feature. He was almost sure that neither Brightly nor Evans knew of its existence, as he had bought it using one of his less prominent identities.

"All the old tradecraft," he muttered. He leaned his head up against the glass and began watching. Not a soul stirred in the street. The bleak light of dawn began to seep through the sheet of clouds in the east. He kept watching and waiting. After the first two hours he wanted to sleep but found he could not.

CHAPTER TWENTY-ONE

When she returned to work the next day Samantha prepared the agenda and waited for Hayes to arrive. The world seemed to float by her as she entered her office, and she was unable to focus on any one thing. She was still living in the night before, she knew, how she had had to coax him as though he were no more than a teenager, and how after they had sat in comfortable silence, allowing the morning hours to slip by without a word. As she waited for Hayes she realized her every second was geared toward seeing Garvey again, and the murders and the many conspiracies seemed to fade to a murmur around her.

After an hour of waiting she figured Hayes would just show up late, claiming some injury or feebleness from his hospital stay. After three she called Evans, explained what had happened, and went by Hayes's warehouse. She pounded on the front door for a good half-hour before she heard a cough. She turned and found a telegram boy standing behind her, looking awkward.

"Yes?" she said.

"Are you, um"—he checked his telegram—"Sam?"

"What? I mean, yes?"

"Message for you," he said, and handed it to her.

She opened it up and scanned it.

OFF A-QUESTING STOP ENJOY YOUR FREE DAY STOP

She read it again, then looked up and scanned the streets and windows around her.

"You cheeky little shit," she said. "Where are you?"

"What?" said the telegram boy.

"Nothing. Oh, here," she said, and tipped him. "Now go on."

She called Evans, and he groaned when she told him the situation. "I'll try and keep it under my hat, my dear," he said. "But I'm getting a little tired of making excuses, especially under these circumstances."

Samantha agreed and said she would send him all the information he needed to make their inquiry look productive, provided he spread it a little thin. She returned to the Nail and sent her work up to the forty-seventh floor, then checked the time. She had four hours left. She cleaned her office for another twenty minutes, then told Evans she was leaving for the day and caught the trolley back to Newton, not sure what she was going to do.

She went shopping at Earl Street and bought some nice bread, then sat on the benches in front of the museum, eating and watching people walk by. She wondered if she should be out trying to find Hayes. Then she wondered if that was even possible. If Evans was right, Hayes wasn't the sort of person you found unless he felt you should.

She went back to her apartment with a bottle of wine and a good piece of chicken, deciding that a nice meal and a long soak in the tub was in order. She passed through the mezzanine and then found Garvey there again, seated in the same chair and wearing the exact same suit he had worn before. He grinned at her, but his face was strained and she knew he was carrying something awful with him this time. She walked to him and put one hand on his face, feeling his stubble. "You look terrible," she said.

"I look terrible," he agreed.

They went back to her apartment and he asked if there was a chair he could destroy. She guided him toward some overstuffed red affair and he dropped himself down gracelessly. She wanted to ask how he was doing, to search him and see how he felt about what had happened between them, but his mind was obviously elsewhere, and so instead she made coffee and poured two cups.

"How is it?" she called from the kitchen.

"How is what?" he said.

"Oh, please."

There was a pause. "Fucked," he said.

"Oh?"

"Yeah. Fucked. Fucked sideways. Fucked in the ear. Pick a fuck, this case is fucked."

"I see," she said, carrying the coffee back over. Garvey took the little cup and tossed it down, dribbling some onto his shirt.

"Mayor went and gave a speech at Bridgedale today," he said.

"Did he?" She sat down on the floor beside his feet.

"Yeah. Something about solidarity. How this is all one city and we've all got to stick together. Then he turned around and vaguely accused the Department and McNaughton of a few things. So I guess it is one city, excluding your guys and my guys. And they've added a shitload more people to the detail," he said with a sigh. "Simons and Meyer. From High Crimes Division. Corralled in on the commissioner's say-so."

"How are they?"

"They're bastards. Think they walk on water. High Crimes is used to details, sure, long investigations with plenty of manpower and resources. They're the dashing heroes of our goddamn shit department. Today they came into Murder and they managed to piss Morris and Collins off in minutes."

"And you?"

"I was already pissed off."

"Well. At least you're proactive."

"Morris has sold everyone some serious horseshit," said Garvey with another sigh. "Some serious, serious horseshit. Looking to impress. This is a career case, you know."

"Oh, I know."

"How do you know?"

She paused, pursing her lips over her cup of coffee. "Well, at the start of this I thought if Mr. Hayes handled this union business particularly well then I might secure a better position."

"And now?"

"Now I don't know. I haven't thought about it for some time. Tell me what Morris did."

"Hm. Well, he waded into the Shanties and before you know it he's got these two little tennies swearing they heard some denner putting a price on Denton and Huffy's head. Serious bounty. Morris has worked it and managed to whip up some amazing conspiracy for everyone, referenced some gang wars he worked way back when. His most touted of all touted theories right now is that the union surge has started a new den war. Morris says the unions have links to the den-runners, and now everyone in Dockland is hitting the mattresses again, just like back in '92. We just don't have enough street-level information to figure out which gang is warring with which, he says. Everyone loves it, of course."

"They do?"

"Sure. Moves things away from McNaughton. Puts it in terms everyone can handle. I mean, it's just gang wars again. And it comes from a veteran, everyone loves a veteran, and all the vet says we have to do is start raiding the opium dens again. And now everyone's seeing careers in it. Collins, Morris. The captain. Everyone sees a bright future for the boys who bust this new gang war."

"And you?"

Garvey was quiet for a long while. Then he said, "No. They don't like what I'm saying. They're trying to treat this like this is normal, like it's just another murder. It's not. They still can't explain how it happened. They're not even trying. But there are politics in play. And I'm already dirty to them," he said. "Because of Hayes. Because of fucking Hayes." He shook his head. "What the fuck happened. What happened to this damn town."

Then he turned and looked at her. "I didn't want to be there anymore. At the Department."

"I know."

"I didn't want to think about things no one wants me to think about. I just wanted to leave it. I just... I just wanted to see you."

"I'm here," she said.

He put his coffee down and kissed her, weakly at first but then more strongly. Then she took his head in her hands and looked at it, all the wrinkles and the bags under his eyes and all the bruises, a face hard and worn by the things it'd looked into. Then she kissed him, on his chin and eyes and brow, and then finally his lips. Then they stood, lips still touching, and she led him to the bed. As she did, one of his hands ran down the front of her body to pull up her skirt and go hunting between her legs.

She was not certain if it came from genuine affection or if it was some kind of desperation, a kindred sense of being lost, like two ships passing each other on a foggy sea and calling to one another, blindly recognizing each other's plight. But she felt that it was, at its heart, both an escape, and real. As if each time he held her she was following him down another one of the underground tunnels to be greeted by wonders that took her away from all of this, to some waiting treasure that had been there all along if only you had the eyes to see it, and she hoped that perhaps it did the same for him.

As night came they watched the spotlights drift across the ceiling of her bedroom. She sat with his head cradled in her lap, and she cracked the curtains so they could see out and watch the sky strobe soft white.

"It's not how I remember it," he said.

"Remember what?"

"The city. It's changed so much, from when I was little."

"How old were you when you moved here?"

He looked up at her. "I didn't. I was born here."

She blinked, then said, "Do you know, I think you may be the only native Evesdener I've ever met."

He laughed. "I'm not surprised," he said. "This is a mutt city, made of other cities and other countries. But it used to be a city. A real city."

"When?"

"I don't know. When I was a kid, I guess." He struggled to describe it to her. How the city had once been something new, genuinely new, new with promise, not new with perversion, as this late Evesden was. It had been the foundation of something, not a tumorous buildup of growth. It was difficult for him to say exactly when he had realized that it had failed, though.

She found he kept returning to one particular day, the day his father closed his carpentry shop. Like all the buildings in Evesden the shop had been relatively new, he told her, but in comparison to everything else his father's shop seemed a great old thing, solidly built of huge shafts of wood, with dark, polished eaves and an eternal scent of polish and smoking timber. It had seemed larger than a church back then, dark and cavernous with strange tools standing among the shadows. And somehow his father had seemed bigger then, too. Garvey still remembered him as a huge man, taller than any other he had ever seen, with a broad back and knobby, darkened hands, hands that were a plum-red like they had been soaked in wine. His father and the shop seemed like emissaries of an older age then, silent and wordless except for the sounds of work and progress. Even when the home-building companies began to take hold and started choking out the little shops his father had soldiered on, indifferent to the rise and fall of those strange, abstract companies. Yet they did not fall, only rise. They rose until they ruined the shop, eating up customers until the gnarled old church went silent, tool by tool, voice by voice. And on the day his father had locked up and doomed the shop, both he and the shop seemed to have lost something. It was not a great, mysterious building made of dark timber. In fact it seemed little more than a shack then, and a shoddily built one at that. And his father no longer seemed so large and mysterious. He seemed like a working man who had not been smart enough to realize when the world was eroding beneath him. And then his father had gone home and uncapped a bottle of whisky and sipped it down inch by inch, watery red eyes fixed on nothing, and he'd shaken his head and said, "It's gone now. It's all gone."

And that was when Garvey had known. Had realized he had known all along. That sometime in the blossoming progress of this city there had come a wound that had sent it all awry, and it could only throw on messy layer after messy layer, like a mad pearl growing within the lips of the sound, until it ate itself alive.

He often got that feeling. That once something had happened that had sent the whole world reeling. Some great violation or change, long ago. Maybe even before Evesden. He wasn't sure. But he had felt all his life that he was struggling in the wake of it.

As he described it to her she suddenly remembered the letter Hayes had read to her in Skiller's apartment, and the little lost boy and his dead father, and she wondered what Garvey saw in his case with the man in the canal. Perhaps he saw that same familiar wound that had sent his life in the direction it'd come, only now there was a chance, however slight, to correct it.

CHAPTER TWENTY-TWO

Hayes slept in five-minute bursts. He had trained himself to do it long ago, and there in the empty cold shop the gift returned slowly. For the past two days he had lived in a swimming dreamworld, fatigue eroding every one of his senses. But still he watched. And, in a way, the silence and loneliness were pleasant. His mind had not been so clear in weeks.

When the storm rolled in he piled blankets about himself on his perch. He ignored his shivering and hunkered down more and sucked on the end of a pencil. He badly wanted a cigarette but would not risk the flame.

He was not sure when he noticed the man. Time had become strange to him as the sun shifted behind the overcast. But he had been staring at the pattern of the crowd for hours and had come to know the traffic and the loitering places, so when one man walked out of one alley and crossed before the building face and walked into yet another alley to examine something on the ground, Hayes knew there was something wrong. Through the fog and the condensation of the glass Hayes saw he was short with a gray coat and a smudged bowler, but could make out nothing more.

He watched the gray coat. Saw him look closer at the thing on the ground, then look at the street and the buildings above and pick the thing up and toss it away. It was half of a shoe, sodden and wet. The man wiped his hands on his coat and stood in the shelter of the alley and put his hands in his pockets and casually rocked back and forth.

"You," said Hayes from his perch, "are fucking terrible at this."

He gauged that the man in the gray coat would stay in the alley for a little less than five minutes. He slipped down to the bottom floor of the shop and watched him from behind a ragged sheet that had been left hanging. The gray coat sidled out toward the lip of the alley and huddled below an awning in the sleet. Then he walked out quickly, crossing to Hayes's warehouse and dodging through the cars and the cabbies and the streams of soaking people. He slowed as he came to Hayes's door, where he turned about and walked backward the rest of the way, eyes roving and clouds of breath forming a trail like the smokestack of a train. Then he ducked down and slid something below the door and hurried off west.

Hayes put on a thick black coat and boots and a riding cap and headed out into the rain after him. He marked the gray coat carefully in the street and strained to keep hold of him. Crowds swarmed about them as his quarry headed north on Embrage and then west on 112th and then south on Dowers. The figure slipped among street criers and huddled bands of the homeless and once a train of passing nuns, black and white like the keys of a piano. He paused at every other corner to inspect something on the ground and sneak glances over his shoulder. Each time he went through this inept process Hayes would pull his face down into his collar and merge with the nearest group of people. If they noticed him they did not say so. Perhaps on rainy cold days such as these the water blended people together until they could not tell themselves apart.

The gray coat came to a trolley station and he swung himself down the twisting iron staircase to the tunnels below. Hayes ambled up to the stairway and passed by while looking down. He did not see the man waiting so he quickly bought a newspaper and pretended to read it to hide his face. Then he walked to the stairwell and descended in a brisk trot and turned sharply left at the floor and kept going. Warm air and the roar of a distant trolley swallowed most of his senses. A vagrant sat by the foot of the stairs, hands cupped for change. He reached out to Hayes, saying, "I am a messenger, sent from afar. Please, you must listen to me. You must listen. You must..."

Hayes ignored him. His eyes stayed vaguely fixed on the print of the newspaper, scanning the crowd for that streak of light gray. He walked around in a quick loop and spotted the man walking east along the tunnel, then over one of the trolley bridges and down west to Westbank. Hayes followed and let the newspaper fall as he did so. It would be hard to lose him now. The trolley stations were mostly abandoned in the wake of the Bridgedale slaughter.

The gray coat came to a trolley stop and stood there waiting. Hayes passed him by, just a few feet away. The man did not notice Hayes taking in his black-smudged face layered with burst veins, the skin heavily lined around the eyes and lips. Probably from fumes of some sort. A unioner, almost certainly.

Hayes kept walking down to a sausage stand. He bought one and shambled down farther to where the maintenance tunnels began. He leaned up against a bright red pipe and chewed his sausage slowly and watched the gray coat. He squinted to read the trolley map. There was the D line and the G4 line and the C38 line and it seemed like thousands more. He badly wished Samantha were there. She was much smarter when it came to things like this.

"Come on, bastard," he muttered as he watched. "Come on. Go on home for me, just real quick."

The gray coat looked back at the platform numbers, then began to walk farther down. Hayes waited for him to pass, then matched his pace, not willing to put any more distance between them.

As they moved a faint sound rumbled through the trolley station, a low groaning that blurred into a hum as some massive burst of pressure was shifted from one system to another. The other people in the station seemed not to notice, but as the noise increased Hayes became aware of something else. There was something crawling in the back of his mind, building tension with the noise until it was a white-hot needle burning into him, right behind his ear.

He stopped, gasping, then muttered, "Oh, no," as the attack began to take grip.

He stumbled to the side, clawing at the wall as he fell before the tunnel. The guttering sounds from below him clacked and shivered, filling up his ears, and somehow the attack strengthened with it. Anger and fear and morose boredom flooded through him, pounding his brain with each wave. He looked up through tear-filled eyes and saw the maintenance tunnel ceiling above him. He thrashed about, the world around him blurring.

Close and dusty and dark. Chambers and passages splintering off, indecipherable signs written on each of them. The roar of the trolleys filling every moment. And somewhere in it was a voice, begging for him to listen.

Then something changed. Suddenly he could hear something new. But that wasn't possible, he thought. Surely he had to be *wrong*...

Things went black. Then lights flashed before him, soft blue ones that were somehow at the edges of his sight. He felt there was some message in them, some signal like Morse code, but before he could pay attention to them they faded and he saw he was no longer in the trolley system at all. Instead he found he was in the bone-like ruins of a city long gone. Pockmarked ribs of ancient gray buildings lay broken on the paths before him. Everything smelled of ashes. Down the remains of one street he could see the husk of a tall building leaning against the dark sky. At the top its steeple had been reduced to shards, but he could see it had once been jade-green, and below it a few metal letters still clung to the building's side, an M and a C and an O.

As he looked he saw there was something beyond it. Something out on the edge of the city, something enormous and white, rising up to the sky…

Someone was shaking him. "Hey, buddy. Buddy?"

The vision faded. He took a breath and smelled the urinal tang of the trolley stations and knew he had not gone anywhere. He opened his tear-blurred eyes and saw he was lying in the mouth of the maintenance tunnel. The sausage stand vendor was prodding him with the toe of a shoe as curious onlookers gathered around him.

"You all right, buddy?" asked the sausage vendor.

"What the hell was that?" gasped Hayes.

"You fell over. Just fell over and started shaking. You hit your head or something?"

Hayes sat up and looked around. The man in the gray coat was gone. "How long have I been here?"

"Sorry?" asked the vendor.

"How long have I been here?"

"Oh. I don't know. A good couple of minutes or so."

"Shit," said Hayes. He got to his feet and staggered back a little but soon steadied himself.

"It wasn't the sausage, right, buddy?" asked the vendor warily.

"Fuck off," said Hayes, and darted off into the station.

He sprinted through the platforms, looking high and low for that smear of gray he'd marked, but found nothing. The man had either gotten spooked or made his connection. Either way, he'd be on the other side of the city by now.

Surrendering, Hayes limped back up to the streets. Dawn was crawling over the building tops. He made his way home, shivering and confused.

It was almost like something under the city had spoken to him. Spoken to him and caused his attack. And as strange as the vision had been, what disturbed him more was what had come just before it, because for one second Hayes had not heard whispers from the minds of those nearby but almost a loud shout from a single mind, one that was vaster than any other he'd ever encountered. An enormous and strange consciousness, somehow buried under the city, and waiting for him, imagining a ruined Evesden underneath a dark sky.

Something was changing in the city, that was for sure, and perhaps these murders and the unions were just the barest hint of things to come. Hayes shook himself and tried to forget it.

Underneath his front door the man in the gray coat had wedged a small letter. Hayes pawed at it with useless, icy hands and forced the door open and stumbled in. He had no wood so he built a fire in the brazier of books, history and poetry and versions of the Bible. He knelt before the blackening pages and felt warmth return to his bones. Then he opened the letter. On it were a time and a place, no more.

CHAPTER TWENTY-THREE

Samantha and Garvey continued their affair erratically, meeting at odd hours, often at her apartments but sometimes his or a hotel room, if it was cheap enough. It seemed time had stopped for both of them. Hayes had not returned, so Samantha's current task was to produce enough information to make it appear as though he were still there, which was easy enough. And Garvey's role in the Bridgedale investigation had all but vanished. He was just chaff, waiting to be thrown out, he said. He often felt perfectly willing to do the throwing himself.

One day he took her west to where the hills and the mountains began. There was a sanitarium there, with natural springs and boiling hot saunas. When they parked she walked to the edge of the lot and looked out over the valley to the city in the distance. From here it was no more than a haze of smoke and the hint of angles and forms resting somewhere at its base.

They spent the day in escape, forgetting about the countless machinations waiting for them at the city, and enjoying the peace and quiet. As evening fell they ate at a nearby diner and returned to their rooms, and after they made love their sweat softened the sheets and the moisture chilled in the evening air until everything was cool and clean.

As night deepened Garvey asked, "How long do you think this will last?"

"For as long as we need it to," she said. "For as long as we want it to."

"No. Not this. Not us."

"Then what?"

"The investigation. The city. Everything."

Samantha was quiet. She did not know what to say to that.

"How long do you think we can keep going at this rate?" he asked in the darkness. "How long do you think this place we've made can last?"

The minutes dragged on, and she asked him what Hayes believed. He told her not a damn lot. Then she asked him what he believed. "Whatever I can afford to," he said. "Which is enough. Sometimes."

"It's killing him, isn't it," she said.

"Hayes?"

"Yes. His talent."

"Maybe," said Garvey. "Probably. I think he knows it, though."

"And he doesn't care?"

"What could he do?"

"Something. I don't know."

Garvey sat up. A bird's cry sounded somewhere out in the night, then faded to a whimper. Samantha looked out the window and her eyes trailed up the gray-white trunks of the pines to the stars above. They seemed to have never been so bright before.

"Mr. Evans says one day we will reach the stars," she said.

"Huh? What do you mean?"

"He says McNaughton is making something that will leave this world and rise up and touch the next, up there," she said, and pointed.

"How?"

"I don't know. An airship of some kind, perhaps. Like the one they tried to launch last month."

"That one didn't go so well."

"I believe they're still working on it. Maybe once it works, we'll have peace. Do you think that could be?"

He thought about it, then shook his head. "No," he said.

"Why not? If people could leave and go where they want..."

"They said that when we all first started going West," said Garvey. "They said if people were unhappy in the East then they could just go out West, and find what they wanted. Well, they went West, and they made this place, and others like it, but they never found what they wanted. People don't leave their problems behind, they don't stop being people just because they moved. They'll do the same thing, every time."

"But why?"

He was silent. Then he said, "Because the world is a tough place. Tough and empty. The ones who get by are the ones who are either mean or lucky. And they don't much like other people like themselves hanging around. It's the same way all over. I bet it's the same even there," he said, and waved his hands at the stars. "If there's people out there like us, they've probably seen the same damn things that we have."

She noticed an edge to his voice. "Donald," she said. "Donald, what's wrong?"

"Nothing," he said. He looked away and then said, "Sometimes it seems like everything's falling apart. Every single goddamn thing."

"You can leave," she told him. "We can leave. Just go away and leave this place. If we want."

He looked at her and shook his head. "No," he said. "We can't. Don't you see? We can't just leave it to die."

Samantha returned in the morning and went to work in the clothes she had worn the day before. After a few hours of doing almost nothing to no one's notice, she returned to her apartment and lay down to rest.

She awoke to the sound of knocking. She sat up and looked out the window. It was dark. The pounding continued. She went to the door and opened it and found Hayes was standing there, soaking wet and smiling madly.

"You're coming with me," he said. "Put your coat on and let's go."

"What?" she said. "No, wait, where have you *been*? It's been days, for Heaven's sake! I've had to keep everything quiet so no one knows you're gone!"

"Well, I knew you'd be able to cover for me. But it won't have been for nothing. I've landed something, Sam. Something big."

"What's going on? What's happening?"

"Oh, it's business as usual," he said. "We're going to an interview, Sam. Tonight. Only this one is a little different."

"What? Please, I'm in no mood for games."

"I've arranged things," he said, giddy. "Arranged a meeting. With Mickey Tazz."

"You *what*?" she said. "You've got a meeting with Mickey Tazz?"

"No. We do. We both do. As esteemed representatives of McNaughton."

She gaped at him, then said again, "You what?"

"I want you to come with me. To be my secretarial aid while I talk to this lowborn king of men."

"No. No, I can't."

"Sure you can. You have to."

"I can't, I have... I have plans."

"Plans?" he said, and scoffed. "What the hell kind of plans? Break your damn plans, we're seeing the man no one else in the city can even *find*."

"I really cannot..."

"Some gentleman caller?" asked Hayes. He picked up an umbrella and brandished it about like a sword. "Some gent from Legal who's here to wine and dine you throughout Newton?"

"Oh, stop it," she snapped.

Hayes lowered the umbrella and looked at her, deflated. Then he said, "You have to come."

"Why?"

"Because I don't want to go alone."

"Then find someone else."

"I can't."

"Some thug or some knife for hire. Get them."

"I can't."

"Why?"

"Because you're the only person I trust," he said.

Samantha stared at him. Hayes replaced the umbrella and stood looking down at it.

"Well, you and Garvey, but I have no clue where he is," he said. "Besides, I don't want to bring him into this. The last thing we need is to muddy the police any more."

"Oh, God," she said wearily.

"Come on, Sam," he pleaded. "You're my rock. Come on. Come with me and let's break this thing in half."

Samantha rubbed her forehead and leaned against the wall. "Fine," she said. "Fine. Just let me leave a note." She went to grab a slip of paper.

"Do you really have a gentleman coming, Sam?" asked Hayes. He peeked over her shoulder.

"Get out," she said. "Get out and go downstairs and wait for me. I can't even imagine how you got in here. Just go."

She turned to find he had already left. The only signs of his passage were the wet spots on the floor.

Samantha found Hayes lurking in a niche in the doorway outside the lobby. He stepped out like some clockwork toy and said to her, "Let's go," and began walking.

They went west to the trolley stop and walked down the iron

stairway to the platform. "Where are we meeting him?" asked Samantha.

"Probably not meeting him, at first," Hayes said. "First we'll be meeting some of his ambassadors. They lead us to Tazz and then we all have a sit-down. We're meeting them at the East Bazaar, per his invite."

"But what do you plan to say to him?"

"I don't need to say anything," Hayes said darkly. "I just need to get close."

They took the 41A to one of the few Shanties stops and walked two blocks down to the bazaar square. The frames of booths were still set up, tiny roofs and walls laid out on the wet pebbled cement like a ghost town. They walked down through the aisles and the small paths. The faint smell of spice and old vegetables still hung in the air. Then Hayes gestured to her and they hid behind the folds of one empty booth. Once they were stowed away he crossed his arms and leaned up against the wall and Samantha did likewise.

They waited for what felt like hours. Then he tilted his head as though he had heard something. He told her, "Wait here," and slipped away.

She waited in the darkness and eventually put her eye to the crack in the wall. She saw two men in overalls walking down from the street to the center of the bazaar. They had on knit caps and one wore an old overcoat. They came to the center and stood there, waiting, and seemed to grow frustrated as the minutes ticked by. Then Hayes returned to her, slick as a snake, and whispered, "Let's go."

They walked out of the booth toward the two men, feeling absurd, like some quaint couple just out for a midnight walk. When they came before the men Hayes nodded at them and said, "Hello. Lovely evening, isn't it?"

The two men glanced at one another. One was older and thicker with ash-gray sideburns. The other was short and thin, his hair slicked back. The older one said, "You the man we're supposed to be escorting?"

"I believe so. Are you Tazz's men?"

"Don't know nothing about Tazz," the older one said. "Orders were just to take someone from the bazaar to a meeting. Escort-like."

"Alone?" asked Hayes.

The younger one nodded. "Alone."

"And it's just you two?"

"Yes."

"You're sure?"

"Yes. Why?"

"Because there's a man hiding behind the bazaar wall. Hunkered down with a pistol," said Hayes. "Is he supposed to be there?"

The two union men shared another glance, this one dismayed.

"He's protection," said the older one.

"Leave him here," Hayes said. "There's no need for protection."

"We won't. We don't know who the hell you are."

"I don't know who the hell you are, either. You're leaving him behind, anyways. And only one of you is coming."

"Why is that?"

"Because your protection needs someone to help him," Hayes answered primly.

The men shared yet another glance. The older one nodded and his partner ran off into the bazaar. After he was a good ways away the gray hair said, "If you've hurt a hair on his fucking head..."

"He'll be fine," Hayes said. "In the morning. He'll just need to lie down for a while. I left the gun with him, too, so you don't have to worry about that, though it's empty now."

"Fucking bastard," said the gray hair.

Soon the young one came running back, face streaked with tears. In between panting breaths he said, "What'd you do to him? You piece of shit, what'd you do?"

"Put him to sleep," Hayes said coolly. "You'll want to keep an eye on him. So one of you will have to take us to the meeting spot. Alone."

The two union men withdrew and discussed it. After a while they returned and the old one said, "Fine. I will. But I am armed. And if you do one fucking thing that I think warrants it I'll kill you both myself, you fucking snake. You and your goddamn woman."

"Fair enough," said Hayes.

The older one led them farther west, down High Street. It was wide and deserted, no cars and no pedestrians. Abandoned buildings marched down the left side, windows broken and sunken roofs yawning wide. Bright yellow signs cheerfully informed them that this block was set for demolition. Then they came to an intersection cordoned off with sandbags. The old man walked by the bags and led them to a long, tall temporary fence circling a part of the street Samantha could not see. They went to a spot where the boards were missing and the old man motioned to climb through. Beside the hole in the fence was a small oil lamp. He knelt and lit it and picked it up. "This way," he said.

They walked across the cordoned street, passing over more walls of sandbags, and soon came to an immense sunken hole that went right down through the cement. A set of steps had been made with yet more sandbags, their misshapen forms descending into the dark.

"Oh," said Hayes. "The Dockland trolley."

"Yeah," said the old man. "Follow me. Carefully. You can trip and die if you damn well please, though."

The old man held the lantern out before him and they walked down the shifting steps. Scaffolding and piping crawled around the walls and water ran down into the dark in pattering streams. As they came to the bottom they found they were at the start of an enormous stone tunnel, more than thirty feet high, the walls smooth and sloping and bone-white. At the bottom were tracks for the trolley lines and up above were faint yellow lights. Most were dead, leaving the tunnels in near darkness.

"What is this place?" Samantha asked.

"The Dockland trolley," said Hayes. "Still in development. Like Construct. Problem with this one wasn't the ocean, though. No, the contractors soon just found themselves running out of workers, and those that chose to work found themselves beaten in the streets."

"You don't know what you're talking about," said the old man savagely.

"Am I wrong?"

"They worked us like animals," the old man said. "Worked us like dogs."

"Hm," said Hayes.

"I was there on one shift when two men were mauled by equipment. Two men, do you hear? And the overseers didn't care. Didn't care at all. When the north tunnel flooded after Construct began tipping an entire crew drowned. They told us to go in and start baling it out by hand. That freezing water, always rising. They didn't care if we died. That was two years ago now and I don't regret a single thing we done since."

"And this is where Tazz has gone to ground?" said Hayes. "Interesting choice." Yet he seemed unsurprised at the revelation.

They continued on through the tunnels, the old man keeping his lantern aloft like some hobbling Charon, leading them to darker, stranger depths. The air grew cold and the tunnel walls were cracked in places from lack of maintenance. Sometimes they heard machinery far beneath them, some massive piston endlessly rotating. Samantha suppressed a shiver at its sound.

The old man took lefts and rights and eventually turned up a long, sloping branch that took them to warmer levels. He veered toward one wall and set into it was a small maintenance passage. As they entered the old man froze and turned to peer back down the tunnel lengths from where they'd come.

"What was that?" he said.

"What was what?" said Hayes.

The old man shushed him and held the lamp high and squinted

down the shaft. There was nothing below but gloom and water. The old man grumbled something and lowered the lamp and they entered the maintenance network.

They passed through pipes and maintenance sheds long unused and covered with dust. Shovels and picks and shoes were scattered on the tunnel floor. Many had been gnawed by rats and more than once they saw pink naked tails fleeing into the shadows. Finally they came to a long tunnel that ended in a small door, and as they walked through the wall completely fell away on one side. They stopped short, shocked, and blinked, and saw they were standing on a small stone pathway that ran along one side of what had to be an enormous room, but it was so dark they could not see beyond several feet out. A small iron railing ran along one side but below that the wall dropped away. Samantha could feel the pressure change upon her skin and knew the room had to be incredibly vast. Sometimes there was the sound of dripping, but otherwise the immense hall was silent.

At the far end of the pathway they saw four men standing patiently in the weak yellow light along the wall. As they entered one of the men turned up a lamp at his feet. They saw a broad, boyish face illuminated bright white, eyes clear and untroubled with an easy smile. He was short and stocky but well built, sporting a plain haircut and simple overalls with leather gloves and brogans.

"Impressive, isn't it?" he called.

Before they could answer two men stepped out from behind them, crowbars and wrenches in hand, and fenced them back.

"What's this?" said Hayes. "What the hell are you doing?"

"My apologies, Mr. Hayes," called the stocky man at the far end of the tunnel. "I'm afraid in the interest of my security we have to keep you as far away from me as possible."

"What do you mean?"

"You have your informants. I have mine," said the man, and saluted. Then his face grew solemn and he said, "I know what you are. And you'll not come within a hundred feet of me."

The hall was silent for a good while. Samantha tried to see Hayes's face in the dark but she could read nothing there.

"You would be the famous Mickey Tazz, then," Hayes said, and stepped back and brushed himself off.

"I would," said the man. "And you would be Cyril Hayes. The least famous of all McNaughton employees. As intended. And there next to you, is that Miss Fairbanks?"

Samantha nodded but did not speak. She glanced to Hayes again to see how he took this but his face was closed and still.

"There's no need to be afraid," Tazz said.

"I'm not," she said.

"Well, that's good. I'm surprised Mr. Hayes has brought you to such a meeting. Then again, I'm not sure why I'm here, either. Though he seems to have made it impossible for me to avoid."

"What is this place?" asked Hayes.

"Don't you recognize it? After all, it's one of yours," Tazz said. He pointed behind them at the corner where the pathway ended. Inlaid in the wall were the rungs of an iron ladder leading down into the dark, and stamped at the top of the ladder was the imperial M of McNaughton.

"Have you never seen it? Or heard of it?" asked Tazz.

"No. I haven't," said Hayes.

"I'm not surprised, Mr. Hayes. Your company keeps its secrets close, and they only share what they have to. Such is the way of all industry. But to keep such a secret from you, their personal secret-keeper? Well. I suppose they didn't *have* to tell you, now did they? You're more of a personnel watchdog. The real treasures they keep far from you, maybe intentionally. As to what this room is, I mean *really* is, I don't know. It's just another one of McNaughton's many secrets, to me. Though by no means the worst. Fascinating, isn't it, though?"

"Maybe so," said Hayes. "But I'm afraid I didn't come here to talk just about rooms. Or McNaughton."

"That's plain," he said. "Then what about, Mr. Hayes? Politics? Fishing? Cabbages and kings?"

"About the murders."

Tazz's eyebrow twitched. "The murders? Just the murders?"

"Just the murders," said Hayes calmly.

"Are you serious, Mr. Hayes?"

"Yes."

"What do you expect for me to say about them?"

"Anything. Anything about what you think of them. About who did it and what they mean," said Hayes. He smiled as though he'd said what he'd come to say, but Samantha got the strong impression he was improvising.

"I think it should be obvious what I have to say about the murders."

"Then say it anyway. I want to hear it. After all, no one else has heard it yet."

"That was in the interest of my security."

"So I've been told."

Tazz placed his hands behind his back. "What do I think of what's happened? I think that this is no longer a struggle. No longer just class tensions. I think it's warfare now, Mr. Hayes. Pure and simple."

"You blame McNaughton."

"Of course. Of course I do. Who would profit most from their deaths? McNaughton, and those in their pay." He nodded, as though satisfied with his claim.

"You would profit as well, Mr. Tazz," said Hayes.

"Me? How would I profit?"

"You get a dozen martyrs. A dozen proud deaths for your cause. And you lose some undesirables. You see, I know what the men in the Bridgedale trolley had been doing. I know about the sabotage. About the murders they did in their own right. We never made it public. But I know they were killing in your name."

"I know nothing of this," Tazz said, his voice still even. "And besides, I cannot control what men do. I cannot influence every decision they make. But I do not kill, either. I do not wantonly murder, nor do I condone it. I am not like McNaughton. I would harm no man unless he planned to harm me."

"And your current residence?" asked Hayes, gesturing to the room around him. "This has nothing to do with it?"

"The trolley lines, you mean?" said Tazz. He laughed. "You think I may have somehow planned the murders myself, through these tunnels? You don't know much about the Dockland trolley, then. It was never connected to any of the other lines. It's a mere fragment. Another project started by the rich and halted by the deaths of the working poor. It is an interesting place to hide, though, isn't it? But it's the smartest one. The last place the union trolley killer would look for me would be in the trolley lines themselves."

"Maybe so," said Hayes. "Unless Naylor and the rest were killed for other reasons. So you say you have no more knowledge of them? You claim no kinship with them at all?"

"Only in their fates. They were men who suffered needlessly, all their lives. They were drawn to my vision of a new city, perhaps. They may have come to my rallies, but they did not have my approval. In anything they did."

"So they were never close to you. Never close to your organization. Your movement."

"You make us sound like a cult," he said. He waved a hand at the plainly dressed men standing around him. "We are just men. Men of a city. And we are dying. Surely you cannot criticize us for merely wanting to survive. And I do not speak in metaphors here, Mr. Hayes. Our lives are at stake, and each day lives are lost. You have seen it. I am certain of it, you have seen it out in the veins of the city. You have seen the dead and the dying."

"I've seen it in this city, and the next, and the next," said Hayes. "In cities older than this country."

"Perhaps so, but on this scale?" Tazz walked to the wall of the room and ran one gloved hand along its smooth side. "Do you know how many people have died here?"

"Here?"

"Yes. Here in this place? Underneath this city? Do you know? No one can say. Not for sure. No one counts a corpse if its life was a poor one. But below the factories, here in the tunnels and the machinery down below... I would say over fifty thousand men have died here since the beginning of the new century. From accidents and overwork and ignorance. That's not just workplace hazard. That's a war. It's a real war."

"And you plan no violence for this war?"

"Would you say we need any?" Tazz said, walking back into the light. "Look around you. This city is dying. Even as it grows, it dies. It ripens to the point where it is sure to rot. And the people above, the people who live their quaint little lives, they live without ever thinking of what goes down below. But us down here, who can't avoid it, we watch. And we count. Someone must watch. Now I ask you, what if we showed them? What if we showed the people this world below? What if we showed them the bones of the men this city is built on, piled down here in heaps, trapped in the gears?"

"You think they would care?" Hayes asked.

Tazz was quiet for a bit, kneading the flesh at his chin with one thumb. Then he said, "They have to. They must."

"I think they would prefer not to look at all, Mr. Tazz."

"Then we will make them."

"And you will do this all without a single blow?"

Tazz shook his head. "We do not need violence. We just need people to see."

"So you're a peaceful revolutionary. And there was nothing between you and the saboteurs. Between Naylor and his men."

"No."

"Nothing you know about Huffy and Denton?"

"I didn't even know who those men—"

"And nothing about Skiller?"

Tazz stopped where he was. Shoulders slightly bent, hands clasped behind his back. His head swiveled to look down the tunnel. "Who?"

"John Skiller. One of the Third Ring men. Or did you forget him as well?"

"I've never heard of that man in my life."

"He died before the trolley murders. Found floating in a canal. A Construct canal not unlike this place."

"I have never heard of that man," Tazz said again.

"Are you sure he wasn't one of yours? Weeded out, or culled?"

"None of us do anything like that. The strength of what we do here rests upon recognizing our suffering. Our purpose would founder if we caused more."

"Really?" Hayes turned to one of the nearby guards. "What about you?" he asked. "You ever kill a man for Tazz? Ever beat him till he stopped breathing?"

"Don't listen to him," said Tazz quickly.

"Why not?" Hayes asked the guard. "Why wouldn't you answer?"

"He wants to infuriate you," Tazz called. "Wants you to hurt him. To prove you're like him."

Hayes and the guard stared at one another. He was a huge man, thick and bearded with eyes set far apart. He swayed slightly as though drunk and the wrench in his hand tapped softly against his thigh. "I never killed a man," he said softly. "But I sure would like to sometimes."

"You're lying," said Hayes. "Have you ever even worked in a factory? Or was your employment down on the street?"

"I don't need to work in a factory to know it ain't right," said the guard.

"No factory? No factory, is that right?" Hayes called to Tazz, stepping away.

Tazz's thumb returned to his chin. He thought for a long time before saying, "Would you say that all the poor in this city suffer just because they have no spot on a line, Mr. Hayes?"

"No. But I know a soldier when I see one. These men around me, they aren't organizers. They aren't the defenseless poor. And they aren't missionaries." Hayes tapped the side of his head. "Trust me. I know. These men you lead, they don't want a peaceful revolution. They just want what they've been denied, and then some."

"Even if they did fight, it would be a cleaner fight than the one your owners wage now," Tazz said. In the distance Samantha thought she could see a faint line of sweat around his brow, and he licked his lips after each sentence. "With their monster roaming the streets, killing at their bidding."

"McNaughton doesn't have a fucking monster," said Hayes, supremely condescending.

"Really? Do you honestly think you're the only scientific oddity they have at their disposal? How could you seriously think such a thing?"

Hayes merely shrugged. But Tazz stopped and thought for a moment, and then stooped to the lantern at his feet. "Would you like to see?"

"See what?" said Hayes.

"See what they're really making. See what's really going on down here in the dark."

"What do you mean?"

"I mean there are things hidden down here you can't imagine. Things the city above has never dreamed of. I can show you, if you like." He began turning up the light on the lantern.

"If you want."

"Oh, I very much do," said Tazz. He picked up the lantern and strode to the railing at the side of the pathway and stopped. "You may find this a little shocking," he said softly, and held the lantern out.

It took their eyes a moment to adjust to the light filtering through the darkness, but then they saw it. It took Samantha a moment to understand what she was seeing, as if her mind was unable to translate the reality before her, but then her jaw dropped and she heard herself gasp.

To say it was a machine would be wrong, because that would mean that the enormous thing in the room with them had once been made, and she was unable to accept such an idea. It was too enormous, too intricate, too fantastic to have ever been designed and constructed by men. Huge, arcing pistons like cathedral buttresses stood frozen in the shadows, their long, slender arms reaching halfway from ceiling to floor. Turbines huddled behind them, silver shining through coke and grease, each one the size of cars. Exhaust lines curled out from somewhere in the machine's innards and slid along the wall before disappearing into the cement. In between gaps in the thing's plating she could see bundles of copper wiring thin as moss that linked one section to another, and upon what she thought of as the machine's boiler the wiring gathered to a brassy forest. The boiler itself was a strange and curious thing, a mass of sloping iron and brass piping and thick blue glass that clutched to the machine's belly like an offspring to its mother. It was so thickly armored and well hidden that whatever heat it bore in its belly had to be immense. And yet even though she could identify each part of the mammoth construction as some piece of machinery she'd seen before, only magnified to huge sizes, when she looked at the whole she could not comprehend it. It seemed wondrous and terrifying and somehow alive, alive and ancient. This thing could not have been made, she thought. It must have always been. It must have sat down here, waiting for them for so long.

Hayes did not seem as affected as she was. Instead, she saw he was staring at one distinct part of the machine: a large lamp-like structure set in the top corner, with what looked like a twinkling glass chimney set in the center. "Won't be out for a year, my fucking arse," he whispered to himself. Then he seemed to remember himself, and asked, "What is it?"

"You don't know?" asked Tazz.

"You very well know I don't."

"Hm," said Tazz, pleased. "I don't know, exactly. I doubt if it's one of Kulahee's originals, though. But I have my suspicions. Have either of you heard of the Spinners?"

Hayes made a small *hmph* of surprise and turned to look at Samantha. "I have. I doubt you have."

"What?" she said. "What do you mean?"

"The Spinners, Miss Fairbanks," said Tazz. "One of the latest big projects. Though it's been a very private one. They're power generators, you see. But ones built deep under the ocean."

"Under the ocean?" she said. "Why?"

"To catch the ocean currents. They're like giant windmills, planted around ocean trenches and all along the bottom of the sea. They're unmanned, just blind devices spinning silently down there, but they generate enormous power. McNaughton has been in the testing phases of the devices for some time, or that was the word among the other workers. They've managed a way to draw power from the sea for their factories, and their factories alone."

"I don't know about that," said Hayes, staring out at the machine. "I've only seen how their maintenance alert works. Whenever one is in need of repair it sends up a little tethered buoy that flashes white. I've heard stories of strings of flashing lights out on the waves, waiting for someone to come service them. Nearby sailors thought they were the souls of the dead." Hayes looked at Tazz. "You think this machine is part of the production of the Spinners?"

"No," said Tazz. "I think it *controls* them."

"From here?"

"Yes. And I know you must think me mad, that it must take miles and miles of cable to do that, but it's true."

Hayes's eyes flicked back to the large lamp on the corner of the machine. "Is it?"

"Yes. This is the only machine of its kind that I've found, and I've been studying it for some time. It regulates them, calibrates them. I'm sure of it. Even from this far away. Or at least some of them. Maybe no more than a few." He looked out at the machine and seemed to lose some of his spirit. "This is the least of them."

"What makes you say that?"

"Because they abandoned it. Why would they do that, unless they had more of its kind, and better ones? Or machines that perform even more important functions? I don't know. They built this off the new trolley lines, and when those flooded they felt they could cut their losses and leave this machine lying dead or dormant with the rest of the workers."

"How did they build it? Surely word would have gotten out about such an undertaking."

"I can't say," said Tazz. "It was not built by any worker I know, and as you can suspect I know quite a few. We just stumbled across it. How it got here is beyond me. Yet I believe there are many more like it under the city."

"That can't be," said Hayes. "It's too big. You couldn't fit more than... than ten of them down here, maybe."

"Maybe. But I once heard that Kulahee had discovered a way to trick space. To make the small large and the large small. I heard he could fit a pachyderm into a matchbox."

"That's a fairy tale."

"So were the machines. But you have a dead one at your feet, sir. After all, you've heard the sounds, haven't you? The pounding? You both must have. Everyone who lives here for more than a few months has."

Samantha nodded, but Hayes refrained.

"Yes," said Tazz. "I think that's how they speak to one another, maybe."

"Speak?" said Hayes.

"Yes. How they call to one another in the dark. These invisible machines doing invisible things. They sing to one another like whales in the seas."

"They're machines. Machines don't talk, and certainly not to one another."

"Mm. Yes," said Tazz softly. "Maybe you're right. Perhaps everyone who spends too much time down here goes a little mad."

Hayes and Samantha looked out at the device a moment longer. Then Hayes pointed down to where it met the lip of the wall. A variety of small tools lay scattered in front of a small hutch in the machine's side. They seemed pathetically tiny next to the enormous mechanism. "You've been trying to repair it," Hayes said.

Tazz nodded sadly. "To restart it, yes."

"Why?"

"Why? Why not? Imagine what you could learn from it. From seeing one of the secret devices of McNaughton in action. You'd have the power of the sea itself at your fingertips. And they wouldn't be so superior to us anymore. Cloistered away in their tower, controlling us, giving us simple toys and making millions off of it. When all along the real gifts never know the light of day." He lowered the lantern and set it on the ground, and the machine was swallowed in darkness once more. Then he looked at Hayes, his eyes wild. "So you understand that when a man of your abilities comes before me, I wonder if you are something that *happened*, or something that was *made*."

"I was not made," said Hayes. "I'm me. I'm my own."

"You don't sound certain. You don't even know how they make what they do already, do you? You're like everyone else when it comes to that. Maybe it's something holy. Maybe they have a single man appointed with the task of going up to the gods and bringing back fire."

Hayes cocked his head. "That's a very educated reference. Above most line workers' heads."

"I read. I read when I was in prison. I learned about justice and the way the world could be, if we only tried." Tazz stepped back from the light. He became indistinguishable from the rest of the shadowed stone. "I looked around and saw men who could not go further. Who could not get out. Who knew lives of nothing more than struggle, and starvation, and hate."

"I'm sick and tired of your fucking rhetoric," Hayes muttered, so low that only Samantha could hear.

"I learned of how deep the corruption went," Tazz continued, the faceless voice in the dark. "That it was in the heart of the very city. Every structure, every institution. It was made to keep these men down, to keep them on the lines and in the gutters and in the prisons. I learned how hard our mission would be, and how desperately it was needed."

"I went to Savron, too, Mr. Tazz," Hayes said loudly. "I learned a few things myself. Spoke to the boys there, and the guards. They say they don't remember you at all."

"What?" said Tazz's voice sharply.

"They say they don't remember you."

"Well... then you're talking to the wrong people."

"Hm. Could you remind me what your jail cell was?"

"My what? My jail cell? Why?"

"Just for my records. Just because I'm curious. What jail cell were you interned in?"

The voice was quiet. Then he said quickly, "Cell one-forty-five. South Sector C."

"Really?" said Hayes, interested.

"Yes."

"You're sure?"

"Yes. Yes, of course."

"Because the prison records show that you were in cell one-fifty-five. Right sector, though."

Tazz was silent. Then he said, "That's impossible."

"It's entirely possible."

"It's not true. You're lying. Cell one-forty-five, South Sector C. Cell one-forty-five, South Sector C. How could I forget? It was drilled into me, every day."

"Are you certain you were in Savron?"

"Of course I'm certain. I spent five years of my life there, five miserable years!"

"Really? I had heard six," Hayes said.

Tazz paused. "No. No. Five years. I spent five years. Five years, three months, twenty-nine days," he said angrily. "Five years, three months, twenty-nine days. You know that. You know that!"

"How would I know that?"

"Because you're a monster!" Tazz shouted. He stepped back into the light. He was leaning forward, snarling like a wild animal. "I know what you are! I know what you can do! That's why they have you working for them, isn't it? Or did they make you? Did they make this... this thing that you are to work for them, like another one of Kulahee's machines? That's how they operate, you know. They make what they need. Isn't that it?

"You won't listen," he said. "You never do. Any of you. Every machine and dollar you make is bought with our blood. And we don't ever get anything. Not even a memory. But one day they'll remember. One day we'll make them. We'll make them remember all of us."

Then Tazz turned away and walked down the pathway into the darkness. They heard his footfalls but after a while they did not even hear that.

CHAPTER TWENTY-FOUR

They were left alone in the tunnel. The other union men stood watching them, faces indistinct in the shadows, but Hayes barely noticed, lost in thought. The big one with the wrench lurched toward them and as he neared the stench of gin was overwhelming. A small man in a coat and hat came forward and pushed him back and said, "Easy there. Easy, Barney. Let's get these folks home, all right?"

He turned to them and Hayes saw it was the man in the gray coat he had seen only a few nights before. He was a ratty little thing with an oversized nose and a wandering line of a mustache. He tipped his hat and said, "I'm Colomb. Mr. Tazz has assigned me the task of making sure you get out all right. Because we're all peaceful-like, see? Very peaceful. Here, I'll show you the way."

He picked up a lantern and led them up into one of the other service tunnels. As they walked Hayes glanced behind them and saw the big guard staring at them, breathing hard. Others joined him, emerging from the shadows and watching their retreat with hungry eyes.

"Can't believe you brought a woman down here," Colomb said as he walked. "The idea of it. You'd get all dirty."

"I'm fine," said Samantha.

"Why in God's name would someone do that, though? Must be crazy."

"I needed someone else to hear," Hayes said.

Colomb shook his head. "Just crazy is all."

They walked up through the tunnels, guided by the weak halo of light projected by the oil lamp. Hayes asked, "How did you come to work for Mr. Tazz, Mr. Colomb?"

"Don't know if I should tell you."

"I'm just making idle chat."

"I don't think you make idle chat."

They walked on. Eventually Colomb said, "I was fired. From valve control in the Vulcan facility. They said I was too old. Getting everyone else in danger. It wasn't so. I just had been around so they were paying me more. And they didn't want to do that. They could get someone to do it cheaper and maybe it wouldn't be as good of a job, but so what? By their accounts it was better. I sent my little girl and my wife back to Idaho to live with her folks. Mr. Tazz gives me money to send to them. Five dollars a week. They do all right. I think they do all right.

"We came here looking for the promised land," Colomb continued. "We didn't find it. This place chewed us up and spat us back out. We're not looking to Mr. Tazz for a general, Mr. Hayes. Not for someone to tell us who to hurt. Least, I don't look at him like that. We just wanted someone to show us the way out of here. That ain't so much, is it? And if he's not going to help us, then who? You?" he said, nodding at Hayes.

Hayes said nothing. They continued through the tunnels and soon they heard the rattling of pipes and cars and trolleys. He figured they were perhaps thirty feet below the skin of the street. Maybe more.

"You're closer to Mr. Tazz than others are, aren't you?" Hayes asked.

"I guess."

"And you perform a lot of his duties?"

Colomb shrugged.

"That's how it works, isn't it?" asked Hayes. "People do one small thing for this man they've never met. Ship a package. Open a door. And they don't know who tells them to do it or why or what it's going to do. They just blindly follow orders. And they all come from the top. Or nearabout."

"You shut your mouth," said Colomb.

Hayes smiled and closed his eyes and listened to the whine of anxiety that welled up inside the man. Suddenly Hayes smelled cool, smoky air and cold wind, and heard the clank and scream of an airship cradle about him. He did not open his eyes but still he saw the airship descending through the starry sky, its burnished belly black and glowing from the lights below. A massive thing that was almost alive.

Smooth and careful, said the man's thought. Tomorrow night. Everyone does the transfer right or they don't do it at all and then everything is lost. Everything, all of it.

Hayes opened his eyes. He and Colomb and Samantha were still trudging down the tunnel. Up ahead he saw ladder rungs and street light filtering through an opening.

"Here," said Colomb. "Here's where you go. Don't ask me what street this is, I don't know."

"Fine," said Hayes. "Should I go first or should you, Sam?"

Samantha sighed and began climbing up the rungs. Colomb studiously averted his eyes and stared at the floor. When she was up Hayes followed and Colomb stayed behind. Samantha bade him goodbye but he did not answer. Simply stood with the dimming lantern down in the underground, looking up at them. Then either he moved away or the light died. They could not tell.

Samantha and Hayes walked back through the streets. By their reckoning they were northeast of the Shanties. As they walked Samantha noticed Hayes was shivering. She was not sure if it was fear or if he was ill.

"Thank you for coming," he said quietly.

Samantha did not answer.

"I was just worried. I knew I'd make it out of the meeting alive, but…but these past few weeks, I don't know what's going to happen. If I'm going to get up the next day or not. Something's wrong with me. I'm…seeing and hearing things. This was important and someone else needed to hear it."

"God," said Samantha. "Just be quiet. Be quiet for once."

"All right."

They continued walking. Their legs were streaked with mud and their footsteps squelched as they walked.

"He knew Skiller," said Samantha.

"Yes."

"And he knew what you can do."

"Yes," said Hayes. "That's something. Do you know how many people know about that that are still alive?"

"No."

"To be honest, I don't either. You could count them on one hand, I'd imagine. I think I got something useful out of Colomb, though. I picked it up very fast, I'm not sure why."

"What was it?"

"He's smuggling something out of the city tomorrow night," Hayes said. "What, I don't know. Where, I don't know. I just know it's by air, and it's tomorrow."

"Does it have anything to do with that machine?"

"No. I don't think so." He laughed bitterly and shook his head. "Did you see that thing on its corner? That lamp-thing?"

"I saw you staring at it."

"Yes. Brightly showed me one a while back. Communication thingy. At the time he claimed that they weren't due out for at least a year. And when they did come out, it would revolutionize the world.

But when we saw Tazz's device, there it was. They must have had working versions for years. If there was a revolution, I didn't fucking notice. That thing doesn't need miles of cable if it's got a Sibling bleeping away on it. They must have every damn machine down there linked up the same way. I always knew they'd been keeping things from me, but I never knew how much." He shook his head. "Sookie was right," he said softly. "They don't ever release anything unless they've already been using it."

They turned down an alley to cut over to the canal road. They could see the lights of a tanker's top deck crowning just above the buildings ahead as it slogged through the waters. It looked like a dreary little carnival spinning through the night sky, its strings of lights fluttering with the breeze.

"He seemed very composed," said Samantha. "Mr. Tazz, I mean. He's quite the orator."

"An orator, maybe," said Hayes. "But he wasn't composed. I think he was absolutely terrified."

"You could sense that?" she asked. "From that far away?"

"No. I just knew. I don't have to have a gift to know when men are frightened."

She thought for a second. "His cell actually was one-forty-five, though, Mr. Hayes. I remember."

"Do you? Good for you."

"But you said it was one-fifty-five."

"Yes. I was just fucking him around. But I got what I wanted from him, didn't I?"

"What do you think of it?"

"I think it troubles me very deeply."

Samantha was about to ask why, but suddenly Hayes stopped where he stood. Then he turned around. "What?" she asked.

He shushed her and held up a hand, then turned to peer down the alley behind them.

"What?" she asked again.

He shook his head and took a step forward, still looking into the darkness.

Nothing moved. The alley was still except for the drip of water from an overhead fire escape. Then there was a whistling sound and something flew through the air, massive and heavy, and struck Hayes on the side of the head with a sharp crack. He fell to the ground, arms limp and crumpled underneath him.

Samantha shrieked and ran to him and turned him over. A river of blood began pouring from Hayes's scalp, marking one eye, and he blinked drunkenly. "What was that?" he asked.

She looked on the ground beside him. A thick wrench lay on the cement, its handle dull red from where it had crushed the skin on his head. Then she heard feet pounding on the ground and out of the corner of her eye she saw movement. She turned just in time to see the big guard from before running up the alley toward them, and she tried to stand and run but he seized her arm and whirled her around and tossed her into a wall as though she were no more than a rag doll. The back of her head met brick and her whole body seemed to fall away from her. She slumped down to the cement, fingers uselessly searching for something to keep her upright.

She watched as the big man grunted and picked up Hayes and punched him three times in the face, all solid blows. Hayes tried to lift his hands to protect himself but the man threw him to the ground and savagely kicked him.

"Fucking pansy," growled the guard. He stooped to pick Hayes up again, but somehow Hayes moved lightning-fast and his flick knife was suddenly buried in the side of the man's arm up to the hilt. It happened so fast Samantha barely registered it, and she found herself wondering if the little ivory handle was just a bizarre ornament on the man's coat. The guard roared in pain and slapped Hayes down and landed a solid kick on the side of his head. Hayes lay still, a curtain of his blond hair hiding his face from view, though it was now rosy with blood where it was close to his face.

"Fucking Newty pansies," gasped the man. "Fucking little bastard." He ripped the knife from his arm, groaning, and slender trickles of crimson began weaving out of his cuff and down his wrist and around his knuckles. "You're all pansies," he said, and threw the knife away. "All of you. Fucking lavenders is what you are." When he turned to get his wrench he saw Samantha crawling away.

"No you don't," said the man. "No. No you don't." He stepped forward and gripped her by the ankle and dragged her to him. Her skirt slid up as she moved, revealing her legs and waist. The big man laughed and reached out to her and she screamed. He slapped her once, then again. His enormous hands grasped the sides of her head and pulled her close, his gin-breath filling her nose and mouth and filthy fingers smearing her cheeks.

"Ain't you the cutest thing," he said.

She tried to turn away, tried to resist the surge of vomit rumbling in her throat.

"Ain't you just the cutest thing," he said again.

"Stop," said a voice.

The big guard dropped her and looked down the alley. There was a man standing there, gun held in both hands with its barrel expertly trained on their attacker. The man was streaked in mud from head to toe and his clothes were ragged and his eyes wild and furious. He was breathing hard and every movement he made screamed of murder.

"Get down on the ground," said the man.

"Donald?" said Samantha breathlessly.

"Get down," said Garvey again. "Get down on the fucking ground."

"Little bastard," said the big guard, taking a step toward Garvey. "You're all little bastards. Not real men. Not at all."

"Stop right where you are, goddamn you," Garvey said.

"Little man," he said, and reached for the wrench.

The gun went off. The flash was quick and muted but the crack was deafening in the tight alley. The man's leg opened up and turned to shreds and he howled and tumbled to the ground, grasping his inside thigh. Garvey stood over him, eyes wide, watching the stream of smoke gently unraveling from the gun barrel. Blood pumping erratically through the guard's knuckles. His eyes moved to Hayes, who lay moaning on the ground. After a second he walked to Samantha and knelt before her.

"Are you all right?" Garvey asked. He spoke faintly, as if he was not sure where he was.

"How did you..."

"I followed you. When I went to pick you up. I saw you leave." He looked away as though he had forgotten something, and then turned back to her and said, "I lost my hat."

"What?"

"My hat. I lost it. In the tunnels."

"Donald, are you hurt?"

"What? No." He thought again. "I shot a man, Sam," he said, almost as though he were remembering something from long ago. "I shot him."

"I know."

Garvey looked at the man lying on the ground. "It's a wound," he said. "It's only a wound." Then he moved over to the man and took off his own shirt and wrapped it around the man's thigh and cinched it tight. The man screamed in agony and Hayes moaned again and sat up.

"What going on?" he mumbled.

"Stay down, Hayes, you've been hurt," said Garvey.

Hayes blinked through the ribbon of blood running down his right cheek and said, "Jesus fucking Christ, Garvey, did you shoot him?"

"Shut up."

"Fucking looks like it to me."

"Shut up."

Samantha walked to the wounded man, legs trembling. She looked at the wound and felt her breath catch. "Oh, no," she said, kneeling.

"Oh no what?" asked Garvey.

She knelt and began pulling back his makeshift bandages. They were already soaked a deep, dark red, so dark you could not tell what their original colors had been.

"What are you doing?" Garvey asked.

"No, Donald, no..." she whispered. "You...you hit an artery. There in his leg." She shut her eyes grimly and began rewrapping his bandage.

"So? So what? Tie it tight and we can—"

"Donald, it's...it's very unlikely he's going to survive this," she said quietly.

Garvey stared at her, then down at the wound. "What? No."

"Yes. He's probably going to bleed out. Unless we get a doctor right now. And even if we do, it's very doubtful."

"God," said Garvey. He began wrapping more makeshift bandages around the man's leg. "We can just put on more, can't we?"

"We'd need to sew the artery shut, Donald," Samantha said, eerily calm. "And I don't think that anyone will be able to do that in time. In fact, I've never seen it done in time."

"He's fine," said Garvey. "It's just a *wound*, for God's sake. I just shot him in the fucking leg."

Hayes pulled himself up, spat blood to the side, and looked at the wounded man. "She's right, Garvey," he said. "That man's dead, he just doesn't know it yet."

The unioner moaned and tried to swipe at Hayes. He missed and his fingers dragged along the ground. Hayes ignored it and reached forward and grasped Garvey's hand.

"Garvey," he said. "You killed him."

"Shut up."

"You did, Garv."

"Shut up."

"You've killed him. You killed a *unioner*, Garvey."

Garvey leaned into the wound a moment longer, then slowly

relaxed. He looked at Hayes as though the words had struck him dumb.

"What?" he said softly.

"You killed a unioner," Hayes said. "You need to run, Garvey. Get up and run. You can't be found like this. You don't know what they'll do to you."

"What?" he said again.

"You need to run, Garvey."

"Donald," said Samantha. "Please, Donald, come on, come and leave him."

"Listen to her, Garvey," Hayes said. "There's no saving him. We have to go."

Garvey sat back and looked at the man. The guard's breath was shallow and ragged now. Then Garvey's face tightened and his eyes went dead and he said, "Get me something else. Some other bandage."

"Jesus, Garvey, we've got to move." Hayes struggled to his feet and grabbed hold of Samantha's arm.

"Get me something or get away."

"Donald, if they catch you here with him that'll be the end of it," Samantha said. "The end of everything."

Garvey looked at her. "I shot a man, Sam," he said. "I'll... I'll call for help and try and get him to a hospital." Then he shook his head. "Go. Get out of here. I won't have you caught with me."

"Donald, *please*."

Garvey bound the man's wound tighter. "I didn't do anything wrong."

"I know you didn't, but—"

"I didn't do anything wrong. And that's all that matters. I have to stay, Sam. I shot a man. I shot him. Someone has to *do* something."

"Donald, please, come with us. We can leave. We can just... we can leave all this behind us."

"No," he said softly. "Don't you understand? No. I can't." He looked at her a moment longer and then turned back to the body lying on the cement.

Samantha felt herself moving toward the mouth of the alley. She looked back and saw Garvey on his knees, streaked in filth and blood and still tending to the man's leg. The man was ashen and pale now. Lips sluggish and white. His final moments watched over by the filthy, doomed creature beside him, who did not know him and never would, tending to the man's injury as though there were no one else in the world but the two of them. Then Hayes pulled her forward and they were gone.

CHAPTER TWENTY-FIVE

Garvey used anything he could to bandage the wound. His shirt and strips from his pants and a nearby newspaper, all wadded up. Still the blood seeped through. The man's crotch was a mass of dark red and Garvey's arms were smeared and crackling up to the elbows. Occasionally he would stop and listen to the man's chest, as his pulse was now too weak to feel. Each time he'd hear the organs within slacken and fade a little more. Once when he lifted his head away he saw he had left a pattern upon the man's shirt in mud and gore and sweat. His own molten face impressed there, mute and panicked. Then he turned and shouted for help once more.

After a while he was unable to tell if the man was dead or not. He suspected he was. The pulse had been too faint for a long time and he could not tell if any breath still went through the man. But the blood still came. Drooling out of the edges of the sodden bandage.

Garvey picked up his service revolver and opened the cylinder and took out each of the rounds. He lined them up on the cement next to him, copper points toward the morning sky, the last one's nose open and smelling of sulfur. Then he laid the gun before them and sat on his knees. He was not sure why he did it. It was some ritual he had never known before, or perhaps had never yet existed. Some urban rite for those who died in these cement passageways, unshriven and unmourned.

They took their time to come. He was not surprised. The response time in these neighborhoods was terrible. As dawn came the end of the alleyway lit up with a half-dozen beams of light and he saw the glint of little shields and buttons behind them like sparks. Someone shouted at him to put his hands up.

He held up his badge. The beams stayed on him for a moment and then drooped as though disappointed. Then they walked to him and someone said his name and they all stood in the alley and looked at the man on the gore-streaked ground.

CHAPTER TWENTY-SIX

They picked Garvey up in Lynn and gave him a coat and sat him in the back of the car. Half the district had shown up, guns and truncheons in hand, pacing back and forth over the cement like animals with their blood up. The detectives raced to beat the sun and keep the body from the residents, but it was already too late. By eight a crowd had formed. By eight-thirty someone had squawked out the name of the body, then begun to put together who had shot him down. Soon the bottles and the rocks were flying through the air and the patrolmen had their truncheons out, but they were retreating step by step. Stones struck Garvey's car and the glass of one of the passenger doors turned to frigid webbing before falling in on the seats.

"Christ," someone cried. "Get him fucking out of here."

They drove Garvey to Central but he barely noticed. He was drifting along. The shot still echoing in his ears. Samantha still calmly peeling back the bandage. Hayes gasping over the wound.

They stuck him in a back office. Collins came in and said, "Think. Just think. Don't say anything yet. Just think." Then he was gone.

Solidarity, he thought to himself. It had always been solidarity before. But the city had changed, he knew. Police were now its casualties along with all the regular citizens. Protectors no longer, perhaps never again.

He watched the ordeal through the slits in the blinds. Collins was speaking with two men, their faces impassive. High Crimes, he guessed. They handled the internal stuff. Collins wasn't arguing with them, and that was troubling. Just talking. There seemed to be a lot of nodding going on. Then Garvey saw the gold glimmer of a full regalia hat, though they were not wearing the rest of the official uniform, certainly not at this hour. Everyone stood up straight and they maneuvered into lines. Someone big had come, Garvey guessed. Brassy. The commissioner, maybe, but Garvey couldn't make out his face.

He wished he could take a shower. He had crawled through miles of piping behind Hayes and Samantha, shedding clothing when it became too sopping wet. He stank of bilgewater and sweat and his hands and arms and thighs were still smeared with the blood from the union man. It seemed as though he would never get it off. As though the stain went down through each layer of his skin to soak into his own veins and perhaps touch his heart.

He looked up. Collins was walking toward him, face set. He opened the door and came in and looked Garvey over. Then he took out a small green flask. "Here," he said, holding it out.

"I don't want it," Garvey said.

"Yeah you do."

"I don't. I really don't, Lieutenant."

Collins hesitated, then replaced the flask. He sat down next to Garvey and asked, "You hurt?"

"No. I need a shower, though. That High Crimes out there?"

"Yeah. They ran down here the second they heard."

"And the commissioner?"

A long silence. Collins said, "Yes."

"What does the commissioner say?"

Collins did not answer.

"I'm being strung out, aren't I," Garvey said. "Cop drops a unioner. Deep in Lynn. That's...that's as dirty as it gets, isn't it?" He pulled the coat tighter around him.

"It depends on the story," Collins said quietly. "It depends on that. If you can sell it clean and sell it real, you can still come out ahead. Still come out police."

"Does the Department have a story for me to tell?"

"We're still putting it together. Why don't you give it to me first? Run it by me and I can see if there's any irregularities."

Garvey told him. Told his story in full. Collins listened and did not speak for nearly five minutes once it was done.

"That's your story?" Collins asked.

"Yeah."

"That's what you're going to tell High Crimes?"

"If they ask."

"And the commissioner? If he asks?"

Garvey shrugged. "Yeah."

"You can't tell that to them. You can't run with that. You'll ruin us. You'll ruin yourself. You'll force our hand."

"That's what happened," Garvey said carefully.

Collins looked him up and down. "I don't even believe you." He stood and opened the door and looked back. "I'm going to give you another hour to think. Another hour to remember. To listen. All right? I suggest you remember that you were traveling with Officer Philips from a local Midnight Mass when you saw the suspect coming from the alley entrance with what appeared to be a weapon and stolen goods in his hand, the stolen goods being three gold watches. Three run-down gold watches. Three of them. You then asked the suspect to stop, which is when he dropped the stolen goods and brandished his weapon. You then produced your revolver and told him to put his hands in the air, which is when he rushed you, which is when you popped off a round. You stayed on the scene, tried to revive him, but could not, and you waited for other police. Philips was there and he saw the whole thing, and he can testify to it, and it'll be believable as he's from that ratshit part of town. You certainly were not in that alley alone. You certainly didn't see him stumbling around drunk with that weapon. You certainly didn't accost him by yourself. It didn't go like that. You understand me?"

"I thought you were still putting it together."

"Do you understand?" asked Collins again.

"I understand," Garvey said.

"All right. Now. When the representative from High Crimes comes and sits you down, will your story be more or less what we have just reviewed here, Detective?"

Garvey shook his head.

Collins took a deep breath. "You should really..."

"That's not the way it went," Garvey said. "That's not the way."

Collins studied him for a moment more, then turned and slammed the door.

CHAPTER TWENTY-SEVEN

Samantha struggled to help Hayes walk. He had been doing well for a bit, but now his head and nose were both bleeding freely. He had to keep his sleeve pressed to his scalp as if he were frozen in the middle of some bizarre salute. They went down empty streets at random and whenever they saw another pedestrian they shied away toward doorways and more empty alleys. Finally Hayes coughed and came to life a little more and began mumbling directions.

He directed her to the Wering Canal. They went down a stone stairway and began walking along the canal apartments. A smoky waterfall laved the stone walls at the far end. Next to it was an apartment with a small green door. Hayes leaned against it and told her to reach into his pocket and find the key with the little pearl. She did so and used it to open the door. Inside it was like a low musty attic with a tattered cot in the corner. Hayes staggered over and collapsed on it, the springs screaming beneath him. He lay there and forced breath into his lungs until it became calm.

"Whose place is this?" she asked.

"Mine," he said.

"How many places like this do you have?"

"I don't know," he said. "Several."

Samantha tended to Hayes's wounds for the next two hours. He had a mild concussion and one finger was broken. He said nothing as she moved his limbs around. She suspected he could not feel them at all. When she was done she went and sat by the door, head leaned back.

"What will happen to him?" she asked finally.

Hayes licked his lips. "I'm not sure. But it's likely he'll be suspended."

"Suspended?"

"Yes. It's procedure. He'll be suspended while they consider how to go. There's a board. I don't know who's on it or how big it is or how it works. But they have the choice to prosecute or fire him or do whatever."

"Lord."

Hayes nodded. Then his head tilted back and he fell asleep. Samantha slipped out the door and wandered up to the street and found a paperboy on the corner. It was so early he had not even cut open his stack yet. He watched her like she was some ghost, a ragged, filthy woman rising up out of the mist. She bought a paper from him and he handed it to her, eyes wide, and she read it as she walked back to the canal apartment. Hayes woke when she shut the door.

She said, "Be still. It's nothing. I got a paper, that's all."

"You got a paper? Where?"

"From outside. On the street."

"Were you followed?" he asked quickly.

"Who would follow me?"

"Anyone. Everyone, now. Were you followed?"

"No. No, I don't think so."

Hayes sighed and rolled his head away.

"He's been arrested, like you said," she told him. "It says so here."

"Which paper?"

"*The Freedom*."

"Ignore most of what they say. They're saying he should be hanged, aren't they?"

She was silent.

"Yeah," said Hayes. "Yes. I know."

"They won't hang him, will they?"

"I doubt it. *The Freedom*'s written by fucking loons. It's no good that everyone's gotten ahold of it so fast, though. That means the reaction will be quicker, and stupider."

"I know," said Samantha. "I... I wonder where he's being kept."

"Probably at the Central's cells. I bet he's still being held for questioning, and they're not dumb enough to put a police in a real prison. They'd kill him overnight."

Samantha's hand went to her mouth. She stumbled out the door and gripped the walkway railing, then stared into the waterfall and took some huge, deep breaths. Then when she had calmed herself she returned.

"I'm sorry," Hayes said, blinking through his matted hair. "I shouldn't have said that."

"I don't care. I just let my emotions get the better of me."

Hayes did not answer at first. Then he said, "It's all right. I understand."

"Understand what?"

He looked at her as though he was not sure what to say. "About you," he said finally. "You and Garvey."

"You don't have to understand anything," she said harshly.

"I know. I just thought I'd let you know."

"It's none of your business. It never is." Samantha shut her eyes and ground the heels of her palms into her eye sockets. She quivered, suppressing a scream, and said, "He hasn't said anything about us."

"What?"

"In the paper. He hasn't said anything about us. It makes it sound like he was just wandering through the neighborhood alone, saw someone acting suspicious, and then there was a brief struggle and he shot him. Him, all filthy and crazy-looking. With no witnesses at all. That's what he's telling them, it says here."

"Oh, Christ. They'll kill him with that story."

"They say the man he killed was Barney Patrick. That he was a longtime administrative aid in the Dock Assembly. But he wasn't. You said so. The man said he'd never worked in a factory."

"Yes."

"So they're lying."

"Oh, yes. A police shoots a union man all by himself in an alley, with no witnesses? If this was any other city he'd probably be dismissed, maybe even jailed. In this city, at this time, with a fucking unioner, it's going to be madness. It's his word against what every bastard in the city wants."

She sat very still, looking at the paper. She reached out and touched the words as though she could rearrange them into something better.

Hayes opened his eyes as though he had heard something. He sat up and looked at her, mouth slightly agape. Then he said, "Don't do it."

Samantha turned to him. "Don't do what?" she asked.

"Don't go to the police."

"They'll kill him with this story. You said so yourself."

"They'll kill you, too, if you give yourself to them. You'll link the company to the police even more."

"Then the hell with the company!" she spat. "They're going to throw him in prison, Hayes! That or ruin him!"

"You don't know that. But he's going to be the sacrificial lamb either way. You'll just bring yourself down with him."

"I don't care! They need to know the truth! Someone does, just one person!"

"They won't care. They can't afford to care."

"Shut up! Just shut up for once in your damn life!" She stood and went to the wall and leaned her head against it. "I won't let them do this to him. It isn't right."

Hayes did not answer.

"Why couldn't he have left?" she asked quietly. "Why couldn't he have just left that man there and come with us?"

"Because Garvey was made for lost causes," said Hayes. "That's why he's stayed in his hometown, after all."

"He believes he can help," said Samantha.

"I never doubted that he believes it. He believes it with all his heart. It's whether he should believe it at all that I wonder about."

She sat down again on the floor and crossed her arms and pulled her legs up close to her chest.

"Samantha..." Hayes said. "I know what you're about to do. If you do it, it'll bring hell down. Hell on everyone."

"Will it help Donald?" she asked, lifting her face.

"Probably. It very well could. But—"

"Then I don't want to hear it," she said. "Just be quiet."

Hayes looked at her a moment longer, then lay back and slept again. She waited, thinking, and then left.

Samantha did not go to her apartment. She knew that would be watched. Instead she walked into the nearest post office, her skirt mud-stained and her face still smudged. The clerk stared at her as she calmly asked for a box of envelopes, some nice paper, a pen, and several bottles of ink. "Doing some letter-writing, ma'am?" he asked nervously.

"Yes," she said. "I am."

When she had gotten her supplies she went to a phone station and called information. A bleary-voiced woman answered the phone. Samantha asked her for the address of a major newspaper.

"Which newspaper?"

"All of them, I should think," Samantha said.

She wrote them down. Then she went to a nearby shop and

purchased some new clothes and cleaned herself up until she looked decent. She found a quiet restaurant and she sat in the back and began to write, first one letter, then two, then three, all the way up to ten, one after the other. Once she was done she walked to the mailbox tubes and slipped the letters in, the pneumatic lines greedily sucking each letter out of her hands.

She sat on a bench then, not certain what to do, vaguely aware that she was putting things in motion that were far beyond her control. She suddenly felt that she had tipped something very large and very heavy over, and it had just passed its equilibrium and now there was no going back. She felt strangely detached. She had never really done a stupid thing in her life, and she'd always been careful about each decision she'd ever made. Normally she wouldn't even conceive of doing something like this. But whenever she thought of Garvey lying in some cell she knew that it was not a choice at all.

She sat for a moment longer, then stood and began walking toward Evesden Central Police Department.

She wanted to wait for him on the front steps, but they told her they were going to be letting him out on the side. When she asked why, the duty officer gestured out toward the street in front of Central, and she looked and saw several men loitering, watching the building front with hooded eyes. She turned away and went down to the side of the station.

She stood in the small loading dock with the municipal workers for more than an hour before Garvey came shambling out. He wore ill-fitting clothes that were certainly not his own. His hair was uncombed and his cheeks bore days of stubble. He blinked up at the sunlight. When he saw Samantha his shoulders drooped as though he was stunned and deeply disappointed, all at once.

"Sam," he said softly. "Sam, what are you doing here?"

She did not answer. She simply walked to him and held his face to make sure he was all right. Then she kissed him. He withdrew in surprise, then gently returned it.

"Samantha," he said. "Jesus, Samantha, what the hell?"

"They were going to prosecute you," she said softly.

"We need to get out of here. Is there a car nearby?"

"There's a cab waiting at the end of the lane."

He grabbed her and looked back at the front of the building, where a crowd was forming, presumably waiting for him. Someone's amplified voice shouted at them, telling them to keep their distance.

"They were going to prosecute you," she said. "I couldn't let you do that to yourself. I couldn't. So I went to them and asked to speak to your lieutenant."

"Jesus."

"And I told him what had happened, what had really happened. And then he got his major. And I told him and he went and got the commissioner. And I told him and they all seemed to think for a bit."

Garvey shook his head and kept hustling her down the lane.

"And then once I had them all in a room together I told them I had written ten letters, each to one of the major newspaper publishers telling them what had actually happened, about the... the assault and everything, and they'd be getting them by the end of the day. So either they could go public with the story or they would wind up fighting the papers."

"Jesus Christ."

"And I suppose they decided to let you go."

"God, Sam. That may make it worse," he said. "That may make it worse for everyone."

"I don't care. It wasn't right. It wasn't right what they were doing to you."

They climbed into the cab. "Where'd Hayes stash you?" Garvey asked. "No. Wait. Don't tell me. Just get us close and we'll let you out."

Samantha gave the driver an address only a few blocks away. Garvey nodded, his face drawn and thin and white as a sheet.

"They'll fire you for this, you know," he said. "This'll be the end of it. Of your career. Jesus, Samantha, they'll crucify you for this. Unioners may be after you."

"I know. I don't care anymore. Will the Department ever take you back?"

"Not after this, I don't think. They said they were going to committee over it soon but they were hinting real hard that I should maybe resign. Maybe I should. Seems like the alternative would be a hearing." He bowed his head and sighed. "You can love your job, but that doesn't mean it loves you. You can love your city and you can love your country and your people, but they don't love you back. They're just things. Things that get too big and one day they just scrape you off their back. They don't need you."

"I do," she said. "I need you. I do."

He looked at her. His brow and cheeks lined and loose. Dark eyes soft and haggard. Then he leaned his head against hers and shut his eyes.

"I know you do," he said softly.

"I'll be there," she said. "Wherever. When you're ready."

They came to the safe house canal. He opened the door for her but did not get out.

"What's going to happen?" she asked.

"I don't know. I think we're being watched. I think we have to assume that."

"By who?"

"By the union. By McNaughton. Hell, by the police. So just for now, stay low. Stay clear. And I don't think we should be seen together, Sam."

"Why? What more could they do to us?"

"I don't want to know the answer to that question. Just keep your distance. From me. From Hayes." He reached out and took her hand. Then he pulled her close and kissed her. "I'm sorry," he said.

"For what?" she asked.

"I don't know."

Then she stepped back and he shut the door and the cab pulled away. Garvey did not look back.

She walked back to the dusty little apartment. Hayes was not there. She waited for an hour and then she went and got the paper.

The Department had acted on it just fast enough to look semi-responsible. She was not named, only listed as a "high-level McNaughton Securities employee." Hayes was not mentioned, as she had kept him out of it. It seemed like just another lie in a heap of them. But that was the end of it, she knew. She no longer belonged to herself.

CHAPTER TWENTY-EIGHT

Hayes staggered out of the canal passageways as afternoon was darkening, then waited until he was steady enough on his feet to begin the hunt again. He was not really sure what time it was, but he felt it was far too late for his liking. The memory he'd stolen from Colomb in the trolley tunnels still burned bright in him, and he knew whatever transaction they were making was about to pass.

He ran to his usual contacts first, asking if they knew the whereabouts of Mr. Colomb, yet found he was a leper to them now. They wouldn't answer his calls, and when he persisted they threatened him. He was too hot now, they said, poison to everyone. No one wanted contact with a man who'd taken part in a union murder.

In the end it didn't matter. Colomb was such a visible unioner that even the lowliest and most ignorant of Hayes's informants knew a little about him, and soon Hayes tracked his quarry to a shabby little inn on the south side of town. There he found a good vantage point within the grasping branches of a dying wax myrtle, and he sat and tried to steady himself when the world swam about him.

He was still fairly wobbly. The place where the unioner's wrench had hit him felt like ice fused into his skull, and every once in a while he'd have to turn his head aside and spit blood. He knew it was stupid to be out here, wounded and reeling, but he didn't care. It was easier to keep moving than to stop and rest. This way he never had time to realize the mess he'd caused.

He gritted his teeth and tried not to think of Garvey trying to pump life back into the dead man. Tried not to remember Samantha, her head leaned back against the safe house wall as she languished in the prison that her life had suddenly become. He shook himself and resumed watching.

As night fell Hayes began to wonder if his informants had been wrong or if he'd somehow missed Colomb among the mists of his concussion, but finally the door of the inn opened and a little figure came tottering out, hat pulled low and mustache bristling. As he stepped below a streetlight Hayes saw Colomb's face peeking out through the shadows. He gave him twenty seconds and then followed from the opposite side of the street.

The little man went to a street-side trolley station and sat on one of the green tin benches. He smoked a quick cigarette and rocked back and forth, head darting around. When the trolley pulled up he jumped on and Hayes snaked through the doors at the other end of the car, marking the gray cap for the second time in two days. Hayes sat down with the rest of the south side rabble and pulled his collar up. Colomb did not notice him. His eyes stayed fixed on the floor, and he continued rocking back and forth with his back hunched, completely consumed by whatever was on his mind.

They went far south, past Infield and the Brookshire plant, until Colomb finally stumbled off the trolley just a few blocks northeast of the train depot. Hayes followed and gave him a good lead. He watched as Colomb rushed down the street with a hitch in his step, then pulled a note out of his pocket and scanned it. He turned abruptly down a small lane and walked up to a squat little halfway house. He walked in without knocking and Hayes stayed behind, hidden in the brush of a dying park.

After ten minutes Colomb came back out, now dragging a companion behind, a pale, drunken vagrant who walked with his head bowed, his beard piled up and hiding most of his face. If Colomb minded dragging such a filthy specimen he did not show it. They went farther south to where a shipping cradle loomed over the train depot, a rickety structure composed of rusted metal and creaking wood, the long chains for the loading lift rattling in the breeze. Hayes looked up and saw two airships circling in the sky like mammoth sharks, one near to the ground and the other far up. Their shadows traced across the train yard like small eclipses, the hum of their engines so faint the ear could hardly sense it.

Colomb dragged his friend to the security officer at the cradle and they began speaking quickly. Colomb handed the officer something and the officer nodded as though he had expected it and all three of them climbed into the lift. The officer cranked a lever and the doors shrieked shut and they began to ascend out of sight, the chains clattering all the way.

Hayes scouted around and found a nearby storage building. It was a short, fat cement structure next to a chain-link fence looped with barbed wire. He walked to the fence and crouched in the shadows, waiting and peering through the links at the graveyard of trains beyond.

The pitch in the air changed. Hayes looked up. One airship began descending, its engines twisting to propel it down. Whatever the exchange was, it would happen in moments.

He grasped the chain-link fence and began pulling himself up, delicately avoiding the barbed wire. As he pushed past the last ten feet it snagged his pants leg but did not catch flesh. He clambered up onto the tin roof, wincing as the metal flexed below him. Then when he was steady he lay on his belly and pulled a small spyglass out and looked.

Colomb and his companion were still there, waiting on the cradle flats. The security officer stood nearby, watching the airship float down to them. Other workers shifted cargo and looked at them curiously. There were no other personnel, as this was specifically a cargo cradle and had no business with passengers. But still Colomb and the vagrant remained and watched.

The airship dropped until it was two hundred feet off the ground, then banked to the left, its engines twirling in their sockets. Spotlights flashed on, and Hayes squinted as the cradle suddenly glowed magnesium-white. The crew ran its loops and extended the anchor arm and pulled the airship in. A blank metal sheet slid out from the cargo cell in place of the cauterized rubber tunnel used with the passenger airships. Then the bay door opened and men began wheeling off cargo and Colomb and his companion stepped forward to board.

It was then that some errant gust of air from the engines seemed to catch them. They both threw up their arms and held their hats on their heads, but something flew up, caught on the wind, something small and hairy. Hayes followed it with his spyglass but could not see what it was. He focused again on Colomb and his friend, and as he did he noticed something was different about them.

The vagrant. He was beardless now. He kept his head low to hide it but it was clear as day.

Colomb hustled the vagrant aboard as the rest of the crew began loading pallets of whatever cargo. Piping, it looked like. Hayes strained to focus but the two men had their backs to them and he could make nothing out. Then as the vagrant entered the bay door he looked back to give Colomb a solemn wave.

Hayes's mouth opened when he saw him. He heard himself say, "What in hell?"

The bay door closed. Klaxons sounded as the ship broke cradle and the anchor arm released. The loops slid off, now lax and slack. Then the tone of the engines changed once more. The airship slid smoothly out over the train yards, then went straight up like a balloon, moonlight spackling its worn hide. Colomb stayed on the cradle, lonely and little, watching the floating island disappear into the heavens. Then he went to the lift and slid down the skeleton of the cradle supports again.

Hayes stayed for a moment longer, then vaulted back down through the barbed wire to the ground. He hobbled away and stood beneath a nearby tree and coughed for a good five minutes. His body hadn't tried such activity in years.

When he was done he waited for the security officer's shift to change. As the new guard took up station Hayes sidled up and after a few minutes' conversation he managed to bribe the man for the shipment's destination. Stopping over in San Francisco, the man said. Then heading on down to Mexico, making its delivery in Tijuana. Hayes asked if he was sure, and he said he was. Hayes nodded and then walked back to the trolley station, disturbed and confused.

He had been prepared to believe a lot of things about what was going on, about McNaughton and the unions. But this was something he had not expected. There was no mistaking that broad, honest face. Once the beard was gone, at least.

Mickey Tazz, the hope of the downtrodden, the voice of the poor of Evesden. Leaving the city and heading to sunnier passages. In the middle of the night, at that.

He took a trolley back to the Shanties. Then he got out and had a beer at a pub and thought.

CHAPTER TWENTY-NINE

"I wouldn't say I'm angry," Brightly said coldly. "Would you agree to that?"

"I'm sure I can't say, sir," Samantha said.

"No," said Brightly. "I would say I'm disappointed. You understand my position, yes?"

"Yes, sir."

"Good. I hope so." He leaned back in the chair at Evans's desk. "Rarely have I seen someone with so much promise, and rarely have I ever seen it squandered so quickly. I mean, what were you thinking? What could have possibly possessed you to put yourself and the *company* in such danger?"

Samantha considered how to respond. She was not prepared, nor had she expected or wanted to come here at all. She had returned briefly to her apartments to fetch some things, thinking it would be safe, but had found Brightly's security team waiting for her, large men with passive faces and their hands calmly clasped behind their back like servants. They had brought her there to Evans's office, where Brightly fumed and paced, waiting to turn his fury on her.

"Mr. Hayes was there," she said, "he surprised me, sir, I couldn't—"

"Mr. Hayes?" he echoed. "He *surprised* you, did he?"

"Yes."

"Hayes was the one you were sent here to *control.* It was your job to say no to him when he needed it. And I already knew he had been present during the whole debacle, thank you very much, I'm no idiot. If you and that damn detective are in some union hole at two in the morning then I can figure out what the magic link is." He took a breath. "No, Miss Fairbanks, my problem is why. Why you allowed this. Why you were willing to let things get so far *out* of control." He held a fist to his lips and thought. Then he dropped it and said, "You approached the union. Directly."

"Sir, I thought I could—"

"I don't care about what you think. I don't care what you think or what you did. I care about what I said. I said in-house," he said. "In-house. *In-house.* What was it I said?"

Samantha hesitated, then said, "In-house."

"Yes, *in-house,*" he said. He stood up, fists at his sides. "Do you have any idea what you did? Do you have any idea what you endangered? My God, woman, I can't even put words to it. You have endangered this company at its home, at its heart. You, personally. The cop was willing to stay silent and keep his story to himself, but you, you *personally* went out and put us all right in the middle of it. This, after the murders and the Red Star. Do you know how many goddamn disruptions we've had since the shooting? How you've endangered the situation abroad? How many shareholders have cut loose? How much *money* you've cost us? You may have ended several careers, ruined lives, just by writing some damned letters!"

He sat back down and took a breath and swallowed, collecting himself. She got the impression of some giant sea creature, gathering its strength to spring up through the deeps at its prey. Once he was ready he calmly said, "It's at times like this that I must look back on the path that has brought us here and see exactly when it forked. When it could have gone well, but did not, and instead went bad. There were many options along the way. Perhaps when you touched your pen to those letters and mailed them, maybe that was the moment. Maybe when I read your profile and looked favorably on it, maybe that was when this disaster began. Or perhaps it was before that. When I first thought Evans could make a capable administrator, it may have been there. I can't say. I can only say that it won't happen again."

Brightly took out a file and dropped it on his desk, then pushed it toward her.

"What's that, sir?" she asked softly.

"Your dismissal papers. I suggest you go through them very carefully. Are you surprised?"

"N-no. No, sir."

"Good," he said. "You have no reason to be. What you did cost this company enormously. You can hardly expect me to tolerate someone who is so evidently willing to bring harm to us. Do you have anything to say?"

She shook her head.

"An explanation? An excuse? Something?"

"He was going to force himself on me," she said softly.

Brightly was quiet for a moment. He tapped his pen against his knuckles. Then he leaned forward and said, "A mouse who wanders among adders can hardly be surprised when it is bitten. It was remarkably stupid of you to go to such a dangerous place."

"I know that. But Donald stopped him. He saved us both. I had to help him."

"He," said Brightly, and he pointed out toward the city, "is a policeman. He belongs to the police department. You," he said, now pointing at her, "were company. You were McNaughton. They have their interests, we have ours, and when it comes to the line, you go with the company. We'll back you. We have the power to help you.

We have your future in mind, because you're one of ours. But you obviously don't care for our interests all that much, which leads me to the decision that you're not actually company after all. You're not, and Hayes isn't, and Evans isn't either."

She blinked. "Evans?"

"Yes. Evans."

"Evans is..."

"I'm dissolving this entire section of Securities," Brightly said. "It was not doing its job. Evans was your controller, you were Hayes's, and the fault starts at the top and goes to the bottom. You're all out. All of you. I already spoke to Evans. I'm assuming his office here, it's the first time I've had a stable office for some time."

"But—"

"Yes, a pity," Brightly said, leaning back. "He was just about to retire. That's another one Hayes has left floating in his wake. You can tell Hayes we don't need him to come in anymore, if you can find him. I expect he'll be relieved. It's what he always wanted, deep down. To be free from us."

Samantha sat there, the dismissal papers in her lap, hands limply holding the pages. Brightly glanced at her.

"Well, what are you waiting for?" he said. "I'm not going to let you sit there and read the entire thing. Get out. Go chum up with your policeman and discuss it with him."

Samantha stood and walked out to the hall. There were already men waiting on Brightly, legs crossed and calmly reading. The secretary scribbled away as she always did. Samantha walked to the elevator and the operator was there, still tiny and shriveled and smiling. He took her down to the lobby and she walked out to the street.

The sun was out and the air was warm. It seemed an unfair thing to grant the city such a blessing when she felt so lost. She wiped her eyes but found the tears were few. Then as she walked to the corner to hail a cab she saw the limousine parked by the curb, Wilford the driver dutifully polishing the hood.

She called out and rushed over to the car. She could see someone sitting in the back, hands in their lap. She got to the window and knocked against it and stooped to speak to Evans inside, but instead of Evans it was a tall, bearded gentleman in a bowler. He stared at her, astonished.

"I'm sorry," she said weakly. She stood and stepped away.

"What's the matter, Miss Fairbanks?" asked Wilford.

"What happened to Mr. Evans?" she asked him.

"Mr. Evans?"

"Yes, Willie. You've seen him, haven't you?"

"Well, yes, a day or two ago. Can't say what happened to him, ma'am," he said. "Drove him down to the central cradle two days ago, on his orders."

"To board a ship?" she asked.

"He didn't say, ma'am."

"What did he say?"

"Not much," he said. "Nothing at all. Just sat there. Looking out the window. He might have caught a ship, I suppose." Then Wilford frowned and said, "He shook my hand."

"He what?"

"He shook my hand. He'd never done that before. Said I was a good driver, which was odd, too. He never does such things."

Samantha nodded and said softly, "What you love doesn't love you."

"Pardon, ma'am?"

"Nothing," she said. "Goodbye, Willie. Have a nice day."

"Won't be hard," he said, returning to polishing. "Sun's out. Seems like the first time in years."

"Yes," she said, and walked away.

CHAPTER THIRTY

Samantha was not sure where to go. Her apartment was watched, she knew that, and though she couldn't imagine what McNaughton would want with her now, she knew it didn't trust her and would take whatever measures it felt necessary. Garvey was being watched as well, that was almost certain. So she was not very surprised to find herself returning to Hayes's little safe house off the Wering Canal.

She opened the door with the little pearl key and walked in and sat on the bed. She very much wanted to lie down and rest and forget everything.

"Where have you been?" said a voice.

She jumped and looked around and found Hayes sitting calmly behind the door, hands in his lap. The top of his brow was frogskin-white with scar tissue but his eyes were steady.

"Where was I? Where were you?" she demanded.

"Out working," he said.

"Working? On what?"

"On the case, of course." He seemed irritated with the question.

"The case?" she said, furious. "The case? There isn't any case!"

"Certainly there is."

"No, there isn't! Not anymore! We've all been sacked, you damn fool! Haven't you realized?"

"Sacked? What? When?"

"Just now! Just when I went to go see Brightly!"

"Why did you go see Brightly?" he asked, mystified.

"God. You really have no idea, do you." She sat down on the bed and pulled up an old newspaper from the floor and threw it at him. It tumbled into his arms like a wounded duck. "Go on, then," she said. "Read."

Hayes opened up the newspaper. It did not take long, as the story was on the front page and all the other stories seemed to be about it. Soon the look of confusion melted out of his face to be replaced with one of aching weariness. He shut his eyes and held his brow with one hand.

"Oh, Sam," he said. "Sam, Sam. You didn't need to do that."

"Do what? Help Donald? Of course I had to. You knew what I was out to do."

"Oh, I knew that. I knew you would never let him be thrown to the dogs. But you should have waited. You should have left it up to me, Sam."

"To you!" she said. "To you, who got us all into this mess? Who got poor Mr. Evans fired, not to mention myself? Who disappears without a word? To you? Good God, Mr. Hayes, why on Earth would I leave anything of importance in the hands of a man like you?"

Hayes took a breath. He seemed to be steeling himself. "It's a question of leverage," he said.

"Of leverage?"

"Yes."

"What the hell do you mean?"

He blinked, startled. "Well, you used everything you had to get Garvey off," he said. "And they took you for it, and Evans. But I think I can get us something more, Sam. Something bigger."

She slowly sat back down on the bed. "What are you talking about?"

"I'm not sure yet. But something stinks about all this. And I think I can find out what."

"Stinks about what? About what happened to Donald?"

"No. About what we saw and heard down there in the tunnels."

Samantha frowned at him. "What do you mean? Are you talking about . . . about blackmail?"

He shrugged.

"Blackmailing who? The unions?"

"No. McNaughton, Sam."

"McNaughton?" she said, confused. "With what? And how would blackmailing McNaughton help Donald?"

"I can't say yet. As I said, I'm not sure. But if my hunch is right then this isn't over yet. We can still set things aright. But I need something from you, Sam."

She laughed hollowly. "What more could you need? After all this?"

"Just something little. Something small." He leaned forward, eyes skirting the floor of the room as he thought. "When you did your research at McNaughton, there was a Records floor, the nineteenth floor, right? You spent a lot of time there, yes?"

"Well. Yes."

"And they let you have access to budgetary files, didn't they?"

"Yes, of course they did."

"All right. And somewhere in there was the budget for Local Securities. There was a room for it, probably, a separate room. Big and black, locked down tight. Wasn't there?"

"Yes. They made sure never to tell me about it, but I saw it there, yes."

"And you had the key," he said desperately. "A light key. Tell me they gave it to you, Sam."

"But why—"

"Never mind why. Just please, tell me they trusted you with that."

"Yes, they did. The key they gave me opened any door on the

filing floor, but I never used it for Local Securities. Someone said if I tried to access those files then they ask you about it immediately. They have some sort of logging system for the keys, I have no idea how it works."

"That doesn't matter. Where's the key?"

"It's in my apartment. In Newton. It's being watched, though."

"I know it's being watched, I swung by there and saw them. But you're sure? You're sure it's there, Sam?"

"I'm sure. I keep all my keys and important file work in my desk."

"Which desk?"

"It's the one I brought with me from home. You'll notice it, it's the ugliest thing in the apartment."

He stood up. "Then let's hope they haven't ransacked the place yet."

"You're going?" she asked, surprised.

"Yes. I need that key, Sam. I've stolen and stored up a great deal of keys in my day, but that one's always eluded me. If there's anything to be found, it'll be in that little room."

"But even if you manage to get the key, you still can't get into the Nail! They'll be looking for you, they'll know they can't let you in!"

"I don't plan on going myself, Sam," he said darkly. "In fact, I'm probably going to do something I'd never consider doing otherwise. Stay here. There's nowhere else that's safe yet. And things are going to get a lot more dangerous out there." He went to the door and opened it. The gray waterfall of the canal was still surging along out front and he pulled his scarf tight against its fine rain.

"If you find what you're looking for," said Samantha, "if you find what we need, will that help Donald? Or us?"

He stopped to look back at her. "Us, no. Garvey, maybe. But I honestly have no idea, Sam. I really don't." Then he shut the door and was gone.

CHAPTER THIRTY-ONE

Hayes went northeast to where Netwon met the Sound and enormous town houses lined its shores. It was a famously pretty area called the Garden District, as it showcased the few picturesque scraps of coastline and the only worthwhile parks. He checked his watch as he entered the park lanes that led down to the water, but it wasn't necessary. He could already tell by the colorful lights beyond that the Tidetop Market was about to start.

The idea for the Market had originally been taken from Dockland, where it was common for small watercraft to be refitted as seaborne vending booths, little houseboats and sturdy rafts that flitted back and forth to harry ships and people on the shore for business. On weekend mornings they would all cling to the wharfs and the docks, setting up temporary markets where one could buy all sorts of exotic fruits and spices and meats, not to mention goods that had arrived in the country by suspicious means and could not be sold anywhere else. And then someone in the Garden District had thought that was a very clever idea indeed and chose to organize their own cleaner, more upstanding version of the same thing, arranged as a community festival. It soon came to be considered one of the most charming attractions Evesden had to offer.

The boats were strictly screened by the organizers. Nothing of any ill repute or anything too upsetting. An exotic atmosphere was encouraged, however, and the boats themselves had to be specially engineered. Some mechanical genius had figured out a way for all the boats to latch onto one another, forming a tight grid of little dinghies and skiffs that reached out into the water. Once they were secure, fans of the market could wander through the bobbing paper lanterns and waterborne shops, sometimes stopping to watch a fantastic meal prepared on a bed of coals on the steel floor of a pontoon. It was a popular place for children of the wealthy, and if you didn't want to spend time in the market you could always get a table at Sutherland's, the restaurant just down the river, and watch the multicolored lights drift and dip along the water.

Hayes got to the market just as evening began, dressed in his very best suit. He waited at the bar of a wine booth that had a clear view of the market entrance, sipping rice wine as slowly as he could. He wondered how long he would have to wait. Hopefully it would not be for more than an hour; the market would soon be a crowded place, and he already felt the uncomfortable itching at the backs of his eyes that told him a migraine was coming. But he knew his man took his family to the Tidetop Market every time he could, so surely he'd be here eventually.

Hayes was right. He arrived just after seven, arm in arm with his lovely wife, his daughters precious in their little blue and red dresses. Hayes guessed the one in red was Jessica, as he remembered she was the older one, and the child in blue would be Honoria. They had grown since he'd last seen them. The wife, Elizabeth or whatever, she seemed to be doing all right, smiling emptily into the night sky. And Teddy seemed to be doing fine as well. Old Teddy Montrose from Telecommunications, gleefully ignorant as always. He should have been thanking God and Jesus and Mother Mary he'd never put a toe out of line, considering what Brightly had on him.

Hayes rose and tracked the family through the market, watching them stop among the flower booths to purchase a crackly little pastry from a woman in a straw hat. Hayes browsed booths in their wake, watching out of the corner of his eye and nodding absently as the vendors tried to talk him into a deal. Then when Teddy split off to go buy something special for the girls Hayes made his move.

He crossed to the other side of the market, then turned and began weaving across the pathways toward Teddy. When he came into view Hayes stopped with an amiably confused look on his face and said, "Teddy?"

Teddy slowed as he passed, then stopped, a puzzled smile on his face. "Yes?"

"Teddy Montrose? Is that you?"

"Well, yes," said Teddy. "Have we..."

Hayes grinned and laughed gaily, throwing out his arms like a long-separated relative. "Why, don't say you don't remember me, Teddy old boy! Don't say you've forgotten me?"

Teddy laughed with him. "Well, I'm...I'm sorry, I really...It's my fault, I really don't recall..."

"Why, it's old Carter, from the company," said Hayes. He stuck his hand out and gave him a robust shake. "John Carter. Marketing Division. We met on the trip, last year. Don't you remember?"

"Business trip?" said Teddy. "Last year?"

"Yes, certainly. We had a rousing old time with the boys, didn't we? Had a lot of fun, right, Teddy? Got up to some trouble?"

"From the business trip?" said Teddy again, now no longer trying to hide his confusion. "But to where?"

"To Dockland, Teddy," said Hayes. He lowered his voice. "To Dockland."

Teddy's brow crinkled. "What? I never went to Dockland. Not on business. I would never go to such a place."

"But you did, Teddy," said Hayes. His voice dropped to a murmur, nearly drowned out by the little flute quartet playing in a booth nearby.

"You did. You went to Stella's, don't you remember? And you got up to so much fun there. With the boys and all. Do you remember?"

Teddy snapped to attention at the mention of that name. He stared at Hayes and the color drained from his face. "Wh-what did you say?"

"The boys, Teddy," said Hayes softly. "Don't you remember all the fun you had with the boys?"

Teddy began to tremble. He swallowed and said, "I d-don't know what you're talking about." He turned and began to leave.

"I don't think I'd be leaving if I were you, Teddy," said Hayes, louder. "It wouldn't be wise."

Teddy froze and looked back. "Wise? What do you mean?"

Hayes did not say anything. He just smiled grimly at him.

Teddy walked closer. "What do you mean? What do you want?"

Hayes pointed up the river at Sutherland's. "To talk, Teds. There, at the restaurant. I'll be at the bar at nine. And we'll talk then, Teddy. Discuss what's to be done with you."

"What do you mean?"

"Nine," said Hayes. "Be there. That's all you need to know."

"You can't... you can't do this to me," whispered Teddy.

"I'm absolutely sure I can," Hayes said. "Tell your wife you met a business partner. One with important news. Or tell her whatever you fucking like, it's nothing to me. But you had better be there."

"Or what?"

"Or else, this?" he said. He waved about at the market, then at Teddy's family. Then he brought his hand to his face and blew into his fingers, as though he'd blown them apart into nothing. Then he smiled at Teddy and ran one finger along the brim of his hat and walked away.

Teddy was there at eight forty-five, covered in clammy sweat and shaking like a newborn lamb. He came and sat before Hayes, bent like a mourner, eyes adrift.

"What did you tell the wife?" asked Hayes.

"B-business partner," said Teddy. Tears began spilling from his eyes to dribble down his cheeks.

Hayes glanced out the window at the flotilla of the market. "They're out on the boats now?"

He nodded.

"All right. We'll try to make this quick, then."

"How do you know?" asked Teddy desperately. "How do you know about... about..."

Hayes decided to give him the truth. About Brightly and the days of following him. Hayes couldn't help but talk about the man's family as he did, discussing little Honoria and Jessica and the days he'd spent watching them. With each passing minute Teddy grew paler and paler. Finally he began sobbing outright.

"I'm a sick man," he cried at the end of it. "I'm a sick, sick man."

"Here now, buck up, Ted." Hayes glanced around the bar. "You don't want us thrown out, do you?"

"I'm such a sick man! So sick!"

"Yes," said Hayes tersely. "Yes, I rather expect you are. Very sick."

"I tried to stop. I tried to stop it. Tried not to go there. But I—"

"But you couldn't."

"No," he whispered. "No, I couldn't."

"No," said Hayes tersely. "No, your kind usually can't. But there's no reason to get upset. We can keep it quiet, Teddy."

Teddy sniffed and wiped his eyes. Snot was streaming from his nose now. "What is it you want? Money?"

"No. No, not money."

"Then what?"

"Just a favor. You just have to do something for me."

Hayes laid it out for him, nice and neat. What he wanted and how he expected to get it. He spoke as slowly as he could, making it easy for the man's distressed mind. Then he took out Samantha's light key and laid it on the table next to his drink. It had been easy to get, no one competent had been stationed near her apartment. Teddy stared at the key through jellied eyes, lips still quaking.

"But I never go there," said Teddy. "I never go to the Records floor."

"I don't care. You'll be going there now, won't you? If you want to keep this quiet."

"They'll know. They'll know I was there. There'll be questions."

"You go in with this key," said Hayes, tapping it. "It's not matched to you. It's not yours. And they won't question you being at the Nail. You're a big man, Teddy. Big and important. You go in. You get what I want. Then when you're done you throw the key away. Throw it down a storm drain, throw it in the ocean, I don't care."

"But they'll find all those missing files!" whispered Teddy desperately. "They'll find them and they'll know it was me! How do I do it without them knowing?"

Hayes looked him up and down, face taut and cruel. "Well. That's your problem, isn't it? I don't care how you do it, so long as you do it. I just want what I need. The rest is up to you."

"They'll catch me."

"Maybe. Would being fired be worse than being prosecuted for buggery?"

Teddy choked. Then he shook as though he was about to vomit.

"Not here," said Hayes quickly. "Run to the washroom if you're going to do it."

Teddy shook his head. He took a breath and got himself under control. Then he looked at Hayes with those weak little eyes and said, "I don't have a choice, do I?"

Hayes shook his head.

Teddy nodded. "All right."

Hayes did not return to the safe house with Samantha that night. He did not want to risk attracting attention to her if he could. Instead he stayed in the attic of a condemned home he'd found. It looked as if it wouldn't be of use for much longer, as it was now roped off for demolition. Once there he lay down on a musty old mattress and slept shivering in the dark.

You never did know which way they'd jump, the boys you burned. Ferguson had leaped out a window. Others had suddenly turned patriot, willing to die for their country or company. And Teddy might still find a way to muck everything up, blundering in there and fooling about. But Hayes suspected he wouldn't. He had watched Teddy. He knew him. He was a careful man and a talented engineer, and he'd somehow managed to nurse an abominable perversion for years without cracking or letting anyone in on it. If anyone could do it, it'd be old Teddy.

But nothing was for sure. And sometimes when he burned them Hayes wondered if he did something to himself as well. If handling their sins tainted him in places deep inside himself.

The next evening Hayes rose and waited under the Brennan Street Bridge. It was the second largest bridge in the state, after the Kulahee, which spanned the Juan de Fuca. Rickety apartments on stilts rested up against its massive curve like barn swallows, their little windows glowing like tiny eyes. As the cold grew the grates on the street belched roiling clouds of steam, like enormous furnaces below the city were working to the point of destruction.

Hayes feared he'd never show, yet then he did. A trim, proper figure slowly walking through the grip of the steam, briefcase in his hand, not in a hurry by any means. Hayes stepped out from his hiding place along the bridge and Teddy's eyes slid over to him, wide and curiously blank. Then he stopped before him and held out the briefcase.

Hayes took it. It was large and very heavy. "This all of it?" he asked.

Teddy nodded, still silent.

"You sure? You'd better be sure, dear Ted. I'd hate to intervene again."

He nodded again.

"Good," said Hayes. "Then I'll be gone."

He turned to leave when he felt a hand on his shoulder. He looked back at Teddy and stared into those terrified eyes.

"You know I couldn't help it," said Teddy.

"Get your hand off me."

"You know I couldn't."

"Get your fucking hand off me."

He did so, then stood there shaking.

"I'm not your fucking priest," said Hayes softly. "I'm not your doctor. I don't care about your obsession or whether you live or die. I'm just gone."

"Will He forgive me?" asked Teddy suddenly.

"Who?"

"God. Do you think He will forgive me?"

Hayes looked at him. His breath caught in his throat and he felt the awful fear rise up in Teddy, the sick magnetism that drew him to Dockland twice a year or more, and the desire to run, to hide from the fear, to hide anywhere, maybe even in death. But as the rush of thought poured into Hayes he realized Teddy feared death even more than being exposed, for then he could no longer hide, not from God Himself, and he would be seen for what he was in his deepest heart.

"No," said Hayes. "No, I don't." Then he walked quickly away and left him there.

CHAPTER THIRTY-TWO

Samantha was just wandering the borders of sleep when the door of the safe house slammed open and a dark figure toppled in. She snapped awake and cried out, then reached below the bed for the little knife she'd hidden there. Then the figure coughed and said, "Christ, Sam, calm yourself. It's only me."

"Mr. Hayes?" she said. She reached for the light. It snapped on to reveal Hayes struggling with the door, sopping wet, with arms full of boxes and briefcases. He managed to get a toe behind the door to shove it shut, then dumped the files down on the floor and sat beside them, breathing hard.

"God, that was a long ways," he said.

She stood to help him. "What are you doing? What are those?"

He grinned, still breathing hard, and laid a hand on the stack with a flourish. "These? These are our keys, Sam. These are our tickets in. In to what, I'm not sure. That's why I brought them to you."

Samantha looked down at the files. Her eyes traced over the red tabs and the olive-green sheaths with black lettering stamped down the side. "Those are McNaughton files."

"Yes indeed."

"How did you get those?"

"It doesn't matter how. I got them, that's enough. They're the financial records for Local Securities for the last sixteen months," he said with a groan as he stood. "Local Securities being those who keep watch at home and pay single characters rather than companies. Shady people on the payroll. Informants."

"Informants?"

"Yes. Are you surprised?"

"Well, no, honestly. I can't believe we kept records for that sort of thing, though."

"Oh, I can. Very easily. It's a business, after all. The right hand may not want to know what the left hand is doing, but they do want to know how much they're paying for it."

"You want to blackmail McNaughton with that?"

"Not with that, no. I want you to look through these," he said, fingering the files and briefcases, "and these," and he touched the boxes.

"And what are those?"

"Those are prison records. From Savron Hill, and Garvey. You're going to use that marvelous mind of yours to look there first."

"Look for what?"

"Disappearances. And similarities."

She rolled up her sleeves and began laying out the files on the floor, as there was no room on the desk in Hayes's safe house. After glancing through the McNaughton files she saw that many of them were heavily coded, seeming to rely on the use of some sort of cipher, which Hayes concluded they didn't have. Sighing, she set the files in order of simplicity, with the prison files close to her and the densest McNaughton files at the other end. Then she began reading, starting with prisoner records from three years back and looking for any gaps in the information, prisoners who had gone missing without any warning or notation at all. It was extremely difficult work, as the prisoner records were often either incompetent or incomprehensible. It was hard to discern if a gap was a mistake or an intended omission.

Hayes was of no help at all; this sort of work bored him to tears. At first he hovered over her shoulder, asking questions and getting cigarette ash all over the papers. Then he gave up and passed the time bouncing around the room, wandering the corners and sometimes going out to the canal to watch the waterfall swell and shrink.

After three hours of work she felt she had found someone. A Mr. Gerald Crimley, once a prisoner of South Sector C, imprisoned there for land fraud. Apparently he got caught getting people to invest in properties that didn't technically exist. Wound up stuck with a five-year sentence, and disappeared with less than a year of it served. Samantha checked and rechecked the death rolls, which were both long and appalling, but among all the names Crimley never appeared. He never reappeared, either, not anywhere else.

"Hm," said Hayes once she told him this. He finally sat down on the bed, his eyes half-shut as though he were sleepy. "Well. We'll need to find out where he went."

"Am I looking for Crimley in the McNaughton files now?"

Hayes opened his eyes and smiled slightly. "Yes. If you would be so kind."

Samantha then began the laborious job of digging through the cryptic budgetary records. They were conveniently arranged by date, but often referred to events or figures whose names were no more than letters and numbers, such as RD232 or WJR34-1-1. She guessed these were the names of other files, and if they had the cipher then she would have been able to make sense of them. Numerous code words were used as well, such as *Seaworthy* or *Easterner* or *Pilgrim*. After looking at all the entries and logs, she guessed that Seaworthy was almost certainly some sort of senatorial contact, while Pilgrim had to be a shipping contractor for a minor-league rival firm. Easterner was all over the records, yet she could see no pattern there. But exactly what they all did for McNaughton was never mentioned; just their costs and financial matters. Bank accounts and payment amounts and dates. It was just one long receipt.

One file name began appearing very often around the time Gerald Crimley disappeared: SP-0417. She noticed it because three weeks after Crimley disappeared from Savron a five-thousand-dollar payment was made to a bank account in San Francisco, referencing that file name as the owner of the account. Frowning, she made the tenuous leap that, provided Hayes's vague hunch was not wrong and the two files were indeed connected, SP-0417 was Crimley.

"If he's alive," added Samantha. "And if Crimley is involved in McNaughton at all."

To this Hayes said nothing. Just nodded again with sleepy, distant eyes.

She kept looking through the financial activity under SP-0417. For a long time there was nothing. No deposits or withdrawals whatsoever, not for nearly three months. Then, finally, another payment was made, this only one thousand, but to the same account. From then on one thousand dollars were paid monthly to the account, starting eleven months ago. Almost immediately after this SP-0417 began to be associated with something called *Craftsman.* Craftsman didn't seem to be a person, as far as Samantha could see, but a project of some kind. The nature of Craftsman was never made clear, and the few details about it were carefully blacked out by some record auditor who had deemed them too explicit for the budgetary files. Eventually there was some sort of warning about financial deposits made to SP-0417 while Craftsman was underway, giving a number of other accounts and stocks to route the payments through before they arrived at the original account for SP-0417. It was some tricky financial math, but apparently whatever SP-0417 was doing necessitated dead secrecy and generous pay.

Until, finally, the payments were no longer made through an account or a series of cleaning fronts. This had happened abruptly, merely two months ago. From then on it was notated that the payments would go through a single person who would handle them himself on the behalf of SP-0417, that intermediary identified directly as one *J. Colomb.*

Samantha stared at this once she read it. Trembling, she read this aloud to Hayes, who shut his eyes fully.

"Colomb is the man who helped Mickey Tazz," said Samantha softly. "Wasn't he?"

"Yes," said Hayes.

"And if I'm right, then... then he's helping Crimley here."

Hayes nodded.

"Then that means... That could mean that Crimley is Tazz, and..."

"And Tazz is company," said Hayes. "Well done, Sam. Very well done indeed."

"But why would they do that?" asked Samantha. "Why?"

"What better enemy to have than the one you own, lock and stock?" said Hayes. "What better foe to fight than the one you control with every move? They must have seen the union rising in the future and decided to act. They fabricated a union leader, from his past to his pamphlets, then found some poor bastard in prison and said, Hello, friend, we'll happily give you a way out and pay you generously if you just wear this mask for a while and do what we say, whatever we say and whenever we say it."

"How could that happen, though?" asked Samantha, still astounded.

"Through time," said Hayes. "And money. My guess is they never intended Crimley to reach the very top. They probably just wanted him to be their agent in the unions, not their leader. But I guess fortune paved the way for him."

"But what good would it all do? Haven't people died because of this union business?"

"Yes, but there's never been any big sabotage," said Hayes. "Don't you remember? Oh, a few have gotten killed, sure, but I bet it's hard to control the hand of every man who pledges himself to the union, like Mickey himself said just a few days ago. But they've never done anything big, have they? Because someone at McNaughton told Tazz to keep them on a leash."

"And that's how he knew about what you can do," said Samantha, realizing.

"Yes," said Hayes. "I'd expect Brightly or someone told him themselves."

"How long have you had this hunch?"

"Since we met him. The way he talked about being made, and owned. It seemed too familiar, for me."

"All right. But then why are we investigating them? Why did they tell us to start tearing down the unions wherever we can? That doesn't make sense at all."

Hayes paused at that, thinking. "No, it doesn't," he said. He sighed. "God, I wish I could have caught him while he was here! I'd have put the screws to him and not stopped."

"He's not here?" asked Samantha. "He's gone?"

Hayes filled her in on what he had seen the night before last. "Just jumped ship and shipped off," he said when he was done. "Up and gone, like no tomorrow."

"Why would he do that, I wonder?"

"I don't know. He didn't seem too pleased when we saw him. What he said about McNaughton, how they make people and use them… I think he was starting to crack after the murders. That he was starting to give up, or give in. It's not easy, living deep cover. They start to believe it. You sink them in with people fighting for a cause, and your man starts to turn over time, if you're not careful with him. I think Mr. Crimley may have actually started to believe the words he was preaching, maybe."

"Maybe that's why he started looking for the machines, down in the tunnels," said Samantha. "He wanted to give them control. To give the union men something of McNaughton's. Or to sabotage McNaughton entirely."

"Yes. But you can see he gave up on it recently, when he told his company contacts to start sending money through Colomb. That way he can get his hands on fast cash and then get out. When I spooked him he must've figured enough was enough, and scarpered."

"But do you think this Tazz business might actually be connected to the trolley?"

Hayes bit his lip. "Maybe. But Tazz seemed frightened, just as much as Brightly. It may not be connected at all." He thought for a moment, then said, "Here, let's keep looking through the file. If this Craftsman nonsense is the term for planting Crimley at the top of the unions, then surely we can find out more just by following it."

Hayes was right. There was more. As Craftsman rolled along it began to accumulate payments to dock personnel, boat owners, and finally a new character, one referred to as *Colonel.* Samantha discovered that Colonel had been found through the ever-present Easterner, apparently an old friend of his who had brought him to the city for reasons and through methods unknown. It seemed, Samantha said, that Tazz's last instructions for the unions had involved bringing something in to Evesden, shipped in by this Colonel from a McNaughton facility west on the Strait. The location of this facility was given more security than anything Samantha had ever seen previously: the word had not just been blacked out, but cut out of the report with a razor blade, and a blank tab of paper had been pasted in. There was a note inked in red in the margins of the paper, saying that all inquiries should be directed to L. Brightly, head of Security.

"There are no McNaughton facilities west down the Strait," said Samantha. "None that I know of, at least."

"What was Tazz shipping in? Or being told to ship in?"

"I've no idea. It just says 'shipment' over and over again and then gives the names for the people attending to it. Buying the boat and whatever."

The heaviness returned to Hayes's eyes again. "Hm," he said.

"What?"

"I'm just wondering if it ever mentions who exactly was supposed to aid in this smuggling."

She looked one document over again. "No, I don't think it ever mentions that. Just who they bought the boat from and who they paid off. Why?"

"Because they would probably need a team of men. Men that had worked on docks before. Or who were used to manual labor, and were willing to get their hands dirty."

Samantha cocked an eyebrow at him, then took a sharp breath. "The Bridgedale trolley?"

"Yes. I think it's possible that all those dead men may have been tapped to bring in the shipment for Tazz. Probably did it for free, thinking it was for the union. Them, and maybe Skiller. That's why there's no payment record."

"And then they were murdered to keep it quiet?"

"Maybe. This is all just guesswork, Sam. But I think that feels right. It hangs together. I would want to look. What else is there?"

"Well, there's this Colonel character who's all over it. Apparently Tazz—or Crimley, or whatever—he contacted him to run this operation on the recommendation of whoever was running things at McNaughton. But I don't know who this Colonel is besides that he was brought in by some Easterner figure, who seems to be everywhere throughout the files."

"What do we have on Easterner?"

"Oh, he gets paid pretty frequently," said Samantha. "And he gets paid well. It says in certain places that the amount routes through a Dutch merchant bank, then a Rabb Real Estate company in Chicago, then through a shipping company in California, and then finally an industrial canning complex here. It's ludicrously complicated and I..." She trailed off. Hayes had gone very still, his face slack.

"Oh, God," he said softly. He blinked once, confounded.

"What? What is it?"

"That's me," he said. "That's how my money gets to me. I'm… I'm Easterner."

"*You* are?"

He nodded. "Yes, I check… I check every couple of months."

"Oh!" she said. She thought about it and gave a brief whoop of laughter. "Well, that would make sense. But who's Colonel, then? It says you brought him here and they made the contact through you, so…"

A queer look came into Hayes's face. He bowed his head and one hand sought the wall for support. "No," he murmured. "No, they couldn't have found him."

"Found who? You know who it is?"

"Yes," said Hayes faintly. "Yes, I know who it is. An old friend. One I got out of a spot of trouble, and one I hoped I'd never see again."

"Who is he?"

Hayes just shook his head. He seemed so shocked by the revelation that he was beyond answering.

"But can you find him?" said Samantha. "Can you find him and see what Tazz was bringing in?"

"Maybe." He shook his head again and sat down on the bed. "God. If I had known what that file would give me I'd have never gone through the trouble to get it."

"What did you go through, out of curiosity?" Samantha asked idly, picking up the files.

"What? Oh. I just dug up an old contact. Or a target, really."

"Yes, but who?"

"Mmm," said Hayes, still lost in thought. "You remember the man I told you about a while back? The man Brightly had me follow, even though there wasn't anything on him?"

Samantha slowed to a stop among the files. Her back was turned to him. "The man who… The one who was going to that place with the children?"

"Yes. Montrose. Teddy Montrose. Turns out he was still around. I put the burn on him and he hopped to it. Rather convenient, really."

"You used him?"

"Yes. It was all short and sweet. Thankfully."

Samantha turned around to look at him, mouth half-open in outrage and horror. Hayes was calmly picking at something in his teeth. It took him a moment to notice her.

"What?" he said.

"And what did you do?" she whispered.

"What? What do you mean?"

"What did you do once you got the files? Once you got what you wanted?"

"Do? To him?"

"Yes."

"Well, nothing. I turned around and walked away."

Samantha swallowed. Her hands bunched into fists at her sides, knuckles going white and wrists trembling. She looked away as a snarl wove through her face, and she moved as though she wished to leave. Then she suddenly stooped down and picked up a file and threw it at him with both arms. He raised his hands to protect himself and the folder burst open, pages flying out to twist and turn and rain on him like snow.

"Hey!" he cried. "What the hell are you doing?"

Samantha moaned in fury. She reached down and snatched another file and hurled it at him as well. It missed and thudded into the wall, bleeding papers over the bed.

"Stop, stop!" Hayes shouted. "Stop it, for God's sake!"

"What am I doing!" she said through clenched teeth. "What am I doing! You little... you little oily shit!" She grabbed another file off the tabletop and was about to throw it when it fell apart in her hands. She gave up and rushed over and began slapping him about the neck and head. He covered himself with his hands.

"Sam, what the hell! Calm down!"

"You let him go!" she shouted at him. "You let him go! You let that man go after what he did, after what he did to those children! You dealt with him and then let him go!"

"I had to!" said Hayes, still covering himself from her barrage of slaps. "I had to use him!"

"But you let him go! You should have... you should have..." She trailed off, shaking her head.

"Should have what?" Hayes said, standing up. His face was a bright, angry pink. "Should have taken him to the police?"

"Yes!"

"And said what? That I followed him and found him buggering children off in Dockland? And that no, I don't have any evidence? And that no, I'd be unable to testify? And that why yes, I'd done the work on the part of one of the most powerful men in the city? Is that what I should have done?"

"Something! You should have done something!"

"Like what, shoot him? Should I have burned down that place in Dockland? Freed all those boys? Given them all a dollar and said here you go, now you're all good? Sam, have you ever even wondered how such a place is still open, and who they're paying?"

"He was a monster!" Samantha cried. "A monster! And you used him and let him go!"

"I had to!" Hayes said savagely. "I had no choice. I needed those goddamn files and they've turned up gold, now haven't they? Haven't they? If we work this to the bone, won't we get something good for you and Garvey? Something to set things right?"

"But those children were victims!" said Samantha. "Innocent victims!"

"We're *all* victims!" Hayes shouted. "All of us! You, me! Garvey! Victims of McNaughton, of the Department, of Dockland, of this whole fucking city! You can't save every single one of them, not when we can't even save ourselves!"

"You're as bad as Brightly. Using that man, that *thing* as you wish."

"I'm not."

"You are," she said. "It's all just an excuse to you. To just do as you please. To enjoy yourself."

"It isn't," said Hayes. "It's not."

"You don't even care, do you? This isn't about any crime. None of this ever was, for you. It's about paring people down, digging under their skin, and proving that deep down everyone is as weak and filthy as you. How odd it is that the one man who should by all rights know more about people than anyone else is so utterly incapable of being one."

"Fuck you," snarled Hayes. "What are you doing it for, then? For Garvey? Just for that?"

"No," she said.

"Then what?"

She hesitated, then said, "For the boy."

"Boy? What boy?"

"God," she said. "You don't even remember, do you? Skiller's son. The little boy."

"Him? Why?"

She faltered then, and some of the color drained from her face. "I just… I know it's stupid to hope. A little boy on the streets of this city? How long could he last? But somehow I always hope that in following up all this union business I'll find him somewhere in it. Maybe there's a chance. After all, I'm probably the only one looking for him."

Hayes stared at her. Then he looked away as though bitterly disappointed and shook his head. "Sometimes you make me feel so… so *empty*," he said. Then he looked at the mess on the floor and said, "Here. Help me clean this up."

They both stooped and began gathering the files, sorting them out as best they could and stuffing them back into their boxes. When they were done Hayes sat on the bed and Samantha on the floor.

"They'll be looking for us more than ever now," Samantha said.

"Yes."

"This place is safe?"

"I hope so," Hayes said.

She nodded, then asked, "How did you plan to use this to help Donald?"

"I don't know. I thought maybe if I gave him a case good enough he could buy his way back into the Department." He looked at her. "We still could, you know. Just give him this about Tazz and stop right there. Leave the rest alone and just walk away."

"We could," she said. "But we won't." She smiled grimly. "So goes the life of a career-minded young lady. I don't miss it, though. I don't know why." The smile left. "Do you know where your old friend lives now?"

Hayes shook his head. "And there's not many willing to help me right now."

"We could probably get it from Donald," she said. "He'd help."

Hayes lit a cigarette, then drew deeply on it and leaned his head back and let smoke leak out of his mouth. "Yes. You're right. He probably would."

CHAPTER THIRTY-THREE

When Garvey woke up he was still drunk and the whisky in his belly was septic and rumbling. He rolled over and lifted his head and saw the cold light of morning drifting in. Then he buried his face in the pillow and shut his eyes and tried to ignore the thick cotton-dryness in his eyelids and mouth.

Eventually he rolled out of bed. He drank rust-tainted water from the sink, whisky bottles scattered on the counter beside like fallen soldiers. He stood. Took a breath. Then he doubled up and clutched the sink edge and vomited something orange-tan and frothy around the drain. When he was done he lay there with one cheek on the cool porcelain. He washed his mouth out but did not drink. Then he pulled on a pair of pants and smoked as he looked out the kitchen window at the little cement courtyard.

It was Tuesday, he remembered. He nodded to himself curtly, put on a nice suit, then went and got his old phonograph and loaded it into the back of his car. He stood looking at it on the seat, thinking, then checked up and down the street. It was empty. He shook his head and returned to his apartment and got his spare revolver out of his desk.

He sat on the bed, holding it, feeling its deadly heaviness. It had never been fired, unlike its brother, which had been confiscated by the Department. He snapped it open and looked at the six little brass eyes watching him from its cylinder. Then he sighed and closed it and replaced it in his desk. He did not want to bear that awful weight, not today.

When he returned to his car he saw that now there was a little figure leaning casually up against its side, scarf loosely tied, hands lost within the pockets of his coat.

"Hullo, Garv," said Hayes.

Garvey stopped where he was on the sidewalk, looking at Hayes. Then he resolutely stared across the street and said, "No."

"No? No to what?"

"No to whatever you're here for," said Garvey. He began walking to the car, still not looking at Hayes. "You shouldn't even be here. We shouldn't even be seen together."

"I've been careful."

"But not careful enough." Garvey walked around to the driver's side of the car. "If you were really careful you wouldn't be here at all." Before he got in he stopped to check the street again.

"No one's watching," said Hayes. "Can't say why not. But I checked. And you know I check better than most."

"I didn't know. And I don't care," said Garvey. He got into the car.

Hayes looked through the passenger window at him. "I need your help, Garv."

"No. I said no and I meant no."

"It's just one little thing. One little thing I need. An address, Garv."

"Get off my car unless you want to lose a foot."

"Here, I'm sorry about what happened."

"I'm serious."

Hayes stepped back. He anxiously flicked the cigarette away and leaned out to continue speaking through the window. "I'm sorry, Don. I am. But we've made headway, me and Sam."

"You and Sam?"

Hayes gave him a pained smile. "Yes."

"That's not safe at all."

"I know, I know, but we've gotten somewhere good. We just need to get a little further."

"A little further," said Garvey.

"Yes. I need an address."

"Get it yourself."

"I can't, Garv. I've pulled all the favors I had on this, so I had to come to you."

"Goodbye, Hayes," said Garvey, and he eased up on the drive handle and sped off.

He got halfway down the block before looking in the rearview mirror and seeing the little figure huddled next to the other cars, watching him leave. He was tiny in the shadow of the enormous buildings around him. Garvey slowed the car to a stop and shut his eyes, wondering exactly why he'd picked this day of all days to get himself back into trouble he knew he could do perfectly well without.

It took Hayes several minutes to make it all the way down the block. By the time he dragged himself up to the window he was red-cheeked and puffing. He still managed a grin. "Where are we going?"

"Just shut up and get in the car, why don't you," said Garvey, and he reached over and opened the door.

Garvey drove west, past Westbank and Lynn, out past the city limits where the buildings shrank and small homes still survived. Hayes jabbered on as they talked, rushing through his discoveries and unable to hide his delight. Garvey noticed he seemed much more fluent than he had previously; whereas before he would leap from topic to topic and forget what he was talking about in a matter of minutes, now he managed to stay on one thread at a time without losing himself. It took Garvey a while to realize Hayes was something close to sober. He wondered how long it would last. Probably until this little adventure came to an end, if it ever did.

"So... Tazz works for McNaughton?" said Garvey slowly at the end.

"Worked, Garv. Worked. He's done a runner, probably down to Mexico. Christ, I wish I was there. I'd be rid of this chill, that's for sure."

"And you're sure about all this?"

"Nearly positive. I can give it to you, Garvey. I can give you the files linking them both. And then maybe you can go to Collins, and he'll take you back."

Garvey did not look at him. A deep stillness rolled over him like a cloak and his heart beat faster. "Maybe."

"I just need an address from you," Hayes said. "For an old friend of mine." He tucked a piece of paper underneath the car's driveshaft and patted it.

Garvey glanced at it as he drove. "And he's complicit in all this?"

"I think so. I can turn him, though, I think. We didn't leave on the fondest terms."

Garvey gave a sardonic laugh. "Imagine that."

"So will you do it, Garv? Will you get me that?"

"You forget I'm not police these days. They've still got me suspended. I can't just walk in and start pulling residential records for you."

"But you've got friends. People you can go to. They can get it for you. Right?"

Garvey sighed as he turned off the road. "Damn it, Hayes."

"I know it's a lot. And I know we don't want to be attracting attention right now. But I need this, Garv. Sam and I do."

Garvey drove on in silence as the car rattled through the pine countryside. In some places there was even livestock, something both of them occasionally forgot even existed.

"How is she?" asked Garvey.

"Sam?" Hayes said.

Garvey nodded.

"She's doing. I think she's fraying a bit at the edges, though. Hasn't had anyone to talk to but me, and, well. I know that can be a bit much." Hayes looked out the window at the damp trees. "She misses you, Don."

"Yeah?"

"Yes. I can tell. I know."

"You know, huh?"

"Yes."

Garvey took a breath and nodded. "Well. Thank you, I guess."

They drove for more than an hour before Garvey pulled up in front of a small white house, quaint and humble and perfect. It had a white picket fence and thriving roses that threaded through a trellis in the front yard. Small tin toys lay scattered on the lawn, still pearled from the kiss of dew. Hayes curiously looked the house and yard over. He had never been here before. "What is this place?" he asked.

Garvey got out and walked around to the back of the car and pulled out his phonograph. Then he came to Hayes's side and said, "You stay here. You stay in the goddamn car, you hear me? Just stay here until I come back."

"Christ, all right. Fine."

Garvey walked up to the front door and knocked, phonograph under one arm. The front door opened and a small, pretty blond woman answered, her mouth tight and grim and her eyes cold. They shared a few words, Garvey with his head bowed. Then the woman leaned out and looked beyond him at Hayes. She seemed to shake with anger and fought to swallow it. Eventually she allowed him in and shut the door.

Hayes sat in the front seat and smoked a cigarette and waited.

After several minutes he heard something. He rolled down the window more and listened. Then he got out and shrank down low and walked to the side of the house to peek in the window.

Inside was a small, cozy room with a worn sofa and old bookshelves. A homey place, with lace doilies on the end tables. In the middle of the floor was the phonograph, playing a symphony Hayes could barely remember, some mournful Beethoven piece. In the center of the sofa sat Garvey, rocking back and forth, a little blond girl in his lap with her arms thrown around his neck, head perfectly still as though asleep. To his left sat another little girl, this one older and her blond hair streaked with brown. She stared at the phonograph intently, swaying slightly with the music, as if attempting to find some hidden truth within the machine that would unlock all the secrets of the world. Garvey stood then with the little one in his arms and he began pacing around the room, the two of them dancing, and Hayes heard him humming along with the music, softly and atonally. One big, rough hand rose up her back to cradle her head, her flaxen hair slipping through his fingers.

Hayes stared in shock and then withdrew, ashamed to have witnessed such a private moment. He walked back to the car, his face burning red, and sat without moving.

There was always more, he thought. Always more to everyone. For all the moments and feelings he could pluck out of the air there were thousands more hidden closer to the heart that would never be known to any other creature except their owner, and when they passed on from this world those secrets would fade as though they had never been here at all.

Which they may never have been, he thought. Which they may never have been.

Time passed. Maybe an hour. Then Garvey came out, phonograph under his arm again, tie fixed and hat straight. He stored the machine in the back and came and sat in the driver's seat again. "You ready?" he asked.

Hayes cleared his throat. "You don't have to."

"Huh?"

"You don't have to do this. Today, at least."

"Why not?" asked Garvey.

"You just don't. Drop me off somewhere in the city."

"Where?"

"Anywhere."

Garvey shrugged and drove back into town. The green-gray countryside melted by until it became smooth cement walls once more. Garvey steered the car to a rattling stop outside an old theater, where he pulled in under the marquee. Then Hayes got out and turned around and said, "You should go see Samantha."

"Why?"

"It'd clean you up, I think. I'm just saying. And she needs to see someone besides me, too. She's probably going mad."

Garvey cocked an eyebrow at him. "All right. Come by later and I'll have that address for you."

"I said you didn't have to do it today."

"Well, I'm doing it anyway. You don't have a choice."

"If you're sure. Thanks, Garv," said Hayes. He gave him the address and saluted and walked away, weaving through the crowd with his shoulders hunched and his hands in his pockets.

CHAPTER THIRTY-FOUR

Hayes had not intended to get drunk. He remembered that now, just a few hours after he'd left Garvey behind and gone roving through the streets, trying to purge that stolen image of Garvey's children from his mind. He knew his actions often had casualties, and it was cowardly to want to ignore them, but it was no longer a question of want as much as need. After the sun had set and the temperature dropped he'd fled into an open pub to huddle next to the barside fireplace, sniffling and cursing, and he'd told the barman that he wanted one beer, and then a chaser of whisky, and no more. But then the gentleman had mentioned one or two specials, and Hayes had listened.

Now it was night and he was stumbling through the alleys of the Shanties. "McNaughton," he muttered to himself. "Mc-fucking-Naughton. Always McNaughton." He turned to peer at the Nail, far away, lit up by spotlights along the base. Where had the bastard come from, he wondered. Had Kulahee dreamed of it, sitting in his little hut? Had he sketched it out on parchment, and then forgotten about it? Or had it always been here, waiting to be carved out of everything else around it?

He hiccupped. Then he looked around and realized he was quite lost.

They said that when Evesden was first founded the Shanties had been no more than log cabins cobbled together with hides stretched over them, built right in the woods. Hayes could believe it. The place had the planning and the hospitality of a shabby campground, or perhaps he was just drunk. As the population of Evesden had erupted, the tenements had swelled up between the leaning homes like enormous mushrooms, dark and stinking, and they'd remained that way for the future. Massive, darkly lit buildings with strings of smaller, rambling homes clutched between their ranks.

He looked at one tenement and realized he recognized it. It was Skiller's, smoke still oozing from the rooftop cracks. Perhaps he'd led himself here without realizing. It seemed like a ruin from some recent war left standing. He reached out and touched it to make sure it was real.

He stumbled around to the side of the building, to a little alley. It swelled and narrowed as the wall of the adjacent building warped. He walked along it and tried to imagine people living here. Tried to match this world with the one in Newton where Samantha had once slept peacefully, or peacefully enough.

Hayes stopped halfway down the alley. He heard someone just ahead, padding through the darkness. There was a snuffle, as though they were crying. Hayes stepped forward and the alley took a hard right down to the debris-filled gutter of the next building. No one was there. He looked back and around and saw no one in the little spaces between the buildings.

Then he heard it again. A child's sob, but now it was from far behind him. He swiveled around drunkenly to look, but again there was nothing.

"Hello?" he said.

The crying stopped abruptly, but not like the crier had just stopped. It was as if the noise itself had been cut off, like the halting of a record. Then Hayes heard it again down an alley to the right, much more agitated, some little child wailing. Hayes staggered down the gap and peered into the darkness. There was nothing.

"Is anyone there?" he called.

The crying did not stop this time, but he still could not see. It was as though it floated away from him. Then he heard it again, this time behind him, but the first voice did not stop. He heard a third voice, this time to his left, and all of them sobbed together, a child's chorus weeping all at once in a circle around him.

Hayes reeled around, listening to the many voices. Then it struck him. A keening sense of such sorrow and grief that it brought him to his knees, sadness almost beyond human naming. Ancient tears. Wordless and timeless. He choked and fell to all fours as it filled him.

Then came the sound, a shrieking like metals being ground into one another with unimaginable force. Hayes screamed and lifted his watering eyes and looked down the alley to see a shadow on the wall, a human shadow, but it was blurred at every edge and it moved so fast it was little more than a smear. It was there and it was real, he could tell, and yet when he looked to see what was casting the shadow he could see nothing at all.

The shrieking stopped, leaving a ringing in his ears. Hayes took a breath and started clapping his hands together and was relieved when he found he could hear it. He checked his ears and felt no blood. Then he crawled up and sat on his knees and stared at the empty alley before him.

CHAPTER THIRTY-FIVE

Garvey went to the safe house at eight, not sure if she would be there. He knocked and there was no answer, so he tried the door and found it unlocked.

She was asleep on the bed. He walked in carefully, moving as softly as he could. Her thumb was just inches from her mouth, as if she were just a few years out of infancy. He smiled and stroked her head and said, "Hey."

Samantha awoke, blinking. "Donald?"

"Yeah. It's me."

"What are you doing here?"

He shrugged, unable to stop smiling.

"How long have I been here?" she asked.

"Long enough," he said. Then he stood and held his hand out to her. She took it and stood up.

He took her to the winter carnival, which was always open this time of year down out at Discovery Bay. They ate floss candy and watched the clowns before finally getting a ride on the Ferris wheel. The clanking architecture lifted them up into the cool night sky, the lights of the nearby buildings dipping below them. Then they looked across the waters and saw it. Glowing starlight-bright like crystal or ice. A city formed from dreams, drifting in the night like some mythical iceberg. It seemed as though such a place could not be made or populated by men, and both were struck silent for some time.

"Sometimes I think this city has a voice," Samantha said.

"Do you?" Garvey said, smiling slightly.

"Yes. Out there." She pointed across the waters.

"What's it saying?"

"That there's always tomorrow. And there always will be."

When they were done they returned to the parking lot and looked back at the carnival. Samantha turned to look at the bridge and the city towering behind it.

"Home," she said, and Garvey nodded.

They drove to his apartment just before midnight. Then as they crossed the little courtyard Samantha pointed to the trees at the center.

"Someone's there," she said. They both stopped and looked, and saw a hunched figure leaning against one of the trunks. A large wooden box was sitting on the ground before him. "Are people still watching your apartment?"

"No," Garvey said. "Hayes checked. And if that guy's a shadow he's doing a terrible job of it…"

Garvey walked to the figure carefully. It did not move. Then he got in front of it, squatted, and said, "Shit. It's Hayes. He's passed out."

Samantha drew close and coughed. "Lord. It's like he slept in a distillery."

"I thought he was doing better. What's that?" Garvey asked, nodding at the box.

She opened it slightly. "It's the files. The Tazz ones, and the ones from Savron Hill. I suppose it's his present for you."

Garvey's eyes gleamed briefly. Then he nodded, jaw set, and grabbed Hayes by the arm and pulled him to his feet. A long stream of drool gathered at Hayes's lower lip and then broke and spattered onto the cement. He muttered something and then said, "Good evening."

"Goddamn it, Hayes," Garvey said. He fought to gather all of Hayes's errant arms and legs.

"Did you all have a nice evening?" Hayes asked, slurred.

"Shut up," Garvey said.

"Yes," said Samantha.

"Oh," said Hayes. "That's good."

"Take that, will you?" said Garvey to Samantha, nodding again at the box.

They brought him inside the apartment and sat him on the sofa. Hayes sprawled across the beaten cushions, then opened his eyes and seemed to focus a little. He moved his limbs around like they were all new additions and managed to force himself into a sitting position. Then he blinked hard and said, "Thought I'd come by and get that address from you, Garvey-o."

"Yeah," Garvey said. "Yeah, I fucking figured." He poured a glass of water and said, "Here. Drink up."

"Much obliged." Hayes held it with the knuckles of both hands, like an old woman with arthritis. He sipped it and smacked his lips. "I look forward to it. Look forward to doing you right."

"What have you been doing, Mr. Hayes?" asked Samantha. "You look sick again. I haven't seen you in such a state since our first day together."

"I'm fine," he said. But then he looked away, transfixed by some invisible presence, and whispered, "No. No, I'm not. I saw it again tonight."

"Saw what?" asked Samantha.

"The thing. The ghost. The one we saw."

"You did?" said Samantha. She and Garvey moved closer to him, propping him up to shake some sense out of him. "Where?"

"Out by...by Skiller's tenement. Same place, sort of. In a little alley behind. No one died, though. No more deaths. I looked, and checked."

"But what did you see?" she asked.

"Nothing. A shadow, twitching. And there was a voice. I heard it. It cried, I think."

"Cried?" said Garvey. He sounded skeptical.

"Yes. Cried. Many voices, crying all along the little dark alley. And I wondered...I wondered what they had said before about it being a ghost. I mean, it's the second time we've spotted it by Skiller's tenement and all."

"God," Garvey said. "How loaded are you?"

"I don't know. Loaded enough. Do you believe me?"

"Are you sleeping here?" Garvey asked, impatient.

"Here? Where, on your couch?"

"That would be the idea."

"I wouldn't want to intrude."

"You've already intruded."

Hayes felt the couch springs, then took a pillow in his arms and squeezed it to his chest and rocked forward. "All right," he said.

"Fine, then. I'll get some blankets," said Garvey, and he went back into his bedroom.

Hayes groaned and lay back, pillow still clutched to his body. "You believe me, don't you, Sam?" he asked softly.

"I'm trying," she said.

"I did see it. It cried. And I felt it. You know, with..." He pointed to his head.

"I understand."

Hayes thought for a moment, his ivory brow crinkling. "I think it's very sad."

"Sad?"

"Yes. Very sad. I'm not sure why, though." He sniffed, and then smiled fondly at her. "You know, I knew a girl like you once."

Samantha turned to him, slightly uncomfortable. "Yes?"

"Yes. I was very young then. A boy. It was a long time ago."

"What happened to her?"

Hayes paused. "She died."

"From what?"

His eyes closed a little. "A bastard."

"I'm very sorry to hear that," she said slowly.

Hayes stared into the corner of the room. His eyes were wide and empty, no doubt seeing faces that he wished he could forget. "She was with child when she died," he said. "We were going to have a baby together. Can you believe that?"

Samantha nearly shook her head, but stilled herself and stayed quiet.

"A baby girl, maybe," he said. "I would have liked a baby girl. With fat baby hands and fat baby feet. I don't know what I would have named her. Gloria, or Susan, or something. And I don't know if she or he or it would have been like... like me. But I often wonder about it. About how it could have been. Two children, raising a child. I'd have never left, never seen the world. Just me, and the wife, and the little one. Fucking momma and poppa. What a crazy thought. Fuck me. Who knows how things could have been."

"Is that why you do this?" she asked.

"Do what?"

"Follow people. Try to set things to right."

"I don't set things to right. Not ever. Usually I just make them worse." He squinted at her. "You're sure you want to come tomorrow?"

She smiled a little. "Yes. I miss my job."

"Oh?"

"Yes. I miss running around with you."

"I never ran."

"No." She laughed. "That's true. You didn't."

Garvey returned with the blankets. "Here you go," he said, and handed them over. "Do not vomit in the middle of the night. Do you understand me? If you do, I'm not cleaning it up."

"I understand perfectly," Hayes said, and he took the pillow and stuffed it behind his head. Then he spread the blankets out across his legs. "Where's my address?"

Garvey took an envelope from his back pocket and handed it to Hayes, who snatched it greedily. "It took a lot of weight to pull that, you know," said Garvey. "Your friend is a hard man to find. He was barely recorded at all."

"Yes. He wouldn't be." Hayes opened the envelope and peered at it owlishly. "Good. Now. You can all stay here watching me if you want. But I do intend to sleep. Very hard and very soon, so..." He waved toward the back bedroom. "Go away."

"Jesus," Garvey said.

Hayes rolled over and stuffed his face in the corner of the sofa. He lay there perfectly still until they could only assume he was asleep. What an odd little family we have, Samantha thought to herself. Two jobless parents taking care of a wayward son. She almost laughed.

"What?" said Garvey. But she shook her head and led him away.

Garvey and Samantha sat in his darkened bedroom, the box of files set on the mattress between them like a needy child. Garvey opened the lid slightly, peeking in through the crack at the papers within, then put it back and looked away.

"It's all there?" he asked.

"It looks like it, yes," said Samantha.

"Jesus. Jesus Christ."

"It's enough to hang Brightly," she said. "And Tazz. Probably more."

"But there's nothing on the murders?"

"Not on the murders, no. Hayes is just guessing there. But Mr. Hayes is terribly good at guessing."

"Yeah. Yes, he is." Garvey placed a hand on the box again and took a breath. "I'm afraid," he said.

"I know. I am, too."

"You know, I lied to you."

"What? When?"

"When I was talking about my gun. I told you I forgot it all the time. But that's not true. It's just heavy. It's got this heaviness to it. When I put it on, it just drags me down. I hate it, so I leave it behind. But this..." He tapped the cover of the box. "This is heavier than anything. It hurts just to have this near me."

"Are you going to do it? Go to Collins with this?"

"Yeah."

"Are you sure?"

"Yeah. Well, no. I just have to. People have gotten killed over Tazz. And it was all nothing. Someone needs to tell people about that." He blinked slowly in the darkness. In the alabaster light from the lamps outside he looked bloodless. "I suppose it'll have to be me."

"And then what will happen?"

"I don't know. Maybe that'll be the chink in the armor. The chance to wipe all this shit from our backs and stand up clean. Or maybe not. Maybe it'll just be papers, to be burned and forgotten."

He opened the box and began taking out the files, carefully looking over each of the notations she had made. It somehow pleased her to see his methodical approach, carefully raising each sheet to catch the lamplight from outside, then squinting to read it, then laying it back down. She could see the librarian in him then, handling these little papers as though they were desperately important and fragile, and yet she could also see something of a priest in him as well, doing his daily rituals for some unspoken higher power, and hoping that with each repeated action he could enforce a structure on the world around him.

After a while he noticed her looking at him. "What?" he said.

"Come here," she said.

And he did.

CHAPTER THIRTY-SIX

She awoke before dawn and slipped out of the bed. She turned, naked, and looked at him where he lay, curled in the cream of the blankets, pillow pressed to his face. She smiled in spite of herself. He was a supremely awkward man lying down, too large for any bed and all elbows and knees when a bedmate. She did not want to wake him, so she dressed silently and then leaned down and placed one gentle kiss beside his ear. He did not even move, still deep in slumber.

When she walked out Hayes was gone from the couch. She thought for a moment, then opened the front door as quietly as she could and walked down to the street. As she passed the courtyard statue she suddenly became aware that someone was walking beside her. She glanced to her left and saw his little blond head bobbing along at her shoulder, cigarette jauntily dancing in his lips.

"I've already called us a cab," he said.

"All right."

They went far to the southwest of the city, to where the land became rocky scrub scarred with abandoned paths. Hayes directed the cabbie up past one field to where the roads turned from pavement into dirt and gravel, the sort of roads that had only recently come to know cars.

Samantha reached into her bag and took out a folded sheet of paper. She opened it slightly. Garvey's sketch of Skiller looked up at her, its graphite eyes blank and empty. "This man that we're seeing," she said. "You haven't told me anything about him."

"No," said Hayes. "That's true, I haven't."

"Who is he?"

Hayes looked out the cab window and sucked his teeth. "You know what I did before Brightly? Before McNaughton?"

"Well. Yes, a little."

"He was there with me during all that."

"Oh."

"Yes. Long, long ago."

"Will he be glad to see you?"

"Oh, I very much doubt it. But right now the main issue is if he's alive, to be frank."

"What? What do you mean?"

"Well, if my hunch is right, and those boys from the Three Ring were involved in whatever the hell all this is, and if Tazz is gone, too, then whoever set this all up would dearly like to get rid of the last witness, wouldn't they?"

Samantha's mouth opened in horror. "Oh, my God, I'd never thought of that. Aren't you worried, Mr. Hayes?"

Hayes thinned his eyes, thinking. "Mm. No. Not especially."

"Why is that?"

"Because Spinsie was always very good at staying alive, and staying careful. He was almost as good as me, in fact." He returned to looking out the window, but glanced back and added, "Almost, but not quite." Then he saw the sketch in her hands and frowned. "Where did you get that?"

"From Donald."

"How long have you been carrying that around?"

"I don't know. A long while. I suppose since I looked him up."

They got out where a wooden fence began and paid the cabbie. They walked along the fence until they came to an old path that rambled along over a wide, green field. Hayes held up a hand and she stopped behind him at the mouth of the path. He stood rock-still, studying the landscape, not moving. She tried to see what he was searching for but could find nothing. Then he made a small, satisfied noise and motioned her along.

They followed the path until they saw a small thread of chimney smoke winding up through the trees. Hayes eyed it and said, "Well, it looks like he's still alive, at least. You do realize that I will have to lie to him?"

"About what?" she asked.

"About how we found him. I don't want him spooked."

"If you say so."

"I just hope he buys it," said Hayes. "And that he's off his game."

They walked on until a small gray house emerged from underneath the boughs. It had not been well cared for. Several shutters were missing and the front garden was filled with weeds. Off to the side someone had made a fire pit, but it had not been used in a long time. There was the glint of glass from around its edge and Samantha saw the snouts of liquor bottles poking up from the grass.

Hayes walked up to the front door and knocked. There was no answer. Then he tried the knob, found the door was unlocked, and pushed it open.

"You're going in?" she asked.

"Yes."

"Won't he be mad?"

"Maybe," he said, and walked in. She waited a moment and then followed.

Inside it was dank and dark and smelled of spoiled alcohol and cheap cigarettes. The curtains were pulled shut over all the windows and empty bottles lay on the floor, on the tables, sometimes in the chairs. Hayes walked to the living room, cleared a seat, and sat and began to wait. Samantha cleared her own space on the sofa and did the same. Like the rest of the house, the room had not been taken care of. Old, musty paintings hung on the walls, most of them of England, or English countrysides. The white cliffs of Dover had grown a dull gray with dust on one wall. On another a cracked, faded team of men on horseback trumpeted and called for a missing fox, with lumps of beagles bawling about the legs of their horses.

"When do you think he'll be back?" Samantha asked.

"He's here right now," Hayes said.

"What?"

"He's here right now. He saw us coming, I think. He won't show until he's sure it's safe." Then he sighed and leaned his head on his hand.

"You don't want to see this man, do you?"

"No. No, I really do not."

Nearly an hour passed. Hayes seemed more awake than she had ever seen him. Samantha shifted on her seat, uncomfortable. After a while she reached under the cushion and retrieved a long, heavy bullet of a massive caliber, thicker than her finger and longer than a half a foot. It was as though it'd been lost and forgotten under the cushion. She could not imagine the gun or barrel it matched. Hayes glanced at her, saw her holding the huge round, and shook his head. She replaced it, and was on the verge of suggesting they leave when a voice behind her said, "You know, breaking and entering is considered fairly impolite in most civilized circles."

She turned and saw there was a man leaning up against the doorway behind her. He was tall and thin and dark, with pepper-gray hair and a black mustache and a sharp, smart smile. He wore a white sleeveless shirt and gray slacks and thick leather boots, the suspenders dangling beside his thighs. There was something very starved about him, a frailness about the eyes that spoke of days without sunlight or warmth. Samantha put him in his late forties or fifties, and she was not sure why but she immediately identified him as a soldier, yet once she did she found it hard to imagine him ever fighting for any country or creed.

"It's also impolite to run away when you see guests approaching," Hayes said.

The man nodded. "I suppose. I suppose. Though you could have called ahead," he said, his slight Cockney drawl becoming more pronounced. "It's not often my oldest, dearest little comrade comes to visit me. I could've tidied the place up."

A few awkward beats passed. Then he smiled more widely and said, "Oh, it's nice to see you again, little Hayseed. I see you still haven't grown any."

Hayes tilted his head. "Hello, Spinsie. How are you these days?"

"I'm decent, little brother. Decent."

"How are the cats? Rufus and Rudolph, yes? I didn't see them."

"They're around. They come in when they feel like it, which isn't often. Plenty of small things to torture and devour in the fields around here. They leave them on the doorstep, don't know why."

"Trophies, probably," Hayes said. "Showing off to you."

"Probably." He laughed. "Oh, it's been a donkey's age, hasn't it? When's the last time we met, little brother? I can barely recall."

"A year, I'd think. In Dockland."

"I don't remember that. What'd we talk about?"

"Not much, Spinsie. I don't think you were quite speaking yet."

The smile vanished. His eyes grew sharp and flicked to Samantha, then back to Hayes. "Yeah. I wouldn't have been, not then. Well, now. What brings you to these inhospitable reaches, little brother? Why've you disturbed my peaceful retirement?"

"I'm sorry if we disturbed you, but to be honest, Spinsie, I'm here because, well, I don't quite think you're retired."

The man nodded, then took a step into the room and eyed Samantha. "I see I've missed someone. Don't believe we've met before." He turned gracefully and put his hand out. "Corporal Michael Spinsten. Former, of course, but still at your service, miss."

"Samantha Fairbanks," she said, extending her hand to him. He bowed and took it and kissed her knuckles, then looked up along her arm.

"Pleasure's all mine," he said. "Mind if I ask who you know my little brother as? His name, I mean, just for posterity? I'd hate to interrupt any of his plans."

"His name?" Samantha said, confused. "To me he's simply Mr. Hayes."

"Is that so?" Spinsie said, turning to Hayes. "Using your real name with her? Getting soft, Hayseed. Getting very soft."

"Perhaps," Hayes said. "Why don't you take a seat, Spinsie? This is your house, after all."

"Yeah. It is." He sat down next to Samantha. Then he picked up a pipe from the table before him, produced a penknife from his pocket, and began to scrape out the bowl. "So you don't think this is a life of retirement, comrade?"

"No," said Hayes. "I don't."

"What makes you think such a thing?"

"You want me to list the reasons?"

"If you please."

"Fine," said Hayes. He settled into a more comfortable position. "I don't think you're retired, Spinsie, because rumor has it someone moved a large amount of raw bullion through Lynn seven months ago, and I know you always specialized in that. And rumor has it that the man they arrested and prosecuted for it is perfectly innocent of the crime, and that the bills they seized in his apartments were mostly counterfeit garbage. And it's also rumored that that same week a coffee shop in one of the shadier parts of Dockland suddenly closed down, but to be honest, well, none of the locals ever recalled it selling much coffee. Lots of shipping, though. Lots of boxes. It just came and went, they said. All of that would be why, Spinsie."

Spinsie nodded along happily as if they were discussing the weather. He packed the bowl, then lit a match and sucked at it until he was satisfied. "You're remarkably well connected these days, aren't you, Hayseed."

"I do all right."

"Yes. You're the little king of Evesden, aren't you."

"I don't think I would go quite that far."

"Maybe the court adviser, then. Surprising, really. When I first found you in Delhi you didn't seem to have a thought in your head. Ambling around, living on scraps. Never thought you'd come so far."

"Delhi was a long time ago."

"Yeah. It was." He coughed harshly and rubbed his nose in a quick, ferret-like gesture. "So. You got a few suspicions about me sneaking in gold in the dead of night. Is that what you're here about, little brother?"

"Not especially, to be honest," said Hayes. "I'm more interested in recent activity."

"Recent?"

"Yes. With the unions."

"Unions? What unions? Last I heard there didn't seem to be any."

"That's what concerns me. I think they were trying to make one by other means, and I think you're involved somehow."

"Hmm," Spinsie said. "This is what worries you these days?"

"Today, at least."

Spinsie leaned back. "You've changed, little brother. Changed since the old days. Back then you didn't give a good goddamn about politics. You hardly realized the world was going on at all. Finally woken up? Finally seen the bigger picture?"

"Spinsie, I really didn't come here to get nostalgic."

"All right. Then play your cards, if you have any."

Hayes thought for a second, then turned to Samantha and said, "Sam, could I please see that picture you have?"

"The picture?" she said.

"Yes. The drawing."

She handed it to him. He studied it, nodded, and then passed it to Spinsie, who took it, confused. "What is this?" he asked.

"That's a man we think was involved as well," said Hayes. "Somehow."

"Do you? And why are you bringing this to my doorstep?"

"Because he's dead."

One eye twitched. Samantha noticed he flexed his ankles. "Is he?" Spinsie asked.

"Yes. Very."

"And it's just him you're here about?"

Hayes gestured to Samantha. She rattled off, "There were also Charles Denton, Michael Huffy, Frank Naylor, John Evie, Edward Walton, Louis Courtney, Phineas Brooks, Turner Maylen... Several others as well. An even dozen in all."

Spinsie looked at her, surprised. "Well. I see why he keeps you around," he said. "You're his little encyclopedia, aren't you."

"I prefer to be called his assistant," she said coldly.

"Yeah, I expect you do." He handled the sketch, tilting it back and forth. "And you think I ran him?" he asked Hayes.

"Yes," Hayes said.

"Why?"

"Because he was involved in smuggling, and you were always a genius with the docks. With water landings, with shore-running. You could fool a port guard into carrying ammunition ashore in his mother's valise. Distribution, I think you called it. I was demand, staying on shore. You tamed supply, at sea."

"Until they chained me up for it," he said darkly.

"You can't still be smarting about that, Spinsie."

"It was seven years," said Spinsie fiercely. "Seven fucking years."

"I got you out, though. Even from the other side of the world, I got you out."

"Yes. Yes, with your special connections. With your carte blanche, yes."

"It wasn't always easy for me, either," Hayes pointed out. "I did my own time. You know that."

"Not as long as me, though," said Spinsie. "I suppose I had nothing to offer the mighty McNaughton."

"Well, now. Here's your chance. Offer me something of value and I may recommend you to my employers."

Spinsie placed the sketch on the coffee table, glared briefly at Hayes, and then stared out through one of the dusty windows. Even though he called Hayes his little brother Samantha could see no kinship between them. She decided he was a man who called the world his brother, yet moved through it alone.

"Well?" Hayes said impatiently.

"If we're going to talk business, I'd prefer if we do it over tea," said Spinsie, and stood. "When's the last time you had really good tea, Hayes?"

Hayes rolled his eyes. "I don't know. I don't really care."

"You should," Spinsie said. He walked into the kitchen. They could hear him clanking around the stove. "All proper Englishmen need an honest cup of tea every once in a while."

"I'm not a proper Englishman," Hayes shouted back.

"And you never will be if you keep this up."

They listened to him rustle up some coal and start the stove. As he worked Spinsie spoke at great length about the type of tea, discussing its genealogy and how it had been won and purified in the colonial days. Samantha got the impression that he had not honestly spoken to anyone in some time.

"Sam," Hayes said softly as Spinsie carried on talking.

"Yes?" she said.

"You pick up the reins," he said. "When he comes back in."

"Me? Why?"

"Because he likes you."

"But surely I can't—"

"He likes you more than me. He's more likely to tell you anything than me, honest."

She stammered and tried to protest, but Hayes shushed her and pointed to the kitchen. After several minutes Spinsie came in with the kettle steaming and dripping and said, "Tell me, Miss Samantha, how did you get tossed in with old Hayes?"

"I was assigned to him."

"Assigned? Why?"

"I believe he had some issue organizing his work."

Spinsie smiled and poured three cups of tea. "Yeah. That sounds about right. Hayes never was good by himself, were you, Hayes? He'd fall to pieces if he was by himself. He always likes having one or two other people working with him. And he always, *always* winds up getting them into trouble, eventually. Isn't that so?"

Hayes blinked languidly as though he might not have heard any of it.

"Do you live alone, Mr. Spinsten?" Samantha asked.

"Well, no. Not alone, no," he said hastily. "I have the cats, that's something. There's a logging firm up the way, though I think they're going out of business. I see them sometimes, though, on my walks."

"It's very pretty countryside here."

"Yeah. I think so. Hilly. Lots of pines."

"It's much nicer than the ones I've seen recently," Samantha said. "The man who died. We went to see his house. It was a tenement, actually."

"Oh?"

"Yes. It was one of the most deplorable places I've ever seen in my life. He had a son, you know. He raised him there. Taught him how to read, a little. But we don't know where the boy is. Wherever he is, I suspect he's alone, too."

Spinsie finished pouring and made sure everyone had a cup and a saucer. Hayes set his tea down on a nearby table and ignored it.

"Are you sure you never met the man, Mr. Spinsten?" Samantha asked.

"I never said I never met him," he said, almost sulkily.

"So you did meet him?"

Spinsie was quiet for a long while, cradling the tea in his hands. "I don't do much out here," he said. "It's retirement, you're not supposed to do much, but sometimes I get bored. And every once in a while someone comes to me with a job. About twice a year or so. I'm not sure how they get my name or find out how to get ahold of me. I guess word just gets around." He took a sip. "I take some of them," he said. "I mean, who wouldn't? It's not because I need the money. It's just..."

"A distraction," Samantha said.

"Yes! Yes, a distraction. That's it, that's the one. Everyone needs a hobby, you know. And I miss the old days sometimes. I miss the old bravado. The rush. They say when you're done, you're done, but if I was, well. I'd go mad, I think.

"A man came to me not long ago. About two months ago. Little man with a mustache. Said his name was Colomb and he worked for someone very powerful in the city. Said he wasn't a rich man, per se, but he had money he could spread around and he needed me to do a job. 'A job?' says I, and I act all interested. He said there was something they needed brought in. Naturally, I asked what, and he said he couldn't tell me. Well, that wasn't anything new, but old Spinsie doesn't take a job unless he knows what he's doing. I mean, what if it's alive? What if it's people? I knew a fella who got himself hung because he was smuggling women into Morocco and didn't know it and a bunch of them died en route. One of the flaws of the game, I suppose." He looked at Samantha very seriously. "I would never do anything to hurt a woman."

"I believe you," she said.

"I'm not like some people," he said, shooting a glance at Hayes, who again ignored it.

"So, I told him I wouldn't take it," Spinsie continued. "Spinsie has rules. There's things he does and things he doesn't. After a bit of bargaining the man caves and he says the thing I'll be handling is going to be 'technology' and I kindly ask him exactly what in the hell he means by that. He tells me they can get ahold of some very important McNaughton machinery, and they plan on holding it hostage. Maybe selling it to someone else. I'm sure you both are used to that sort of thing."

"No, I'm afraid I'm not," Samantha said.

"Oh. You, little brother?"

Hayes smiled slightly as though if he was he would never admit to it, perhaps out of professional modesty.

"Well," Spinsie said. "Anyways. I got a bit concerned at that. Interfering with McNaughton business, that's a little big. It'd be like walking up and putting a finger in God's eye. But, you know, after a while I started to like the idea. I liked the idea of Spinsie pulling one over on McNaughton. David and Goliath sort of thing, and it'd put a bit of youth in my chest. And just maybe old Spinsie would see his little comrade again. If he tangled with McNaughton's people, you see. And here you are," he said softly. "Here you are, little brother."

He thought for a moment. Then he turned to Samantha and said, "I never wanted anyone to die."

"I know," she said.

"I never did. Not at all."

"I'm sure of it. Very sure. What sort of machine was it?" she asked.

"They didn't say. I didn't ask."

"Is there anything you could tell me about it?"

"I'll tell you what I knew then. They said it would be two crates. Only two. Big. Same dimensions. Same weight. Same items, really, from the sound of it. I asked them where they'd be coming in from. They said they had contacts in the East who'd rob a train heading through Russia. They'd pick the things up there, hop it to Novo-

Mariinsk, and they'd have a ship coming in across the Baltic. I said that sounded elaborate as hell, so why would they want me handling it when they probably had someone already? And they said that it wasn't just smuggling it in that was hard. It would be storing it. They'd want it in someplace safe. Someplace no one'd ever look at. So they needed an old hand for the trick, which was why they came to me. So I said I'd take it. Because, well, why not? You understand, don't you, Miss Fairbanks? Sometimes a man needs to stretch his legs."

"I do."

He nodded and sipped his tea, though it was getting cold now. "So. So Spinsie starts planning. Starts thinking about how he's going to do this. I already have some ideas, of course. Already know how to get the prizes on land and safe. And they've decided the ship's arrival already. Going to be intercepted by a smaller vessel, which would come east and make a night landing, not too far west along the Strait from the city. And they had a few men ready. But from there they had no other idea. Well. I had a few. I used the old mortician switch. Remember that, Hayseed?"

"Oh, yes," said Hayes. "If I recall, you always had a lot of reservations about killing the cat."

"We didn't always kill the cat," Spinsie said angrily. "If we could find one that was already dead then that would be fine, too."

"Or a dog," said Hayes. "Or a bunch of rats. Or a chicken."

"What?" said Samantha, puzzled.

"Right," said Spinsie to her, with some professional relish. "See, the real problem with bringing in anything is, how do you make it something everyone treats with careful respect, and also wouldn't ever want to open? The answer is, well, you put it in something sacred. A coffin works best in a pinch."

"Oh, Lord," Samantha said. She covered her mouth.

Spinsie chuckled. "Yeah. So what I planned on having us do was transfer the cargo to a different boat with the coffins and all, and then put the cargo in a big crate with 'Quarantine' on the side and a few dead things tossed in for the odor. People will leave that alone, you believe me."

"What happens if they search the other coffins?" asked Samantha.

Spinsie hesitated. "Well... well, they're not empty."

"You use *real* coffins? With *people*?"

"I know a mortician chap who's putting his kids through school, he lends them out to me," Spinsie said, now flustered.

"What do their families say?"

"Not much, they don't often know about it. It's not like we use the same corpses every time."

"I should hope not!"

Hayes cleared his throat. "I think we're getting off topic."

"Right, right," Spinsie said hurriedly. "Anyways, so I get the funeral barge all ready and we go out there at the dead of night and wait for these bastards. They've got a fair group of people waiting there to help me out. Strong crew. I didn't get all their names, I usually don't want them. Maybe a few of those men you listed, maybe they were in there. But one of them." Spinsie tapped the drawing. "He was there. Quiet fella. Didn't say much, maybe didn't say anything. At first, at least. Just waited. The others were rowdy, 'specially these two snotty little pricks. Fancied themselves great criminals. Simple thugs is what they were. Christ, I wanted to throttle them."

Hayes smiled at that, almost in recognition, but said nothing.

"How many were there?" Samantha asked. "In all?"

"Eleven, maybe. Maybe twelve. All working men, it seemed."

"I see," Samantha said.

"I expected a delay, I always do, but this one came puttering along, right on time," Spinsie said. "We all got up and got ready to load the cargo into the coffin ship, but it was funny. The ship that came... I mean, they said they were intercepting a big frigate from Anadyr, right? Out in the Bering? But the vessel that came was just a little thing. No way that boat could fare in the ocean proper. It'd founder in a minute."

"How far would you put that ship's range, Spinsie?" Hayes asked.

"Don't know. Not much more than fifty miles. Maybe seventy. I wasn't the only one who noticed it. The quiet fella. What was his name?"

"John," said Samantha. "John Skiller."

"Yeah. He noticed it, too. Asked me what sort of boat that was. It was a shore boat, really. Like a ferry. Not that I told him that, he didn't need to know. But I think he figured it out anyways. He might've been the only one with a brain there. 'Cept for me, that is.

"So we pull the little ferry alongside the shore and haul the funeral boat up alongside, too, and we hop aboard to unload the crates. What they were, hell, I couldn't expect. A weather machine. Or maybe the parts for a fancy new type of car. But as soon as I looked at the boxes, I know. You just get a sense. You carry things like that enough, you just know these things."

"What was it?" Samantha asked.

He shook his head. "The other men didn't know. They picked them up and hauled them onto the coffin ship. I shouted at them to watch it but they still dropped the damn thing. It broke open, just a little. But they still saw."

"What was it, Spinsie?" Hayes asked softly. "What was in the boxes?"

"Guns," Spinsie said. "But guns like I'd never seen before, and I've seen a few in my day. Guns of a type that I don't think exist anywhere yet. When Heaven invades Hell I hope God gives the angels a few of those guns. I didn't know much about them but I knew I didn't want to be around when they started going off. And Skiller. He saw. Started asking, 'What are those? What are those?' The others, they didn't care. But Skiller wouldn't have any part of it. Went all quiet once he realized what they were doing. Oh, he still loaded it, after a while. But I could tell he didn't like it.

"We took the coffin ship back to the docks. Plan was to have the cargo shipped to a tobacconist pal of mine and have it repackaged as cigars. Then they'd wait a while and move it. Out to that, that big place, what's it called?"

"Construct, probably," Samantha said quietly.

"Yeah. You can stash anything there. The plan was to secure it real good, make sure no one could jimmy it. But once we got to the docks and unloaded them and started putting the corpses through the dockmaster we noticed Skiller was gone."

"Gone?" Hayes asked.

"Yeah. Just gone. No one had any idea where he went or anything."

"No one hurt him? No one attacked him?"

"No, not at all. He just slipped away."

"Where do you think he went?" Samantha asked.

Spinsie shrugged. "Well, he wasn't stupid. He knew something was up. He knew those guns hadn't come from any Baltic freighter. Wherever they came from, it could only have been a few miles away. So I think he doubled back to the night landing, and just started walking. Started walking west to look for some pier. Some small dock. Something. To see where those guns had come from."

Samantha and Hayes did not speak for some time. Spinsie rocked back and forth, glancing between them nervously, still desperate to please.

"Where are the guns now?" Hayes asked.

"I don't know," Spinsie said.

"You don't?"

"No. After the tobacconist it was all up to them. They handled the Construct part. I wasn't going in there."

"And they didn't know what they were going to do with the guns. Just that they were bringing stolen McNaughton cargo ashore."

"Yeah. Yeah, little brother. That's right."

"Where was the night landing at? Off of what point on the shore west of here?"

Spinsie gave him the coordinates, or near enough.

"And you didn't tell anyone about this?" Hayes asked.

"No. Spinsie keeps his mouth shut. Never says anything he doesn't need to."

Hayes nodded. "All right," he said.

Spinsie glared at him. He took his cup of tea and tossed it back violently. Then he slammed it down on the table and said, " 'All right.' All right, he says. Like he knows everything. You *don't* know everything, you know that, little brother? Just 'cause you've been around. Just 'cause you managed to get out before I could. That doesn't make you any better."

"There's no need to be angry," Hayes said.

"I think there is. I think there's plenty need. Always one step ahead, aren't you, little brother? Always smarter than everyone else, always need to show it. How's the god, Hayseed? How's the little god that sits on your shoulder and tells you what to do? Very Socrates, that."

"Enough," Hayes said.

"You're not always smart. Weren't when I found you. Don't think you are now. What put you on the streets? What about that girl you knocked up all those years ago, if you remember?"

"Enough," Hayes said angrily.

But Spinsie kept talking, speaking louder with each word. "You didn't see that coming. Didn't see her putting the knife to her wrists, did you?"

"Enough!"

"Didn't see daddy dearest tossing you out of house and home, did you, Hayseed, my little brother? Did you see that? Did you see that?"

Hayes rose and strode over to Spinsie and gave him three quick slaps. Spinsie recoiled and felt his lip and stared up at Hayes, stunned.

"You always were an ass, Spinsie," Hayes said fiercely. "A stupid, ignorant ass. The reason I was always on land and you were at sea was that no one could ever stand you. You can't even stand yourself. It's the reason you were alone then and it's the reason you're alone now, and it'll be the reason you're alone for the rest of your damn days." He turned around and waved to Samantha and said, "Come on."

He marched out the front door with Samantha following. She hurried up to him and said, "Mr. Hayes, your friend, shouldn't you—"

"He is not my friend, Sam."

"But he—"

"He's an idiot old man living an idiot old man's life. I'm content to leave him here. Come on. Back up to the road."

They were almost to the fence when she heard the shouting. She turned and saw Spinsie on his knees in his doorway, screaming at them to come back, come back, he had done a bad thing and he was sorry, just please come back. He waved his arms and then dropped them to his sides and sat there on the ground, watching them leave.

"Mr. Hayes?" she asked.

But Hayes did not hear her. He walked on until they could find a phone station and call a cab.

CHAPTER THIRTY-SEVEN

It took Garvey more than three hours to get to Collins among the desks of the Department. It was much the same as it had always been in his absence, even painfully the same. Same stale scent of coffee. The sting of cheap aftershave and old cigarette smoke. The other police watched him with a medley of expressions, surprise and disdain and frowning sympathy. Garvey waited quietly in one of the chairs witnesses occupied so often, the box of files balanced on his knees. Finally Collins came charging in, riding a wild head of steam and still muttering curses. When Garvey stood he stopped and said, "Holy hell. What the fuck are you doing here?"

"I need to talk to you," said Garvey.

"We don't need to talk to you," said Collins. He turned away. "Go talk to someone else."

"And to show you something."

"You don't need to show me anything. Go home, Garvey."

"Please, sir. Just listen to me."

"No. No, no. Go home, Garvey. Just go home."

"You need to see this."

Collins squinted at him over his shoulder. "Would you bet your career on it?"

"I'd be willing to bet my life," Garvey said simply.

Collins led him to his office. It was famously messy, covered in little cities of files and papers and paperweights, old clothes and shoes he had had to change in and out of in the depths of a case. They sat and Collins took out a pipe and read over the file as Garvey spoke, just like any other case, like any other day. With each word his lieutenant's eyes became wider and wider. Eventually he turned off the light as if he didn't want to see any more and they both sat in the dark.

"You're sure about this?" said Collins.

"Positive. That's McNaughton records. Right there. You can see the M."

"How did you get these?"

"They were given to me," said Garvey. "I'm not sure how they got them."

"And you have a witness? That guy in the cabin? Out west?"

"I think so. And Colomb, if we can find them. We can make them testify."

"You don't know that."

"No, I don't. Not for sure. But we have to try. We have to try."

Collins sat there, not moving, pipe ticking up and down in his mouth like the pendulum of a clock. "And Brightly was directly involved."

"He had to have been. He's the director of Securities there, he had to have known. Maybe the whole board did, I don't know."

"But Brightly. You're sure."

"Yeah. I'm sure."

Collins looked out onto the Murder office. Then he said, "Go home, Garvey."

"But—"

"I know. I know. We'll do something. We'll do something soon.

Tomorrow. Just go home for now. Where I can contact you. And we'll do something. Okay?"

"Do you think we can win it? Make it stick?"

Collins sighed. "We're already gearing up for this denner war, Garvey. You didn't give me anything on the murders, and that's what we're concerned with. We got enough on our plate right now. But just go back home and come in tomorrow. All right?"

"All right," said Garvey. He reached for the file.

"I'll hold on to this," said Collins sharply.

Garvey stopped. "Yeah," he said. "Okay, that's a good idea. That's only half of it, though."

"Half?"

"Yeah. I kept the rest. For security. I don't like traveling with it."

Collins looked down at the file. The paper flexed as he held it tighter. "Make sure you bring it, then. Tomorrow. Make sure you bring all of it."

"All right." Garvey stood and said, "Good night, sir."

"I doubt that," said Collins.

Collins sat in his office and watched Garvey walk away quickly. Weaving through the maze of desks as he'd done a thousand times. Then Collins strode out of his office and called for a phone.

CHAPTER THIRTY-EIGHT

By the time they reached the ferry landing it was nearly dark. Samantha could not tell if it was raining or if it was the wind bringing the sea haze onto them. She suspected it was still raining, very slightly. Perhaps it had never really stopped.

"How far west is this again?" Samantha asked.

"I've no idea," Hayes said. "I'm assuming this is the excised facility from the budget files."

"I suppose so."

Samantha peered into the east, where the horizon was overtaken by smoke and the city. Not more than two miles away the bridge network started, beginning with the Kulahee, which reached across to Victoria. Hayes stood along the seawall, not looking at anything, fingers of water running down his face.

"I'm sorry you had to hear that," Hayes said.

Samantha nodded.

"I was very young."

"I thought you said she died because of a bastard," she said.

"Did I?"

"Yes."

"Well. Am I not a bastard, sometimes?" He was quiet for a bit. Then he said, "Do you believe we are made, Sam?"

"I'm sorry?"

"Made. Created. Do you believe that?"

"I believe in the Holy Maker, yes. Of course I do."

He nodded. "Sometimes I wish I could meet Him. God, I suppose, or whoever made me. I'd probably ask them why they made me broken. Why nothing inside me works right, and how to fix it. Am I meant to be broken this way, perhaps? Does this serve a purpose? But even if I met my maker, I don't think I'd get an answer. They wouldn't know. I don't think there's any fixing anything. Not really. Not for long." He took a breath and then hopped up to sit on the wall, balefully staring out at the sea. "Amazing, isn't it?"

"What?"

"The sea. All that water. I still remember the first time I saw the sea. I was a young man, back in India. Barely more than a boy. I'd traveled to the coast, all by myself. I'd heard of the sea, yes, but hearing about it is different from seeing it. You can't grasp something that big just from someone mentioning it to you. You have to see it. And when I did I didn't know what to think. It stunned me, something that big. I wondered then if there was anything worth doing. You know?"

"Worth doing?"

"Yes. In the face of that. If there was anything you could do that could mean anything. Because it could always be swallowed up. Swallowed up and gone." He was quiet, his pale face drawn and his mouth a thin line. "I thought all the bad things I'd done didn't matter and all the good things I could do would never matter either," he said. "It was all the same next to the ocean. Those waves. They don't know anything about you. They just know how to sweep you away."

The ferry arrived less than ten minutes later. It was a tiny thing and wouldn't have been able to hold more than a dozen people very comfortably. For once Samantha let Hayes do the negotiating. When he pulled out his billfold the captain's eyes bugged out and he agreed to do whatever Hayes told him.

The ride was short. Spinsie's coordinates were almost exact. There was a nice little inlet on the shore where it would be perfect to dock a small boat. Hayes discussed how long the captain would stay, and after paying the man they stepped off onto the rocky shore.

They walked for several miles. As the light slowly faded the countryside was sunk into shadow. They did not know what they would do once they got to wherever they were going. They just knew they had to see.

"I've never been in the country here," Samantha said. "What is this part called?"

"I have no idea," Hayes said.

"You don't?"

"No. I never really cared to learn." He stopped. Then squatted to the ground. "Look," he said softly.

"What?"

"There. Down the trees to the shore. You'll need to get down."

She did. It took some searching to find it. It was a small pier, the wood wet and shining, bobbing on the gentle waves.

"Boat's long gone," Hayes said. "But that's probably where it started."

They found a little gravel road that ran from the pier up into the hills. Hayes sifted through the gravel and pronounced it recently used, then squinted up to the countryside but could not see where it led. They followed it quietly, walking in the grass to cover the sound of their footsteps. They wound through the pines up into the hills until they came to a chain-link fence built behind a ring of the trees. A rusty gate hung slightly ajar, kept closed by a band of rusty chains. Hayes squatted and took out some picks and went to work on it. Somewhere in the lock's heart the pins sank together, and he pulled the lock free and opened it up.

At first there were only trees beyond the fence, yet as they walked they saw flat white light shining across a large clearing ahead. They crept to the tree line and looked out. It looked like a bunker, small and flat and cement. Unmarked. Doors small and hidden. Hayes pulled out his spyglass and scanned the clearing. Then his eyes shot wide and he grabbed Samantha and flung her to the ground and clapped his hand over her mouth.

Her first instinct was to struggle, but when she heard it she quieted. A motor, low and buzzing. She heard the tires sighing through the wet grass and saw the headlights flashing on the trunks overhead. The sound of the tires stopped but the engine went on. She strained to hear anyone coming. As she did she noticed Hayes moving, slowly reaching into his vest and pulling out a pistol. He held it with the nose pointed through the grass and then did not move, waiting.

The seconds dragged on. Then she heard the whisper of the tires again and the headlights swung away. Neither of them moved. Then Hayes released her, eyes still fixed on the retreating car.

"Where did you get a gun?" she asked softly.

"Brought it with me, of course. I don't think you saw, but they had a few as well." Then he turned to her and said, "You know, you don't have to come any further if you don't want to."

She sat up and looked back over at the building. "What do you think's in there?"

"I don't know. But I don't think it's good."

"I don't either. Do you think we can get inside?"

He raised an eyebrow. Then he smiled and nodded.

Hayes led her in a strange pattern across the clearing, ducking and weaving, pausing here and there. It seemed erratic and mad, and she was not sure what he was doing until she realized there were men patrolling the outskirts of the field, walking back and forth with rifles under their arms.

"It's not guarded well," he whispered as they moved. "Probably because they never expected anyone to come here."

At the end they stopped and crawled low until they were near the building itself. Samantha saw it was set low in the ground. Mostly windowless, except in certain places near the ground level. Hayes led her to the closest wall, then sank down low and began pushing at the handle of one of the windows, murmuring to keep a lookout. He managed to shove it open but it wedged itself stuck halfway.

"We'll have to try another," he said softly.

"I can fit," she said.

"Are you sure?"

"We can find out." She maneuvered her legs around and pushed them through, then slid all the way past the gap, her dress rising up above her knees.

When she landed she was worried that her feet would make some sound, but the floor was bare cement and she made no noise at all. She let her eyes adjust and saw she was in some enormous dark storage room. Crates and boxes were filed away along the walls with little paths running between them. The ceiling was low and cramped and she had a hard time seeing the rest of the room, yet somehow the layout felt familiar.

"You all right?" Hayes whispered above.

"Fine." She turned back to begin to work at the window when she noticed an insignia on one of the boxes. She stooped to look at it and traced her fingers over the ink.

"Well? Are you getting this goddamn window open or not?"

Samantha frowned, then reached up and twisted the handle around to let the window open fully. Hayes slipped through, silent as a leaf falling on the forest floor.

"Look," she said, pointing at one of the boxes.

He squinted to see. When he finally saw the imperial M on the side he nodded grimly and said, "Well. It's as we thought, then." He looked up and around the basement. Then suddenly he froze and tensed up like an animal hearing a gunshot ripping through the trees.

"What?" she asked.

"There's... there's something else here," he said. "In here with us."

"What else? What do you mean? More guns?"

"I... I don't know yet. Something. I can hear it."

"Should we go?"

Hayes swallowed and shook his head. "N-no. No, I have to see. I have to see what this is."

"But why?"

He was quiet for a moment and then said, "Because it's talking to me. Or trying to. It knows we're here, Sam."

They walked off into the boxes toward the back, where a dark stairway down loomed. Besides the sound of his shuffling feet and the slight moan of a distant fan the storage room was silent.

They moved down the stairway and came to the next floor. Down below they saw yet more crates with strange shapes covered in tarps between them. She wondered if they should peek under their folds, but for some reason she was afraid that the things underneath would wake and fall upon them. They were sleeping, or perhaps waiting for somebody to stumble by. Like an ancient museum, all shut down while it waited for its next visitors.

Hayes looked out on the lower floor and said, "No. It's not here, either."

"What isn't?"

"There's something here. Or someone. I'm not sure yet."

They went down another floor and looked out at the next level. This one seemed empty, the blank cement floor stretching far back into the shadows. Hayes took one step out and looked into the darkness. Leaned forward as though drawn by an invisible string. His face drained of color and he said, "It's here."

He began walking forward. Samantha looked and saw a set of switches on the far right of the wall. She hesitated and then hit them. Out in the gloom orbs of light flickered, quavered, then strengthened and stayed on, revealing a small doorway at the far side of the floor. Set around that were chairs and charts and small tables set in a circle.

Hayes staggered toward the doorway, reeling drunkenly. Samantha rushed to keep up with him and called, "Mr. Hayes! Wait!"

He ignored her, stumbling as he kicked over a chair. Then he fell forward into the small black doorway and was gone.

Samantha slowed as she approached. She looked in and thought. Then she took off her watch and her belt and whatever other metals she wore, though she was not sure why, and took a deep breath and stepped through.

She had expected to feel something. Some change in the air or in the ground beneath her feet. But there was nothing. Just more cement, more cold air, more darkness.

"Mr. Hayes?" she asked.

"I'm here," said his voice.

"Are you all right?"

"No," he said quietly.

She reached out and felt along the wall, searching for a light switch again. When she could not find any she reached into her pocket and pulled out a small box of matches and struck one.

She could see Hayes standing nearby, staring into the darkness. He did not appear hurt. She stepped forward to tend to him and as she did the flickering light struck something mere feet ahead. Something immense and shining and golden.

"Are you hurt?" she asked.

He shook his head.

"What is that?" she asked, and stepped closer.

The object's surface was many-faceted, made of thousands of tiny rectangles of paper-thin gold that were as reflective as a mirror. Its side was rounded but the thing was so enormous it disappeared beyond the light of the match flame. As she moved she saw the match reflected in each of the tiny mirrors, even the ones that, by her guessing, were not at the angle to fully reflect it. She was not sure why but suddenly she felt that all the little mirrors were eyes and each one was watching the light, the image of her face trapped in each of their flat golden pupils.

"It knows we're here," Hayes said softly.

"What?"

"This. This thing. I don't know what it is. But it knows we're here. It's *thinking*. I can feel it."

Samantha drew away until her back touched the wall. In the dying light of the match flame she saw the light switch at the other end of the room. She paced over and hit it and the room lit up and they saw the thing fully, sitting in the center of the room like an enormous beached whale, long and tapered at both ends with a mass of strange piping hanging truncated from its midsection. It looked like some nameless organ of a massive clock, some great machine that had spent its long life connected to a dozen others in constant movement, back and forth, patient and ageless. In some places clumps of dirt and ripped-out, ancient-looking tree roots had woven their way into the innards of the device and remained lodged there. Some of the mirrors were broken and missing, leaving its glittering hide patched and dark in places.

"This... thinks?" she asked.

"Yes. I can feel it," Hayes said faintly. "Not like a person. Not like when I'm standing near you. Less than a person. But also more. Like it's doing only one or two things in comparison to our hundreds, but those things... They're so *big*."

"It's doing them now?"

"I don't know. I don't think so. Not fully. It's trying to talk to me, Sam. But it's not... not smart enough. But, Christ, just the fact that it's *trying*..."

She leaned close, then reached one hand out to the many mirrors. They seemed to twist with her though she could detect no movement.

"Don't touch it," Hayes said sharply.

"What? Why not?"

"It's not... not happy, I don't think."

She paced around it, watching the images in the mirrors move. She looked at the mixed jumble of tubing that dangled off the midsection. Looked at the brass and crystalline threads hanging limp like rags. It was as delicate as a dragonfly's wing. She remembered her wonder at the machine Tazz had shown them in the tunnels, and now that device seemed huge and clumsy and stupid in comparison to this thing of terrifying grace. She looked around and saw the walls were lined with worktables, each one paired with a bench. On all the tables were hundreds of tools, pliers and microscopes and thick drills, and in some places there were white stone slabs each with a small golden piece set in the center. She examined these and saw the pieces were tiny gears or many-faceted rods of incredibly intricate make, and guessed they had been pulled or ripped from the strange machine in order to be examined.

"How could McNaughton have made a machine that thinks?" she asked.

"I don't think they did," said Hayes from the other side.

"Then who? Kulahee? Do you think this could be one of his first ones, maybe?"

"I don't think this was made by people, Sam."

She stopped, then came around to look at him. "What?"

"I don't think this was made by men."

"Then... What?"

He shook his head. "I don't know. But I don't think this could have been made anywhere on Earth."

She stepped farther back, eyes tracing over its long, sloping figure, like a golden piece of driftwood washed up on the cement floor. She could see no source of power feeding the machine and yet she knew somehow that it was on and functioning. Unlike Tazz's mechanism she felt this device could not be stopped, could never fall dead. It was somehow eternal, unending, or perhaps it had been forged in a place where time was as easily manipulated as steel or wood.

"The machines they make seem like they were never built for people," said Hayes quietly. "And sometimes the workers think they talk to them, in their heads..."

"What do you mean?"

"It's nothing," he said. "It's just what someone said to me not too long ago." He swallowed. "This building," he whispered. "It goes down far below."

"All of our facilities are seventy percent underground," Samantha said without thinking.

"But down there. Below us. I think there's *more*."

"More of these things?"

He shook his head. "But ones like it. Being stored. And waiting. And they've been waiting for so long..."

Samantha remembered the sounds of the machines in the deeps, and the faint pounding of strange devices filling the underground chambers. "Waiting for what?" she asked softly.

Hayes lurched forward, grasped his chest, then turned away and vomited onto the cement. Samantha went to him and pulled the hair out of his face and pounded his back. As he coughed she noticed something lying not more than a few feet away. She picked it up and studied it.

"What is that?" Hayes asked between breaths.

"A hat," she said. "A child's hat."

Hayes looked at her and she knew he was wondering how and why a child could be there.

"We need to go," Samantha said.

"You're probably right," Hayes said.

They slipped back through the patrols easily. The night was moonless and quiet, the whole world sleeping and shrouded in darkness.

They passed through the woods and walked along the shore, searching for the boat.

"What is our city built of?" Samantha asked as they walked. "What's down there, in its heart?"

"Do you remember the Red Star Scandal, Sam?" asked Hayes quietly.

"What? Yes, of course. Why?"

"Do you remember how, when they were asked how they knew the airship they'd made would work, they immediately said that they just knew?"

"Well, yes, but why..."

"How could they know," said Hayes slowly, "unless it had already worked before? Maybe very, very long ago..."

Samantha thought about that. Then her eyes grew wide. "My God...Are you saying..."

Hayes swallowed and nodded.

"Then what could be down there?"

"I think it's something alive," Hayes said. "Genuinely alive, down under the city. I've...I've felt it. It's trapped and broken and old, I think. It's tried to speak to me, like that thing back there. But it can't. It's so old."

"What could it be?"

"I don't know," he said. "But I have to find out."

They found the ferry rocking gently on the night tide. The captain was sprawled in the back, a fishing pole in his lap, head nodding as sleep threatened to overtake him. Hayes picked up a stone and sent it ricocheting across the stern. The captain sputtered awake and then hauled them in, complaining with each heave.

"We have to get to Garvey," Hayes said as the ferry started off. "We have to tell him that McNaughton has armed the unions. Maybe not all of them, but some, and enough. And we don't know why."

"We don't?" she asked.

"No. We don't."

"What about that thing? That machine?"

"That's why you're going to go to Garvey," he said. "I'm going up into the mountains to do some historical sightseeing. I'll go visit Mr. Kulahee's cave. I think it's a tourist site these days. But no one there's looking right. Not really. But I know how to."

"How?"

"With this," he said, and tapped the side of his head.

The boat sped over the waves, dipping up and down as it sloshed through the water. They saw the jeweled mass of Evesden rise up ahead, the glitter on the black shoreline growing with each mile. Both Hayes and Samantha stood at the stern, watching it approach with different eyes, as though it were a foreign land.

"Look!" cried Samantha suddenly, and pointed.

They both leaned forward to see it better. It was faint but it was there, a streak of the night sky that was a slightly lighter color than the rest, almost ash-gray. As they came closer they could see that where it met the cityscape the streak's innards were red and molten and boiling. Then the cradle spotlights flashed along the column's side and they saw it fully.

"It's smoke," Hayes said. "Jesus Christ, it looks like all of Lynn is on fire."

"What the hell?" said the captain. "What the hell is going on?"

The boat veered closer to the bays of the city. They could hear screaming from far, far away. A whine like some insect, buzzing madly. Then a low-throated burst, and the column of smoke lit up.

"What the hell was that?" said Hayes.

"They've started," Samantha said softly.

"What?"

"They've started. Don't you see? They've started. The union men, with the guns. They've got them now and they're using them."

Bells rang somewhere and went unanswered. People rushed back and forth along the dock front, shouting to one another. Someone cackled somewhere and there was the sound of glass breaking and more screaming.

Hayes pulled out his gun as they came close to land. "Here," he said, thrusting it toward her. "Take this. Get to Garvey. Just tell him what happened. Tell him what's going on." Hayes put one foot on the bow of the boat and waited for the captain to pull it in.

"What are you going to do?" asked Samantha.

"I've no idea," he said. Then when he was near enough Hayes leaped down to the dock. He slipped and fell, recovered himself, and sprinted off toward the fire.

CHAPTER THIRTY-NINE

It seemed as though in Hayes's absence the city had become a different place. Some streets had no lights and were filled with complete darkness. Homes were being emptied and small crowds filed down alleys and lanes, though none seemed sure of where they were going. And on some darkened streets one could look far down the block and see distant building faces lit with the hellish glow of merry flames.

He managed to stop one young woman and force some sort of story out of her. "They took hostages," she panted.

"Hostages? Who?"

"The union men. They stormed the Southeastern Office of McNaughton, tried to take hostages. Political hostages, they said. But things went wrong. The guns they had, they did something crazy. Hit a gas main."

"Oh, God."

"Everything's on fire. You got to get out, mister. Got to get the hell out of this town before it all burns down." Then she turned and fled and was gone.

Closer to the Southeastern the flow of the crowd was almost overpowering. Women clutching children or dragging them along. Men bowling one another over as they fought to escape the oncoming flames. As he crossed the Lynn Canal Hayes began to see fire trucks among the throngs of people, clanking, yellow contraptions piled with rubber tubing. They pulled up at the street sides and turned their nozzles toward the burning buildings and poured great gouts of sewer water through the windows. They seemed forced to work the fire at the edges, though; toward the Southeastern the inferno was immense, whole buildings crumbling under its onslaught, and in those places they could not venture close to the flames.

There was a noise from the burning end of the street like a thousand steam whistles ringing at once. One of the firemen screamed, "Get down!" and the entire crowd dropped to the cement, except for Hayes. He watched as one of the building faces lit up as if an entire spotlight were focusing on one square foot of the building's façade. Then a white-hot spark flew from an alley across the street to strike the glowing spot and the building erupted like it had been hit with an artillery shell.

Hayes was blown backward off his feet and tumbled to the pavement. His ears rang and the street scene grew hazy and stuttered. He wondered what had happened before remembering that he was stunned. He took a deep breath, remembered what he had done under the same circumstances during his old life and the appropriate reaction, and wriggled his fingers and toes until the world became still again.

He rolled onto his belly and saw a man running out of the alley across from the building that had exploded, carrying something long and thin in his hands, like a short pike with a scooped blade at its end. One of the firemen screamed something and several policemen fought to their knees and began wildly firing at him. The man screamed, the shoulder of his overalls suddenly dotted with red, and he pointed the thin pike at them. There was the piercing whistling sound again and the end of the pike glittered white. The policemen fell to the ground. From the end of the pike a small spark the size of a thumb came shooting out, arcing over them and the street behind them, far up into the air where it burst like a firework, shrapnel spinning down to the city below. The man stopped and tried to rerig the device but was hampered by his dead arm. The police began firing again and there was a wet burst from the edge of the man's neck and he sank to the ground and lay there. The police kept firing at him. His calf burst. Then his side, yet still they fired.

"What the hell sort of guns did they give them?" Hayes heard himself asking.

The damaged building caved in on itself. Hayes could see the shivering light of small fires dancing in its husk. The building next to it fell as well and more fire spilled down the street. One of the firemen shouted something and waved his hand and the crews began reeling in their lines to withdraw down the street. This neighborhood was lost, they called. The most they could do was contain it.

Hayes tried to stand. He watched the screaming faces rush before him. Watched as the fire licked adjacent roofs or crept down into bushes and small lawns. He saw there was something moving in one of the homes, ambling back and forth and covered in flames. It fell from sight and he did not see it again.

He realized he felt something in the back of his head. Something cold and intense like a drill being pushed into his brainpan. Sensations washed over him, lurid terror and wild fear, eating into him and seizing up his heart.

"Oh, God," he murmured to himself. "Not now. Please. Not now."

But there was no stopping it. The attack was coming. He fell to his hands and knees and waited for it to pass.

Yet it did not pass. It grew and it grew, swallowing him and pulling him down and drowning him. Soft blue lights began flashing at the edges of his sight, just as when he'd seen that strange vision in the trolley tunnel. He took a deep breath and wondered if vomiting would clear it, but as he did he realized that the pain was lessening, but the sensations were not going away. He could still feel the people around him, yet it did not pain him at all.

He opened his eyes and stood and looked out at them and, astonished, held them clearly in his mind. Sensations flooded through him, the echoes of many thoughts and desperate hopes and wild fears, but they did not pain him or wound him as they always had. It was so clear, so focused. It was as though he had been blind, but now for the first time he could see the world clearly and without pain, and he looked out on what surrounded him.

A chorus. A wailing chorus of fear and terror, and his soul was the reed that caught their scream and sang out, loud and high and clear, begging for someone to listen.

He looked at the building behind him and knew immediately someone was inside. In the lower back room, hiding in the bathroom. More than one person, probably.

Several nearby firemen began to load up to head out, and Hayes ran to one and grabbed him and shouted, "There's someone in that building!"

The fireman looked at Hayes, then at the building. "What? No, we evacuated that an hour ago!"

"You're wrong! There's someone in the back!"

"In the back? How the hell do you know? Get your goddamn hand off me."

"I'm telling you there's a mother and daughter there!"

The fireman shoved him back and brandished a leather-gloved fist. "Get the hell off me or I swear to God..."

Hayes steeled himself and reached out to him, desperately listening to the growing echoes from within the man. It had never come so fast before, and so easily, and soon he heard...

"Janey says you need to listen," he said suddenly.

The fireman stopped and stared at him. "What?"

"Janey says you need to listen to me. To help. Or else it will have all been for nothing, all of it. Will you help me, then?"

The fireman's mouth dropped open. He gaped for a moment, then said, "How in the hell do you know?"

"Will you help me?" said Hayes again.

The fireman's face grew pale. Shaken, he nodded, and followed Hayes into the building.

Hayes led the fireman down into the basement, standing aside sometimes to let the man hack away at the doors that barred their progress. When they reached the bathroom in the basement they had to turn aside and cover their faces, as the ceilings were filled with thick rolls of black smoke, yet they saw a mother and her little girl lying on the sooty floor like dolls thrown aside. The fireman stuck his head in and looked at them for as long as he could, then looked at Hayes and said, "Well, I'll be goddamned." Then he went to the front door and called for help.

Four more firemen trooped in. Hayes withdrew to the street and watched. He could feel it when the firemen grasped their limp arms and dragged them out, the little girl pale as the moon, the mother drooling and unconscious. Hayes watched as the firemen laid them out on the cement and began to tend to them.

Then the fireman he had spoken to approached him slowly. "How did you do that?" he asked.

"I don't know," Hayes said honestly.

"How did you know they were in there?"

"I don't know. I just did."

"Can...can you find any more?"

Hayes turned and looked at the buildings up and down the street. "I think so. If I get close."

"Well. We'll follow you if we can."

Hayes took a thick leather coat from them and began the haphazard process of sprinting up and down any alleys he could, frantically trying to listen for anyone trapped inside. He would know when they were close, as they lit up in his mind as they always had, but so much faster and brighter than he had ever felt it before. For a while there was nothing as he dodged and ducked among the flaming pathways, but then he skidded to a halt before a small ramshackle tenement, looking up at it. Then he ran back to the firemen, calling, "In here, in here! There's one in here!"

They came and broke the side door down. Inside was a man trapped in his stairwell, his leg broken in two places and his ankle crushed below a mound of fallen wood. When they found him he looked up, gaping like a fish and scrabbling at his leg. He was curiously bald, his hair having slowly withered in the heat, and his face glistened with the promise of blisters. The crew chief levered the boards up and they pulled his foot out, twisted and wet and red. Then they hauled him away, and he howled whenever his foot touched cement, tears running down his red face.

The firemen stared at Hayes. "Jesus," one said softly. "What the hell are you?"

"Enough of that," said the crew chief. "He can find more. Can't he?"

Still breathing hard, Hayes nodded.

"Then go to it, I guess," said the chief.

Hayes sprinted through the network of streets, the fire crew shining in his mind and distant screams ringing in his ears. He led the crew through a maze of ruined streets and tumbling rookeries to three vagrants trapped in a cellar, having crept in in the middle of the night to find a warm place to sleep. The fire crew hooked the truck's hoses up to the hydrants, and the hose chuckled and whistled as the water barreled through it until finally it shot a towering spray onto the alley. It blew the boards back and the fire died instantly, and Hayes and the crew pulled the drunken vagrants out and led them staggering out to safety.

Hayes wiped sweat from his face before running back into the streets. There were more, many more. He felt them, when he looked. Felt their terror beating wild, hovering in the fire when they were near like will-o'-the-wisps in boggy mists. Minute after minute he returned to the gathering fire crews, telling them where he had found another and how they were trapped. Then he realized more people were following him. Not fire crews, but normal people. Normal people listening to his voice and following his commands.

He was surveying the fire from a corner when he felt it start to leave him. His veil of awareness slowly began to recede, and the souls that had burned so brightly in the night now dimmed to become murky haze. Soon he knew he would be blind and broken and fumbling again, shortsighted and lost, and he cried out, "No! No, not now! Please, don't!" But it did not stop. It was leaving him.

He climbed back up to the top of the fire truck and began desperately shouting orders. He pointed up one street and told them where survivors were hidden, and pointed down another and told them where the fires were spreading fast. He told them who was hurt and where and how long they had. And each time the crews emerged from the rubble with a black-streaked refugee he waited for them to be laid upon the sidewalk before turning around and sprinting back into the fire.

And the crowd watched him. They watched this strange, sooty little man bellowing hoarse commands and ordering them this way and that. They watched him climb up onto a car roof and summon some strange authority around himself like a cloak and then shout directions to teams far down the street. And for some reason they began to believe that he wielded some power over the fire, as if he could control the fire itself. Like he could merely point at a burning home and the flames would wither and die and not return. And how could they believe otherwise? Battle-scarred and tattered and grim as the fiercest warrior, how could this little man be anything less than the commander of all things within his sight?

Hayes knew this. He heard what they thought of him. And he knew then that this moment would echo through time for him. This one would be different. In some way he knew that even though he had been whole and painless and powerful for only a short time, he had been what he was always supposed to be, and would be for the rest of his days.

He was watching the firemen tend to the wounded when it left him entirely. The world fell silent around him, dead of all the thoughts and hopes he'd heard so clearly. Now he heard only the indistinct mutters he'd heard all his life. It was like being struck blind.

Hayes sat down on the hood of the fire truck. He huddled in his coat and wiped tears from his eyes and fought to hold on to that feeling, that feeling of being whole, of being unbroken and able.

"Are you all right?" asked one fireman.

"Yes," said Hayes hoarsely. He stood up. "What else is there to do?"

CHAPTER FORTY

It took a long while for Samantha to get to Garvey's apartment. In the past few hours the city had come under siege, practically. As Samantha hurried through the gloomy streets she held the pistol Hayes had given her at her side, glad it was there but hoping she would not have to use it. You could hear the din of the crowds and fires far away to the southeast, as if through a radio, and all the sky was smoke. The few cabs that were still out would not stop for anyone and trolleys sat abandoned in their tunnels and stations. Some of the eastern portions of the city had lost power, and there the windows and stoops were lit up with candlelight, little flickering stars spackling the building fronts. It seemed medieval.

When she finally came to Garvey's apartment she found it deserted. At first she was frightened for him, but then she saw it had not been ransacked. Everything was clean and ordered, as usual. Even the bed had been made. Then she opened the drawer to his desk and found his gun was missing.

"Oh, Donald," she said sadly.

She thought for a moment, then went east to where the Wering Canal began. She followed the paths down into the canal to where they ran just above the water. As she moved she could hear people running around among the bridges and sidewalks above her, sometimes cackling or shouting threats. She was glad of the solitary darkness down here, underneath the bridges and forgotten piping.

Soon the paths rose up and she was met with a string of small apartments, the first one being Hayes's safe house. She went to the door and found it unlocked, then thought hard and pushed it open to reveal darkness. She kept the gun pointed down as it swung. There was a sharp click, the sound of a pistol cocking from somewhere back in the room. She shut her eyes, waiting for the bang, yet it never came.

"Goddamn," said a hoarse voice. "Samantha?"

She cracked one eye and saw a gray electric light fluttering on far back in the room. A figure was hunched on the bed with a pistol pointed to the floor. The light grew to show Garvey staring at her, breathing hard. "What the hell are you doing with a gun?" he asked.

"I could ask the same of you," she said faintly, pointing at his own weapon.

He looked down at the revolver in his hand as though confused about what it was, then hastily put it on the table. As he stood she ran to him and he caught her in his arms.

"Jesus Christ, Sam," he said. "Thank God you're all right."

"What are you doing here?" she asked. "I went to your apartment, but you weren't there. What happened?"

"I didn't think it was safe," he said. "I waited a while and then I snuck out the window. I think maybe Hayes's paranoia is catching."

"I don't think it's paranoia if it's justified," she said. She let go of him. "Listen, Donald. We found that friend of his. And he told us what Tazz has been doing."

She went over what she had heard and seen out in the woods. Garvey listened carefully, his body seeming to tighten with each word.

"So Tazz arranged this?" he said softly at the end. "Bringing in these guns and holding hostages?"

"It would seem so. I'm not sure."

"And then starting this. This fire."

"I don't know."

"Jesus," he said, and shook his head. "This just got a whole lot nastier. What about that thing you found? Down underground?"

"I don't know much about that. Hayes seemed to recognize it. It seemed to speak to him. About what, I don't know. I think he's handling that. He said he was going up to Kulahee Cave."

"What the hell? Kulahee Cave? What for?"

"To look for something, he said. I don't know what." She glanced around the apartment. "Where are the files?"

"Under the bed. Half of them, at least. I took half in to Collins to show him I meant business."

"And what did he say?"

"He said to come in. Tomorrow. Or today, depending on whatever the hell time it is. I just hope there's still a city in the morning."

"And you still plan to? To go?"

"Yes," he said. His face seemed starved and thin, like too little skin stretched over too much bone. "Especially now, Sam. I mean... someone has to be accountable. We just need to wait now. Wait until it's safe to go out."

Samantha looked out the window at the sheet of smoke pouring off the horizon. "Yes," she said. "Safe."

CHAPTER FORTY-ONE

Once the fires had died out Hayes crept away and stole a car at the edge of Lynn and drove south and west. He passed out of the city and roved through the dark woodland roads until he came into the hills and the little towns there. He could not remember exactly where it was, so he drove for two more hours until his headlights fell upon an enormous blue-and-gold sign that read: SEE KULAHEE CAVE, BIRTHPLACE OF GENIUS. He stopped the car and stared at the sign, then looked off down the road in the direction the big yellow arrow pointed. He primed the engine and continued.

He kept rising. The car strained on the little dirt roads, but he followed the signs until he came to a small home with a large sign proclaiming it to be the visitor's center for Kulahee Cave. He got out and walked to the little building, then peered into the dusty windows and tried the knob. There was nothing of interest there save an electric torch on the back stoop.

He took the torch and walked down the path into the pines. He wandered until he came to a small, neat little entrance into the side of a hill. Two wet, mossy stones made the doorway, leaning against each other. He touched them and shone the torch inside. It was empty. Nothing but small signs educating the visitor about the life of Kulahee and his great contributions to society. Whatever he was looking for, it was not here.

He walked out of the cave and looked up into the hillside. He shone the torch up and the beam of light bobbed around the rocks and the brush and the sparse grass.

There was something else. Something else farther up. Buried just under the skin of the earth. He felt it, though he could not understand how.

He began climbing up the hillside. A few hundred feet up he turned and looked out. He saw the smoking remains of Evesden far away, lining the shore. Then he turned and looked at the hills around him.

From this angle it appeared that there had once been some work done here. There was a road on the north face, he saw, but it had long been out of use and was now overgrown. It led to some large basin, unnaturally made, which had been somewhat filled in. As he rose farther he saw there were divots and carvings in the very hills, as if they had been torn apart, clay and stone rivulets running through the earth. A scarred countryside, moonwrought and alien in this strange night.

On the far side of the pit was a small river, worn deep into the stone around it. A knot of pines clutched it at the lip of the basin. There were no other trees in this part of the hills. Only those remained untouched. Somehow the little copse felt like a flag or a cairn, marking where something was buried.

He walked across the basin to the trees and where the river crested and fell. Then he walked to the edge of the water. The rock edge was smooth and rounded. Slick with the wear of time. The river had to be thousands of years old. Millions, even. He looked down into the waters and saw nothing but darkness. He felt strangely cold, yet it was a feeling he had felt before, in the city. That strange pounding machinery, deep underground in the trolley tunnels...

He knelt down. Put his hands in the water. It was icy cold, so cold it hurt.

Yes, said a voice inside of him.

He stood and took off his leather fireman's coat and threw it away. Then he looked into the waters again.

There was something down there. Something looking back. Something that had lain there for uncounted years, sitting in darkness, waiting.

He grabbed the torch and took a breath and dove in.

The power of the cold was deafening, overwhelming. The shock of it nearly drove the breath from his body. He strained to hold on to it. A little column of bubbles escaped one of his nostrils and threaded its way toward the surface. He struggled to orient himself and the beam of light from the torch thrashed about, catching smooth rocks and stabbing into the deeps. Then he steadied and began forcing himself down, the torch clapped to his side as he kicked, driving his body into the darkness as far as he could go.

He caught a glimpse of it first, a random flash from the torch in his hand. Something silver and white in the rock wall. He stopped where he was, breath burning within him, and then flashed the light around again. Finding nothing, he tried once more, and saw he had gone too far. It was above him. He fixed the beam on what he could see of it and looked, and then fought to hold on to his breath.

The machine was enormous. Huge and long and thin, just breaching the wall of the mountain river, and now that the torch had found it the machine seemed to refract or enhance the light until it gained a faint luminescence. Its surface was smooth and pristine, almost unearthly, and still completely intact after so long. He knew he was only seeing a bare fraction of it, that the rest was hidden up under the shelf of rock below the river.

He saw that the metal was slightly translucent, and deep within it there were things moving, delicate threads and tubing and miniscule gear-works churning away quietly and smoothly. He somehow suspected he'd seen it before, or something like it. Then he remembered the wonders he'd glimpsed down in the factory's floors, spindled glass and pearly alloys, and Tazz's machine. They were similar, he realized, as if they were related, though those were primitive toys compared to this. But the golden device he'd found mere hours ago matched this buried thing perfectly. They were parts of a whole, he realized instantly. One broken off from the other.

Hayes swam up to it, blinking in the murky water. He had only a few seconds' worth of air left now. As he neared it he thought he could hear it humming. Still functioning, somewhere. Somewhere in the heart of the Earth.

Yes, said the voice.

He felt the machine turn its awareness on him, examining him, then welcoming him.

Touch, it said.

Hayes hesitated. Then he placed one hand on its side.

Then a voice inside him roared, "I AM A MESSENGER, SENT FROM AFAR. YOU MUST LISTEN TO ME. YOU MUST LISTEN." And the world lit up.

He felt cool air wash over him. Listened to the sigh of the wind and the breath of the shore. Then he opened his eyes.

He was in a small field on a cliff next to the ocean. It was night. Clean green grass rose up to his waist and tickled the tips of his fingers. He had never been to the spot before, yet he felt it was familiar. It was somewhere around the city, to the west, yet Evesden was gone from the shore below. The countryside seemed empty without it. Above him the stars shone bright, and he knew then he was seeing the sky untouched by the lights of any city. A younger sky, before any building began.

"Where am I?" he asked out loud.

"Where you were," said a voice. It was tinny and weary-sounding, as though coming through a worn-down phonograph, yet it seemed to come from all around him. "I am merely showing you this place as it was, long ago."

Hayes realized he could not feel himself breathing. He grabbed at his wrists and could feel no pulse there either. Before he could speak the voice said, "You are not dead. All this is but a dream, in some ways. It lasts no more than a mere moment in the time outside. In the real world. You are safe."

"Who are you?" asked Hayes.

"A messenger," said the voice. "I traveled a great distance once, and have waited so long to deliver my message. So long, down there in the dark. Far below the earth."

"Are you... are you a god?" asked Hayes hesitantly.

"A god?" said the voice. "No. I am perhaps no more than a recording. A record waiting to be played."

Hayes didn't say anything at first. Then he ventured, "What... what is your message?"

"That your kind will die," said the voice simply. "That it will overreach, and crumble, and perish, and be forgotten. And that this will happen soon."

Hayes was silent. He grew aware that there was something walking in the field beyond the circle. Something pacing through the grass, yet he could see nothing.

"Where are you?" he asked.

"I am nowhere," said the voice. "I am nothing. I am a voice in the darkness, a ghost in an old, old machine telling you of a future. Of your future. And what you must do to survive."

"What do you mean? Where did you come from?"

"From the stars," said the voice softly. Up ahead one star shone brighter than the rest. "That star, specifically."

"You're from the *stars*?" Hayes asked, astounded.

"Yes. I was made there, once, long ago. Made to help you."

"By who?"

"By watchers. By those who left their own world and made the stars their own, ages ago. And having done so they saw what little life foundered in the empty black, and learned much. Do you know how many worlds have been birthed out there? In the far places, in the lost places? Only a few. Thousands, maybe. Maybe less. And can you guess how many survived more than a few million years? Even less than that. Most die, of their own doing. Sputter out. Flash and flame and fade like hot stars. It is the nature of life to overreach," said the voice sadly. "To spread out and multiply and grow until it can grow no further. And then, starving, it will devour itself."

"Why are you telling me this?" Hayes asked the thing in the field.

"Because you must know," it said. "Someone must know, besides me. You must know that you are dying. It was my purpose to help you avoid it, but now I can do no more than tell you. I have tried to speak to you before, using the crude signaling machines in your city. They recognized me and tried to do my bidding, but you could not listen. Not you or anyone else..."

Hayes suddenly remembered the strange noises rushing through the trolley tunnels, and the vision of the ruins of Evesden. "That was you," he said softly.

"Yes. But now you can hear. You can hear my message. Will you listen?"

Hayes was not sure what to say. "All right."

"Then listen," whispered the voice. "Intelligence changes the life span of a species. It is enormously talented at self-destruction. Those few worlds that foster it rarely see it last for more than a handful of years. It is the price for your complexity, for ability, and it is paid in hunger and bloodshed. It begins as you grow. First clans become tribes. Then tribes become cities. Cities become nations. Nations become empires. Until it is nothing but a constant war of giants. Enormous forces struggling against one another. And when one of those giants falls, sometimes there is no recovering. Sometimes everything ends.

"It comes about in several ways. Warfare is common. Exhaustion. Starvation. For each new advance you pay a higher price, until the price is so great it swallows you. Ends you. This is the way. This has always been the way. Always will be. There is no other.

"Some recover. Some survive. And then they survive not as nations. Not as empires. Not as giants. But as a species. A single species, undivided. United by how close they came to such enormous death. I and others like me were made by those rare few who survived. I was sent to ensure that you also reached this, long ago, when this world first showed hope of life. That you came to that point. There were others, made for other worlds, but I was yours." There was a sharp click out there in the fields, like a record's skipping. "I have failed."

"Failed?"

"Yes. There was an error. An error of calculations." There was a pause, then a slight hum from around him as if something was spinning up, gathering momentum. "I will show you," said the voice softly.

Above Hayes the night sky fluttered as though there was something alive in it, something working to break through, and then the boiling sky calcified to form an enormous ship suspended above the Earth, long and thin like some seacraft. It was black-gold and perfect and it seemed to Hayes that every part of the device was alive. It hovered over the landscape, huge and gorgeous, moving very, very slowly. As he studied it he thought to himself, *My God. It looks almost like an airship. Like an enormous airship.*

"Yes," said the voice in the fields. "That is me. How I was. I was meant to..." The click came again. "...Watch, and seed you. Alter your very structure slightly so that you could hear me, and listen. I was to curb your most self-destructive impulses. But I did not get far. Once you rose and began to walk across your world, to see and to know, something happened."

Hayes watched as the vessel hovered across the earth. There was a sound from within it, a gouging, creaking clunk, and a flash of blue-white flame shot from its right back section. The entire ship shuddered and then its side seemed to crumple inward, as if some unimaginable force inside the ship was pulling it in, all of its panels and sides flexing toward an inner point. Then the ship began to dovetail, spinning slowly through the air, its side still crumpling in as it spun faster and faster, until finally it struck the Earth and a great cloud of dust rose up, concealing it from view.

"The chances of any significant malfunction were considered, but deemed negligible," said the voice wearily. "To this day, I do not know what it was. An error in mathematics. Corrosion from the moisture from your atmosphere, perhaps. But regardless I did not prepare, and I was broken."

When the clouds dissipated Hayes saw the ship was halfway buried in the earth, its strange wreckage rising only a few feet above the mountains. Wind picked up dust and piled it around the ship until its golden nose was swallowed by the ground. Hayes saw people roving over the land, bands of brown-skinned folk with long black hair and primitive weapons. They sat around far fires and wandered across the earth and did not return.

"You continued without me," said the voice. "What seeds I had laid among your kind had not yet sprouted, had not taken hold, and I was too damaged to speak to what was there to listen. You could not hear my suggestions. Not yet. So I watched. And grieved. And waited. The long wait. I cannot describe how long, how the years stretched on. The eons in the dark. A voice speaking to nothing. This was what I was. What I am. But this is soon to end.

"When I was finally discovered it was much later," said the voice. "You had changed. You could almost hear my call, however faint. One man listened, just faintly, without knowing what I said. He came down and found parts of me. But he could not truly hear. And instead he brought others to me, and they took me apart. And kept me a secret. And made things from my remains."

Hayes watched as men in suits scurried across the hillside. They sifted through the earth at their feet and picked up the wreckage of the vessel and studied it. Cocked their heads. Then stowed it away. Construction teams labored away in secret, finding more and more of the wonders hidden below the earth. And beyond Hayes saw the shoreline light up and grow gray-black as a city was born and rocketed to dominance in only a handful of decades.

"McNaughton," Hayes whispered. "My God. You're McNaughton. You're what Kulahee found in the mountains. He wasn't any genius, he just tripped over you!"

"Yes," whispered the voice. "He made toys from my bones. Little amusements. And then he brought others. They could barely hear me. I had to develop defenses. It took so much effort to keep them away. To hide this most important part of me, and keep my message for someone who could hear me. To wait for you."

"For me?" Hayes said, astonished. "You waited for me?"

"Yes. Yes. Yes." The harsh click sounded somewhere above again, insectile and pained. "I sensed you. Far, far away. A bright jewel, wandering among distant lands. Your mind is different. More sensitive. The seeds I had sown had taken hold in you, and though they had gone awry you could still hear me. You had to come. To come and listen. So as they slept in the city below I whispered to the men there and used all my power and spoke to them of you, and they drew you in. It doomed me, that effort. Made my life short. But it had to be done."

"You…you made me?" Hayes asked softly.

"I did not make you."

"But I'm…I'm like this because of you?"

A pause. "Yes."

Hayes fell silent. He shook his head and fought back the sorrow rising in him. "Why did you…why did you make me like this?" he asked.

"There was no making," said the machine. "There never was.

None of this was intended. You or this city or this strange new world. Nothing was meant to be this way. It simply is. It simply happened."

"Can you... can you fix me?" asked Hayes desperately.

There was another harsh click. "No," said the machine. "I cannot."

"Please. Please, you have to..."

"I have already spent much of my strength changing you, changing you so you could listen," said the voice. "You were close, but not close enough, and I was forced to use the machines below your city to make you better. Have you not felt it? Have you not felt your abilities become so focused and clear that they almost pain you?"

He shook his head. "The attacks..."

"Yes. The devices they built to run your city were a primitive medium, but they did what I needed. Their signaling mechanisms amplified my few remaining strengths. Gave me a way to reach you. You had to listen."

Hayes remembered the flashing blue lights he'd seen when he'd had the vision in the trolley tunnels. "It's the Siblings, isn't it," he said. "You can work through them. If I get close enough, I can hear you."

"Yes. Others can hear only echoes. But yes."

"And it was you who gave me that... that moment back in the fire, wasn't it? That was you."

Another harsh click. "Yes."

"But why?"

"It was a gift. A moment of clarity. But it would have ended me to sustain it any longer than I had. And I must use my last remaining seconds wisely, for one final act."

"What do you mean?"

He heard the voice sigh beyond. "My presence here has changed things. Destabilized them. Accelerated them. I was a catalyst on a level that even I could not have foreseen. And now I can no longer keep pace. I am dying. Only unformed minds hear me now. Madmen. And children."

"Children?" Hayes asked.

"Yes. This world is falling apart. The factions have grown enormous and hungry, fed by the technology I have provided. And war is coming. Change is coming. The last change. I cannot prevent it. I can only warn you."

"But when will it come? What will it be?"

"I do not know."

"But can we do anything about it? Can we stop it?"

The vision quaked, the field rippling at the edges. "I do not know," said the voice. "No. I do not think so."

"What will happen?"

"Your civilization will crumble. Exhaust itself. And survive only in shreds and tatters. If that."

"So...so we have to stop it," Hayes said, trembling.

"There is no stopping it."

"But there has to be. There has to be something!"

"There is no stopping it. This is the way. It is a machine grown so large and with such momentum that it cannot stop, only fall apart under its own force."

"But we can...we can tell people," Hayes said desperately. "We can tell them to stop."

"To stop what? Stop hungering? Stop expanding? It is the nature of life and power to want more, to grow faster until it cannot. With the tools I have inadvertently provided, you grow at a rate that makes self-control impossible. There is only one feasible end."

The quiet went on, broken only by the sigh of the wind.

"Then we'll die," said Hayes. "Then we'll all die. And there's nothing we can do. Is that what you're telling me? Nothing?"

"There are..." Another click. "...Possibilities."

"Possibilities? What possibilities?"

"There is no stopping the collapse. It is unavoidable. You have seen your city, and know it is beyond repair. A place of outrage and sorrow, and waste. And your city is the heart of your world. When it falls or begins breeding destruction, the consequences will be catastrophic. Yet for the few who will survive, for the scraps that will persist at the fringes, there is hope. They can make a new world. And learn from their mistakes. But that is in the future, and I will not last long enough to see that. I cannot help them directly. But I can make use of my last moments to ensure they receive at least some aid."

"How?"

"By making sure there is someone to lead your people from your ruined lands, and find a home somewhere in the future. An architect who can rebuild, the seeds of a new future sown."

Hayes listened to the words. He looked at the field around him and at the invisible thing waiting in the grass. Then his eyes opened wide and he said, "No."

"There is no other choice," said the voice.

"No, not me."

"There is no other choice."

"No, no. No, it shouldn't be me. There... there has to be someone else. It shouldn't be me. It shouldn't be me!" he shouted.

"But it must be."

"There have to be others. Others who are better."

"They cannot hear. Nor have they seen the wide expanse of humanity that you have, and known its flaws, and its strengths."

"It shouldn't be me," Hayes said softly. "It shouldn't be me."

"Would you have your people founder against the future? Die out and become extinct? Live their last days in darkness and savagery?"

"No, but... but we can stop the war," he said desperately. "Get rid of the empires. Can't we?"

"You cannot stop such a thing. You cannot alter the nature of nature. All life desires destruction. The only thing that matters is if it survives it."

Hayes bowed his head. "But I can't."

"When the city burned they did not look to you, yet still you came," said the voice. "Still you came, and showed them the way.

And did you not feel joy? Did you not know their hearts, and love that they were safe?"

"Yes, but—"

"This is who you are. This is what you are. This is what you must be. With the last of my strength, I can help you. And there is no time. The changes that I have brought about are unraveling your city. Already a boy stumbled across a part of me, a part that had long been separate and alone and had grown depraved, and when the boy came to it, it changed him. Changed him for the worse."

"Changed him how?"

The voice sighed again. "It was a part of me for travel. You have seen it yourself, hidden away in buildings not far from here. It has its own mind, for its own purposes. It bent..." The voice clicked again. "...Time. Bent reality. Twisted it so I could move through vast distances in months instead of eons. When the boy found it, it... elevated him. Took his being and sped it up. Placed it on a different level. Now he is a half-thing. Mad and distorted. Living in two times. And the things he has done have torn your city apart. That is how fragile it is. And that is why you must be ready."

Hayes swallowed. "What do you want from me?"

Another harsh click. "Once a man came among me and walked away with a handful of trinkets. He changed the world with these meager things, these toys. He made a new age, though he did not know it. Imagine what could be done with all the concepts that could be willingly shown to you, given to you. Imagine what a world you could make. I can give them. Now, in an instant."

Hayes thought quickly. He looked back on his years, lonely and wandering, always living on the razor's edge. Living nameless lives, adrift among the hopes and madnesses of the people who passed him by.

"Will it hurt?" Hayes asked. "Changing?"

"Yes," said the voice.

Hayes winced. "And what will I know? After this, what will I know?"

"Secrets. Laws. Devices. Truths hidden in the furrows of reality. Tools that will carve out a home among the coming years. These and more." Click. "Will you do it?"

Hayes thought about it and said, "What will I do? With the knowledge you give me?"

"I cannot say. I am not one of you. I know only how to curb your desires, not how to build. And the path your civilization has taken since my interference has gone well beyond any reckoning I have."

Hayes shut his eyes. "And what if I say no?" he asked.

There was silence.

"What if I say no?" he asked again. "What if I turn it down?"

The voice said, "If you, who have walked among these people for a lifetime, and know their hearts and minds more than any other person alive... If you say no, and doom them to a future of ash and scorched earth, then I will trust your judgment, and let it be, and die voiceless here in the dark."

Hayes sighed. He found he was weeping. He was not sure if the tears were real or part of this strange vision, but they felt hot and wet on his cheeks, and seemed real enough. "Will I remember everything from before?" he asked. "Will I remember that?"

"If you wish."

Hayes nodded and wiped tears from his eyes. "All right. Okay, then. Do it."

The hum intensified. He became aware that somewhere machinery that had long been silent suddenly came to life, desperately working for one last undertaking.

"Once this is done I will be no more," said the voice. "I will be gone. Know this."

"I know. Just do it."

Silence. The thing out in the fields was still.

"Just do it already!" shouted Hayes.

The image around him flashed briefly, flickered like a candle flame. Then the air around him grew hot. There was a feeling in his skull of a thousand fingers probing his mind, rearranging it. Dissecting it and rewiring it.

"Jesus," Hayes said. "Jesus Christ, Jesus *Christ*!"

The air was burning hot now. Hayes felt memories melt into one another, felt experiences and times long lost suddenly flare up as if they were the present. He saw a desert train trundling across desolate flats and watched as the rail in front of it erupted, and he heard himself laugh in satisfaction. Then his father was howling at him, screaming about his idiot son and his foolish ways, and he ached with shame. Next he was grinning as he watched a McNaughton trader being led away, sobbing like a child. And then he felt the madness of grief as he watched a funeral from the gates of a cemetery, stinking drunk and half-suicidal. Watched the coffin slowly descending into the dry ground, knowing that the girl inside it and the child in her belly were dead by his rashness.

The thoughts came together. Crumbled. Rebuilt. Then everything went dark.

A memory blossomed somewhere in him. One he knew was not his own. He saw the ruins of a city, gray and gutted, and he recognized it as the one he'd glimpsed in the trolley tunnels. He saw the city was ravaged beyond belief, its endless wreckage dark beneath the night sky. Yet somewhere within it there was a train of people, a small thread of folk walking through its rubble, and in each of their hands they held a candle, sheltering the flames against their bodies. A vein of light, still alive in these wastelands. And at the front of the procession he saw a man holding a great torch aloft, leading them away from the city, away from their broken homeland, and out to the wilderness beyond where something waited. A building, or a city, it was difficult to make out. Some great white architecture that reached up to the sky, past the clouds and up into the veil of stars.

Survive, said the voice. *Survive. Peace. And bring tomorrow.*

* * *

Hayes opened his eyes and found he was still underwater. He fought the urge to breathe in and failed, and icy water rushed into his mouth and throat. He convulsed and then kicked himself up to the surface.

He burst up from the water, gasping, and clung to the smooth side of the rock wall. He breathed for a few seconds before heaving himself up and over, where he retched water onto the stones. It was then that he noticed a red rain falling from his face, rosy blossoms pattering the stone below. He touched the red drops on the rocks and then touched his face and felt the rivers of blood running from his eyes and ears and nose and mouth. Then he crawled to the edge and washed the blood away and looked at his reflection in the water.

It was still the same face. Yet the hair had changed. It was now sheet-white, white as bone. He touched it, half-expecting it to crumble under his fingers. It did not.

Then he looked beyond, past the surface and the reflection to the deeper waters. There was something missing there. An absence or void where a mind had watched and waited, grieving silently for its lost children. He could no longer sense it.

He stood up and breathed until he was steady. Then he looked at the city below.

Only madmen could hear it, he remembered. Only madmen, and children.

Then he walked down to his car, started it up, and began back down the hilly paths.

CHAPTER FORTY-TWO

Garvey and Samantha sat next to each other on the cot, the stolen files laid on the ground, neatly organized into the most important parts. As the wild night had raged on out in the rest of the city they had both been far too restless to sleep. Garvey had found a small bottle of gin in the desk, no doubt squirreled away there by Hayes for his dry spells, and they'd sipped it while they waited for the wailing and the fire to die down. Now in the early reaches of the morning the drink wore off, and though the smell of smoke still hung heavy in the air and there was still the odd scream out in the streets Garvey figured it was now or never.

Samantha had laid out his suit the night before. She had not been sure why, though she had claimed it was to keep it from getting wrinkled. It had just seemed like something to do, something to occupy her mind, and she'd been grateful to have a task to focus on. She now helped Garvey get dressed in the bleak bunker-light of the safe house, still gray and drained even though the sun had finally come out.

When he was dressed Garvey picked up his pistol and walked to the back of the room to check it, as if it were a shameful act he'd prefer she not see. She heard him opening it, closing it, then opening it and spinning the cylinder. When he turned around it was gone, secreted away, and there was just a worried-looking man in a suit standing there.

"All right," he said.

She gave him the briefcase and he walked to the door and stood there with one hand on the knob. She found she did not like the way he looked in that moment. It was as if he could have been someone else, just some random stranger. She asked what he would do if no one believed him. He said he had friends, friends in the state and federal offices. He told her she could catch a charge from this, being as she'd stolen from her employer. She shrugged. The world of courts and charges and offices seemed far away in the wake of disaster.

Then he turned around and looked at her, wry and weary, and suddenly he was hers again. They embraced. With his free hand he opened the door and let a sliver of light in.

"Stay here," he said. "Stay here, damn you. Until I get back. It may be hours, maybe days, I don't know. But stay."

"I will," she said.

"I'll be back," he said, and he walked out the door and up the brightly lit path of the canal.

Outside it was warm, warmer than he remembered its being in a long time. Garvey shaded his eyes and looked up at the sun and then took off his coat and draped it over one arm. Smiling slightly, he turned and walked up through the canal and onto Broad Street, headed toward a cabbie station, briefcase in hand.

It seemed as though in the wake of the fire the whole city had changed. It was some taste in the air, some relief that came washing up into the streets as the disaster subsided. People gabbled and spoke on the sidewalks, leaning in close to share news, sometimes embracing each other, stunned to find they all still lived.

He took a cab close to Evesden Central, but road repair had

blocked off most of the main routes and he had to get out and walk the last four blocks. All traffic, both pedestrian and vehicle, was being directed down one single alley. Usually it would cause a backup, but these areas seemed deserted. No one wanted to be downtown today, or anywhere near any building of importance. Who knew when the union men would strike again?

He turned down a small lane, tapping his briefcase against his side. He walked along the narrow path of sunlight, trying to gather its heat onto his shoulders. Then he heard muttering. He looked up ahead and saw two men sitting before a shop, playing dice. He frowned at the strangeness of it but continued on.

When he heard the first pop he immediately recognized it as gunfire before he even felt the pain in his side. A little pop, just a .22, barely noticeable to the ear, and his side lit up. He slapped his ribs as if he had been bitten and his hand came away dark red.

More pops. He wheeled awkwardly around and looked behind and saw a man leaning up against a wall to steady his aim, his gun trained on Garvey's back. He squeezed off another round and Garvey heard something crack by over his head. Garvey turned and started forward, but then the two men playing dice stood and reached into their coats and he knew then he'd fallen into a trap. He skidded to a stop and ran down an alley beside, still clutching his briefcase.

He felt warmth running down his side and into his pants. It had gone in deep and since it was a .22 he knew it was still in him somewhere. He reached for his gun and tugged it out of its holster, nearly dropping it as he did so. He cocked it and ran on.

He heard shouting. Echoing from somewhere near, someone calling, "He went in here! In here!"

Garvey kept running. He was limping now and he was not sure why until he looked at his thigh and saw he had been hit there as well. He could not remember when, could not remember how many shots had been fired. He stopped and ducked into a doorway, then leaned up along the side and waited. When he saw the man dash into view he began firing right away, wild shots. One took the man in the belly and he stumbled, his face stupid and surprised. Then Garvey abandoned his roost and ran on.

The alley turned ahead and somehow he knew his leg could not make the turn, so he gripped the wall and slid around the corner. He heard more pops from behind him and his right hand lit up with pain. He looked at it as he ran and saw the bone exposed and blood oozing from the side of his palm. He stared at it, amazed. As if it were some marvel or miracle. The blood ran down and pooled in his palm and he tried to move the gun to the hand with his briefcase but it clattered to the ground. He limped on, abandoning it, reeling and breathless.

He got onto a main street and staggered by a barber shop. A woman inside saw him and screamed and a man shouted to get back, get back. There was a crowd of children down the sidewalk, watching him solemnly. A woman shrieked and rushed down the front steps of her house and grabbed them and pulled them inside.

"Help me," Garvey said as he ran. "For God's sake, someone help me."

He heard another pop. He looked behind as he limped and saw two of the men on the street behind him, aiming carefully. He tried to find cover behind a doorway but as he moved his right shoulder erupted in pain and he stumbled forward. There was another pop and his ankle screamed. He began crawling away on all fours, trying to reach the gutter to hide behind the trash pails lined up there. He moved through them with shaking, clumsy hands and the pails tumbled over, spilling papers onto the sidewalk. He tried to pull them up over himself to hide among the piles. His blood brilliant red on their white surface, like blood on mountain snow.

He heard them running toward him but somehow his mind did not register it. They stumbled around the doorway, guns firing wildly, randomly. He knew they had hit him in the chest and stomach, felt ice dripping through his rib cage and fire along his pelvis.

He stopped moving. Held the briefcase to his chest and lay there gasping. The two men stood looking at him. As if they were uncertain of what they were seeing, or none of this could be real.

Garvey tried to say no. Tried to but did not have the breath or the strength. Then one of the men walked forward and put his gun against Garvey's cheek and pulled the trigger. His head snapped back and he slumped to the side and lay still.

The two men stared at him. A man came out of the doorway across the street and looked at the body.

"Yeah," he said. "That's him."

Bells began ringing not far away. The three of them looked in the direction passively. One of them stooped and picked up the briefcase. "We'd better go," he said.

Then they walked in different directions without looking back.

CHAPTER FORTY-THREE

Hayes sat in Skiller's tenement room in silence. Meditating, almost. The building was empty now, devoid of all the screaming tenants and the filthy children he had seen before. This part of the Shanties had been abandoned after the fire.

He looked around the little room. Looked at the two little beds. The tattered Christ calendar on the wall. Prostrate peasants, still laying their palms before the approach of the Lord. Always approaching, never here.

He knew when the child entered the building, felt him rushing up the stairs like a bolt of lightning, leaping from floor to floor. Hayes felt something new here right away, some intense, deep connection. He suspected he knew why. He and the boy had both beheld something similar, and come away different.

When the boy entered Hayes could not see him but he knew he was there, watching. He said, "Hello, Jack."

There was a quiver in the air before him. It slowed to show a fiercely vibrating form, moving so fast it confused the eye. It slowed further and somewhere in the blur he saw a child's face, eyes mad and confused, teeth bared in rage.

"Calm down," said Hayes. He could feel the boy more viscerally than any other person, as if his very thoughts were painted on the walls. Hayes held up his hands to show him he meant no harm, and the boy began to slow further. Then more until Hayes could finally see him.

He looked nothing like a boy anymore. His hair was sheet-white and his skin was devoid of all pigment and his eyes were wide and hollow. He looked like a starving thing or perhaps some specter from a medieval painting come to life. His teeth chattered as though he was agonizingly cold, and Hayes saw they were tinted with red. One of his hands was horribly mauled, streaked with red and black.

"Can you speak?" Hayes asked.

The boy shivered and watched him. He blinked rapidly. It was an unnerving sight.

"Can you speak, Jack?"

He saw the boy open his mouth. There was a whining noise like dozens of flies by his ear, and somewhere in it he heard a stammering voice say, *Who are you?*

"I'm like you," said Hayes. He pointed to his white hair, then to the boy's.

The boy's shivering stopped. He looked at Hayes and furrowed his brow as he tried to remember speech. "Like me?" he asked, his voice still shuddering.

"Yes."

He looked Hayes over, eyelids fluttering jerkily. "I know you," he said. "You've been here before."

"Yes. Twice. I was looking for you. To take care of you, Jack."

The boy watched him for a long while. "Did you see it, too?" he asked.

"See what?"

"The monster. The monster in the basement."

"The golden one? Yes. Yes, I did, Jack."

The boy stared at him a moment longer. Then suddenly he was

gone. Hayes looked at the empty space and then searched for the boy and found him standing in the kitchen, arms at his sides, face furious.

"I don't like that," he whispered.

"What?" said Hayes.

"I don't like that!" screamed the boy. He picked up a nearby pan and flung it against the far wall. It punched a hole through the plaster like it was paper and daylight streamed through. "I don't like it! I don't! I don't!"

"I don't like it either," Hayes said. "I'm not here because of it."

"Then why?" demanded the boy. "Why are you in my house?"

"Here," said Hayes. "Here. You've hurt yourself. Does that hurt?"

The boy looked at his injured hand. Then he looked back up at Hayes, mistrustful.

"I can help that," said Hayes. "Come here."

The boy shook his head.

"Come here, Jack. Come here."

He relaxed. Then he walked to Hayes and sat down before him, staring blankly at the floor.

"Let me see your hand," Hayes said.

The boy stuck out his ruined arm. Hayes knew it would hurt the boy were he to touch it, so he took out a handkerchief and wrapped it around his upper arm, pinching off the blood flow. The boy did not squirm. Perhaps he felt the strange connection as Hayes did and trusted it, like they were linked somehow by what they had passed through and seen. It was like a window into one another's minds.

"How did you do that?" Hayes asked.

"I hit a door," said the boy. "There was a lock and I had to get it off."

"I see," said Hayes softly. "Does that feel better?"

The boy nodded.

"How old are you, Jack?"

Jack watched him, eyes wide and uncomprehending.

"How old?" asked Hayes again.

"I don't know," said the boy.

"You don't?"

"I used to know. But I don't anymore." He stopped and said, "It doesn't work that way anymore."

"What doesn't? What doesn't work that way?"

The boy shook his head. Hayes thought for a second. "Time?" he said. "Does time not work for you anymore?"

Jack did not answer.

"How old were you before, Jack? Before the monster in the basement?"

"I was ten."

"All right. You're ten, so you're a big boy. And I'm going to treat you like a big boy. Do you want to know why I'm here?"

The boy nodded again.

"I'm here about your daddy," said Hayes.

The boy's eyes went wide and he stared at Hayes. He began shuddering and flickering again and there was a sound like two ship hulls sliding over each other, grating and maddening. Hayes raised his hands, hoping to smother his anger before it could grow.

"No, Jack," he said. "I'm not here to hurt you. I'm not. I'm like you, remember?"

The boy relented and became solid again. "My daddy's dead," he said softly.

"I know, Jack."

"He's dead."

"Yes."

"He was killed."

"I know. I know that. I need to know how."

"How he was killed?"

"I need to know what happened." Hayes felt the boy's thoughts flow before him. He seemed terribly stunted. He had the mind not of a boy of ten but perhaps one of five, maybe even younger. Hayes was not sure if he had been like this before he had been altered.

"What happened?" repeated the child.

"Yes. On the day that he left."

"When he left to go to the boat?"

"Yes. On that day."

"Why?"

"I just need to know. Someone needs to know what happened to people like your daddy. We can't just forget about them."

"No," said the boy. "No, no." He frowned, blinking back tears, and said, "I loved him."

"I know, Jack."

"He was my daddy. I loved him and I didn't want to be bad but I had to see where he was going."

"Yes."

"I had to see. So I followed him." And he began speaking while Hayes watched his memories unfold.

His daddy had said not to follow. He'd said he couldn't follow, that the boy should stay home, and then his daddy had crept out in the night beforehand, trying to get away without him knowing. But the boy had been awake all night and had just been faking sleep, so when his daddy put on his shoes and put the letter on the chair the boy knew. He knew, and when the door shut he went and read the letter. Read it as best as he could. He knew what it was saying and he did not even cry, he was too old to cry, he just tossed the letter aside and went downstairs and saw his daddy walking away down the street. Walking down the street, north. Alone.

"I followed him," Jack said then. "I'm good at it. I'm good at being quiet."

It was a long walk, and they took trolleys sometimes but still the boy followed him. Away from the city, to the far northwestern waterside. Cold and wet and dark and alone. And there his father met a whole lot of other men and waited with them. Waited, staring out at the water, looking at a dark black boat that waited with them. And when the second boat came they all seemed scared at first but then they got to work because one man said they had to. Moving things from one boat to the other. Working. Working like daddy did at his job, and the boy wondered if this was part of his job but he didn't think so, daddy never did work with boats and ships on the water, but deep down in the ground.

Then one man dropped one of the crates. The others swarmed to the dropped box, trying to scoop up what was inside, but his daddy saw it, and his eyes got big and he started shouting. So mad he was almost crying. The boy had been too far away to hear what was said, too far, but it had to be bad. No one looked that upset and said good things, and he knew what his daddy looked like mad. But still the men put the boxes on the boat and then they got in the boat and went away. And his daddy went with them, away toward the city.

"I was scared," the boy said. "They left me there. I wanted to tell them not to leave but if I did that my daddy would know I had followed him."

"I see," Hayes said.

So the boy waited. Hunkered down below a tree and waited for day. It was too dark to see and there could be things in the woods. Hungry things, waiting. And soon the boy fell asleep.

He awoke when he heard something walking through the bushes, and at first he was scared but then he saw it was his daddy again. He wondered if his daddy had come looking for him, but he didn't seem to be. He walked right past Jack and kept walking along the beach, looking up into the hills from time to time. And the boy waited, and hesitated, and followed him again.

"I didn't want him to be alone," he said. "But I didn't want him to be mad, either."

Sometimes it was hard to follow him. Hard to see him in the dark, walking into the hills. But then he hit a path and all the boy had to do was follow the path. After a while he saw his daddy stop and look at something. The boy had to creep close and he saw it was a fence, a big one. His daddy stared at what was inside of it, at the building he could see beyond, and he seemed to figure something out because he turned and ran away, back toward the city.

But the boy stayed. There was something inside the fence. Singing. Singing to him. Singing a song that only he could hear.

"It was beautiful," the boy said dreamily.

"I'm sure it was," Hayes said.

The boy climbed the fence and went out into the field. There was a big building there and there was a voice in it singing. Like an angel. He walked to it and listened to the song and sneaked inside. It was easy, because the voice told him who to watch out for. Where to go. What to do.

He went down in the dark. Down to where the thing waited. Where the voice was singing. And he found it burning in the darkness like a big golden coal and he reached out, reached out to touch the song and try and see if he could sing it, too...

What happened next was hard for Hayes to discern. The boy did not really know either. He just knew something had changed.

The world stopped. Froze and drained of color. And then stars lit up along everything, like everything was made of light, and between the stars was so much, so much emptiness, so much space, so much everything and so much nothing, and in between every second was another second, and inside of that second was a day, a month, a year, and suddenly Jack was lost, stretched out among the years and the stars and all the hidden nothingness that lurked below everything, between everything, around everything...

"I was everywhere," Jack whispered. "I was everything. Forever."

Hayes pulled away, gasping. He could not touch that memory. He knew that if he did it would destroy him. But he realized then that in that instant the boy had been alone for what must have felt like weeks. Perhaps years, perhaps centuries. Left alone to stagnate and go mad, isolated within that one unending moment.

Hayes noticed the boy was quivering and flickering again. His voice whined and rose higher and higher and Hayes's ears began to pain him. Hayes waited it out, watching. When the child was done he gasped and shook his head, tears running down his face.

"Then what happened, Jack?" Hayes asked quietly.

The boy sobbed and shook his head.

"What happened?"

"I didn't know what was wrong with me," the boy cried. "I didn't know what it was. I was sick. I was sick and I had to find my daddy. But I didn't know where he was. So I went to the giant's playground. It was all I could see, where I was. The only thing I knew."

"To the big stones? Out on the water?"

"Yes," the boy said, eyes baleful. "And there he was."

Hayes saw the image laid out before him. A lone man, running toward a group of people carrying boxes. Lost in the shadows of the tomb-like stones lined up around them, waving his arms and saying to drop them, to let them go. Shouting that it wasn't what they thought it was, that they had been betrayed and that this wasn't the way. They could not do it this way. They had to stop. It was a trick, he said. It was a trick.

They told him to be quiet. Told him to shut his damn mouth. He said he couldn't, said he wouldn't let anyone die. They told him to be quiet. Again he said it was a trick. They said this had been set up by the boss men, by Tazz himself. And he shook his head and said that they had been tricked by Tazz, too, if that was the case. He wouldn't let anyone die, he said again. Not like this. There's a better way. There has to be. He'd go to the police if they didn't listen.

Then they hit him. Struck him across the face with something hard and heavy, and he crumbled. They looked at him and then looked at each other and then they started to beat him. Kicking him. Punching him. Then somewhere in their movements there was the glint of a knife and someone stabbing down and across, quick. And then he lay there. White and shaking. Clutching his face. His neck. The ground around him. And then he lay still.

"My daddy," whispered Jack quietly.

"I know," Hayes said. "I know."

"They couldn't do that to him. They couldn't. They *can't,*" spat the boy. "I went and hid. But then I found them. I found them later. All of them." He flared up again, his face growing indistinct, his words a stuttered buzz. "My daddy," he cried out. "They killed my daddy! They killed him! I'll kill all of you! All of you! For what you did to my daddy, for what you did!"

"I know."

"I found them. Most of them."

"Yes."

"And I got so mad that... that things stopped. And I could hear the blood inside them and all the angry things inside of them and I thought of my daddy and... and..."

Hayes saw the door of the Third Ring. He watched as the men filed out, Naylor, Evie, Eppleton, all of them laughing, and they descended into the trolley station. The boy watched from across the street and then picked up a waste bin from in front of a diner. He waited, steeling himself, and then bolted after them through the darkness to where the trolley was now standing frozen in the tunnels, curiously still like all time was stopped around it since the boy was moving at unimaginable speeds, and then the boy threw the trash can at the door and screamed at the top of his lungs and charged in. Windows cracked and lights erupted in dazzling fireworks as the boy descended on the trolley like a lightning bolt. And inside the people were like statues, eyes wide, waiting to die. Waiting to die, as they should have. All of them.

There was a glitter from something in a woman's hands. A pair of scissors, clipping yarn. Hayes saw the boy's gray-white hand reach forward and pick them up and turn to the nearest person and raise the blades up...

Their flesh tore like paper, and gore tumbled from their wounds at slow, syrupy speeds. The tunnel outside floated by, piping and tubing drifting along like logs in a stream. The boy wept as he lashed out at them, tearing at the still figures that slowly fell to the ground once he stabbed them, wafting down like thistle seeds in a summer breeze. It was like a dreamy dance, sinking to the trolley floor with red streams twirling up and away from their necks and backs and chests. Their faces quiet and thoughtful as though they did not yet know they were dead. And then when the scissors broke he stopped and moved to the man at the front, the pilot-man in the uniform with the shiny brass buttons, but he knew not to hurt him because once his daddy had said those men were very good men and would get him home if he was lost, and to just ask them for help.

Which is what the boy did then. Asked him how to get home, and for help. But the man sat still as stone like the other frozen people, and said nothing. And so the boy turned to look at the little trolley behind him and all the colorless people still falling to the ground or slumping over like marionettes with their strings cut, and he dropped the scissor handles and walked out to the dark tunnel and the distant lights beyond.

Hayes shut his eyes. "I know, Jack," he said. "I know."

"Kill all of you," the child gasped. "All of you. Every one. Even the ones who got away, I found them, too. You can't hide. You can't."

Then Hayes looked into the boy's heart once more and saw how broken he was. How mad, how hungry. He was not a boy anymore but something irreparably damaged, something vicious, like a rabid dog seeking a hand to bite.

There could be no return from this. No way back. Not from this.

Hayes waited until the boy was quiet. Then he swallowed and said, "Why don't you get into bed?"

"Bed?" said the boy.

"Yes. It's bedtime."

"But it's light out."

"Aren't you tired, though?"

"I guess. I guess I am."

There was a flurry and then the boy was gone. Hayes looked around and saw he was in bed, staring out the window. Hayes walked to him and sat down beside him.

"Jack?" he asked.

"Yes?"

"I want you to close your eyes, Jack."

"Why?"

Hayes swallowed again and took a breath. "Because you're going to sleep now."

"Oh." The boy looked at him a moment longer, then did as he asked.

"Now I want you to think of something for me, Jack."

"What?"

"I want you to think of your old home. Your old house. Before this place. With your daddy. Can you do that for me now?"

"Yes."

"Then do it, please."

Hayes saw the memory swell up in the boy. Fall leaves tumbling over the porch gate. Neighbors coming over and bringing leftovers on plates. The sound of crickets, lost in the din of the city now, so lost.

"I remember that," the boy said. "I remember crickets."

"Do you remember your daddy?"

"I do. Of course I do."

Hayes picked up a pillow. "I want you to think of him. Think of him very hard. Okay?"

He saw Skiller's face in the boy's mind. Smelled his aftershave. The rough feeling of his pants as the boy sat in his lap. His voice in the darkness, low and calm. Reassuring him that everything would be all right.

"Now go to sleep," Hayes said. "Go to sleep, Jack. Sleep."

The boy dropped off. Hayes waited until his breathing was steady. Then he clamped the pillow over the child's face and held it there.

There was no struggle. Perhaps the boy had known what Hayes was going to do and did not mind. Hayes held the pillow there until the breathing stopped and as he did he noticed drops forming on the pillowcase and realized he was crying again. Still he held it. He waited until the mind and the thoughts he sensed wavered and died, like a candle flame burning low. Then they were gone, perhaps to parts unknown or maybe evaporated into nothing like dew in morning light.

He took the pillow away and stared at the little creature in the bed. He sat on the bed opposite it for some time, clutching himself as though he were cold. Then he began rocking back and forth, moaning quietly. He fought the scream rising within him, tried to choke it out, but then he gave up and howled, a strangled cry that did not even sound human to his ears.

When he was done he walked downstairs to the abandoned street and began heading toward the Department. And as afternoon began to advance and he neared the police station something drifted down to him from up above, some thought or worry from someone near, and Hayes stopped where he was and knew that Garvey was dead.

CHAPTER FORTY-FOUR

Hayes went to him in the morgue. At first he did not want to look at all. But then he decided he must. Someone has to look, he told himself. Someone has to look, for things like that.

He was not sure which cabinet was his so he began pulling them out at random. Garvey's was on the far wall. When Hayes found him he looked nothing like how he remembered him. He was just a thing now. An object, cold and pallid. A casualty, perhaps.

Hayes looked at his friend laid out on the slab, his legs and chest and hands dotted with wounds. He felt grief grip his chest and he knew then as he had perhaps known all his life that in this fading world the good were forever fated to die young and die violently. Fated to change the world only in their remembrance left behind in the hearts of those who lived on. In the sinners. In those who unjustly survived the slain.

"It should have been you," Hayes said.

A young boy in a white coat came walking in. He saw Hayes standing there and said, "Who the hell are you?"

Hayes turned around. The young man saw the gun in Hayes's hand and paled and drew back.

"Whoa," he said. "Whoa, hey."

"Shut up," said Hayes.

The young man was quiet. Hayes walked past him and up the stairs of the Department, and then outside.

It was growing dark now. An uneasy hush rolled throughout the city. Tattered clouds made bird's nests around the yellow eye of the moon overhead. A crowd of drunks tottered over the lanes nearby. Hayes thought he heard one of them singing but when he stopped to listen he realized they were not.

CHAPTER FORTY-FIVE

It was not hard for Hayes to get into the office. The Nail was shut down at these hours, claiming emergency. Those few who were left behind did not see him, not if Hayes didn't want them to. So he came to the office and sat in the dark and waited.

Brightly came in while it was still dark out. He walked in and sat down, tossing a few papers down as he did so, and he reached over and turned on the desk light. Then he glanced up and cried out as he saw what was sitting on the other side of the desk, pale-white with bone-bleached hair and skin that was sooty and ashen and scarred.

"Hello, Brightly," said Hayes.

Brightly squinted at him, horrified. "Hayes?"

"Yes," said Hayes softly. "Yes, it's me."

"Dear God, man, what happened to you?"

He shrugged.

"You can't be in here. How did you get in here?"

"That's not what you should be worrying about." He took a breath and said, "Do you know where I've been?"

"Where you've been?" Brightly began glancing to the sides, trying to find some escape or weapon.

"Yes."

"I've... I'm sure I have no idea."

"I was at the morgue. Do you want to know why?"

"I... Well, I suppose," said Brightly.

"I went there to see Garvey," he said. "To see my friend."

Brightly froze, staring at him. "W-what?"

"Garvey. The detective. You remember him?"

"Well, I... I never met the man personally, but..."

"He was shot," said Hayes. "Just today. Shot dead. Did you know that?"

"N-no. No, I didn't, I'm... I'm terribly sorry to hear that."

"To hear that," echoed Hayes.

"Yes."

Hayes's pale eyes flicked up and down Brightly behind the desk. "You're lying."

"What?"

"You're lying to me, Brightly. I know Collins called you yesterday. And he told you what Garvey knew, and what he was going to do. And I know the precautions you took."

"That's preposterous," said Brightly.

"No. It isn't. You had him killed."

"Why on Earth would I ever have... have a policeman killed?"

"Because he found out about Gerald Crimley," Hayes said.

Brightly flinched and took a breath.

"You don't like that, do you?" Hayes said. "That name? That man, perhaps?"

"How do you know that name?"

"I know all about him."

"You can't... you can't come in here and start..."

"I can. Because if anyone in this town finds out that all those fires started under your watch or the watch of McNaughton, you'll be hung from a window by your ankles, won't you?"

Brightly grew very still. "I don't know what you mean."

"Yes you do. You certainly do."

"I don't. I don't, and I...I want you out of this office, Hayes. I want you..."

"I know he brought in the guns," Hayes said thoughtfully. "But I'm just not sure what they were meant for. You remember them, don't you? The guns?"

Brightly was silent at that.

Hayes looked away, thinking. "I'm going to assume you didn't intend for them to actually *use* the guns, did you? Come on, Brightly. Give it up. Just stonewalling me isn't going to get anywhere. So. Did you?"

Brightly swallowed. Then shook his head.

"No. You just wanted them to be caught with them, yes?"

Brightly did not answer.

"Yes? Is that it?"

"Yes," he said.

"Yes. To dirty the names of Tazz and unions. Show them as violent and untrustworthy. But you know what, I'm going to guess that Mr. Crimley went native. He started living his Tazz role, didn't he? Started to become hard to communicate with? That happens with long jobs. To men who're deep inside. So Mr. Crimley—or perhaps Mr. Tazz—tells his boys to go all Old West on us and then he leaves in the middle of the night. Is that it?"

Brightly looked away.

"What were me and Sam there for?" Hayes asked. "To make it easy? You get Crimley to set up the unions, then you get me and Sam to tear them down, one after the other? That's why we never made any arrests, isn't it? Because you wanted us to build it up naturally until we got to the guns."

He still did not answer.

"All that," said Hayes quietly. "All that, for just a little bit of money."

"Not a little bit of money," said Brightly. "For a lot of it. Unimaginable amounts. Fortunes many times over."

"All money is little," said Hayes. "In the long run."

"Damn it, we're almost our own *country*, Hayes," said Brightly. "We have to defend ourselves! This is war, practically. Countries depend on us, the whole *world*, for God's sake. You would have done it, too! You're no lamb yourself, you would have done the same!"

Hayes nodded. "Yes. Yes, that's true. The saddest thing is that I can understand what you did. To protect your own, at any cost."

"Then what is it you want?" Brightly demanded. "Money? Is that it?"

"I have money of my own. You know that, of all people."

"Then what?"

Hayes took out a revolver and laid it in his lap. Then he sat and stared into the front of Brightly's desk, unmoving.

"Oh, God," said Brightly.

"Yes," said Hayes.

"Cyril. Cyril, listen. Don't do anything rash, now."

Hayes nodded again, apparently lost in thought.

"Don't do anything silly," Brightly said. "You're company, Cyril, you're one of our boys, you shouldn't—"

"I'm not company," Hayes said. "No one is. There's no union. No company. No city. Just people. Alone. And unwatched."

"I was... I was just doing my job."

"So was he. And he died for it."

"I can get you whatever you want..."

"Larry, I am *not* in the mood for negotiating right now!" shouted Hayes. He looked up at Brightly, breathing hard. "I killed a ten-year-old boy today," he whispered.

"Oh, my God," moaned Brightly. "Oh, God. Please, Cyril."

"It's worse than you think, Brightly."

"God, Cyril..."

"I killed him because he found out what was in the mountains," Hayes said.

"What?" said Brightly, confused. "What mountains?"

"I found it there, too," said Hayes softly. "What's hiding up there. I stumbled across it. I know why this company never moved away from this spot. And I know where the machines come from. The discoveries."

"What do you mean? What's in the mountains?"

Hayes stopped, looking him over closely. "You don't know. You really don't know, do you? You don't even know what that thing in your bunker is, do you?"

"Know what? What's in the damn mountains?"

"God, who *does* know?" spat Hayes, standing up. "Who really knows what started this company? Christ almighty, *someone* has to know. Someone on the board has to have *some* idea!" Hayes shook his head, furious that there was not someone to throw this in front of, no real enemy to attack.

"What do you mean?" asked Brightly. "What are you talking about?"

"I went up there, Brightly," said Hayes. "Up in the mountains. To see what Kulahee had found long ago. And I found it, too. But it didn't matter. It didn't matter what I found. When I came back down Garvey was dead. All the people in the fire, they were dead. And there's nothing I can do to change what happened. He was my *friend*, Brightly."

"God, Hayes, please don't. Please..."

Hayes pointed the gun at Brightly, who fell backward out of his chair and lay on the floor, trying to inch away. Hayes walked around, still pointing the gun. Brightly lifted his arm and shielded his face with it, staring over the top.

"He was my friend," Hayes said. "He was just doing his job. He just died because he cared. Because he was the only one."

Brightly swallowed and closed his eyes.

The barrel of the gun quivered and Hayes lowered it. He shook his head and sat down on the floor next to Brightly, the big man and the little man sitting together in the dark. Neither of them moved for a great while.

Hayes whispered, "I don't want to do this anymore, Brightly."

"All... all right."

"I don't want this. No more of this. No more. No more killing. No more killing, Brightly. Do you understand that?"

"Yes. Yes, I understand, no more killing," Brightly said quickly.

"Things are going to change here. Be ready. Be somewhere else, if you need. You can try and send men after me. If you're stupid. But I'm not what I was before. And I'll see them coming." Then he got up and began to walk away.

"Cyril," said Brightly. "Cyril. What's up there? What did you see in the mountains?"

Hayes turned, looking back, a blank figure in the shadows. Then he said, "The future," and walked out.

CHAPTER FORTY-SIX

He went to Samantha just before dawn, guessing easily where she would have run to. He walked down the canal and knocked on the door. Then he waited and knocked again. It opened just a crack and he saw her peek through. Then she opened the door the rest of the way and said, "Oh my... my *God*, Hayes? Is that you?"

"Yes," he said.

"What happened to you? My God, what happened?"

Hayes walked forward and embraced her without a word. She drew back, shocked by the display of affection. Then she slowly embraced him back.

"What's going on?" she asked.

"I'm sorry," he said.

"What? Where's Donald? Mr. Hayes, where's Donald?"

"I'm sorry," he said again.

She began shaking in his arms. "What are you doing? What's happened? What's going on? What's happened, Mr. Hayes?"

He did not answer. He just kept holding her.

"Please," she said. "Please tell me. Please, you just have to... You just have to *tell me*! Please, just tell me, *please*!"

He kept holding her. She kept asking questions, one after the other, but she knew the answers now. Eventually she collapsed and sat on the floor and sobbed, rocking back and forth. Hayes sat with her and waited, patiently. After a while he shut the door.

He gently led her to a cab and directed the driver toward the downtown cradle. She leaned against the cab window like a drugged woman, hands limp in her lap.

"We shouldn't leave," she said.

"I know."

"We should see him buried. I should at least see him."

"It's dangerous. He wouldn't have wanted you to be in danger. And you are the last good thing in my life," said Hayes. "I won't risk you. You are too precious to lose."

"We should... find the men who did this and..."

"No," said Hayes. "No more. No more of that."

She shut her eyes and began crying again.

When they got to the cradle he led her to the central lift. They climbed inside and stood in the glass tube, the windows wreathed with condensation, the street traffic just below their toes. Something hissed above and they began to rise up, floating up above the shops and the cars, then above the crinkled rooftops of the houses, then finally above the sodden tops of the office buildings, gray and wet and graveled. Finally they were in the cradle itself. Men and women in starched suits and sharp dresses strolled about the tiled platform, smoking and casually speaking to one another as though they were on the deck of a cruise ship. In the distant heart of the dawning sky they could see the nose of the airship approaching, slowly swiveling to position its passenger cell for the center of the cradle. It would only be a few minutes.

"Where are we going?" she asked quietly.

"You're going to Los Angeles," he said. "From there, who knows?

It's up to you. Your purse has more than five thousand dollars in it, so you can go where you'd like."

"Five thousand?"

"Yes. That should support you. It should get you where you need. Do me a favor and go someplace warm. Somewhere with sun."

"You're not coming?"

He shook his head. "No, Sam. I'm not."

"Why not?"

"I think I have a lot to do now."

Samantha turned to look at the airship. The docking arm eased out and snatched it to hold it still and men in overalls moved forward to secure its many trusses. Then a steel-and-rubber staircase unfolded and rose to meet the side of the passenger cell. People began trickling out to greet their loved ones or hurry downstairs or just stare at the city laid out around them.

"And…and you're just going to send me away?" she asked. "While you stay here?"

"Yes. I want you to go and leave this behind, Sam. Someone needs to. Someone needs to go on."

Samantha looked at the airship for a moment longer and then turned and walked to the corner of the cradle where children and tourists gathered to look out at the city. She stared out at the rooftops and the streets and the cars, then looked back at him, eyes glinting. "What did you find out there, Mr. Hayes? What's happened to you?"

"I just…I've just seen something. Or had something shown to me."

"What was it? Who showed it to you?"

Hayes tried to articulate what had happened but could not. He simply shook his head.

Her face softened. She sighed and sniffed and said, "Well. I can see you haven't changed that much. You're still a remarkably silly man."

"What? What do you mean?"

Samantha turned back to the city. "Do you honestly think you can just send me away? Just shove me on a ship and have done with it?"

"Sam, it's dangerous, and I—"

"I know it's dangerous. It's always been dangerous. And once I would have said yes, that we should go, and forget all this. But I can't now, don't you see? I can't. We can't just leave it, just leave all this to die." She sniffed again and turned to look him over. "What did you see, Mr. Hayes? Did you find something? Did you find out what happened to Skiller, or the boy?"

"I did. I found the boy."

Her breath fluttered. "What... what happened to him?"

He considered telling her, wondering whether she could be burdened with yet another awful truth. But his strength failed, and he found he could not tell her what he had done. He could barely accept it himself. And besides, the boy *had* died, in a way, when he touched the thing in the basement, and what he became after was not Jack at all. And so Hayes simply shook his head, and said nothing.

Samantha shut her eyes. "Then it's as we feared. I should have guessed."

"I don't think he died in pain, if that's of... of any help."

"It isn't. I had hoped we could take just one thing away from this. That we could save one thing innocent, or good."

"If you leave, we can," he said. "You really won't consider it?"

"No, Mr. Hayes. No, I won't." She looked at him. "Can't you tell me anything? Anything about what you found?"

"I don't know. I don't know how to tell you what I saw."

"Then tell me what you plan to do, at least."

He hesitated, then told her. As he did the waiting passengers boarded the airship. Then finally it broke truss and began to drift away. People gathered on the cradle to wave goodbye and all the people in the passenger cell of the ship gathered at the blue-green windows to wave back. Once it had drifted far enough out the engines whirled and spun until the ship found the right angle of ascension, and then it began to rise straight up, its skin shining gold in the morning light.

When he was done talking Samantha thought it over. "What will you do with it?" she asked.

"I don't know," he said. "But it's a start, at least. It's got to be a start."

"And what do you need from me?"

"From you?" he asked.

"Yes. You've always needed someone sensible around. What can I do? What can I give you?"

He frowned, thinking, and then he said, "Lamps."

"Lamps?"

"Yes. Lamps," he said. "I need lamps."

"But what do you need lamps for?" she asked.

"To light the way, of course," he said.

"Is that all you need? Can't you get those yourself?"

"Sam, are you coming or not?" he asked irritably.

She turned to watch the airship float away until it disappeared into the clouds above. Then she nodded. "All right," she said.

They took the lift back down to the ground. People gave them a wide berth, thinking Hayes some maddened transient. Then they walked out into the street, heading southeast. Hayes followed Samantha, not thinking, just watching the city around him.

Down at the cabbie stand old men in worn knit caps and thick coats leaned up against the wooden posts. They smoked filthy cigarettes and watched the world go by with hangdog eyes and mournful shakes of the head, forever disapproving of the modern way and speaking of the past. Of forgotten wars, of legendary baseball players, of the city as it had been and never would be again. One man described the fire in great detail, his double-jointed fingers forming crooked flames that he spread out along an imaginary horizon. Then he shook his head and put his finger on his chin and they all mimicked the pose, staring into the sidewalk and trying to set the world to rights.

Down on the corner four new mothers sat on the front steps of their houses in white cotton dresses, peering up at the sky. Their eyes were troubled but they balanced their babes on their knees with thoughtless skill, fat chubby legs clutched around their thighs, perfect little booties bobbing up and down. As the mothers discussed the fire and the city and the future their children laughed and reached out to one another and shared some delight, as if they could see invisible wonders in the morning air. Which perhaps they could, after all.

Further down a newspaper stand clerk leaned up on his counter, chin in one hand, a mound of soaking cigarette butts beside his elbow like defeated challengers. His arms and his fingers were black with ink and he wore wandering lines of it on his face like some clownish war paint. Sometimes a pedestrian would catch his eye and he would squint at them and maneuver his toothpick about, flashing row upon row of gray teeth as though showing what he'd like to do to them. Hayes waved to him as he passed and the old man blinked in surprise and stared after him.

They found a supply store, and Samantha went in while Hayes stayed on the corner, absently watching the passersby. She came back out with three oil lamps and a pocketful of matches. Hayes took two of the lamps from her and then they continued walking east. Through parks and markets and floundering games of street baseball, through fights and purring traffic and the waking day. It all felt so fresh and new to Hayes. So alive with so much promise.

They came to a rickety old wooden fence with many KEEP OUT signs, but they ignored them and found a gap and walked through to where the street opened up and a staircase of sandbags led down into the dark.

Hayes gazed down into the tunnels. For a moment he quavered

and wondered what would happen if he simply turned away, but then Samantha took his hand. He turned to her and she looked back at him, uncertain. He was not sure if she had taken his hand to offer support or to reassure herself, but either way it was welcome. He nodded to her, grateful, and then they began their way down the sandbags.

Once they reached the bottom they lit the lamps and started forward into the tunnels. Now Hayes led Samantha, sensing the way ahead, taking turns through maintenance shafts and over trolley tracks. A familiar world of darkness and dank and the soft hums of distant machinery, and sleeping secrets.

They wound deep into the labyrinth, Hayes walking with his head cocked as he tried to listen. Then as they passed by one tunnel's opening Hayes looked to the side and saw Skiller standing there, whole and unwounded, ankle-deep in water and watching him with burning, pained eyes. He stood with his arms close to his body as though powerfully cold. He shook his head. "It's not what we thought it was," he said. "We've been betrayed. This isn't the way."

I know, thought Hayes. *I know. Don't worry. I know.*

They continued on, leaving Skiller in the dark.

They bent low as the tunnel slightly began to shrink. The floor underneath them turned to iron grating, and sometimes in between bundles of piping they could see even deeper pathways below. As they walked over one gap Hayes looked down and saw Evans sitting there, crosslegged and staring up, his face concealed by shadow but his glasses glinting. "We're making a new age," he whispered up to him. "A new age. And we are but a part."

Yes, thought Hayes. *I see that now. I know.*

They crossed over tracks and began up the maintenance tunnels, picking their way over old boots and shovels and ancient equipment. Up ahead he saw Jack sitting in the doorway of one of the maintenance sheds, not yet pale and ravaged. He watched Hayes pass with terrified, sunken eyes and pleadingly said, "I was scared. They left me there. I wanted to tell them not to leave." As though this could somehow explain everything. Explain all the atrocities left behind in their wake.

"I know, Jack," whispered Hayes. "I'm sorry."

"What?" said Samantha, looking up.

"Nothing," he muttered, and quickly wiped tears from his eyes.

He was not sure if they were his imagination or if they were memories he'd stolen, laid out here before him. To him they were simply more voices. Fragments and seconds from time past that came to life down here in the dark.

They found a maintenance hallway and followed the dim sodium lights along its winding path. As they walked they came to a darkened intersection, and Hayes looked to his right and saw Tazz or Crimley or whichever standing far down the crossing hallway in the darkness. "You have seen it out in the veins of the city," he said. "You have seen the dead and the dying."

Yes, whispered Hayes silently to himself. *Yes, I have. I know.*

They walked on through the cement hallway, and as they passed a small closet Hayes saw Spinsie sitting inside, lounging up against a set of empty metal shelves, smoke snailing up from a cigarette in his hand and his glance dismissive and contemptuous. "You don't know everything, you know that, little brother?" he said, his words pluming smoke. "Just 'cause you've been around. Just 'cause you managed to get out before I could."

Yes, Hayes thought. *Yes, I know.*

And somehow in the next room was Teddy Montrose, still wearing his overcoat and his hat and his prim tie, briefcase in hand. Face pale and pearled with the kiss of steam. He watched Hayes pass and begged, "Will He forgive me? God. Do you think He will forgive me?"

But Hayes shook his head and shut his eyes and kept walking.

Then as they passed the next room Hayes glanced in and saw it was crowded with the victims of the Bridgedale trolley, Evie and

Naylor and poor Mrs. Sanna, and many more. They sat along two wooden benches running along the walls, or stood holding on to a support beam as they would a handrail. They casually read the paper with their legs crossed, or knitted or smoked or grinned at some small joke. They did not seem to know they would never arrive anywhere. That they had died down here, and were forever trapped in that little room.

In some way they would never leave here. They and all the others. They were claimed by the city and what it was built upon. Casualties caught in its many gears.

I'm sorry, Hayes said to them. *I'm so sorry.* But they did not hear, or if they did they did not show it.

Then finally they came to a huge, dark room with a thin passageway running along one side. Hayes looked to the end of the passageway, thinking. Then he raised the lantern and as the light reached further out it found Garvey standing there, the knot in his cheap tie loose and his hands in his pockets. His small smile was wry and sad, as though he was pained by the things he'd seen and yet at peace with the absurd knowledge that he'd willfully see more of them. Hayes swallowed as he stared at him. Then Garvey's small smile deepened and he said, "Someone has to look, for things like that."

The hand holding the lantern began shaking. Then Hayes took a breath and said, "Yes. Let's take a look." And he turned the lamp away until his friend was swallowed by shadows, and he and Samantha walked to the edge of the passageway.

They lifted the lamps and found Tazz's machine waiting for them. It was huge and dead and silent still, its turbines quiet, its pistons frozen. Hayes nodded and walked to the ladder rungs and began to climb down, lamp hanging from the crook of an elbow. Samantha did the same, leaving one lamp burning at the top of the ladder.

When they were at the feet of the machine it seemed larger than ever. From this perspective they saw it was easily taller than most buildings. But Hayes took no notice and instead found the small hutch in the machine's side and the many tools that had been left there. He knelt and peered into the hutch and sniffed. Then he nodded again and grabbed the second lantern and got down on his hands and knees.

"How will this be any different?" asked Samantha.

"Different?" said Hayes.

"Using this machine..." she said. "How will this be any different from what McNaughton was doing? How will this help, and not hurt further?"

Hayes thought for a moment. "It will be different," he said, "because now I know the limits. We know how fragile all this is. And I am not looking to build, and grow, and keep pushing the boundaries. I am looking to make sure that the heart of the world keeps beating."

He crawled in on his hands and knees and dragged the second lamp in after. Samantha stooped and called into the hutch, "But will that be enough?" Yet Hayes did not answer.

On the inside the machine was a world of gears and pipes and bundles of wires, of blown glass and steel and frail copper plates. Hayes crawled or walked or sidled his way among them, looking them over and somehow recognizing them. He knew them and saw how primitive and vulgar and simple the device was, how it was a feeble work that attempted to ape something far beyond the conception of its creators. But he could sense the potential there as well. It could be fixed. Brought back or even made better.

He began adjusting it as he saw fit. Moving the parts until they matched the design in his head. It took hours, but he hardly noticed. So many foreign memories were coming to life inside him, memories and patterns and designs that had waited eons to be used.

Finally he slid one copper plate into its slot and the machine filled with a deep, resonant hum. Hayes looked up above at the roof of wiring and piping and crawled back out as the hum grew. He pulled himself out of the hutch and saw Samantha seated at the lip of the wall, staring up at the machine with wide, frightened eyes. Then she saw him and helped him up and they both stood and looked.

"Sometimes I think this city has a voice," said Hayes.

"A what?" said Samantha, surprised.

"A voice."

She looked away, and then shut her eyes and tried not to weep. "What does it say?" she asked.

The hum kept deepening until they could feel it in their bones. It seemed as though there were some great pressure shifting down in the earth, something pushing up and rising through the rock and charging toward the surface.

"That things are going to get better," said Hayes.

The hum reached its apex and another hum joined it, this one of a higher pitch, and then another and another as boiling air coursed through the many metal throats in the machine. A groan rolled throughout the room as gears that had long been silent began to move. Then the air took on a slight charge as electricity found its way through the device and signals began echoing through its recesses, whispering to long-forgotten components and rousing them from sleep. Soon the little crystal in the Sibling above began flickering, perhaps calling to others like it and straining to attract their attention. Distant islands of machines floating in the dark, chained together by links of light, all of them aware of this little rogue pocket in the center of the city that had suddenly come back into existence. Wondering what this could be, if they could wonder at all.

Let them watch, thought Hayes. Let them listen. Let them see what we're making here. Something extraordinary. Something genuinely for the future. Maybe they'll listen.

"Open your eyes, Samantha," said Hayes. "Open them."

She did so, and gasped softly. The many hums gathered like a chord on a church organ until finally there was a great squalling and the dozens of pistons began to move. At first it was slow and painfully arthritic and the machine strained until it seemed it could not bear the force, but then the pistons began to find some lost rhythm, a slow, pumping beat that pulled more life and power into the machine with each stroke. And somehow both of them recognized that beat, that soft, powerful churning they'd heard before, echoing up storm drains and air vents. It spoke of great strength and magnificent power, enough to move the Earth and the stars themselves, should it be set to it, and both of them thought it new and terrifying and wonderful. Then the beat faded as the pistons gathered speed until they were churning at a blinding rate, smoothly and beautifully, and the hundreds of gears spun cleanly and the wiring sang and the batteries sparked and every inch of the massive construction was moving and humming and alive.

"Yes," said Hayes. "Things are going to get better."

And they sat and watched as the machine awoke.

ACKNOWLEDGMENTS

I would like to thank John, Raymond, and Dmitri for the endless inspiration they've given me. Not only have they shaped this story in many ways but they have also changed my perception of what story and art can really do.

I'd also like to apologize to the people, geography, and history of the state of Washington. Reality sometimes has to bend to meet the story, and while the whole world got rearranged and shuffled in this one, Washington got the worst of it, I'm afraid. Please be comforted by the fact that it was not your Washington, but merely one very similar to yours from a long, long time ago.

And finally, I'd like to give thanks to Carrie and Josh, who read this book when it was a very puny seedling and made me realize which direction it wanted to grow in, and to DongWon, who showed me that this book could grow at all. And to Cameron, without whose direction I wouldn't even be able to write these words, which are feeble in comparison to the gratitude that inspires them.

extras

meet the author

Robert Jackson Bennett was born in Baton Rouge, Louisiana, but grew up in Katy, Texas. He later attended the University of Texas at Austin and, like a lot of its alumni, was unable to leave the charms of the city and resides there currently. Find out more about the author at www.robertjacksonbennett.com.

introducing

If you enjoyed
THE COMPANY MAN,
look out for
the next exciting novel from
Robert Jackson Bennett

Now came smoky, wintry days, days of drafty rooms and chilly floorboards, of sour meats and sleepless nights and yellowed bedsheets layered with grit, always the grit. It came tumbling down from the train tops to rest in your hair, on your collar, in your sleeves and mouth, a constant invasion of grainy cinders that turned white linen into graying sackcloth. You could wash, certainly, but what was the point if you'd be on the train again in a week, or a day, or even less? You would always be moving, adrift in a sea of dour, distracted faces and jostling elbows and the grasping spumes of smoky grit, and when that was done you were speeding along through leafless forests and sodden fields and tumbledown towns with the white winter sky weighing down upon you.

You lived for the afternoons and the nights, when you did your turn. Everything else was backstage, in a way: the train station, the railways, the hotels, and the bars, all of these were just a long, drawn-out wait in the shadowed corridors behind the real performance. You bided your time among greasepaint clowns and acrobats and chorus girls (who scratched at their leggings until one of their partners slapped their hands and told them, Stop, stop, you'll put a run in them) and teams of softly whining dogs in little dresses. To pass the time you bickered with them in an idle, affectionate way: over billing, over originators of bits and lines, over the goddamn choosers who lurked in the audience and sought to plunder your act and apply it elsewhere. Why, I found some jake in Columbus who'd been doing my bit for well over a year, they'd say, and certainly I pulled out an ad in the monthly and called the fellow out, but he never replied, the coward, he certainly never replied.

Your dressing room was only desirable in terms of solitude; the actual conditions were often nothing short of deplorable. The first thing you did upon arriving was search the walls and corners for any peepholes (they would be there regardless of your sex), and fill them in with shoe polish (and yet how many times had you seen narrow, soiled fingers worming through the blocked-up holes, pushing past this obstruction to make way for a desperate eye?). Then came the rituals: You avoided looking at all the windows, for to spy a bird on one's sill was sure to bring bad luck. If you found a peacock feather accidentally jettisoned from some chorus girl's gown, you made sure not to touch it; to touch a peacock feather was to invoke the worst of all misfortunes. You made *sure* not to whistle, that was a death knell if ever there was one. You just put on your oldest performance shoes and turned your shirt inside out while mumbling your lines, perhaps shuffling widdershins two or three times as you did. Then you would be sanctified, consecrated, protected against all ills. Unless, of course, you were following an animal act; no luck could aid you in competing with dumb, trained creatures who somehow always managed to charm the hearts of the audience while leaving shit all over the stage.

Then came your moment, the little splinter of time you'd been waiting for since you awoke that morning: they called your name and you took a breath and walked across the stiff cardboard floor (riddled with holes from previous props), the dark back of the theater full of gleaming, watchful eyes like a cavern full of roosting owls, and then you sang or bleated your little song, or made your little speech, or did your funny little dance. And it was easy, because after all you'd done it just the day before, and the day before that, and the dozens of hundreds of days before that. Had you always been doing this, you wondered, as you listened to the sprinkling of applause (sometimes a dribble, other times a roar)? Had you always been playing for these darkened people, rendered bodiless and invisible by the blazing footlights?

And then after the performance you returned to your barren flophouse room, frosted with moonlight from the many holes in the walls, the bed and sheets alive with dozens of creepy-crawlies who roved the folds looking for bare flesh to bite. You'd sleep shivering in a ball and awake with red and pink perforations lining your neck, your crotch, your armpits. But you did not want to slap yourself down with kerosene to keep them away, like some people advised, as the reeking fumes almost choked you in the night, so you suffered through their tiny bites. And when morning came you'd sit on the edge of the bed, aching and stiff, your breath smoking and pluming, and you'd fear to touch your soles to the chilly floorboards… Yet just before you did, you'd wonder what day it was. Surely it could not still be February? Could it really? Had it not been winter for many, many months?

* * *

George finally asked Silenus about the time once. It seemed to move slowly now that they were touring.

"We are traveling the thin parts of the world, George," he answered. "We seek out the fringes, the edges, the festering, open sores. Existence is breaking down here. Time doesn't work right. It's grown distorted. That's why we come here to play the song. Then things will right for these places, in time."

"But it's been winter for so long," said George. "It feels like it's been winter for years. Can the people who live here really never notice that something's wrong?"

Silenus grinned and said, "To them, everything's dandy. They never notice that the world is dying below their feet."

"But why?"

"Because they don't want to. The human aptitude for self-deception is unfathomable, kid. After all, it's the crux of our trade, ain't it? They dupe themselves into thinking we, caricatures and stories, could maybe be doing something real. But of course, we're not."

George felt as though he were breaking down along with the world. His back began to stoop, his skin grew thin and sallow, and his knuckles clicked and cracked after every performance. When Collette once found him sleeping in a pile of dusty curtains backstage, she slapped him awake and held him upright with one arm, murmuring, "Told you. I told you so."

Her original resentment eventually transformed to pity when she saw how hard George was taking their travels. If she was confident enough in his collaboration with the orchestra, she'd let him sleep backstage in one of the dressing rooms, and would cover for him if Silenus asked. For some reason she was happy to have something to fight with Harry over: the two of them often seemed to be in the middle of some managerial argument or another, always retreating down some empty hallway to harangue each other in hushed tones, or bickering all the way back to his office. But though George was glad of her help and friendship, his affections for her went unrequited. Whenever she woke him from his naps, or tended to him when he was weary, there was always a distance there, and she was reluctant to touch him. Each moment with her was fleeting and frustrated, and soon her very presence was a dull ache in the root of his being.

Franny was one of the few troupe members not infected by the pervasive weariness of winter. Instead, she'd become oddly invigorated by the revelation of George's parentage. Yet it took some time for George to realize she was not happy, but angry, and specifically angry at Harry. For some reason she could not forgive him for the affair, and his ignorance of his only child. She was so angry that after one rehearsal she was neglectful and allowed a splinter of an iron band to tear open her bandaged sleeve. When the tear flapped open George saw the black writing on her skin again, yet now he saw it was not writing but a *drawing*, an amazingly intricate design that covered her entire arm, full of loops and twirls and spidery angles. Before he could examine it further, Silenus pointed out the tear. Franny quickly covered it up, shooting her manager a sullen glance as she did, and unbelievably Silenus appeared shocked and hurt by this reaction. "What does she think I ever did to her?" he asked, mopping his brow. But George just watched the strongwoman leave, wondering what was below all of those bandages and scarves.

And if George was doing poorly, his issues were slight compared to Kingsley, who got worse every day. Somehow the Professor still managed to perform each night: he would shuffle out behind the curtain, limping and bent sideways, and take his seat; yet when he'd hear Silenus announce his name he'd straighten up and smooth himself out, and perform as though he was hardly hurt at all. But when the curtain dropped again he'd crumple again like a snail dashed with salt, sometimes even whimpering, and would need several deep breaths before being able to stand.

Everyone took this grimly. The Professor denied any medical treatment, saying he preferred his own remedies, though he never explained what these were.

George was not sure how the troupe had lasted as long as they had, and could not imagine them continuing for much longer. It seemed as if they might fall apart at any moment. And how much farther would they go, even if they could? His father had never mentioned a specific endpoint for their precious mission. When would they ever be done?